Right There All Along

SAPPHIC IN SEATTLE
BOOK TWO

ELEE ROSE

For anyone who thinks they are unloved.
This one's for you.

Ps. Get yourself a Lemon vibrator and thank me later ;)

Content Warnings

This book contains episodes of PTSD. There are also mentions of parental death. This book contains sexual content and graphic language. There is a scene briefly depicting a car accident and a life threatening injury. Reader discretion is advised.

Playlist

Stargazing teddy swims
Dusk til dawn feat. Sia zayn
The only exception Paramore
Lay me down sam smith
Love me like you do Ellie Goulding
You are the reason Calum Scott
Clothes off feat. kwn kehlani
Funeral teddy swims
Wet Lauren Sanderson
Lose control piano version teddy swims

Chapter One

DREA

"Oh, for fuck's sake, where is my dildo?" I was trying to be as quiet as I could so I didn't wake up Carla? Kylie? Kameron? Whoever. I wasn't going to see her again, so what was the point of remembering her name? I was more focused on taking off her underwear with my teeth.

The curvy blonde stirred on the bed as I found my favorite pussy-pleasuring pal—neon green, double-sided, and vibrating—hiding under my discarded clothes.

Without looking back, I snuck out of her room, dressed quickly, and made my way out the front door, hoping I wasn't forgetting anything. Not that I'd go back for it if I was.

I finally stumbled into my house just after seven in the morning, thankful it was Sunday. The bookstore I owned, Open Book, was closed on Sundays, and moments like this, I wanted to thank past Drea for making that decision. That also meant I had all day to recharge before opening the store on Monday morning.

Not thirty seconds after I had settled into my pillows and closed my eyes, my phone rang. Ignoring it, I snuggled further back into my bed, waiting for the room to become silent again. After a few minutes passed, it rang again, and I picked up the infernal phone, desperately trying not to hurl it at the wall. *Who the fuck calls at this ungodly hour on a Sunday?!*

"Hello?" I asked with bitterness coating my tone without looking to see who the caller was.

"Drea, I'm so sorry to bother you, but I was just wondering if you were coming in to work today? Of course, I can handle it if not. I was just asking." I rubbed my eyes, straining to see the clock on my phone. Please tell me I was dreaming.

"Kaia, sweetie, why are you calling me at ten in the morning on a Sunday? We are closed today. Enjoy your day off." I groaned at the sound of my own voice. It should've been illegal to be awake that early on your day off.

A soft chuckle sounded through the phone. I wanted to be mad that she woke me up, but Kaia was so adorable, I could only roll my eyes in silent irritation.

"You went out last night, didn't you? It's Monday, Drea," she replied softly.

Well, shit. "Yes, I'm coming in," I groaned, tossing my blankets off me." I'll be over in a little bit. Call me if anything happens before I get there."

I didn't think anything would happen, though. We'd been fairly slow these last few months.

I hated to admit that being late happened more often than it should've recently. The bookstore was my life, and I took being the owner very seriously. It wasn't until my ex, Skylar, left for the other side of the country, that my tardiness became a more recurring issue.

The bookstore was busy when I got there, and I felt like a complete shit head for leaving Kaia to deal with it. I was the boss. I wasn't supposed to fuck up.

"Good morning, Drea," Kaia greeted me breathlessly as she carried a box from the back room to the counter.

"Sorry I'm late," I apologized as I reached for the box to help her remove the books inside.

Once it was empty, Kaia broke the box down and added it to the pile I hadn't noticed behind the counter.

She wiped a bead of sweat dripping from her brow. "No worries, I had it handled."

She was always so cheerful, no matter what was going on, and I needed to make a point to tell her more often how grateful I was to have her here.

"Well, I'm here now. Go take a break." I shooed her off to the back, and she didn't argue. But to be fair, she never argued about anything.

Kaia was like an adorable baby deer. She had wavy brown hair down to her shoulders and big brown eyes. I wanted to wrap her up in a blanket and rock her to sleep.

She was only a few years younger than me, but she was the baby of our group. Her bright eyes held sweetness and innocence without a hint of darkness, like she had never had anything terrible happen to her.

$\sim$

Five draining days had crawled by, and I was ready for a day off. I loved my little bookstore, but not all the little problems that could arise, especially when they all seemed to happen within the same week.

By the time the third Karen had come in to request a refund on a book they didn't like, I was ready to punch something. So, I was pleasantly surprised when Mackenzie, my best friend's fiancée, had invited me to a rage room.

Kenz: Hey bestie! Want to go to a rage room with me? I really need to smash something.

Me: Don't worry about me. I've got my own way of coping 😝

Kenz: A way that doesn't involve sucking clit?

Me: Okay fine! Smashing shit it is!

Kenz: See you at 5 😚

. . .

She said it seemed like we both could use some stress relief, but I disagreed. With the things going on in her life, I understood how she could be under stress, but me?

I was perfectly fine. I had been relieving stress almost daily for the past two years, but she demanded I pound my frustration into something else.

Mackenzie and I were finally on good terms again. She came to me with the idea of proposing to Fallon, and although I had good reasons to question it, she convinced me that she had nothing but good intentions.

I was finally at a point where I didn't want to choke her every time I saw her. I wouldn't call us best friends by any definition of the word, but she was safe with me, as long as Fallon was happy.

After checking in and choosing what we wanted to smash—me an old box television, Mackenzie a few glass bottles—we took a seat in the lobby, watching the groups before us on the monitor take their turns in the rage room.

"Tell me, how's the wedding planning going?" Mackenzie and Fallon were set to get married in a couple of months.

Fallon still had a long way to go to repair the damage that her ex had caused, but Mackenzie was there right behind her to help rebuild her shattered heart. She was great for Fallon, and I truly believed they were soulmates.

I was happy for my best friend. She deserved her happy ending and I was glad to have a part in it.

Mackenzie sighed contentedly, the corners of her lips tipping up. "It's good. You know I love her, and I can't wait to call her my wife. She's been really getting into the whole thing and talking with her mom on the phone almost every day about everything from colors to dresses. As long as I get to marry her, I wouldn't care if we went to city hall, but you and I both know Fallon deserves the wedding of her dreams. Speaking of the wedding, we have the cake tasting coming up in a few weeks, so don't forget!"

"Of course. I am her maid of honor, you know. I would never forget!"

She snorted. "I don't know, Dre. You've been kind of out of it lately. I was just making sure. Fallon will kick both of our asses if you miss it, and I'm not getting into trouble for you."

"Relax," I said, nudging her shoulder with mine. "You won't be sleeping outside anytime soon, at least not because of me. Anyway, I haven't been out of it. I'll be there Kenzie, scout's honor." I jokingly saluted her.

She glared at me. "I know, I'm sorry. I think I'm more of a bridezilla than she is. I just want everything to be perfect for her. Both of our bridal parties will be at the tasting. It's going to be a full house for a damn eating appointment!"

I could understand the horror written on Mackenzie's face. Cake tasting and wine with the girls was definitely going to be memorable.

I laughed. "Yeah, I know. Let's go, it's our turn." I angled my head toward the monitor that showed our names.

That was the most fun I'd had in a while, but I might have taken too much aggression out on that poor television.

At one point, I threw my bat and started screaming and cussing until I could feel the tears coming, and I had to leave, not stopping to speak to anyone.

It was safe to say Mackenzie's idea was effective. I started channeling all of my anger from the past five years, from all the fights I'd had with Skylar.

I wish I regretted it. I wish I regretted not going to New York with her. But I didn't, and I think that was part of the reason I was upset about our breakup, because I should have been devastated, but I wasn't —at least, not about that.

I was upset because I missed having someone to take care of. I was angry because I missed her, and I missed being needed. I was Drea Voss. I shouldn't need to depend on anyone for anything, yet a part of me did. My father would be disappointed in me, and I couldn't blame him.

Then, as if I weren't angry enough, a memory crossed my mind. My rage exploded, and that thought was just the icing on the cake. My whole childhood came rushing into that room.

I was angry with my parents for killing any hopes of happiness. I was angry at them for allowing me to think I was too weak for someone to love. What kind of person— Not right now. I wouldn't give that thought any power.

I was walking out when Mackenzie stopped me. "Drea!"

I stopped and schooled my features before turning around. "I was wondering if you were going to catch up."

She walked closer to me and spoke in a gentle voice. "Do you want to talk about it?"

I narrowed my eyes, hoping she couldn't see how red they were becoming. I needed to get a hold of whatever was going on. "Talk about what, Kenzie? It's a rage room. You're supposed to smash things. That's kind of the whole point."

"Yeah, but you aren't supposed to throw your weapon at the wall and scream at it. Come and sit down with me." She angled her head toward a bench just outside the building's front door.

I sighed and relented, taking up the seat next to her.

"Okay, you are in a safe space. Put your walls down. What's going on, Dre?"

I was not in the mood to talk, but it was also hard keeping everything in sometimes, and I knew if Fallon could trust her with her heart, I could trust her with this.

"I don't know, I guess I'm still dealing with the breakup. Sky was all I knew for three years, you know? I don't know how to move on from that."

We had our final piece of closure a few months ago, when she came back into town to visit her parents. I ran into her at Brewed Awakening one morning, and we sat and talked. She was doing really well, and she was happy in New York. My heart cracked when she mentioned she was dating someone, but I was happy for her. She deserved it.

"I know it's hard, Drea, and I'm sorry you're going through this. It will get better, though, I promise. Things happen for a reason, and you did the right thing for both of you." She smiled and rested her hand on my shoulder.

"You know, that's the same thing I told Fallon when she first met you, and look where you two ended up. I'm doing fine, though, really. I knew we had an expiration date. I just wasn't expecting it to end the way it did, but I'm enjoying the single life and trying to mend a broken heart."

She sat back and got a dreamy look on her face at the mention of her fiancée. "I'm so thankful she listened to your advice. I cannot imagine where I would have been if things turned out differently. But seriously, Drea, I don't think you are okay. You've been enjoying the single life a little too much."

What was that supposed to mean? "What are you talking about?" I frowned.

She glared at me. "You know what I'm talking about. The drinking, sleeping with different women almost every night, being late to work, if you show up at all. That is not you. Well, the sleeping around is, but you would kick Kaia's ass, and most definitely Fallon's, if either one of them pulled some shit like that. I know people grieve in different ways, but the way you are going about it is not healthy, Dre."

"Sex is in fact extremely healthy, Kenz. Look it up." I was in the best shape of my life, and my mood had been pretty peppy these days. Maybe not like it used to be, but still something.

"Drea, be serious for a second. You know I am never one to talk down on having sex. Next to Fallon, sex is like my favorite thing in life. Especially sex *with* Fallon, I mean you saw, she can really—"

"Get on with it, please," I cut in, desperately trying to avoid the topic of my best friend's sex life. I loved the details from Fallon's side, but I really did not need to hear about how freaky my best friend could get. She was like my sister.

"Interrupting is rude, Voss!" She huffed, as if I had just ruined her whole day. "Like I was trying to say, yes, sex is healthy, but sex with a lot of random women is not, especially when you're also getting intoxicated, and it's affecting your everyday life. And showing up late to work, or not showing up at all, is affecting your life."

She wasn't wrong. About the sex part, yes, but the other part, it wasn't like I was proud of the way my life had been going recently. I would just start drinking to forget about Skylar, and when that didn't work, I drank some more until I found a warm body to comfort me.

"You're one to talk. If I remember correctly, you were the expert on sleeping around before you met Fallon." I glared at her.

"Yes, and you see what happened when I stopped? I found my

reason for breathing. I'm not proud of that part of my life, and I don't miss it at all. After a while, it just got to be too much. Keeping track of who I'd slept with and who I hadn't, on top of getting tested frequently. Not to mention, making sure I didn't scream out the wrong name. And don't turn this around on me. We're talking about you. Your work is your life, and something is really wrong if you're letting anything or anyone get in the way of it."

I really hated when she was right. "Okay, so maybe I'm going through some things. I'm just trying to find myself again."

"That's all fine and dandy. You're allowed to miss Skylar and you're allowed to figure your shit out, but you can't do that when you're face —or strap—deep in someone else. You need to take some time to find yourself. Alone."

"Alone? What exactly are you suggesting, Mackenzie?" My voice was laced with weariness. I was pretty sure whatever she was suggesting, I wasn't going to like it.

She rolled her eyes. "You need a restraining order against sex, to clear your head."

I gaped at her and tried to suppress a snort, dumbfounded that she would even suggest such a thing. "No sex?! Oh, for fuck's sake, you have to be out of your mind! I should make Fallon ban you from sex for that horrid suggestion!"

She laughed. "First of all, good luck with that. She would be just as miserable without it as I would be. Our sex is way too good. You remember the book sign—"

I threw my hands up in the air, shaking them violently across her face. "No, no, no, I believe you, Mackenzie. I told you we were never to speak of that again! I should have thrown the damn chair out, or burned it!"

She shook her head. "Fallon was right, you are dramatic. Anyway, my point is, you can't find yourself if you can't see where you are going, and you can't see if your head's between someone's legs. Just give it a try, Dre."

I thought about it for a moment. Could I actually give up sex? Would it even help anything? "What are the terms of this challenge, then?" I was a little curious, I admit.

"No sex for..." She paused in thought, and I hoped she didn't say anything longer than a month. I didn't know if I could survive that. I really enjoyed sex.

"A year."

My eyes almost popped out of my head and this time I couldn't hold back a snort. "A year?! You have really lost it. Please tell me this is a sick joke?"

"Drea, I believe in you. No sex for an entire year. Find other things to fill your time. Take a class or something. Find yourself and who you are without sex."

"Is masturbating off the table too?" I prayed not, or I was screwed.

She laughed. "Of course not. I'm not that cruel." Thank fucking God!

I frowned. A year without sex sounded fucking terrible. "A whole year? That is impossible."

She rolled her eyes and let out an overly dramatic sigh. "No, it's not, Drea."

"Then you can do it. Honestly, Kenzie, was this Fallon's idea? It sounds like a stupid idea she'd have rolling around in her head."

Fallon was never one to sleep around, so it wouldn't have surprised me if she came up with this plan.

"She may have suggested it, but I agreed with her—"

"As you always do." It didn't matter that Fallon was always right, and right now I despised her for it. The woman had a freaky ability when it came to knowing someone, but I supposed, as her best friend, I was a little easier to read.

She rolled her eyes. "Drea, I'm trying to be nice and supportive here, and you're ruining it! You need to stop silicone-dicking around and get your shit together! Fallon hates seeing you like this, and it's pissing me off, too. This isn't you!"

I sighed. She was right, Fallon must be rubbing off on her. "I should never have helped your ass get her back. I retract everything I ever said or did to help."

She nudged my shoulder. "I know you love me. She told me so."

I groaned. "Goddamn her. Are none of my secrets safe anymore? Ugh, fine, you guys win! I'll give it a try, but I honestly don't see how it's going to do any good."

Chapter Two

DREA

"This fucking sucks!" My chaste year started fifteen days ago—yes, I was counting the literal days—and I already wanted to quit.

As Mackenzie had suggested, I found some local classes, trying to find something else to fill my time. The first class I tried was yoga, and that was an epic fail. Not only was I terrible at it and had zero flexibility, it was an incredibly erotic class. All those women in their tight-ass leggings bending over? Jesus Christ! Needless to say, I wore out several batteries that week and decided yoga was not for me.

Last week was glass blowing, another erotic class. Blowing a hot rod? Who came up with that idea?!

I should have known taking Mackenzie's suggestions was going to piss me off. She couldn't have suggested painting or knitting? I should learn to make birdhouses or something. Birds can't be erotic, right?

This week, I was going to start finding my own activities to try. When I mentioned Mackenzie's great plan to Cara at lunch, she almost choked on her drink.

"Let me get this straight. You're going to go a whole year without sex? You? I give it a week, tops," she had said in a fit of laughter.

Cara and I had worked together since I opened the store five years ago. Cara was the CEO of Wells Publishing. She also took on a few clients herself.

She published several of the authors I had signings for over the years, and she had become not only a colleague but a close friend.

I scowled at her, but eventually she calmed down and actually started being useful. She suggested trying a more physical approach, like pickleball. Physical activity was a good way to relieve stress, and boy was I full of it.

When she introduced me to the sport, I laughed. The only physical activity I enjoyed required a different set of grunting noises. But Mackenzie's stupid voice was playing in my head, so there I was trying to better myself or some bullshit.

~

Twenty-two days later, I was dripping in sweat, and not the good kind.

"Fuck you, you suck!" I grunted out. We were ten minutes into our pickleball game, and I was not having a good time.

She laughed, hitting the ball back over to my side. "I'm winning, so I think it's you who sucks. Maybe if you were getting laid, you would have the stamina to keep up and I could actually have some competition!" She laughed when I almost tripped trying to hit the ball.

"That was a low blow, Wells!"

"You walked right into that one, or tripped into it!" She was laughing so hard I wanted to throw my paddle at her.

I cursed under my breath when I missed my next shot. "Did you come to talk shit, or play a game?" I yelled through gritted teeth.

"Seeing as how you're losing by a long shot, I think I'm the only one playing. And shit talking is part of the game. I'm pretty sure it's the first rule, actually."

"I thought the first rule was not to talk about the game?"

"That's fight club, Dre. Come on, one more round and I'll set you free." She laughed when I flipped her off. "Tempting, but you're banned from sex." She winked.

She was attractive for sure. She had the perfect combination of blonde hair and blue eyes, and don't even get me started on her boobs. But we had been working together for years, and I didn't mix business with pleasure. Besides, I just didn't see her that way.

By the end of our game, I had lost five to one, but at least I got a workout in. We turned in our paddles to the front desk and headed for the parking lot.

"You're getting better, but you seem a little off today. Is everything alright?"

"Besides my self-inflicted dry spell, yes. I'm perfect." The lie flew out.

I knew she didn't buy it. "Drea."

I sighed. I hated being vulnerable. "Fine. I'm a little on edge today, okay? On top of not getting laid, the store isn't doing as well as I would like and I'm just a little stressed."

"How bad is it?" Concern laced her voice.

"We're not in the red or anything, but it's not doing as well as it has in the past, and I would like to see it get there again. I don't know what's been going on."

"It can be like that sometimes, especially with social media and access to ebooks. You just need to do something to gain attention and bring people in."

I knew she was right. I just didn't have a clue where to start. I'd been thinking about adding a little cafe or bar. Maybe a live music night or something, but it was expensive and risky to invest that kind of money if the store wasn't already doing well enough.

"We had some speed dating events, but they didn't bring in enough to change things, and I'm stuck. Do you have any ideas on where to start?" I asked.

"This is perfect timing, actually. I might have a business proposition for you, but I need you to hear me out before you immediately say no because I don't think you're going to like it, but I think it could be just what you need."

I had a strong feeling that I knew exactly what she was going to say, and she was right, I wouldn't like it. Not one bit.

Chapter Three

BLAIR

"Absolutely not. Forget it! Not a chance in hell!"

I was pretty sure my publisher had smoked something insanely strong before calling me, because she could not have suggested what I thought she was.

I heard a long sigh on the other end. "Blair, calm down and hear me out."

I scoffed. "Calm down? Why don't you calm down, Cara? I mean that respectfully, of course."

Cara Wells had been my publisher for the past seven years, since the first book of my fantasy romance series had been released.

"Look, I know you're upset. You two don't have the greatest track record, and I get that, I really do. But I'm doing this as a favor. You're a best-selling author now. It can only help your career, and it's also good publicity for the bookstore."

Saying we didn't have the greatest track record was the understatement of the year. The first time I worked with Drea was a mess. It started out friendly and professional, but by the end I wanted to forget the whole thing. Every small request was like trying to run in quicksand.

She bought plain decorations that looked like they belonged behind a window of a second-hand store. I asked her for fresh baked goods and colorful flowers, but on the day of the book signing, it was a complete disaster.

The pastries looked as if they were baked by someone's five-year-old, meant to be secretly thrown away after you praised the child for a great job. I was embarrassed and horrified.

When I confronted her, she accused me of being demanding and hard to please. Apparently, she had reviews from other authors praising her choice of vendors. Clearly, they were just trying to kiss her ass for a discount.

I reluctantly agreed to work with her a few more times after that, but after the last time, I vowed to never work with Drea Voss again.

She thought that just because she was British and had the legs of a Greek goddess, she could do whatever she wanted, and I wouldn't stand for it.

"I don't give a shit about what's good for her store, and making me work with her is not doing me a favor!"

"Blair, I know it's not ideal, but it's business. She is willing to put her differences aside and start over."

I scoffed at the absurdity. "Yeah, right. I'm sure she's jumping up and down at the opportunity to work with me again."

I'd done a few signings at Open Book, and it was a nightmare every time. The owner was unprofessional and incompetent.

She sighed. "Look, I'm going to level with you here. I'm doing this to help the both of you. It'll be good for the store, and you need to keep up the momentum. If you want me to play hardball, just remember that you signed a contract, so I could've pulled rank here and made you do the signing without asking. But I came to you as a friend first. I'm asking, as your friend, to please do this favor for me."

I groaned. "It sounds like I don't have a choice either way, but you did ask nicely, so fine. I will do the signing. But I swear if it doesn't work out, it's the last time. I mean it, Cara!"

She squealed. "Thank you, Blair. Everything will be fine, don't you worry. We are meeting with her tomorrow morning at nine a.m. before the store opens to go over the legality of everything. Just try and be nice, please."

Be nice to Drea Voss? That was going to be a challenge. "We have a meeting tomorrow? That was quick. You didn't happen to schedule this meeting assuming I would say yes, did you?" I scowled into my phone.

"I might have. You have a heart of gold... somewhere, and I knew you would see it my way one way or another. Listen, I have to go. See you tomorrow, doll."

I hung up the phone and threw it across my couch. This was my living hell. The last time I worked with her, I swore to myself it would be the last. I might as well open my own bookstore if I want it done right.

Releasing a long sigh, I stood up and headed for a much-needed bubble bath. If I had to work with that woman again, I was going to get all of my ducks in a row and make sure I started off with a clear and calm head.

The next morning, I woke up before the crack of dawn for my regular yoga class. I did yoga every morning.

Normally, it would set my day up for success, but since I knew I had a meeting with Drea today, it didn't help as much as I had hoped.

To say I was not looking forward to this meeting was an understatement. The last time I saw Drea was about a year ago at my last signing at her store. Her assistant was professional and friendly, nothing like her boss.

The one and only thing I had in common with the insufferable bookstore owner was the fact that we were terrible at hiding our emotions. I could always tell when she was pretending to be nice, which was anytime I interacted with the woman. The feelings were very much mutual.

I hoped she was dressed more professionally this time. She wore a low-cut brown halter top and white jean shorts the last time we had a meeting, and showing that much dark and creamy skin was inappropriate.

A car horn pulled me out of my thoughts, alerting me my ride had arrived, and when I got into the car, I texted Cara:

> Me: Good morning. I'm on my way. Are you there yet?

> Cara: Morning, doll! See you soon. Not yet, grabbing coffee from BA. Want anything?

Brewed Awakening was a cute coffee shop a few blocks down from the bookstore, with the best coffee and the sweetest barista.

> Me: That sounds amazing. My usual please?

> Cara: Of course! Chai latte with cinnamon. Some things never change!

> Me: Why fix something that isn't broken? It's delicious! And thank you!

> Cara: 😊

When I made it to the bookstore, Cara was standing outside the door holding my drink with a grin on her face.

"Good morning. Here's your latte!" She held out one of the two cups in her hand.

"Thanks, Cara. Take it out of my next book," I teased as I took a tentative drink.

She laughed. "Don't mention it. Are you ready?"

No, I wanted to say. I was not ready for this guaranteed disaster of a meeting.

Instead, I rolled my shoulders and took a sip of my latte. It was like Christmas in a cup, in the spring. "As ready as I'll ever be. Let's just get this over with." I put on my best professional smile.

"Just be nice, please. We are all professionals. Can you keep your personal feelings outside?"

I turned to her and widened my smile. "I can if she can."

Groaning, she opened the door, motioning for me to go inside.

Chapter Four

DREA

There were countless other things I could think of that I would rather do instead of attending this meeting with Blair. For example, getting a pap smear from Edward Scissorhands came to mind.

I agreed to this? I was really about to work with Blair Sterling again? The last time I worked with her was torturous.

She was arrogant and overbearing, and nothing I did made her happy. Finally, I put Kaia in charge, and told her to give the princess whatever she wanted.

I tried to be friendly, and I strived to create a relaxing environment for anyone I handled business with, but she wouldn't know "friendly" if it bit her in her perfect round ass!

The store wasn't in any sort of major financial trouble, but it wasn't doing as well as it had been the previous years, and I wanted to do something to get it back on track.

Unfortunately, working with a pain-in-the-ass best-selling author was my only option at the moment.

I'd wanted to throw my pickleball paddle at Cara when she'd mentioned it. I almost did, actually. She knew I couldn't stand the woman, but she pointed out the fact that I kind of owed her, so I really couldn't say no.

Before Fallon met Mackenzie, I tried to set her up with Cara, and it sort of worked. They went on a date that ended horribly when Mackenzie also happened to be there and ruined it in the only way Mackenzie knew how at the time—by letting her jealously get the best of her and embarrassing both Fallon and Cara in the process.

This was when Fallon and Mackenzie were just keeping things casual, but it turned out that Mackenzie also went out with Cara. Small world. Also, those two wouldn't have known casual if it stared them in the face.

From the moment I saw them together, I knew they were lying to each other just as much as they were lying to us.

Mackenzie used to be a serial one-night stander like me, but one look at Fallon and that life was out the window. As for Fallon, she *never* slept around, so I knew nothing about them was actually casual.

After the whole thing, I talked to Cara, and she was surprisingly okay with everything. She was laid back and understood that these things happened, but I felt like I owed her for unintentionally putting her in that weird situation.

I shouldn't have pressured her so much into asking Fallon out. Luckily, it all worked out for everyone involved, except for me.

Because there I was, roughly thirty-three days into my sexless year, and I was forced to work with the last person I wanted to.

At least I wouldn't have to worry about breaking my promise. Even if I was drunk and she was the last woman on Earth, I would never have sex with Blair freaking Sterling.

Her ears must have been burning, because the bell above the door chimed, and when I looked up, my entire body tensed for a multitude of reasons. It had been over a year since the last time I'd seen her, but not a lot had changed.

Her strawberry-blonde hair was still in long waves, but she'd replaced her studded nose ring for a golden hoop. *That's new.*

Hazel eyes stared back at me with intensity. Her sun-kissed olive skin was surrounded by a cream-colored off-the-shoulder sweater dress so tight I had to clear my throat in hopes of erasing the dryness that had crept its way in.

"Are you going to go say hello, or do you plan on just staring at them all morning?"

I jumped, turning my head to see Kaia's arched eyebrow. To be honest, I had forgotten she was standing there.

I scowled, trying to cover how red my cheeks were getting. "I was hoping if I stared hard enough, she'd get scared and leave."

Kaia rolled her eyes. "You wish. Go be a professional boss lady!" She nudged my side and I groaned. I didn't want to.

"Good morning." I smiled tightly as I walked toward Blair, with Cara following a step behind.

"Morning, Dre. I got you a chai latte, your favorite."

"Thanks, Cara. Hello, Blair, you're looking nice." It was the best I could do. It was too early to deal with her, and she did look nice. Really nice.

I had to admit, for a pain in my ass, she was gorgeous. *That's just the dry spell talking. Pull it together!*

She looked at me with narrowed brows. "You drink chai?"

"See, something you both have in common. Aren't we off to a great start already?"

We both looked at Cara, who put her hands up in surrender. "Okay, fine. Let's go somewhere and talk."

"We can talk over there," I said pointing to the couches in the corner. "Is that alright with you, Ms. Sterling?"

Cara gave me a cutting look, but I only shrugged in response. At least I was pretending to be nice.

Blair's lips curled. "Of course, Ms. Voss. Thank you so much for asking." Her response was sarcastic, and I barely suppressed an eyeroll. *This is going to be a long project.*

I grabbed my laptop from underneath the counter and followed them to the couch, ignoring the way my body heated watching Blair's ass move in that dress.

Cara and Blair sat on one couch while I sat on the other with Kaia. I didn't really need Kaia for this meeting, but it was always helpful to have an extra buffer between us.

"I want to start this meeting off by saying how appreciative I am to both of you for agreeing to this. I'd like the signing to be in a few months, so you won't have that long to deal with each other. I know it's not an ideal situation, but we are all grown adults, and I think we can put our childish differences behind us for the sake of business, don't you agree?" Cara looked directly at me the entire time she spoke, as if I were somehow the problem.

I narrowed my eyes. "May I ask why you're looking at me like that? It's not like I'm the one who started this whole thing."

"And what exactly does that mean?" Blair crossed her arms.

"Ladies, ladies, please. I think it would be a good idea to run some promotions before the signing. You know, really get the word out not only about Blair's books, but about the store as well. This is a partnership, ladies. You are both getting something out of it."

I tried, and failed, to hide my eye roll. What exactly was I getting out of it? More business, which meant more money, I guess. But working with Blair again, I wasn't so sure it was going to be worth it.

It was all I could do to put a smile on my face. "Of course."

Cara looked at me and sighed before turning her attention to her best friend. "Blair, is there anything specific you expect from Drea and Kaia?"

Her shoulders slouched slightly and she sighed. "I expect professionalism and competency. The bare minimum, but still somehow too much to ask for when it comes to Ms. Voss."

I scoffed, but Cara didn't let me protest before she cut in. "That is easy enough. Drea, what about you?"

"I can't speak for Kaia, but I expect to work with someone who has a shred of class and knows when to get off her high horse." I sighed when Cara shot me a threatening glare. "I expect communication, honesty, and patience. We can only do so much. We do still have a business to run after all."

"Okay, see, we're getting somewhere. All of that sounds reasonable. I'll draft up a contract with estimated capacity numbers, as well as a blueprint for our typical signing set up, and you can let me know if you have any questions. Does that sound fair?" she asked.

"Perfect. Are we done here? I have things to do, and I don't want to take up anymore of the queen's time."

Blair rolled her eyes, but Cara interjected before she had a chance to say anything. "I think that covers it for now."

"Good. Well, Blair, as always, it was not a pleasure, and I look forward to when this whole thing is over, and you can take whatever stick is glued up your ass and—"

"Drea!" Cara interrupted through gritted teeth.

"Talk about class. I'm sorry, but I'm pretty sure I'm helping you more than you're helping me, so you really need to watch who you're talking to!"

"First of all, little miss best-seller, you have no right to come into my store and act like you run the fucking show. I don't care if you're Oprah Winfrey—you will show some respect. I may have to put up with you as a favor to Cara, but I will not put up with your attitude, so leave it at the fucking door!" I stood up, ready to walk away from this whole thing.

"Okay, ladies!" Cara said, standing up. "I think that is enough for one day. Drea, I'll call you later and we can go over the next steps."

"Fine." I didn't bother acknowledging Blair as I headed for my office, giving Kaia a short nod on the way.

"Well, I think that went okay, don't you? No one got hurt," Kaia said as she shut my office door behind her.

I glared at her and sighed. "It went about as well as it always does. Why did I agree to this again?"

She sat down and smiled sweetly. "Because, Drea, you're a business woman, and you know it will benefit the both of you. And you're doing a nice thing for a friend."

"Some friend if she's making me do this! How am I going to survive this project?" I groaned, reaching for a bottle of water.

"If anyone can get through this, it's you. You are one of the strongest women I know."

"Your ass-kissing is improving, Kaia, but thanks. I swear, this is the last time I will ever work with Blair Sterling. Now, if you'll excuse me, I need some time to reset before we open. Also, don't forget I'm leaving early for my boxing class."

After Cara's genius idea to work with Blair, I decided a more physical approach was necessary, so I signed up for boxing. Tonight was my first class and I was looking forward to beating the shit out of something.

Chapter Five

BLAIR

Just as I'd expected, our first meeting went horribly. I stepped out onto the busy sidewalk, the cool spring air hitting me like a splash of water, a stark contrast to the heated bookstore from minutes ago.

I took a deep breath, trying to shake off the lingering irritation. I didn't get rattled. I was poised and collected, and I tended to let things roll off my back. It was just... Drea Voss.

She had a way of getting under my skin, and I couldn't control it. If there was one thing I liked having in my life, it was control, and every time I was around her, I felt like I had no control of anything. I couldn't control the words spilling from my mouth, or my body's reaction to her smooth skin, or that fucking accent—

"What is wrong with you two?" Cara's yelling broke me free of my internal thoughts. "You are one of the most professional authors I have worked with. Why is it with Drea, you can't seem to channel that professionalism?" Cara threw her hands up while we walked down the street.

I shrugged. "You should be asking her that. She started it!"

"Oh, I plan to, but right now I'm asking you. You two need to pull it together. If other businesses hear about your little rivalry with her, it is going to be harder to get them to work with us."

Damn, she had a point. I sighed. "I'm sorry, Cara. I know, and I don't want that for either of us. I'll try harder, I promise."

"Good! Now, I have to run. Do you need a ride?"

I smiled and hugged her. "No, I'm good. I'm going to walk around for a little."

As I walked down the street for some much-needed air, my phone buzzed in my pocket. When I saw it was my brother calling, I hesitated before answering.

I loved my brother, of course, but I knew he would want to talk about the meeting, and I wasn't in the mood. Even though my brother lived in California, we still talked a few times a week if we could.

Guilt swirled inside my chest as I thought of declining the call. What if something was really wrong? What if something happened to the boys or his wife?

I sighed rather dramatically before answering. "Hello, Christopher."

"Ugh, you know I hate when you use my full name! How'd it go with the new project?"

I grimaced, looking back toward the infuriating bookstore. "Terrible. The bookstore is beautiful and one of my favorites in the city, but the owner is... difficult."

"That bad, huh?" He chuckled. "Well, if anyone can handle it, it's you."

"Sure," I muttered, not feeling as confident as my brother was in me. "Anyway, what's up? Why'd you call?"

"Oh, right! I was just checking in. I wanted to make sure you came out in one piece!"

I snorted. "What, you don't think I could take her?" I could have totally taken her!

"No, of course you could take her. I'm sure you could totally kick her ass! Anyway, I gotta take the boys to soccer. Stay safe in Seattle. Love you. Bye, little sister."

I rolled my eyes. "Love you, too. Bye, you big pain!"

After hanging up, I found myself at a nearby park. I took a seat on the bench, my mind drifting back to the meeting.

There was something about her—something more than just the

initial animosity. She still had that same snarky personality, but something was different underneath her exterior. There was a sadness in her eyes, like something had changed her within the last year.

But before I could ponder it further, I noticed a woman with a dog walking by. The dog, a fluffy golden retriever, trotted over, wagging its tail enthusiastically.

The dog reached my lap and demanded attention in the form of a belly rub. "Looks like someone made a friend." The woman giggled as she gently pulled the leash back. I reached out to pet the dog, smiling for the first time since leaving the bookstore.

"Well, at least someone's happy to see me," I murmured. No sooner had the words left my mouth than the dog decided even he was done with me, and walked away without so much as a goodbye.

As I sat there, watching my new furry friend walk away into the distance, I decided I needed a distraction. I pulled out my phone and opened a dating app I hadn't used in months. Maybe it was time to put myself out there again, even if it was just for a little while.

After my last relationship, I had tried a different approach. During one of our lunch dates, Cara had convinced me to try something more casual, but when the time came, I freaked out. I couldn't bring myself to be comfortable enough to have sex with a random stranger. I never mustered up the courage to tell her. Anytime she asked about it, I would deflect and change the subject.

I swiped through profiles, but my mind kept wandering back to Drea's fierce eyes and the way she'd stood her ground. Not to mention, that thigh-clenching accent.

"Great," I muttered to myself, shaking my head. "I'm already obsessing over the one person I can't stand."

With a resigned sigh, I stood up. I had work to do and a book signing to survive, and I wasn't about to let her stand in my way.

Chapter Six

DREA

Mackenzie picked the worst time for this sex ban! Dealing with Blair and not being able to relieve some tension was not ideal.

She was insufferable, she was a pain in my ass, she was a fucking bombshell of a woman and I didn't know how to handle myself around her.

I was still on the hunt for a class to take my mind off not being able to have sex. I enjoyed boxing, but the bruises didn't look good on me, so I went back to playing pickleball with Cara for now.

I was actually getting pretty good, and the workout was great. It kept my mind off of things it had no business being on, like the way someone's outfit hugged every curve of their body.

Cara called me shortly after the meeting and tore me a new one. I honestly thought my phone had cracked from how loud she was. I apologized for being rude, but I couldn't help it. Blair just rubbed me the wrong way. I promised I would try harder the next time I saw her, which, sadly, was tomorrow. Cara had another meeting, so it was going to be just Blair and me. Fucking perfect.

When I stepped out of my office and into the bookstore, my heart warmed.

"Babe!" Fallon rushed over from the counter and gave me a warm hug. It felt like ages since I'd last seen my best friend. She had been busy with her fiancée, and I guess I was simply a peasant to her now. Kaia was busy with a customer, but she looked up and smiled at us.

"Love! Oh, how I've missed you, my queen. I'm so glad you deemed us worthy of an appearance on this glorious day," I joked.

"Oh, fuck off!" She swatted my arm. "Catch me up. What's been going on?"

"If you bothered to make a phone call, you would know what's going on, love. But you have more important people in your life now, I suppose." I shrugged.

"Drea Elise, lose the attitude, please. You know I have a lot going on, as do you I'm told. I guess I don't have to ask how your sex ban is going. You seem a little on edge these days." Her grin was irritating.

I resigned my irritation with an exhale. "Sorry, love. You're right, I'm a little testy these days thanks to your fiancée's great plan. Not to mention, I'm only in the beginning stages of the 'Blair Bitch Project' and I want to scream! We had our first meeting a few days ago, and spoiler alert, it ended in a fight. If it were anyone else besides Cara, I would have vetoed this great business arrangement immediately."

Fallon seemed to find my crappy life hilarious. "I'm sorry, Dre. Yeah, Kaia told me you're working with Blair again, and I have to admit I was surprised. But if it's for the good of the store, I know you'll figure it out. You're still coming to the cake tasting next week, right? Kenzie said she talked to you about it?"

I sent Kaia a glare, who blushed from embarrassment and only shrugged. "After the two of you ganged up on me and decided my sex life needed to cease? Yes, she did, and yes, I will be there, love."

She smiled softly and gave me another hug, which nine times out of ten, calmed my anger. "Good. I can't get married without my sister."

Damn allergies! I wiped my eyes and cleared my throat. "Enough sentimentality. I have work to do. Are you going to be around?"

"Of course, babe. Go do your big boss shit. We got this." She laughed, bringing Kaia in for a side hug.

I rolled my eyes but grinned as I headed back to the solitude of my office.

The next day, after a round of pickleball, which I lost, by the way, Cara and I were sitting in the club's café having lunch.

"Okay, so Blair is stopping by the store around three today. Does that work?" Cara asked.

I blinked at her with a closed smile, trying to be as calm as I could be. I was not looking forward to seeing her again, especially if Cara wasn't there as a referee, but I didn't have a choice. "That's perfect." It was far from perfect. No good could come from Blair and me being in the same space together unsupervised.

"Good, and you're going to be nice this time? I cannot have you two fighting every second. This is business, so can you act like mature adults?"

"Yes, Cara. I told you I was sorry. She just gets under my skin. But I will try, for you and for the store."

"Excellent. So, when she gets there, maybe don't go to your office? Stay in a public place. I know if you have customers you won't raise your voice in front of them." She grinned.

Clearly she didn't know about the time I yelled at Mackenzie in the middle of my store. The circumstances were different back then. The store was my life, but Fallon was my family.

"You got it, boss. Anything else?"

She sighed. "No, that's all. I'll talk to her and make sure we're all on the same page. I will also talk to Kaia, and she will let me know if even a hair is out of place between you two. I expect her to come back in one piece with a final drafted copy of the signing schedule. Usually we would handle that, but Blair and I have more of a relaxed professional relationship than I do with my other clients, so I give her more say in how things are done."

I snorted. "Relaxed? I didn't know she knew the word."

She rolled her eyes. "Anyway, I've got to go, but good luck, and please be nice. She's been through a lot."

"Haven't we all?" I asked dryly. When she glared at me, I added, "Fine, go. You'll get her back in one piece, I promise."

She left and I sat there, unable to finish my salad. I put my fork down in annoyance as I had lost my appetite at the thought of seeing Blair again.

There was no way this meeting wouldn't end with someone getting hurt, especially with how the last one ended, and that was with witnesses.

I made a promise, and I always kept my promises. I would go into this meeting with a positive frame of mind, but if I had any say in the matter, she would get her back a lot sooner than originally planned.

Chapter Seven

BLAIR

"Yes, Cara, for the millionth time, I will be as nice as I can be. Strictly professional." I groaned while Cara reminded me for the third time about my meeting with Drea. Like I could forget.

Cara had another client to meet, so it was going to be just the two of us. I attended two yoga sessions and even went for a facial and a massage. I needed all the serenity I could get.

I was in my cab headed to the store when she called.

"Great! Call me later, and good luck." The line went silent, and I groaned before heading into the bookstore.

When I walked in it was pretty quiet. A few people were sitting around reading, and Kaia was at the counter with a redhead I'd seen once or twice.

"Hey, Blair, welcome in," Kaia greeted from the cash register. I squared my shoulders and smiled. Strictly professional. I could do this.

"Hello, Kaia, it's nice to see you again." I turned to the redhead who was on her phone doing something. "Fallon, right?" I asked.

"Yes, hi again, Blair. I'm so sorry, I'm being rude. Wedding brain. Kaia, tell Drea I'll see her later? Enjoy your meeting, Blair," she said with a smirk.

"It's alright, I understand. Congratulations on the engagement." There was a softness in her eyes, and it made something in my chest ache. I longed to have that feeling. Of being with someone who made me look that way when I talked about them. That made *them* look that way at someone when they talked about *me*.

"Thanks. Bye, guys." And with a blink, she was gone.

I turned back to Kaia, who was looking at something within the bookstore. I tried to follow her gaze, but as soon as I turned my head, her throat cleared. "So, Drea is in her office. You can go on back."

I whipped my head back in her direction. "Oh, thank you. Can you just let her know I'm here? I think it's best if I don't go back there, considering how the last meeting went."

She frowned. "Nonsense. You need a private setting to discuss business. Go on back. She knows you're coming. It'll be fine, Blair." She motioned to the back toward Drea's office, and I hesitated. Drea and I had never been alone together before. It seemed risky, but what choice did I have?

Did I want to sit and argue with Kaia, or relent and go back to Drea's office? Arguing with Kaia would be like kicking a three-legged puppy, and even I wasn't that cruel.

"Sure." I decided it wasn't worth the fight. Besides, I was an adult. Surely I could handle myself around her. I took a deep breath and rounded the counter, heading toward the back.

I was a little nervous, but I couldn't let Drea see that. Our initial meeting with Cara was a nightmare. I went into it with a clear head, hoping to end on a positive note, but that didn't happen.

When I walked into that first meeting, I almost dropped my latte. I hadn't seen her in so long, but she still looked the same. Same shaved head, same dark caramel skin, same labret piercing. What was it about that damn piercing that made me want to circle it with my tongue? *Woah, where did that thought come from?*

I remember so vividly what she had on that day. She wore the shortest pair of black jean shorts I had ever seen someone wear, exposing her mile-long legs. If she had bent down, I would have seen more of Drea Voss than I needed to.

She paired them with a white button-up shirt with the sleeves rolled up, the shirt tucked into her shorts. She looked casual but still somehow professional. The closest she'd ever gotten to professionalism so far.

Before today's meeting was over, I would need to remember to tell

Drea to install an air conditioner. I was sweating outside of her office in the middle of spring.

I knocked on the office door and waited.

"Come in." Drea's voice came through the door, and I rolled my neck. I could do this.

I took a deep breath and opened the door. She was wearing a low-cut maroon button-up shirt that accentuated the perfect shape of her breasts and hugged her natural curves. I couldn't look away even if I wanted to.

I blamed the lack of protein from my breakfast for the way I fanta-sized about what was underneath her shirt and how they would feel in my hands, or in my—

She was looking at her computer screen when she spoke. "What is it, Kaia? Is that—" She stopped when she looked up and saw me, and I quickly looked away. I hoped she didn't catch me staring.

I crossed my arms. "Don't stop on my account. Please continue. What were you going to say? Is that bitch here yet? Is that pain in the ass best-selling author still coming in?"

"Your words, not mine," she mumbled.

"What was that?"

She cleared her throat. "Nothing, apologies. Please, have a seat." She motioned to the two chairs in front of her desk and went back to her computer, typing away at something. The room was as silent as a library, only the soft pounding of her fingers on the keyboard filling the space. I hated myself for wondering what else those thumping fingers could do. *Seriously, Blair?*

I was anxious to break the silence between us. "Nice office. It's very... simple," I said, looking around. The walls were bare, and the only furniture besides the desk and chairs, was a small couch in the corner. Simple wasn't necessarily bad, but I couldn't bring myself to give her a proper compliment.

"I prefer simple over complicated." She looked up from her computer, and I'd never noticed how dark her eyes were before. They were like warm pools of chocolate, and I could get lost in them if I wasn't careful.

I shook away my thoughts about any part of her and cleared my throat. "And what is that supposed to mean?"

"It means exactly what you think it means." She exhaled before continuing. "Listen, we're supposed to be playing nice, so can we just get down to business and get this over with, please?"

"Wow, she has manners. I'm very impressed." I sighed. "You're right. Our spy out there is probably listening to every word." Kaia was a sweet girl, but Cara informed me that she had asked her to make sure we stayed in line.

"Exactly. Cara wants us to come up with some sort of plan for the signing. Did you have anything in mind?"

"Well, I always like to do a small Q&A before the actual signing. Is that going to be a problem this time?"

She rolled her eyes. "No problem at all. Anything else?"

I sighed, irritated by the fact that she should have known by now what I like. This wasn't my first signing with her, but God, did I hope it was my last. "You know I always have a dessert table set up."

She wrote something down in her notebook, gripping the pen a little tighter than she needed to.

I frowned, already feeling like I was a burden to her. I was contractually obligated to work with her, but Drea? I wasn't sure why she'd agreed to work together if she hated me so much. If a simple request was a big deal to her. "If that's too much to ask for..."

She looked up at me and shook her head. "No. A dessert table is fine."

"Then why are you gripping the pen like you have a personal vendetta against it?" I was honestly beginning to feel bad for the poor pen. She had quite the grip.

She looked down at her victim and lessened her hold. "It's nothing. I'm fine."

"Are you sure?" I wasn't sure why I was pressing.

"Yes!" she bit out. That was what I got for trying to be civil.

She didn't look fine, but I didn't ask anymore questions. I didn't care, anyway. "Okay... Well, if that's all, I can get out of here and tell Cara no one got hurt." I stood up and headed for the door.

She stopped me as my fingers wrapped around the door knob. "Hey, Blair?" When I turned around, she stood up and cut the space between us.

My pulse quickened when she got closer. I didn't know what to expect. We had never been that close before, and I wasn't prepared for whatever she was about to say or do.

She was quiet for several moments and the air felt thick. "Thank you... for doing this. I know it's not what either of us really want to be doing, but I appreciate it."

I swallowed. "Yeah... sure." I turned to walk away but paused when I heard her speak again.

"Also... that color looks good on you."

I looked down at my forest-green sweater dress. I didn't think about turning around to let her see my heated face. I left the bookstore for the second time that week, feeling the need to cool down.

Chapter Eight

DREA

I was fifty-six days into my sexual shutdown, and I was starting to lose it. Why on earth did I compliment Blair Sterling of all people? *That color looks good on you?* What was that? I must really be on something if I'm starting to find her attractive.

Still, I couldn't get that first meeting out of my head. Of course it didn't start off great; they never do.

But the way she looked, the past year had been very kind to her. I couldn't stop thinking about how I wanted to take her on my desk and use my double-sided dildo while ripping that sweater dress wide open.

Which was ridiculous, because I had absolutely no feelings for Blair. But the way that dress hugged her ass, I could pretend to like her, just a little.

I could pretend to like the way her tongue darted out to wet her bottom lip when she was anxious, or the way she looked like she owned every room she walked into wearing those infuriating fuck-me black heels. *God, I'm really losing it!*

I rubbed my face and fought the urge to lock my door and do something about my desperate need to fuck something, anything.

Then, as if the universe had read my thoughts, my dad called, immediately extinguishing the roaring fire building between my thighs.

"Hello, Father," I answered with a peppy voice.

"Hello, darling. How are you? How's Skylar?" I sighed, forgetting that I still hadn't told my parents about the breakup, even though it had been two years. I was over it by now, but it had just never come up.

"I'm fine. Skylar and I broke up a while ago. She moved to New York."

I could finally talk about it without spiraling into a drinking and fucking frenzy. Banning sex was one of the hardest challenges I'd ever had to endure. I had to admit, it had been keeping my mind clear and sharp, for the most part. I could still drink, though, and thank fuck for that.

"Oh, I do apologize. But I know you aren't broken up about it, are you? You were never the settling down type, not like your sisters."

I groaned. My sisters were the epitome of the all American dream. They were only a few years younger than me, but they had always wanted marriage, with kids and white-picket fences.

They were too young to understand what was happening when our parents divorced. I wasn't as fortunate. I had just started high school when my parents sat me down and told me the news of my father's adultery. After so many years of marriage and four kids, even my parents couldn't commit to each other. What chance did I have?

"How are you, Father?" I needed to turn the topic somewhere else.

"I'm splendid, dear. I just saw your sisters, and now I'm headed to Brighton for a few weeks to visit family."

My father had been in the military, and we'd moved out of England when I was ten. He got stationed in Portland until he retired, and had been there ever since. I'd been wanting to go and visit him, but with the bookstore, and dealing with Skylar leaving, I just didn't have the time to take off.

"That's good. Well, I have to run. I'm meeting Fallon for her cake tasting in a few minutes." We were meeting at our favorite bakery, Sugar-leaf, which was only a short drive from the bookstore.

"Okay, dear. Please be safe, and come visit soon. I miss you."

I smiled into my phone. I really did need to plan a visit to see him soon. "I will. Love you, Dad."

After my phone call, I was looking forward to taking my mind off things and spending time with my best friend.

I waved at Kaia as I headed out the door and down the street. It was a gorgeous day, so I thought the walk would be good for me and would clear my head.

Mackenzie was right, it was going to be a full house just to eat cake. When I got there, Fallon and Mackenzie were already sitting with Penelope, and Harper, Mackenzie's sister. Mackenzie's two best friends were arriving any minute as well.

"You made it!" Fallon shouted from inside the bakery. They were already sitting at a table, each with a glass of wine.

"Of course I did, babe!" I grabbed her shoulders and kissed the top of her head. "Good to see you again, Harper. Mackenzie, always a pleasure." I took my seat across from the happy couple.

After a few minutes, Rylee and Roxxy arrived and sat down, joining the various conversations. I couldn't help but feel warmth in my chest at the scene. My best friend found her forever home in Mackenzie, and I couldn't be happier for her.

After the shittiest two years of her life with her ex in Portland, she deserved to find happiness. Even two years later, the way Mackenzie looked at Fallon made me smile. She proved time and time again that she would do anything for this woman, even when they weren't together, and the love they had for each other had only grown.

After a while, the owner came out to greet us and he asked questions about what they were looking for, what size cake they wanted, and how they'd met.

The owner was a hopeless romantic and loved to hear about a happy ending. His wife overheard the story from the kitchen and giggled. When caught, she blushed and rushed out to refill everyone's wine glasses. That story still makes me laugh to this day.

Fallon still had a ways to go before she could laugh about it, apparently, because when I snorted, she kicked me under the table.

"What? I'm sorry, love, but it's still funny! You were so drunk and so pissed off, and yet you couldn't stop talking about her."

Her face turned the slightest shade of pink, and Mackenzie pulled her in closer. "I guess I made quite an impression." She grinned.

I laughed about it for a little longer until the owner came back with our first samples.

We started with the classic vanilla, but Fallon requested they add raspberry filling and top it with vanilla buttercream.

Harper wasn't a fan, so Fallon immediately said no to that one. Up next, Mackenzie wanted to try the lemon cake with blueberry and cream cheese frosting. Roxxy wasn't too keen on that one, so Mackenzie declined that choice as well.

We also tried a carrot cake and a champagne cake with strawberry filling and whipped vanilla frosting—which was my personal favorite.

As I was savoring my last bite of the champagne cake, I noticed Mackenzie looking at me with concern in her eyes.

"So, how's it going with Blair?" Mackenzie asked. My body tensed at the mention of her name. I couldn't go one day without someone talking about her. "Any sparks flying?" She winked.

I glared at her. "It's going and nothing is flying, I can't stand the woman. You already know this."

"Right, I've heard about your little rivalry, and it sounds like these two at the beginning. Give it some time and we'll all be here again in a few years." Mackenzie's sister, Harper grinned.

Mackenzie had told me about Harper prying to get information. I bet she and Fallon had become really close.

I laughed. "That is definitely not going to happen. She is not my type, and I hate her!" I sounded like a preschooler, but it was true.

"I think we can all agree that Blair is hot!" Fallon said, earning an arched brow from her fiancée. "Obviously not as hot as you, baby." She smiled and kissed Mackenzie, and my heart warmed.

"I hadn't really noticed," I lied. The first thing I noticed about Blair was her captivating hazel eyes, but they were a distant memory as soon as she opened her mouth.

"I agree. I may be straight, but even I can't deny she is gorgeous," Penelope added.

For no reason at all, my jaw ticked at my friend's words. "Can we talk about literally anything else, please?!"

Five heads snapped to me, and I cleared my throat. "What's our next flavor?" I was begging for this conversation to be over.

No one mentioned my little outburst, and for that I was grateful.

Chapter Nine

BLAIR

After my morning yoga, I walked into Brewed Awakening a few minutes earlier than my scheduled meeting. Other than Kaia, Rylee was the sweetest person I knew, and I always gave her a good tip when I went in for coffee.

I was meeting Cara and Drea to discuss the book signing. I still couldn't believe I'd agreed to work with her. Things hadn't started off the best, but after the last time I saw her, I would be lying if I said I didn't go home and do inappropriate things. Her smooth caramel skin, mixed with that accent, should've been illegal. I hated the woman, but the things she did to my—

"Blair?" A familiar sweet voice cut through my dirty thoughts, and I whipped around to see Kaia smiling at me.

"Oh... Hey, Kaia. How are you?" My heart was pounding so loud, and I was thankful she couldn't read my thoughts.

"I'm good. Just getting some coffee before heading to work. Are you waiting for Drea?"

I cleared my throat. "Yeah, in a few minutes, actually. I don't know how you put up with her, Kaia. You are too good for that woman!"

She pushed some hair behind her ear and shrugged. "She's not so bad. I love the store, and she's actually a really good person once you get to know her. You should give her a chance."

I laughed without thought and then my face heated. "I'm sorry. That was very rude of me. I'll just have to take your word for it."

She sighed. "Well, I better get going, I'm opening today. Have a good meeting, and try to be a little patient with her. She really does have a good heart." She waved goodbye and floated out the door.

She has a good heart? I'd pay good money to see that.

Shortly after my conversation with Kaia, Drea and Cara showed up and ordered their drinks.

I ordered a salad and my usual—a chai tea latte—as did Drea, and I wondered if I might have to find a new favorite drink. I couldn't stand the thought of thinking about Drea every time I ordered it. Cara ordered a salad with a shaken espresso.

"Good morning, doll. Glad you could make it." I hugged Cara and gave Drea a quick glance before sitting down at our table. I had chosen a table in the back of the coffee shop so we could have a little privacy.

"Wouldn't miss it," I said through a fake smile. That was a lie, and we both knew it. I had spent the entire car ride over thinking of possible excuses to get out of it, but none of them were good enough to work.

Having your best friend as your publisher was a blessing and a curse sometimes. She knew everything about me, so unless I was really sick or dead, there was no way out of this meeting.

She only sighed in response. She'd put herself in this position by forcing us to work together, but I felt bad about adding more stress to her life. I had to make a mental note to try a little harder at tolerating Drea, at least in front of Cara.

"I'll start today," Drea demanded after I sat down.

It's okay, I don't need to get settled in or anything. Let's just get right to it!

Cara nodded. "Of course, Drea."

"I was thinking of setting up the display and getting our website aligned with the signing two weeks before the event. Do you have a specific vision in mind?" It seemed like it was a chore for her to smile or even look at me, and I couldn't say I didn't have the same difficulty.

"The only thing I would like to see are violets, seeing as how the book is titled *The Last of the Violet Thorn*," I replied, trying to not remind her of the horrendous rose incident that happened during my first book signing.

"Noted. Cara, you're up." Drea was all too quick to avert her gaze to anything besides me. I wondered if she regretted her slip up of politeness in her office. I knew I regretted how my body reacted. I really needed to get out more.

"Thank you, Drea. We need to settle on vendors for the flowers you want, Blair, as well as a bakery. I'll let you two handle that, and you can let me know what you've decided. Sound good?"

We nodded our heads in a silent agreement, as I was desperately trying not to roll my eyes at the thought of working alone with Drea again.

"Before I forget, Blair, we have that book festival coming up in a few weeks."

I lit up, nodding enthusiastically. Finally, something I actually wanted to discuss. "Yes, I remember. I can't wait. I'm looking forward to it."

"Good. And Drea, I want you to go as well."

Our heads snapped to Cara. and I almost choked on my drink. "What? Cara, I don't think that's necessary," I protested. There was no way we would survive a weekend together without murdering each other.

"I agree. That's sort of an author thing. I think I should sit this one out."

Cara sighed. "Must you two make everything so difficult? Drea, it's a literary thing, and you own a bookstore last I checked." Cara grinned as if she thought she was so funny. This situation was anything but funny. "There will be hundreds of readers and authors there. It'll be good publicity for the store. It can't hurt to go."

I begged to differ on that point, but kept my mouth shut anyway.

"Listen, I appreciate the thought, but I have a store to run. I can't just leave for a few days."

Cara glared at Drea, and it pleased me more than it should've. "Kaia is more than capable of handling things for two days.

Drea was quiet for a long moment before she nodded and sighed, causing dread to fill my body. "Fine. If you think it'll be beneficial."

"Perfect! I'll have Eloise send you all the details. It's going to be a fun little girls weekend!" She smiled, and I groaned as she sat there, looking pretty damn pleased with herself.

Drea and I gave each other a look. Her stare was unreadable, but I knew she could see the terror building in my eyes.

I could barely stand to be in the same room with the woman for more than five minutes, but a whole weekend with Drea? That should be fun...

Chapter Ten

DREA

"How are you, love? I feel like it's been ages."

Penelope and I were sitting at Reids, a local bar a few blocks down from the bookstore. I needed to get out and find a distraction. Since I was banned from my typical method of stress-relieving fun, I invited my friends out for a girls night.

Fallon, of course, declined. She had something to do for the wedding with Mackenzie. At least, that was what she told me. Truthfully, I think they just wanted to watch *Stuart Little* and fuck on the couch.

Penelope was busy with work and her husband most of the time, so we didn't spend as much time together as I would like, and I was looking forward to spending some time with her.

"I know! I've been busy with work... and Greg." She chuckled, a slight blush creeping over her cheeks.

"From the look on your face, I can tell that Greg is taking up most of your spare time." I grinned, and Penelope's cheeks continued to turn a brighter shade of pink.

"Dre! Keep your voice down, and yes, my husband has been showing me a great time. That hasn't changed in the twelve years we've been married," she said with a smile that stretched from ear to ear.

"I didn't want to say anything because I don't want to take away from Fallon's big moment... but Greg and I are trying to get pregnant."

"What? That's amazing, congrats!" I hugged my friend and smiled. "I cannot believe you two are going to be parents. I'm so happy for you, babe."

"I'm nervous but excited. Like I said, I don't want to overshadow Fallon getting married and I don't want to jinx anything, but we felt like it was the right time, you know?" she said as she took a sip of her cherry coke. Now I understood why she didn't order alcohol.

"Of course! I'm sure everything will work out the way it's supposed to." My best friend was going to make an amazing mother, and I was going to spoil that kid shitless.

"I'm sure it will. So, what's been going on with you?" Penelope asked with curiosity in her voice.

I groaned. "I have to go out of town next weekend. There's a book festival that Blair is attending, and Cara thinks it would be a good idea for me to go, so I'm being dragged along with them."

"Oh, come on, I'm sure it won't be that bad. Won't Cara be there, too? You can ignore Blair the whole time, if you want."

"Yeah, she'll be there, but I mean honestly, a whole weekend with Blair? That sounds awful. Cara definitely won't let me ignore Blair the whole time. She's been trying to get us to get along since day one. I keep telling her it's never going to happen, but she doesn't give up once she sets her mind to something." I took a long drink of my whiskey, hoping the burn would cure my irritation. I was three whiskeys in and so far having no such luck.

Penelope laughed. "Then why did you agree to it? Just don't go. It's not like you're contractually obligated."

I rolled my eyes. "Because, as always, Cara was right. It'll be a good place to do some networking for the store. But that doesn't mean I'm not allowed to bitch about it the entire time."

I was going to make Cara think twice about ever inviting me anywhere with her and Blair again.

"That's true. How did your first meeting alone go? I see you're not injured or dead, but I can't say the same for the other party." She laughed as I glared at her.

"We survived. I was nice, if you can believe it. I used my big girl manners and even complimented her."

"How nice of you... Wait, you complimented her? What did you say?"

Why did I admit that out loud? I looked down at my half-empty whiskey glass. No more for me.

"I was just trying to be nice. I promised Cara I would at least try, and her dress was a nice color. So what?" I shrugged.

Thankfully, I wasn't drunk enough to tell her that the body clothed in the dress looked even better.

Penelope gave me a look that said, *what the fuck?* and I wanted to shrink into my chair.

"What? Am I not allowed to be nice? We have to work together, you know."

"Drea, in the almost twenty years I have known you, you have never been nice to someone you didn't like. You make it a known fact that you don't like them. And Blair is not someone you tolerate at all. So I'm sorry if I'm just a little confused here."

I sighed. "Look, I made a promise to Cara to at least try and be civil, so I complimented her dress. It's not a big deal. It's not like I took her over my desk and tore the dress off her or anything." I let out a nervous chuckle, hoping Penelope didn't see how red my cheeks were getting. It was definitely the whiskey talking, fantasizing about Blair like that was crazy.

She arched her brow. "Drea, that sounded very specific. Is that something you've thought about?"

I definitely have not thought about Blair in any way or position. Definitely not. "What? No, of course not. Don't be ridiculous, Pen. It was just an example. Let's get the check. I think I've hit my limit for the night." I motioned for the waitress and ignored eye contact with Penelope.

"Drea?"

I risked a quick glance, and my shoulders sagged at her soft expression. She wasn't judging. She was just concerned, and so was I. Thinking about Blair with anything other than irritation was downright ludicrous. "I'm fine. Too much whiskey."

Thankfully she didn't press anymore and we paid our tab and left.

～

When I walked into the bookstore on the following Monday morning, Kaia was already there opening up.

"Good morning, Drea," Kaia cheerfully announced as I walked toward the counter.

Her personality was always sunshine and rainbows, but in the morning, it was on a whole other level. I loved Kaia, but I needed at least two cups of coffee before I could handle those sprinkles of positivity.

"Hello, Kaia."

"Are you ready for another great day?!" She beamed and I wanted to throw my coffee at her, but I refrained—for now.

"Oh yeah. I can't wait," I answered in a sarcastic tone.

"Well, everything is already done for the morning, and we are ready to open."

I smiled as I headed to my office. "Good. I'll be out in a bit. Call me if you need anything. I have a few things to finalize before the end of the day."

"Sounds good! Oh, are you excited for your weekend off? I know you'll technically be working, but you'll be in a nice hotel with Cara and Blair. It'll be so much fun!"

I had told her about the festival yesterday, and she seemed a little too excited for me to be gone for two days. She insisted that she would have it all taken care of and I had nothing to worry about. I knew I could trust Kaia, but I was still nervous.

I glared at her, suppressing an eye roll. No part of that weekend was going to be fun, except maybe the end of it. "Thrilled."

A few hours later, I left my solitude to check on the store. A few customers milled about, but Kaia seemed to have a hold on it.

"How's it going, Kaia?" I asked.

She turned to me after her last customer left. "It's been pretty steady so far, but it's nothing I can't handle."

"Good. Do you want me to take over? You look like you could use a break." She was starting to look a little flushed.

"Well, I guess I could go... check up on some customers. You know, make sure nobody needs anything." She smiled and headed toward the center of the store.

I chuckled. "Have fun." I knew exactly who she was going to "check up" on.

Chapter Eleven

BLAIR

"Good morning, Marcus!" I waved as I walked into Furever Homes Rescue.

I'd started volunteering at the animal shelter when I was twenty. I tried to help out at least once a month, but sometimes my schedule wouldn't allow for it. I hadn't been back for two months, and I felt horrible.

"Hey! We've missed you around here, Ms. Best-selling Author!"

I blushed. Yeah, I was a best-selling author, but I didn't let it get to my head. It wasn't like I was making millions, anyway. Even if I was, I would still come by when I could.

"Where do you need me today?" I asked as I hung my coat on the hook.

Marcus was the only volunteer who had been here longer than me. I had called last minute to see if I could come by to help. I usually called in advance, but these days I just hadn't had the time. Especially with dealing with Drea.

My body was hitting its emotional capacity, and I needed to decompress and focus on something that wasn't an infuriatingly attractive British store owner or writing my next series.

"Well, we're pretty good on volunteers these days. It's been a little slow, but if you want to take Milo for a w-a-l-k, he's been waiting for you." He grinned, pointing to the crazy German shepherd who was wagging his tail in agreement.

I smiled. "Hi, Milo. I missed you, too. Want to go for a walk?" He tilted his head and started barking loudly in enthusiasm.

"See what you did? Now you *have* to take him!" Marcus shook his head with laughter, handing Milo's leash to me.

I put my coat back on and got the necessities before letting Milo drag me down the street to the nearby park.

The park was only a few blocks down from the shelter, which was a few streets over from the bookstore. Luckily the park was in the opposite direction from the store. That was the last thing I needed on my decompressing day.

I had to spend two days with her, and over an hour with her in a small car. I fully planned to get some writing done and tune her out the whole way. She could talk to Cara and pretend I wasn't even there.

The storm cloud brewing in my head slowly began to evaporate. Walking to the park was a small pleasure of mine. When my thoughts became too great, walking would help me make sense of things.

Writing my novels was a passion, but it could get lonely sometimes. Walking Milo had me thinking I could get used to this. Maybe not walking Milo specifically, although I wouldn't complain if he somehow found his way to my house. He was still a puppy, but he would be grown by the time I could adopt him.

I owned my house, so I could have adopted a dog already if I wanted to, and I did want to. I had always been an animal lover, but I never had any growing up. That was just something we never had. My mother was a lawyer and my father was an attorney, so they were rarely home as it was.

My grandmother, Amelia, took care of me after school until one of them got off work to come get me. She worked for city hall until she retired in her early sixties, but taking care of my grandfather and his dementia took up all her free time until she passed six months after him. I was twenty-five when they passed, but my grandmother had become like a second mother after she took care of me when I lost my parents.

After my parents died, and on top of losing my grandmother, I was terrified to get attached to anything that could leave me, so I never had any type of pet, not even a fish.

If I were to ever adopt, it would be a German shepherd like Milo. I was alone, though, and whoever I adopted deserved to be raised by two parents.

I wanted to share that experience with someone. I wanted kids someday, but I wasn't an idiot. Being gay made it a lot harder to have children, and made it more expensive. I was willing to try all the avenues I could someday when I found the right person, though.

But I would be content with a dog before adding children to the mix. Taking morning walks together with our coffee. Sitting at the dog park together while they played and ran around with the other dogs. Snuggling up together on the couch while watching movies...

None of that was in my near future, so I got my fix volunteering and walking with Milo.

We sat at the park for an hour. He ran around like crazy, chasing his tail until he developed a case of the zoomies.

I guess it was contagious, because all the other dogs started running in circles, and playing their own version of tag with each other.

At one point, it seemed like Milo made a best friend. A tiny, jittery bug-eyed Chihuahua. They were inseparable.

Turned out the chihuahua had a crush on Milo, humping his leg at any opportunity. He didn't seem to mind, though, and I wondered if I was going to need to take him with me to the next pride festival.

We started heading back to the shelter when it was time for lunch for both of us. I usually walked several dogs at a time, but today I just wanted to spend some time with my furry best friend.

I started feeling sad and wishing I could take him home with me. I always hated leaving him at the shelter—any of them, really. I knew they were well taken care of, but I still wanted them all.

We were halfway to the shelter when Milo somehow broke out of his leash and started running down the sidewalk.

"Milo, no!" I yelled after him, begging for him to stop, but he kept running. *This day was going so great!*

I took off after him, but he was a fast little booger. He finally stopped at someone's feet, and I was thankful for the distraction. At least if he tried to take off again, one of us could catch him before he ran out into the street.

"I'm so sorry about him. He got out of his leash somehow, and—" I looked up to apologize to the poor person Milo was sniffing all over and came to a crashing stop. All my words died a painful death as I looked into a pair of mesmerizing brown eyes.

"Drea... hi." I couldn't think, couldn't move. She was the last person I expected to see today, and yet I couldn't stop my stomach from doing an impromptu breakdance as she looked me up and down.

"Blair... What a nice surprise." Her tone didn't sound like it was nice at all.

I cleared my throat, trying to gain back control. "What are you doing here?" I winced at the stupidity of my question. She sure as hell wasn't riding an elephant.

"On a public sidewalk? I'm walking to lunch... I didn't know you had a dog." She squatted down and petted Milo, who jumped in her lap and started licking her face. It was adorable, but I was nervous she was going to yell at him for ruining her extremely short brown shorts or something. I mean seriously, did this woman not own pants? Her legs were miles long and so soft looking. Jesus!

"Hello, aren't you a cutie?" She looked at Milo as she continued to rub his belly. I wanted to kick myself for the tenderness I felt in my chest as she continued to sweet talk him. At least I had confirmation she could be sweet to someone.

"I don't. He's a shelter dog. I volunteer at Furever Homes and was just taking Milo back after our walk to the park. He got off his leash. I'm sorry about that." I reached for Milo and put his leash back on, making sure it was secure.

"You volunteer?" she asked, something unexpected in the way she was looking at me. Did she think I thought myself too good to volunteer?

I hadn't talked to her or seen her since our meeting with Cara, but that comment in her office still left me confused.

In the years I'd worked with Drea, she had never once said anything remotely nice to me. I never understood her animosity towards me, but since the feelings were mirrored on my side, I didn't care enough to ask.

I shrugged. "Since I was twenty. I try to volunteer once a month if I can."

She nodded in response. "Well, I better go. See you Thursday, I guess." She gave a faint wave and took off.

"That was Drea, Milo. Yeah, I know she's pretty on the eyes, buddy. You don't have to worry about her, though. I'm sure you'll never see her again." I shook off that encounter and took Milo back to the shelter.

Chapter Twelve

DREA

"Hey, Cara. I was just about to call you. Are you guys on your way?"

I had just arrived at the bookstore, and I pulled my phone out to get an ETA from Cara. Not that I wanted them to get there any sooner than necessary. I was eagerly waiting for this weekend to be over with.

I was leaving Kaia in charge while I was away. She had looked after the store for a day here and there, but never two days in a row, and I never went out of town. I was a little nervous, but I knew I could trust Kaia. She would call me if the slightest thing was out of place.

Besides that, I had access to the cameras on my phone. I had recently upgraded my camera system thanks to Fallon and Mackenzie's... anti-literary activities in my backroom.

After a brief moment of silence, hesitation surrounded Cara's voice. "Actually, that's what I was calling for. So, Blair is on her way, but something came up and I am not able to make it."

Please tell me this was a prank call. There was no way she was suggesting that Blair and I go to this festival... alone. "I'm sorry, what now?"

"Drea, don't start with your dramatics, please. I'm sorry, but it'll be fine. The reservation is under Blair's name, and everything is already taken care of. I'll call to check in as soon as I can, hopefully once you're already settled in."

"I'm not being dramatic. I think I'm reacting exactly how I should be, Cara. You cannot be serious. You can't leave me alone with her for two days. This better be an emergency!" Cara was usually very hands on when it came to work, so I hoped nothing was seriously wrong.

"You'll be fine, but I gotta go. Have fun and please don't kill each other! I love you both." She hung up before I could get another word out.

Blair was walking up as I got off the phone with Cara. "Cara isn't going to make it; something came up. She said everything is under your name at the hotel, though, so we shouldn't have any issues," I said dully.

"Of course." She sighed.

"What does that mean? She doesn't usually bail on work things last minute unless she doesn't have a choice." I scowled.

"No, I know. I just meant... nevermind." She shook her head.

I wanted to press, but I knew it would just cause a fight. Besides, we had the whole weekend for that. Why rush things?

"Well, it's about an hour away. Do you have everything you need?" I asked, noticing her one suitcase and purse.

I knew it was just a two-day trip, but I had expected her to pack for the equivalent of a two-month trip.

She saw me looking at her bag and rolled her eyes. "We're only going to be gone for two days. I'm fine."

"Alright then. Do you want to drive?"

"I don't drive, actually."

I blinked at her. "What do you mean you don't drive? You're how old?"

"I'm thirty, and I just don't, okay? Can we go now, please?"

I could tell she was getting more irritated by the second, and I couldn't help but notice how cute she looked when she was mad.

"Fine, Jesus, let's go." It was no use arguing with her. *Of course Her Highness doesn't drive...*

It wasn't that I minded driving; I actually loved it. I just wasn't in love with the idea of chauffeuring the princess around like I was her personal servant.

The entire car ride was an agonizing hour of awkward silence. Every so often I would get the urge to look at her. I couldn't stand the heat that passed through me when I did. She was devastatingly beautiful, and I had no right thinking about her like that.

Anytime I stole a glance in her direction, she would be doing the same and we would sharply turn away from each other.

I wanted to say something, anything to break the horrible silence, but I was at a loss of what to say.

I was put out of my misery when we arrived at the hotel. It looked as if someone had lit a fire underneath my ass with how fast I bolted out of that car. I was counting the minutes until I was alone in my own room and I wouldn't have to deal with her until tomorrow.

"Hi, we have a reservation. It should be under Blair Sterling?" She spoke with a sweet smile. *Good to know she knows how to do that.*

"Of course, we have your room all ready for you. Will you be needing one key or two?"

"Wait, room? As in singular?" She looked between me and the receptionist.

I stood frozen as I let the words sink in. *One room. As in sharing a room... with Blair freaking Sterling!*

This had to be a sick fucking joke. If this was Cara's doing and not just an unhappy accident, so help me God...

The reservationist chuckled. "Yes, ma'am. One room, two queen beds. That's what the reservation says. Is there a problem?"

She scoffed. "Yes, there is a—"

"No, there is no problem. That's perfect. Thank you so much..." I leaned in closer to read the name tag the woman was wearing. "Teresa. We will definitely be needing two keys, though."

I took the room keys, leading a very ruffled-looking Blair to the elevator. I usually reveled in anything that caused her perfect life to be off-balance, but not when I was also suffering.

"What the hell was that?" She glared when the elevator door closed. "There is a problem. I am not sharing a room with you."

I rolled my eyes. "First of all, Your Highness, relax. It's not like we have to share a bed. It's for two nights, and you aren't paying for it, so calm down and enjoy the free room."

"Unbelievable," she muttered under her breath, and I resisted the temptation to say more. At least there were two beds.

We didn't get fully checked into our room until a little after six, and by then I was in desperate need of some liquid stress relief.

"I'm going down to the bar." I waited as long as I possibly could before hesitantly continuing. "Do you want to come?" I promised Cara I would at least try to be nice.

"I'm fine. I don't really drink." She looked up from where she was sitting on her bed.

"Of course you don't. God forbid you have any fun." I rolled my eyes as I turned away, shutting the door on my way out, not giving her a chance to respond.

The hotel bar was empty and I welcomed the silence.

"Hey, what can I get you?" The bartender came up to me as soon as I sat down. He was tall and had a blond buzz cut.

"I'll have a whiskey please, neat," I replied. That was my typical order whenever I went out. It was sophisticated and smooth.

I was enjoying my drink when I felt a warm presence slide into the seat next to me.

"Hi, there. Can I buy you a drink?"

I turned to see a curvaceous blonde smiling at me. She wore a very short red dress that did little to hide the pair of double Ds that were begging to be released. That fiery red lipstick was a tempting invitation... *Out-of-town sex doesn't count, right?*

I smiled. "Sure, what's your name?"

She motioned the bartender over to us and stuck out her hand for me to shake. "I'm Destiny. What's yours?"

I grinned. "I'm Drea, but my friends call me Dre."

We sat and traded flirtatious lines for a while until I finished my drink.

"So, how about you come up to my room for a night cap?" She placed her hand softly on my arm, and my skin heated at the touch.

Mackenzie didn't have to know, and I could just send a quick text to Blair and let her know not to expect me back. It wasn't like I owed her an explanation.

Destiny stood and lightly brushed her fingertips down my back. It felt like my skin was on fire as her fingers trailed lower and lower. Then she motioned me to follow her.

Something deep inside ate at me at the thought of Blair upstairs and alone. She would be alone all night if I went to Destiny's room, not that I cared, but...

We were miles away from home, and it didn't seem right to abandon her. What if the room caught fire or there was a burglar? Deep down I knew I was making excuses. As much as I didn't like her, I knew what it was like to feel alone. Not to mention, Cara would be so pissed if I left Blair on her own.

I sighed. Fucking Blair Sterling. "I'm sorry, darling, I can't. I have to get back to my roommate."

She shrugged and slid me a card. "If you change your mind, that's my room number." She kissed my cheek and walked away. I wanted to cry when I saw her juicy round ass walking away.

I have to get back to my roommate? What a fucking idiot! *Why do I care how she feels?*

I closed my tab and headed back upstairs. I wanted to take a cold shower and relieve some tension...

When I got off the elevator, I opened the door to my room and almost tripped over my own feet.

Blair was standing in the corner of the room, digging through her bag, completely naked. Holy fuck, I was not prepared for that. I only saw the back of her body, but what I did see had me clenching my thighs together and suppressing a groan.

Her hair was wet and curly, and her tan skin had water droplets trickling all the way down to her... Yup, I can confirm that her ass was in fact perfect. I was glad I stopped after a few drinks.

I quietly went to the bathroom without Blair noticing and took a cold and very long shower.

Chapter Thirteen

BLAIR

It was the morning of the literary festival, and I shot Cara a text, trying to be as nice as I could be:

> Me: It's festival day, and where is my publisher?!

> Cara: I'm sorry, doll. There was a family emergency. I'm upset that I can't be there. How are things going? Is Drea still alive?

I looked over to the other side of the room. Drea was getting dressed. She had on a white sports bra and black boxer briefs, and I had to peel my eyes away. Good God!

> Me: Yes, still alive. I need to get ready.

> Me: Also wtf, Cara... one room?!

Cara: 👀

Cara: I'm sorry. I thought it would be good for us to spend more time together, and for you two to try and get along.

Me: 😳

Me: Hope everything is okay 😔

Things were definitely not okay over here. Drea had invited me out for drinks, but I knew she was only doing it to please Cara. After that silent car ride, it seemed like she wanted nothing to do with me. I didn't lie, though. Since I'd lost my parents, I rarely drank.

I should have ventured out on my own because I was losing my mind in that room! She was several feet away from me, her half-naked caramel skin glistening from her shower. We used the same hotel body wash, but why did it smell so much better on her? I quickly brushed that thought away.

I had decided to listen to a podcast last night so I wouldn't have space left in my brain to think about what she was doing in the shower for so long. I tried not to think about what she looked like, all wet and—

"Are you going to keep staring at me, or are you going to get ready?" Drea's voice shook me from my fantasy.

I scoffed. "I was not staring at you." I got up and took off for the bathroom. I hoped she couldn't see the burning on my face.

Ink and Imagination was one of my favorite literary events to attend. It was always set up so beautifully, and they were so warm and welcoming. Drea could learn a thing or two from them.

The event was held every year at the Hidden Library. It wasn't really hidden, but it was located near the coast of Seattle. It felt as if you were driving to the edge of the world as you drove up the winding road.

The library looked like a medieval castle with its beautiful architecture, surrounded by a blue-green sea. I loved hearing the crashing of the waves against the rocks and the salty scent of the sea.

When we got to the festival, the organizers—an older married couple in their late forties—greeted us. They were the cutest couple, as they seemed to gravitate around each other.

One was a short, plump woman with a salt-and-pepper pixie cut—Margot. The other was a tall, lean woman with flowing brown hair and the biggest blue eyes imaginable—Penny.

They walked us inside and gave us a small tour, pointing out where the panels were going to be held and where the meet and greet would be located.

The auditorium would be used for the panels, showcasing the best-selling sapphic authors around the country. Although this was one of the biggest libraries in the world, they made a safe space for the rest of the arts. It was an honor to be invited.

The room was elegant and full of color. The windows had stained glass, so as the sun rose and moved across, the reflection gave the room a multi-colored hue. The rooms were decorated with an array of flowers and art pieces that looked historic and priceless.

The meet and greet was located in the library gardens. As I stood in the garden with Drea, I could see the astonishment in her eyes as she looked across to see the majestic trees and the full, blooming blood-red roses.

Dozens of little booths were lined up, filling the entire outer edges of the garden. My booth was located near the edge of the garden. If I looked down, I could see the waves crashing into the rocks below.

"The panel will be starting within the hour. Please make yourself comfortable and find me when you are ready," Margot said with a soft smile on her face.

"Thank you, Margot. You and Penny have been very helpful."

Margot's wife beamed as she added, "It's our pleasure, we are so excited to hear about your story. Please call us over if you need anything at all."

As the lovely couple walked away, a small stabbing pain shot across my heart. It made me wonder if I would ever find my person, someone who shared the same passions that I did.

Drea broke the silence. "Wow, this place is amazing. In all my time in Seattle, how had I never heard of this place?"

I laughed. "It's called the Hidden Library for a reason. You can't just google it. You have to be invited."

Drea rolled her eyes. "Okay, smart ass, I'm sorry I'm not as cultured as you. Let's hurry up and find your booth. The faster we get settled, the faster I can walk around to meet other authors. It's time to drum up some new business."

My eyes shot to Drea's. I was about to throw her off the cliff. She was so insufferable. Why did Cara think this would be a good idea?

I kept my mouth shut and walked away. She was not going to ruin this event for me.

During the whole panel, I was so nervous. It wasn't my first one, but I still didn't like talking in front of a lot of people. I enjoyed them every time, though. After they were done, I felt better. I felt accomplished.

Every time I looked out into the crowd, my eyes immediately found Drea's. Her expression was unreadable, but she never took her eyes off me. It made the event all the more nerve-wracking.

They always asked the same questions, and for that I was thankful. Everyone usually stayed on the topic of the books and no one asked personal questions.

But this time, a brave soul decided to ask a question that I wasn't ready to answer.

Margot, the sweet event attendant, stood and began to speak. "Ms. Sterling, my wife and I have been married for ten years and we really enjoy your books. I'm sorry to be so frank..." she said as a blush crept up her cheeks, "but your books have helped bring more spice into our marriage. Tell me, how do you come up with these brilliant ideas? You and your wife must have stories to tell." She motioned to Drea in the crowd.

The room grew silent as the hundreds of attendees looked from Drea to me and back again.

My soul left my body and my cheeks became stained with a bright-pink blush. "M-Margot... Ms. Voss and I are not married. We are strictly business partners," I said as I glanced toward Drea, who was clearly trying to contain her laughter.

"I am honored that my stories have helped. It brings me joy that I was able to spread a message about love. I write these stories because it's something that I craved when I was growing up. My parents died when I was very young, and these stories helped me escape into a fantasy. But now I see them as the love that I could potentially show someone," I replied, trying to hide the trembling in my voice.

I shot a glance over to Drea, and her expression once again became difficult to read.

Why did I care so much about her opinion? It wasn't like it mattered. Knowing her, I would never hear the end of this.

"I'm so sorry Ms. Sterling. I apologize for the confusion. You both just look so perfect together. I think I need to get my eyes checked," Margot said with a bewildered look on her face. "I'm so sorry to hear about your parents, but I know they must be proud of who you turned out to be. You turned a terrible memory into something positive for everyone to enjoy."

I am not going to cry... I am not going to cry! Come on, Blair, you can talk about your parents!

"Thank you Margot. I... I appreciate your loyalty as a reader and your support," I said, with tears threatening to escape.

"Now if that's all the questions that everyone has, I will meet you at my booth to sign my new novel, The Last of the Violet Thorns."

After the Q&A, everything was a blur. I usually wasn't so open about my past, but Margot's question had completely thrown me off guard.

I signed a few books and answered a few other questions from some fans. I even mingled with festival attendees. Other than the actual writing, these events were my favorite part of my job.

The walk back to our room was silent. After the mortifying observation that Margot had made, I had no idea how I was going to face Drea, let alone sleep in the same room as her.

Cara was one of the few people who knew about my parents' deaths. I felt uneasy sharing that vulnerability in front of Drea.

Even though she was kind enough to let me board first, that elevator ride was pure torture. Of course our floor couldn't have been ground level or even on the second floor. We had to be on the fifteenth floor.

Being confined in a small, hot space with only Drea and her delicious scent, I was half-tempted to hold my breath the whole way so I didn't breathe her in.

When we got to our room several excruciatingly long minutes later, I headed straight for the bathroom. I needed some time to clean up and to shake these ridiculous feelings.

I was washing the makeup off my face when I heard Drea just outside. "You did good during the panel, but I'm a little bummed you didn't trip or anything. I was hoping for some entertainment today."

I turned off the water and dried my face. "I see you forgot to pack civility for this trip." I rolled my eyes. "I'm sorry to disappoint you."

"Apology accepted... Mrs. Voss." I could hear the roaring of her laughter through the bathroom door.

"Not even in your wildest dreams!" I said through gritted teeth.

I should have pushed her off the cliff when I'd had the chance. But I'd be lying to myself if I said for a second I didn't think about Margot's assumption and what being tied to Drea would be like. Then I started thinking about being tied in a different way, and I quickly threw that thought away.

She shrugged. "I was only kidding. Relax." She paused for a second, like she was having a debate with herself, and sighed. "Do you get nervous doing these things?" She rested her hands on the doorframe of the bathroom.

The way she stood there in a white tank top and shorts, dominating the room, I couldn't hide my attraction to her, and I wanted to throw up.

She was insufferable, rude, unprofessional, and she smelled better than anyone I had ever encountered. It really should've been a crime to smell that delicious.

I swallowed, clearing my throat. She had never asked anything about me if it wasn't business related, and I wasn't sure what to make of it. I knew we promised Cara to be nice, but to me, that meant ignoring each other instead of arguing.

"Sometimes. I still find it hard to believe there are so many people who have read and enjoyed the books. I know I can be hard on myself, but it's difficult for me to understand just how much impact a book can have on people."

She shrugged. "I know. I've read a few of your books and I don't get it either."

In the blink of an eye, any chance of having a decent conversation vanished. I guess the compliment in her office was a one-time slipup.

I rolled my eyes. "Of course you don't."

She frowned. "What's that supposed to mean?"

"Nothing, just forget it." I went to pass by her, but she stopped me with a hand on my wrist. I froze in place and looked down at the contact.

It wasn't enough to hurt by any means, but it did something to me I didn't have the courage to explore. Heat flared in my eyes as her hand burned into my skin. This was the first time any part of her was touching me, and I didn't know how to react.

"No, what exactly are you saying, Blair?"

"Don't. Touch me," I bit out.

She released her hold on me and I turned back around to look her in the eyes.

"You wouldn't understand. You don't know what it's like to put something out there and worry people won't like it. You own a bookstore; your job is easy. Everyone loves bookstores. I have to actually create something and hope it's good enough for someone and deal with the criticism from those who don't like it. And of course you don't like my books. You have made it perfectly clear that you don't like me. I told Cara this trip would be a waste of time. You don't like anything except yourself!"

She laughed. "Please, anyone can make up a story. Do you want a key to the city, Mother Teresa? And just because you aren't one of the things I like doesn't mean they don't exist. You're right, but I know the feelings are mutual, so don't pretend you're the sad little victim. I'm sorry you have to deal with the fact that someone doesn't find anything about you appealing, as hard as I'm sure that is to swallow."

I scoffed. "You are unbelievably insufferable, do you know that? I was trying to have a civil conversation, and you couldn't even put in that much effort. I don't know why you have to make things so difficult. At least I was trying." I was becoming more frustrated with every second.

"Excuse me?! You're the one who makes everything so frustrating. Nothing is ever good enough for little miss perfect!"

"Me? I'm sorry, I'm not the one—"

My words died off when she cut the distance between us and backed me against the wall. I took in a breath when she leaned in closer.

She had one hand braced on my hip, caressing it delicately with her thumb, just a whisper of a touch, and the other was pushing a piece of hair back behind my ear. The softness of her touch was vastly different from the harshness of her words.

The movement was so quick I had no time to think, and the feeling of her fingers on the skin above my shorts was sending the wrong kind of messages to the wrong kind of places.

I was breathing like I had just run a marathon, and my face was on fire. Inhaling her scent was causing my heart to pound faster. She had a musky scent mixed with cinnamon and cardamom, and I could have sworn my knees started shaking... actually shaking.

Our eyes were fixed on each other without a word, the tension growing thicker and thicker with each passing breath.

Was she going to finally take her frustration out on me? Would I do the same? Would she slap me or throw me on the bed and show me just how frustrated she really was? Whatever the answer, a part of me was dying to find out.

"What the hell are you doing?" I demanded in a hushed voice.

"You seem to have a lot to say, darling, but I'm sure we can find something more useful for you to do with that mouth of yours. For example, I bet it would look so good wrapped around my clit," she whispered.

I couldn't find any words to say, and I was embarrassed to admit the image she painted turned me into an aroused mess.

"I'm..."

She leaned in a little closer, our lips only inches apart as she brought her hand to my face, and I instinctively wrapped her shirt in between my shaking fingers, closing my eyes.

Was she going to kiss me? My heart was pounding erratically, and it showed no signs of slowing down the closer she got. We were so close that one inhale from either of us would bring our mouths together.

I should've stepped back, but I was frozen in place with need. I needed her to kiss me. I needed our bodies to collide. I needed our clothes—

I jumped when the phone rang. When I opened my eyes, she was still extremely close, before she slowly took a few steps back. She covered her face with her hands and muttered a curse I couldn't hear, before she turned around and headed to the bathroom.

"Drea..." I called out to her, but she didn't turn around.

"Great," I muttered softly before walking over to pick up the phone.

"Hello?" My tone was a little clipped, and I wasn't sure if it was from the fact that I was going to let her kiss me, or because we didn't get the chance.

"Hey, Blair, how's it going?" Cara's voice on the other end brought me back to reality.

"Cara, hey. It's going fine. No big news to report yet." I hoped she didn't hear the deflection in my voice.

"Good. Can I talk to Drea? She wasn't answering her phone. Is she okay?"

I cleared my throat, tearing my gaze away from the closed bathroom door. "Of course she's okay. Why wouldn't she be? She's in the bathroom, but I'll tell her you called, okay? Call you tomorrow." I hung up the phone, still sweating with nerves.

Nothing had happened, but I felt the guilt sinking in, like I was hiding something from her.

Eventually I got tired of waiting for Drea to come out of the bathroom, and I went to bed.

I was glad we were leaving tomorrow, but that car ride was going to be the longest hour of my entire life.

Chapter Fourteen

DREA

The car ride back was similar to the one on the way there—quiet and weird. Neither of us spoke the entire way until we got back into town.

She refused to let me take her home, so I dropped her off at the bookstore and she got a car from there. I wasn't willing to argue, and it wasn't like I wanted to see where she lived anyway.

I was lying when I said I didn't understand how people liked her books. I was ashamed to admit that I had read most of them, more than once.

I found her novels well-written and inspiring, but I couldn't exactly tell her all that now without getting a snarky comment.

～

A week had slipped by, and I was sitting in my office, staring at the blank walls, still thinking about the festival. Cara owed me big for that weekend. I wouldn't tell her exactly why, but she did.

My mind hadn't stopped spinning since the phone interrupted what would have inevitably happened. I had been seconds away from kissing her, from knowing what her lips tasted like.

My fingers still vibrated from the feeling of her soft skin underneath them. I had been inches away from the hem of her shorts. It would have been so easy to slide underneath and—

"I'm sorry, Drea, but she insisted." My door flung open, jerking me out of my thoughts and causing a damn near heart attack.

Kaia's frantic voice forced me to look up and see her standing next to a furious looking Blair. But when was best-selling author Blair sterling not looking at me furiously?

The night you pushed her against the wall, and wanted to kiss her until you both forgot your names...

"Kaia, it's all right. Why don't you go take a little break? I'll keep an eye on the store."

Her eyes ping-ponged between us hesitantly, but I nodded reassuringly. She put on a faint smile before closing the door.

Blair was still standing there, staring at me with a burning intensity in her eyes.

"Please, sit down and tell me what I've done to piss you off this time. Would you like me to start a list?" I said dryly, reaching for a sticky note and a pen.

She gave me a curt smile. "Cute. You know what you did... or... almost did!" She stormed over, slapping her palms on my desk. The audacity she thought she had, coming into my office—*You promised Cara...*

I took a calming breath before responding. She wasn't going to get a rise out of me today. "I'm sorry, but I'm afraid I don't actually know what you're rambling on about. So, could you just tell me and get it over with? I'm very busy today."

"With what? The imaginary long line of customers circling the building? I'm talking about the festival, Drea. The kiss?"

I froze. I wanted to say something about her little dig about my business, but all thoughts flooded out of my mind at her mention of the kiss. "I'm sorry, the what?"

She rolled her eyes. "You are many things, Drea Voss, but dumb is not one of them! You know exactly what I'm talking about. After the festival, when you pushed me up against the wall, you were going to kiss me."

"I..." I was speechless. I hadn't stopped thinking about that night since it happened. I'd been so sexually frustrated, I'd had to lock myself in the bathroom until I knew she was asleep. I couldn't risk the temptation, and if Blair Sterling was anything, it was extremely tempting.

I didn't know what I was thinking. I guess all the tension built up, and when she was yelling at me, all I could think about was how I wanted to take her up against that wall and fuck the attitude right out of her. She looked so—

"I've been trying to come up with a reasonable explanation as to why you would have thought that would've been a good idea in the first place. I mean, seriously, what the hell, Drea? What exactly were you trying to do? Were you trying to make me think you actually had feelings for me or something? Maybe I would get so offended that I would break my contract. Am I really that difficult that you would try any tactic you see fit to get rid of me?!"

I sat there, still speechless. I didn't know what to say. All the frustration was building back up, and being alone together was not a smart idea.

I needed her to leave or I was afraid I would do something regrettable. Would it be so bad to give in, though? *Yes, Drea. It really would be!*

"You had a lot to say that night, and now you're quiet?"

I stood up and walked over to her, finally having had enough. I was done talking. "Are you done yelling now?"

"What? You're not serious. You are the most enraging, insufferable—"

I cut her off, pulling her in from the waist. "Are. You. Done. Yelling?" I articulated every word slowly, demanding an answer with my tone.

"Y... yes," she replied breathlessly.

"Good." I grabbed the side of her face, gently feeling her bottom lip under my thumb, before I kissed her.

I could have disappeared in that kiss, not even a shadow of me to be seen for the rest of eternity.

She kissed me back with such intensity, I could hardly catch my breath. She gripped my shirt and pulled us closer together, and I almost came apart.

I should've stopped and pulled away, but I was glued to her. She tasted like strawberries and cream, and I could have forgotten my own name.

Nothing short of the earth caving in on itself could've pulled me away from her as her hands started clawing my back.

I moaned and deepened the kiss, gripping her hips and pressing her into me. I needed more. I was desperate for more.

I had thought a lot about what it would be like to kiss her since the festival. Hell, possibly even before then. But nothing could've prepared me for the reality of feeling her lips on mine.

The kiss lasted only a few seconds, but I was sure the heat I felt would linger for hours. I didn't think Blair was the type for a quick office hookup, but as her lips stayed pressed against mine, I was getting closer and closer to wanting to find out.

It was Blair who finally broke the kiss, her cheeks flushed and her breathing heavy. "Drea."

"I..." I stammered to find something to say but before I could, she turned and ran out of my office without a word, and I slumped back in my chair.

"Fuck," I muttered to myself, rubbing my face in my hands.

Something was seriously wrong with me. Was I trying to mess up everything?

"Drea, are you okay? I just saw Blair run out of here, and she looked upset."

I jumped at Kaia's voice. "Uh... yeah, everything's fine. She got a call and had to go." I hated lying to Kaia, but I couldn't tell her what had happened.

"Oh no, I hope everything's okay."

"I'm sure it will be. Are you heading back to work?" I asked.

She smiled. "Yeah. I just came in to tell you I was back."

I nodded. I was anxious for Kaia to leave the room. I had to wrap my head around what I'd just done.

"Oh, Drea? You have a little something on the corner of your mouth." My head shot up to see a wide grin.

I brought my hand to my lips, seeing the telltale sign of red lipstick smeared on the pads of my fingers when I pulled them away. Well, fuck me into next week!

"Goodbye, Kaia." My face burned as she shut the door, and I was left alone with my thoughts.

Chapter Fifteen

BLAIR

I took the coward's way out, I know. I didn't know what else to do. I had to get out of there. I let her kiss me... Was I trying to make a mess of things?

My body was still buzzing from what had just taken place in Drea's office. One second, I was angry at her for giving me mixed signals and confusing me. Then the next second, I was getting lost in her kiss. Truly, helplessly lost.

She was claiming me with that kiss, and by God I was letting her have me. What was wrong with me?! I needed a cold shower, or something... electronic.

~

A few days later, I was headed to a lunch meeting with Cara and Drea. At least we would have a buffer.

We hadn't spoken since I fled her office. I couldn't breathe, and I didn't know what else to do. I still wasn't ready to face her, but I had to stay professional.

When I got to the restaurant, Cara and Drea were already there. They were talking, and I stopped when Drea turned to look at me.

I sucked in a breath, feeling her eyes rake over me. I unintentionally wore a low-cut, blue ruffled dress and regretted it immediately. She didn't look away, and I couldn't move. It was like my deceitful body wanted her to take everything in and examine me inch by inch.

When Cara finally waved me over, I cleared my throat and forced a smile, continuing my steps to their table.

"Hey, doll. You're just in time. Sit, sit."

"Thanks. Hey Cara." I slowly turned to Drea, who was still staring at me. "Drea," I said shortly.

"Blair," she replied, her tone giving nothing away despite the way her eyes bore into me.

"Okay, now that you have been formally introduced, tell me, what's been going on? How was the festival?"

"Fine," we both answered suspiciously too quickly and at the same time.

Cara laughed. "Okay then, good. Well, I wanted to talk about our capacity for the signing."

During the entire lunch meeting, Drea and I hardly spoke. We exchanged a few words between each other, but I could feel the strain and hesitation in her tone. The rare times I looked over to her, she caught me looking, and I turned away, pretending to find something else equally as interesting as her.

Cara did all the talking and kept looking between us both. She never asked what was going on, so I assumed she was oblivious.

After the meeting, Drea headed in the opposite direction, and Cara stopped me as we were walking to her car. "Okay, talk. What's going on with you two?"

I tensed. "What do you mean? Nothing's going on."

"Something is clearly going on. You wouldn't even look at each other. What happened?"

I groaned. "You know we don't get along. I'm trying to be nice, but it's hard, okay? Nothing happened."

If she didn't buy my half-assed attempt at a cover up, she didn't lead on. She glared at me and sighed. "Fine. At least no one's gotten hurt yet."

"Not yet, but there is still time." I grinned.

"Blair Amelia, do not even joke!" she scolded.

I laughed. "Using my government name. That's serious. Relax, Cara, everything's fine." *Totally fine...*

When I got home later that night, I paced around my kitchen, contemplating doing something utterly stupid.

It was a terrible idea. The worst idea in history. Nothing good could come from this idea. And yet, I was contemplating it anyway. I was clinically insane; I had to have been. Why else would I even consider it?

After a five-minute debate with myself, I caved. I was risking my sanity, but I couldn't help it.

One ring. Why was I doing this? Two rings. *Hang up, Blair!* Three—

"Hello?" a sleepy-sounding Drea answered, and fuck if that sound didn't scratch at something deep inside.

This was such a bad idea. I shouldn't have called her. I shouldn't have been talking to her outside of meetings with Cara at all.

I cleared my throat. "Hey, Drea... it's Blair."

The line was quiet for a minute, and I thought she hung up. "I do have caller ID, you know. Can I ask why you're calling me after hours, which is against our contract, by the way. You'll be lucky if I don't call Cara and—"

"I know, I know. I'm sorry, I just... I was hoping we could talk about what happened in your office." The line went quiet again, and I checked to see if she'd actually hung up. Nope, still there.

"I apologize for that. It was extremely unprofessional. I shouldn't have kissed you." Gone was her previous irritation. She became soft spoken, and I didn't know what to make of the drastic change.

I blinked. "What? There's nothing to apologize for, Drea. I kissed you back, so clearly it wasn't one-sided. I wanted to apologize for running out like that. I..." I didn't know what to say. I didn't expect any of this to happen.

"It's okay. I should've stopped it, but you were right, I was going to kiss you that night. I didn't think it was a good idea and I did it anyway. I realized after I kissed you that I made a mistake."

I frowned and spoke softly. "Oh. It wasn't good for you?" God, I sounded so pathetic. I didn't know why I cared.

So what if that kiss changed everything I thought I knew about the world? So what if it shook me to my core, and I went home fantasizing about her soft lips on other parts of my body—

"No, no, that's not it at all. It was good. It was really good." She laughed. "I just meant... was it not good for you? The way you ran out, I figured you thought it was a mistake."

I chuckled. "No, it was really good. I... I didn't know what else to do. I just wasn't expecting it." And I wasn't expecting to like it so much.

"Oh, well, again, I'm sorry. I don't want it to complicate things further," she added.

"There's no need to apologize, and yeah, I don't either. Anyway, I better let you go. I just wanted to say I'm sorry, and please don't tell Cara I called. It won't happen again. I'll see you tomorrow?"

"I won't," she said softly. "Goodnight, Blair."

"Goodnight, Drea."

I was heading into dangerous territory.

Chapter Sixteen

DREA

After our kiss, I enrolled in some more classes. I tried tai chi and knitting, and I even took ice skating lessons from Fallon. Anything to get Blair off my mind.

What was I actually thinking? It wasn't enough to fantasize about kissing her, I had to actually do it?

Fallon would have a field day with this situation I found myself in. Too bad she would never find out. For all the shit I gave her about Mackenzie, I would never hear the end of it.

The woman I complained about even months after our contracts were over—the one woman I couldn't stand—and I kissed her?!

I blame it on Mackenzie. If she would've just let me have sex with a stranger, I could've gotten rid of these ridiculous feelings.

Speaking of...

"Mackenzie Thompson, as I live and breathe. What perfect timing. I was just thinking about you," I said with a mischievous grin.

She narrowed her brows at me. "I'm flattered, but as you know, I'm taken. Which is why I'm here. I came to check in on your ban. Also, Fallon told me Blair ran out of here the other day upset? What did you do?!"

I groaned. "I love Kaia, but she cannot keep a secret from that fiancée of yours for anything."

"We both know my fiancée. She can get anyone to tell her anything she wants to know." She winked.

I blanched. "Gross! And yes she can. It's a gift, really."

"So..." she pressed. "What did you do?"

"Why do you assume I did something? You know what, don't answer that. I didn't do anything. Something came up and she left." *Yeah, your feelings for her!*

"Well, how's your sex life going, or rather lack thereof? Learn anything new about yourself?"

Several things I would rather not get into right now, actually.

"As a matter of fact I did. I learned that you hate me. I don't know how I'm going to make it through this. I'm taking a lot of classes and buying a lot of batteries. My accountant is going to be very concerned come tax time.

She laughed. "You still have a ways to go, but you can do it. It'll be good for you. You'll–"

The bell above the door chimed, causing us both to stop and look up. When my eyes locked with the most perfect pair of hazel eyes, I took in a breath.

Her lips parted slightly and my cheeks heated. Mackenzie cleared her throat, forcing me to tear my eyes away from Blair.

I turned to Mackenzie, who was giving me a look. "What?" I asked.

She smirked. "You know what."

"No I don't, and neither do you!"

"You better not get any kinky ideas. Keep it in your pants, Voss." She nudged my arm, and I rolled my eyes.

"Oh please. I'm not that desperate."

The thing was, I wasn't desperate enough to go fuck the first person I saw. I was actually taking this challenge seriously. Kissing was not the same as sleeping with someone, but if the opportunity presented itself, I wasn't sure I'd be able to say no.

She opened her mouth to say something, most likely sarcastically, but Blair approached the counter before she could. I had never been more grateful to see Blair in my life. As much as I loved Mackenzie, she had a way of pushing my buttons.

"Hey, I'm Blair." She smiled and held out her hand to Mackenzie.

The things I would've done to keep that smile around were unsettling to think about.

"I've heard so much about you. I'm Mackenzie. Her best friend is my fiancée, who I want to get back to, so I'll let you get to it." She gave me a wicked grin, and I wanted to throttle her.

"Bye, Kenzie. Thanks for dropping by."

She turned around and winked, and I just hoped she didn't go run to Fallon about what she did or did not see.

I cleared my throat, turning back to Blair, who was looking devastating in a yellow sundress. *Get it together!*

"Hey, she seemed nice," she noted with a grin.

I laughed. "She can be. What's up?"

"I was hoping we could talk? Cara said she sent over the finalized schedule, and wanted to know if you've had a chance to look at it yet."

"And she sent you instead of calling?" I asked.

"Not technically. I told her I was in the neighborhood and offered to drop in for her. She seemed happy I was attempting to do something nice. But I can go if you don't want me here." She motioned to the front door.

"No, it's fine. You're already here. We can talk in my office."

When we got to my office, she sat down. She moved slowly, hesitating with almost each step. She looked nervous sitting there, fidgeting with her dress. The dress that clung to her sexy-as-fuck curves. The dress I wanted to feel between my fingers and scrunched up to her hips—

"Can I get you something to drink?" I asked.

"I'll take a water if you have one. Thank you." She smiled, and I had to turn away. I should have put in our contract that she wasn't allowed to smile at me.

I grabbed some water out of the fridge and handed it to her before leaning against the desk with my own water in hand.

I took a drink and licked my lips when I caught her looking. I knew I shouldn't have. I also shouldn't have felt a pulse in my clit at the reddening of her cheeks when I did.

"So..." She cleared her throat. "The email?"

I scrunched my brows, confused. "Oh, right." I stood up and rounded my desk, pulling up the email. "Let's see. Okay, that sounds doable. You can let her know I sent over my signature. Was there anything else?"

On one hand, I wanted that to be it. I didn't want to spend any more time together than necessary. But on the other hand...

She stood up, smoothing her dress. "I believe that was all." She paused for a moment, looking a little shy. "Unless you had something?"

Oh, I had something all right, but nothing I was sure she wanted. *What? You don't want it either, Drea! It's the dry spell talking, that's all.*

I walked over to her and leaned back against my desk. "You asked if we could talk, Blair. I assumed you had something specific you wanted to discuss?"

She gave me a confused look, like she had forgotten all about what she was doing in my office in the first place. "Right. It was about the email from Cara. That's all." She licked her lips, and I wanted to reach out and feel them underneath the pad of my thumb.

"Well, if that's all, then I guess we're done here," I said in a low tone.

"I guess we are."

She made no move to leave, so I made the first one, pushing off my desk, ready to see her out. I wouldn't make the mistake of kissing her again, despite how desperate my body was to feel hers.

"Goodbye—" My words were cut short when she grabbed my shirt, slicing the distance between us, and kissed me. I guess she didn't have the same thought.

I instantly melted into the kiss without so much as a second thought. She tasted like a mixture of promise and regret, and I wanted to drown in it. I would have been perfectly content if kissing her was all I was allowed to do until the end of time.

I instinctively grabbed her arms, pulling her closer, the warmth of her body grounding me as the world seemed to fall away. I wanted our bodies fused together, just as our mouths were.

Every swipe of her tongue sent lightning bolts through me. She let out a soft moan when my hands traveled down her back. Oh, that was a delicious sound.

I grabbed her hips and turned her, lifting her onto my desk. Fuck, it was a sight. She shouldn't have come here, not back to my office, and definitely not by herself.

I was playing a dangerous game, but seeing her like this was doing something to me. God, was it ever.

I should've pulled away. The second our lips touched I should've, but I couldn't. If she'd let me, I wouldn't have stopped until she begged me to.

My hands were still on her when they moved up her dress and rested on her bare thighs. Her arms were wrapped around me, pressing our bodies closer and closer.

Just feeling her smooth legs underneath the palm of my hand was doing things to my body that I had no business feeling with Blair.

"Drea, are you in there?" My hands froze in place when Kaia's voice followed a knock on my office door.

"Shit," I muttered as I leaned my forehead against hers. I was equally thankful and irritated at the intrusion. If it weren't for Kaia, I wasn't sure how much further we would've gone, but I knew it would've been too far to take back.

We were both out of breath, and my hand was still on her thigh.

"Yeah, Kaia, give me a minute." When I didn't hear a reply, my shoulders sagged.

"I better go," she whispered. I took my hand off as she stood up and fixed her dress. "I'll tell Cara you signed off on her email," she added.

"That... sounds good. Hey, listen, Blair, I'm—"

"Don't." She shook her head. "This was a mistake. I shouldn't have come here." She turned around and opened the door without another word.

"Oh, I'm sorry, Dre. I didn't mean to interrupt," Kaia said when she saw a flushed Blair floating past her.

"It's okay, we were just finishing up." It was not okay. I was deeply horny and getting more irritated by the second.

She followed my gaze to where Blair had disappeared out of the store. "She looked pretty today, didn't she?"

I glared, clenching my jaw. I saw her. I knew exactly how she looked in the dress that showed off her sexy shoulders, but I didn't like the idea of anyone else noticing those things.

"Was there something you needed, Kaia?" My tone was harsh and devoid of any calmness. I needed to relax. I had no right to get short with Kaia. It was just my hormones talking. It had nothing to do with

Blair specifically, and everything to do with the wetness between my thighs. It was making me irrational.

She turned back and cleared her throat. "Oh, right. I was wondering what you wanted me to do about that woman that comes in almost every day and doesn't buy anything? She's been coming in for a while now. She's not bothering anyone, but—"

"Her name is Daisy, and she's deaf. If she's not bothering anyone, then what harm is she doing? Is she bothering you?" I knew the answer to that already. The number of times I caught Kaia looking in the same direction as the woman was outrageous.

"No, not at all! I was just trying to be helpful. I feel bad that she's always alone. I could go talk to her if you need me to. I know sign language. Not that I would know if she does or anything. I don't know anything about her. I—"

"She's fine. But if you want an excuse to talk to her, just make one up." I grinned when her cheeks turned red. "If there's nothing else, I'm heading home." I needed to get home fast to finish what Blair and I had started minutes ago.

She shook her head, trying to hide the blush creeping its way up her neck. She was never good at hiding her emotions. "No, that was all. I got it covered, have a good night."

I chuckled. "Goodnight, and Kaia? Go talk to her. She probably just needs a friend."

She smiled and walked away.

Chapter Seventeen

BLAIR

"Bend over and take a deep breath," the yoga instructor said in a soothing tone. I had to squeeze my mouth shut to keep from making a sound that could've gotten me kicked out.

I needed to get a hold of whatever was happening to me. It was like every time I was around Drea, I either wanted to slap her or rip her clothes off. She was insufferable, but anytime she kissed or touched me, I lost control.

It wasn't like I was deprived of pleasure. I had an array of toys that got the job done, and I supposed I had options if I really wanted them. It was just... I didn't want anyone. I wanted her, and the thought made me want to punch my stupid horny vagina.

Those warm chocolate-brown eyes. Her small, yet still perfectly sized chest. That damn piercing below her plump suckable lips...

I cleared my throat and squeezed my thighs together. This yoga class was not helping me relax. I needed to get my mind off of her, but it was impossible.

The universe kept throwing us alone together like it wanted bad things to happen. Really filthy but, if I had to guess, extremely pleasurable bad things. *Enough! I hate Drea Voss. I hate Drea Voss. I HATE DREA VOSS!*

I forced my thoughts to go elsewhere. To think about our first meeting together and about all of the times she made my life so infuriatingly difficult. About how rude, pig-headed, and unprofessional she was.

There, that was better. I was starting to get annoyed, and I would take that over lusting after her any day of the week.

After my yoga class, I had a meeting with Cara. We called it a business lunch for tax purposes, but it was really a girls lunch. Even though we were colleagues, we were friends first.

Today, we were meeting at The LunchBox. I was excited to spend some time with her, without Drea, and catch up on life outside of work.

"Why do you always look so good?" I asked as I saw her approaching.

She laughed and threw her arms around me. "Stop, you flatter me. But please, keep going. You look stunning, too, doll."

I wasn't as put together as she was. While she looked flawless in a navy-blue form-fitting dress with black heels and her blonde hair in a high ponytail, with ruby-red lipstick, I was wearing a plain black dress and black flats.

Still, I blushed and sat down. The waitress came, and we ordered lemon waters while glancing over the menu.

"I'm so glad to have this time with you. I feel like it's been nothing but work for the past few weeks, so it's nice to take a break from it." She smiled and took a sip of her water.

I nodded, mirroring the gesture. "I agree. I love my job, but I needed a little break."

"We both do! You and Drea aren't my only clients giving me a hard time. Two others are being extremely difficult. I have a few other authors releasing books around the same time, so it's been a challenge scheduling them without the signings colliding with each other." She groaned, and I felt bad for her. She worked really hard to build her business up from the ground, and she still took it just as seriously as she did in the beginning.

"Excuse me?" I scoffed. "I am not difficult!" She gave me a look that said she disagreed with that statement. "Okay, so maybe sometimes. I just know what I like! But I'm your favorite client and you know it!"

She laughed. "That you are! So, besides the signing, how are things going?"

"They are fine. I'm finishing up this next book and planning a new series, and I just spoke to my brother not that long ago. We're planning a trip to see our parents on their anniversary."

Her smile fell. "It's coming up already? What's it been, eight years now?"

I nodded. "Almost. It still feels like I lost them yesterday. I really miss them."

There wasn't a day that passed when I didn't think about my parents. Growing up without them was really hard. I was lucky enough to have a grandmother who loved me and supported me, but it wasn't the same.

I didn't get to have father-daughter dances at school. I wouldn't get to have my dad walk me down the aisle when I got married or have our own dance. I wouldn't have my mom there to give me her wedding dress, or tell me stories about her wedding. It sucked. It fucking sucked.

She rubbed my arm in a comforting gesture. "I know, I'm sorry."

I shrugged. "No more sadness. Let's change the subject please."

"Okay, well, don't forget we're meeting Drea in a few days to go over the outline of the setup."

"Can we go back to talking about my parents again?" I groaned.

"Blair, do not forget!"

"How could I forget? You've only reminded me a few times this week, Cara. I'll be there with bells on." I sent her a fake smile.

She rolled her eyes. "You two will be the death of me, I swear. I thought things were getting better? You both told me the festival went okay. Did something happen that you're not telling me?"

I groaned. "For the millionth time, nothing happened. We aren't best friends despite your plotting. But I can promise we won't bicker— at least, not in front of you." I winked. "I know you want us to get along, but I'm sorry, it's just not going to happen. We will never see eye to eye, but for you, I can put all of that aside, at least until this project is done."

It wasn't a lie. Technically, nothing did happen, besides her pushing me against the wall and painting a very pleasurable picture, causing my legs to nearly give out. But Cara didn't need to know that. I was trying to pretend like it never happened anyway. It couldn't happen.

What happened in her office, again, still played on repeat in my mind, but that didn't mean it was a good idea, or something to ever be repeated again.

She sighed in defeat. "Fine. It was worth a try. You both are important to me, and I just wanted us all to get along. I won't press it anymore as long as things are at least civil between you two."

"I assure you, they are." And they were, at least for now.

Chapter Eighteen

DREA

"Okay, so, I was thinking we could set the table up here so the line would be out of the way."

We had been walking around the store for over an hour with Cara, trying to map out the signing and where everything would be. Cara had just left when Blair and I were discussing where to put the table for the signing.

"I think that's a good idea. That way it won't interfere with the line at the counter, and we can set up the snack table over there." I nodded.

"Wow, something we agree on? Better film this or Cara will never believe it." She laughed.

I rolled my eyes. "Don't get used to it." It was still weird for us to have this mutual civility toward one another. Complimenting her in my office was like pulling teeth, and now, here we were working together, alone, and no one had lost an arm. At least, not yet.

We were just about finished when there was a flash outside, followed by the boom of thunder.

I jumped. "We better put a pin in this until later. It looks like there's a storm coming." She must not have heard me, because she didn't respond.

"Blair, did you hear me?" I turned around and saw her frozen. She wasn't moving and was staring out the door. "Blair, are you—"

Another loud boom. This time, she flinched. *Okay, so she doesn't like storms. Good to know.*

"Do you want to call it quits for the night and get going before the storm gets bad?" I asked.

She was still standing there, but she was trembling slightly. "Blair?" I asked again, but no response.

There was another boom, a louder one this time, followed by the sound of heavy rain, and that caused a bigger reaction from her.

Her breathing quickened and she started sweating. Her eyes looked like they were filled with tears, and I didn't know how to help. This situation felt like something her best friend, or even a stranger, would be more helpful in than me.

Another loud boom, and she flinched again, and I could see she was getting weak. I rushed over to her when her knees slowly gave out.

"Shit! Blair!" I shouted, catching her before she hit the ground.

She stood back up on trembling legs and looked at me. "Dre... Drea."

"Shh. It's okay, I've got you." I didn't say anything else as I held onto her and walked her to the back room, away from the storm.

I sat her down on the couch and covered her with the blanket, keeping her warm. I put some earmuffs on her to block out the thundering sounds, and sat next to her. I didn't know what I was doing: I just wanted to make it better. She was still hyperventilating and shaking, so I wrapped my arms around her and held tight until everything settled.

It felt awkward, holding her so intimately. We might have kissed in heated moments, but we were nothing more than colleagues. But at the same time, it felt right. It felt... good. It had been a long time since I'd held someone like that.

I couldn't help myself. I had to draw circles on her back. I wanted to comfort her, and a part of me wanted her to comfort me. This was her time to be taken care of, but I admit, I was a little selfish and wanted to feel needed in some way, and I wanted to feel her.

I inhaled deeply, which was a mistake. I was trying to center myself, and not think of Blair in any way, but all I could think about now was how she smelled.

God, did she smell fucking delicious! I was trying desperately to not think any impure thoughts about her, which was a challenge.

Feeling her skin on mine as her hands rested on my bare legs. Breathing in her vanilla perfume. I was so totally fucked.

What I did seemed to have worked. After a few minutes, her breathing had slowed to almost normal, and the shaking subsided.

"Drea, I'm so—"

"Don't you dare apologize. You can sit here as long as you need to. Come get me when you're ready." I stood up to go, but she caught my wrist.

"Wait!" I stopped and turned to look at her. "Please don't go. I... I don't want to be alone."

Being alone with Blair in the back room of the empty store was not what I should have been doing. I should have left her alone. I should have called Cara and told her to come deal with her best friend. This moment seemed too intimate, and our relationship wasn't that.

Instead of doing any of the things I should've, I sat back down next to her. She shifted on the couch, and I wondered if I'd made a mistake.

"So, you aren't a fan of storms, then?" I teased, but my smile fell when she looked down and didn't have a witty comeback or insult. "I'm sorry, Blair. Do you want to talk about it?"

She sat, not making a sound for a good while, until she finally shifted in her seat and looked at me. "I was thirteen, and we were on our way home from my grandmother's. We went there every Sunday for family dinner. My parents, cousins, aunts, and uncles, all of us. It's been that way since I can remember. Well, it used to be."

I put my hand on her thigh reassuringly. I wasn't sure what compelled me to do so; I just felt the need. The need for her to know someone was there, and she wasn't alone. I was expecting her to scowl at me or throw my hand off her, but she only sat there, barely acknowledging the contact.

"We had just left dinner when the storm hit. It was raining hard, and visibility was low. The road was slick, and our car was sliding across it." Her eyes started to fill with tears, and I wanted to hold her until it stopped.

"It all happened so fast. One minute we were singing in the car, and the next, a drunk driver behind the wheel of a truck ran a red light and smashed into the passenger-side door. It killed my mother instantly, and my father died shortly after. He passed away in the ambulance heading toward the hospital. I had a nasty concussion and a few broken ribs, but nothing else. I walked out of the hospital as an orphan. Anytime there is a storm, I have a flashback to the accident, and I can't breathe, I can't move. That's why I don't drive. If it happened while I was driving..." She shook her head and wiped the tears away.

I was still touching her leg, but she didn't back away. "I'm so sorry that happened to you, Blair. No one should ever have to go through that. I shouldn't have asked you to drive the weekend of the literary festival."

Without thinking, I reached out and gently wiped away a stray tear. She sat there unmoving as I did so, and I wasn't sure what to make of that.

I wasn't sure what possessed me to do such a thing to begin with. It wasn't like we were friends, or anything close to it. I just... I felt like it was something I had to do. I had to comfort her in some way.

Seeing her upset was unacceptable. I shook my head at myself. When did I start caring about Blair?

"It's okay, you didn't know. Thank you for staying with me. I know you're not my biggest fan, but it still means a lot." She started caressing my wrist and I was afraid to move and ruin the moment.

"Drea?" She was quiet, and there was something in her eyes I couldn't place.

Her fingers were still circling my wrist when I responded. "Yeah?"

She looked deep into my eyes, searching for something. Did she want me to back away? Did she want me to pull her close? I wanted to do it all.

She started to inch closer and I didn't even think about protesting as I felt her breath on my lips.

"I want..." The thought must have died off in her mind, because she grabbed me and kissed me, and once again, my body didn't belong to me anymore. It belonged to her.

Every thought, every action, wasn't my own. My body did whatever she commanded it to.

Every swipe of her tongue compelled my throat to moan with pleasure. Every touch ordered my body to react and connect deeper with hers.

When she started to reach underneath my shirt, my body tightened and sent a very dirty message to my clit, but before it could make it there, alarm bells began to ring in my mind.

I couldn't do this with her. As much as my body was begging me to, it was wrong on so many levels, and not only because of the sex ban. I would've been willing to throw that away, but we couldn't do this, not like this.

I pulled us apart. This wasn't right. "Blair, I can't. You're upset, and if you keep kissing me, I won't be able to stop. I don't want to be the person you blame for anything you might regret tomorrow." I wanted to kick my own chivalrous ass!

"Of course."

Seeing how embarrassed she looked, I added, "Please don't think it's because I don't want you, Blair. I just don't think—"

"I should go." She went to stand up, but I stopped her with a hand on her leg. She looked down at the touch, and I instantly removed my hand, losing my confidence from earlier.

"Let me take you home. It's late."

She shook her head. "No need. I'm a grown woman. I can handle a little darkness. I've been dealing with you for years, you know."

I took her hands in mine. "Trust me, I am well aware. Please let me take you home. I need to know you're safe." The admission came out like it had been there all along.

She sat quietly for a while, contemplating my offer. Eventually she sighed. "Fine."

I helped Blair gather her things before we headed to her house. Part of me wanted to stay back there with her, holding her until she fell asleep and the nightmares of her past didn't haunt her.

I didn't want anything sexual in that moment, which was weird, in a way. I had never been around a beautiful single woman and not thought about sleeping with her.

Granted, I'd thought about Blair that way quite a bit recently, but being in the back room with her? It just felt good to comfort someone and to be held after I hadn't been for so long.

It was weird to think about, but something about that situation, the vulnerability of being with Blair, it felt different than any moment I'd had in the past few years. It felt easy.

Before Skylar and I broke up, our relationship felt like a rollercoaster. It ranged from intense passion to bitter arguments. She wanted to settle down, but my gut told me that it wasn't my time. Our time together never felt easy, and with Blair, I felt I could be vulnerable.

Her house was exactly as I'd expected it to be—small and quaint. It had a triangular- shaped roof with green trim around the windows and door frame. Slim trees and other various shrubs lined both sides of the few steps leading to the front door.

It was a very whimsical cottage, but it looked like it had personality. Everything about this house shouted BLAIR!

"Well, I made it safe and sound. Goodbye, Drea." She went to open the door, but I stopped her with a hand on her thigh.

She looked down at where my hand rested, but I didn't pull away. I should've because it was itching to move up her dress. She really needed to invest in some pants. As much as I wanted to reach higher, I couldn't allow myself to.

"What are you doing this weekend?" I asked.

There was no reason for her to say yes. There was no reason I should've asked her, anyway. We'd already gone too far.

Just kissing her once was a mistake, but did that stop me from wanting to do it again? Did that stop me from hoping she wanted to do it again? The only thing that stopped me from inviting myself inside was Cara and my stupid ban.

I was really trying to take it seriously, and one night of intoxicating sex wouldn't be worth it, no matter how badly I was desperate for it. I didn't need sex; my body just thought I did.

And Cara. She was one of my dearest friends, and she knew how much Blair and I hated each other. If anything were to happen between us, it could cause so many problems. Most of which were business-related.

Cara took her business very seriously, and anything that jeopardized that was not okay with her. It was bad enough that we'd kissed a few times, but as long as nothing else happened and she never found out about it, we'd be okay. But if anything more happened, she'd blow a fucking gasket, I was sure.

She frowned at me, turning her whole body to face me. "What? Why?"

Fuck! That little frown was the cutest thing I'd ever seen. I really needed to stop seeing her as anything more than a business partner I sort of tolerated now. A colleague, not a woman with the most mind-blowing body I'd ever seen and the lips of a goddamn angel.

"Let me take you somewhere."

She arched an eyebrow. "Are you asking me out?"

I told myself it wasn't a date. That it was strictly platonic. It wasn't a date. I was not asking Blair Sterling on a date. Definitely wasn't happening.

"No, just... an apology for the entire time we've known each other."

She let out the cutest little laugh. Jesus Christ! I wished she'd stop being so fucking adorable. It wasn't helping matters. "That could take a while."

I rolled my eyes. "Is that a yes or a no?"

She sighed. "Sure. Pick me up Saturday, around six?"

I smiled. "Sounds perfect. Goodnight, Blair."

She leaned in to kiss my cheek, and I turned at the last second, causing her delicious lips to make contact with the very edge of mine. She pulled away, but only slightly. Just enough to look into my eyes.

I took a shaky breath and raised my hand to caress the side of her cheek, wishing I could do so much more, but at the same time, nothing at all.

I dropped my hand and gripped the sides of my legs so I didn't reach up and pull her down for a real kiss. Things were getting out of hand, and I needed to get a hold of myself.

Blair cleared her throat and whispered, "Goodnight. Thank you for taking me home."

She got out of the car, and I watched her walk away. The way her dresses always hugged every curve of her body, and the way her ass looked when she walked away, caused my mouth to go a little dry.

I breathed deeply before I drove away. Those little, short dresses were going to be the end of me.

Chapter Nineteen

DREA

When I asked Blair out, I didn't really have a set place in mind. I honestly thought she would say no.

I was laying in bed, reading her first book, Roses and Runes, and it gave me the idea of the perfect place to take her.

I was taking her to Mythos Cafe, a fantasy-themed cafe just outside of Seattle. The cafe had a mixture of soft and neon lighting.

There were hanging lanterns and plants draped across the ceiling, creating an almost magical forest vibe. The menu stayed on brand with themed food and drinks, offering even more to the fantasy experience. The seating areas were each unique and never duplicated, with an organic feel—like they'd been carved from nature.

When we got there, I was worried I went about it all wrong. She still seemed on edge, and I couldn't blame her. Not only did she have a PTSD episode in a public setting with someone she probably didn't feel safe around, but she made herself even more vulnerable by making a move, and I shut her down.

I was still upset with myself for saying no when I wanted nothing more than for her to be screaming yes all night long. I couldn't bring myself to think about anything else other than how she was feeling.

I wouldn't take advantage of her like that. She was not in the right headspace, and trying to make a move on her was not what she needed. When I took Blair Sterling, I didn't want there to be any regrets.

The outside of Mythos looked like an ordinary unmarked building. She sat in the car, confused.

"Where are we? The only place I see is a church. Unless you're asking for forgiveness from someone else, and I don't think they have enough holy water to wash away your sins."

I chuckled, shaking my head. "Oh no, love. There aren't enough hours in a lifetime to ask for forgiveness for the sins I've committed." Not to mention the deliciously sinful thoughts I'd had about Blair.

No! Shake it off! That's not ever going to happen, and that's not why you're here!

We got out of the car and headed around the wall-sized fence that caged the cafe. I never understood why there were no signs out front indicating the business. I guess it didn't matter, because when we walked inside, it was nearly packed.

My previous worries disappeared as we walked further into the space and Blair's eyes lit up brighter than the sun. She was looking around, captivated, taking in the details of every surface.

"Drea, where did you find this place? It's incredible." She was still taking in everything when she spoke.

I placed my hand on the small of her back, guiding her to the counter so we could place our orders. The contact seared into my skin, causing my breathing to quicken. I wondered if she was affected by the gesture, or if she even noticed.

"I've heard a few people talking about this place at the store, so I looked it up and thought it might be worth checking out." I shrugged.

I didn't dare tell her exactly how much research I had done, including coming in here myself to get the lay of the land and to talk with employees about their menu, convincing them to make a few tiny changes for one night.

When we finally made it to the counter, the employee greeted us and I motioned for Blair to order first. "Can I have the faerie blossom tea, please, and the pixie dust shortbread? Thank you."

I didn't want to examine the way my chest felt, seeing her bright eyes as she ordered, still looking around the cafe.

"Of course, and for you, miss?"

I turned to the man behind the counter, forcing my gaze away from the true beauty of the cafe. "I'll have the violet petal tea and a thorn-berry scone, please."

Blair gave me a questioning look, to which I shrugged. "They sounded interesting."

She took out her wallet, but I stopped her with a hand. "I've got it."

"You didn't have to do that. I can pay my own way, you know," she said as we found a table in the corner. It was a small wooden table shaped like a tree stump.

"I am well aware, Ms. Best-Selling Author." I winked. "I asked you out tonight, as an apology, and part of that is paying for you."

"I'm still waiting for that apology," she teased as she took a bite of her bread, causing my throat to become dry when her eyes rolled back. "Oh my God, this is amazing!"

I definitely agree. "You're really going to make me work for it, aren't you? Can't I just say bringing you here is an apology, you accept it, and we become the best of friends?" I laughed when she rolled her eyes.

I washed my smile away and turned serious. If I was going to apologize, I was going to do it right. "Fine, but tell anyone, and I'll deny it," I teased.

"Don't worry, I wouldn't dream of it. No one would believe me, anyway." She grinned.

Relief flooded through my shoulders as I began to speak. "I'm sorry, Blair. Since our first time working together, which didn't end in the best way, I've been nothing but rude and unprofessional toward you, and I know the feelings have been mutual. I've been holding onto that animosity for years, and considering my outburst from our first meeting this time around, it had only grown."

I could have sworn that I saw a slight glitter forming in her eyes as a soft smile spread across her lips.

"I also want to apologize for forcing myself on you at the festival, and again in my office. That was inappropriate and should not have happened."

"Drea, please stop apologizing about that night. If I hadn't wanted it, you would've known about it. And seeing as how I came back into your office and forced myself onto you, that's not the case." She grinned sheepishly.

I blushed, remembering that day clearly. "Believe me, you didn't force yourself. I have wanted that for a long time, probably longer than I care to admit. Anyway, I don't expect things to just change overnight, but I hope you can accept my apology and maybe we can try to start over?"

She nodded while taking a sip of her tea. I had barely touched my drink or my scone besides the initial first tastes. I had my eye on something more delicious than anything they served at the cafe. Jesus, I sounded so lame!

"I'd like that. Hating you has been exhausting. I'm not saying I like you, but hate seems like a strong word these days."

I frowned. "So do you just go around making out with people you don't like? I'm intrigued to know what you do to people you do like." I winked and chuckled when her face turned a shade of dark red.

"Funny. Too bad you'll never find out." She winked. "Are you about ready to go? It looks like they're closing soon.

I looked around, noticing the workers cleaning up around the cafe; wiping tables and taking out trash. I hadn't realized we'd been sitting there for over an hour. Time flew when you were having fun, or in beautiful company.

"Yeah, we should probably get going."

We walked in silence until we got closer to my car.

"Did you like the cafe? It was cool how they had menu items that sounded like they belonged in one of your books, huh?"

She rolled her eyes. "Yeah, what a coincidence. You didn't have anything to do with that, did you?"

I smiled. "What? Me? No, not at all."

She didn't seem to buy the lie at all. "Sure. Well, I guess you weren't lying when you said you read my books. That place was amazing."

"I don't lie. And just because I don't like you doesn't mean I can't appreciate talent. You're a really good writer, Blair."

She smiled. "Wow. Thanks for the backhanded compliment, I guess."

She scowled at me when I opened the passenger-side door for her. "What?" I asked.

"Are you sick or something?"

I laughed. "Oh, for fuck's sake, hasn't anyone ever been nice to you?"

"Of course, just not you." She smirked.

"Fine. Remind me to never do it again, then." I took a step closer and lowered my voice. "Just get in the car, Blair."

Her breath hitched and her eyes darkened. She didn't say anything as she got in, but I didn't miss the subtle lick of her lips. Did she like being told what to do? And why did the thought turn me on?

I shook away the thought and rounded the car to the driver's side.

"Thank you." My only response was a smile. I really had to pull it together.

I rested my hand on the gear shift as I drove, but my fingers were itching to reach out for her.

"I feel like I'll never be able to eat again." She groaned.

After the cafe, we stopped at a bakery and ended up sharing an abnormally large piece of chocolate cake.

I laughed. "I'm sure after some sleep, you'll be starving again."

"Nope. Not going to happen."

We were silent for the rest of the drive until I pulled in her driveway and stopped the car.

"Well, this is me," she joked. "Thanks for today. I had a lot of fun. Who would've thought?" She laughed.

"So funny! But I'm glad. I did too."

My smile disappeared when she became serious. "And thank you for the other night. That was so embarrassing, but you didn't have to be nice to me. I haven't done anything to deserve it." She shrugged.

"Even if I didn't like you at all, I'm not some neanderthal who can't see a lady in need. You went through something horrible. I don't blame you for feeling the way you do. Don't ever feel embarrassed. After seeing you handle those comments at the festival... You are one of the bravest people I know."

A tear slid down Blair's cheek, and she quickly wiped it away. She made a motion to grab the door handle, but she pulled her hand back.

"I'm sorry, I'm usually not this emotional. I don't open up like that to anyone. You must think I'm crazy." She laughed nervously

"I could think of a number of things to call you, but crazy isn't at the top of my list," I joked.

"You are insufferable!" she said as she rolled her eyes in amusement. "But seriously, Drea, I really had a great time with you tonight. I got to see a side of Drea Voss I didn't know existed."

I looked at Blair's lips, then at her eyes. I could see fire burning inside them. "I don't know, maybe your kiss has put me under some kind of spell." I shrugged, but it was true. Kissing her had opened something that had been closed inside me for a long time.

Blair licked her lips and stared into my eyes. In that second, she closed the space between us as she crashed her lips into mine and pulled me toward her.

I moaned into our kiss, desperately wishing for more. After a few fantastic seconds, I knew I had to break away sooner or later.

"Well, do you want to come in? Maybe your apology doesn't have to end so early," she whispered, bringing me in closer.

Did I want to? That seemed so very risky... "So tempting," I murmured.

I wasn't supposed to be having sex with anyone, let alone Blair. But I had to admit, I was a little curious. Was she as feisty in the bedroom as she was with work? Besides, I wasn't blind. I would've been a damn fool to say no.

"You don't seem like the type to hesitate when someone offers you sex, Drea. Just so you know, I'm not in the headspace to regret anything tomorrow," she whispered as she played with my earlobe.

I cleared my throat, very aware of the tingling sensation happening between my legs. "I mean, if you're absolutely sure, Blair. Once we cross that line—"

"Why don't we see if we can put your mouth to better use." She smirked before she kissed me again.

All common sense crumbled within me as our lips touched. Everytime any part of me connected with her, any practical reasoning seemed to be a thing of the past. I had this insatiable hunger for the woman sitting next to me.

I broke the kiss and groaned, wanting this more than I would admit out loud. I stepped out of the car, rounded to her side, pulled the door open, and offered her my hand. She took it with a smirk and led me inside.

As soon as the door closed, I was on her again, backing her against the door. I grabbed her waist and tilted her chin up with my fingers. "Is this more useful, sweetheart?" I asked before I kissed her as if she were the last drop of water on earth.

At this point, my resolve had shattered, and there was no piecing it back together. Not when she took off my jacket. Not when she unbuttoned my shirt, and certainly not when she grabbed at the waist of my pants and pulled me closer to her, our bodies touching.

She broke us apart and walked past me, taking off her coat. I grabbed her wrist and pulled her to me again, connecting our mouths once more. They were apart for far too long.

She walked me backward down the hall, leading me to her bedroom. We left a trail of clothes in our wake, never tearing ourselves apart for very long. I made a mental note to ask for a tour of her house later. I was very curious to see if it matched what I had envisioned it would look like.

She pushed me onto the bed, and I scooted back until I reached the headboard, and I had the sexiest view of Blair crawling up to me.

Holy shit. I was so screwed. She was the most perfect woman I had ever laid eyes on. I'd seen her perfect ass before, but that was nothing compared to the rest of her.

Her soft kissable skin was as perfect as I had imagined it to be, not a flaw in sight.

Her tits were fucking unreal. I had always thought they were fake, but as I looked at them in person, there was no denying that Blair was a natural goddess. They were perfectly C-cup sized, and her nipples were begging to be flicked by my greedy tongue.

She had an athletic build with faintly toned muscles. Her stomach was flat leading down to her sweet glistening pussy. I could see her desire from where I sat with my own desperate need. I wanted to take in every inch of her and devour her until we were both left a pile of ruins.

I was pretty sure I was breaking my vow tonight, but I had no intention of caring as this gorgeous woman straddled me and kissed me again. The sight of her was enough to wreck me.

I broke the kiss, breathless and so fucking wet. "Are you sure, Blair?" I needed her consent before I showed her what years of built-up tension and animosity looked like.

She nodded. "Yes. I've never been more sure of anything."

"Get up here," I demanded.

"Are... are you sure? You don't have to—" I muffled her hesitation with a kiss. I, too, had never been more sure of anything in my life. I was going to demolish any lingering doubt either of us had.

"Get up here, sweetheart," I whispered.

She moaned and straddled my face but didn't sit down immediately. She was hesitant, but I grabbed her hips. "Sit the fuck down, love. I'm thirsty," I said, and I pulled her down onto me.

I moaned my pleasure into her at the taste. I wanted to shatter from the first gentle swipe of my tongue. Feeling her clit above me was like my own personal heaven.

"Oh my God!" She moaned as she arched back, her soft strawberry-blonde waves flowing down and tickling my stomach.

I groaned when her hands found my breasts. I wanted this vision of her riding my face imprinted on my brain.

When I grazed her clit with my teeth, she let out a moan and tangled her hands in my hair. "Fuck, that feels so good," she whined, and the sound caused a moan to escape from me.

I grinned when her breathing became rapid and her moans became more frequent.

All these years of bickering and hating each other, and we could have been doing this?! Holy fuck! I was going to come just from tasting her.

I grabbed her ass while my mouth went to work, and as I could feel her about to lose control, I squeezed and sucked harder, causing a series of shudders from the body above me.

I slowed down my pace as she came apart on top of me, and I relented her sensitive clit before she got off me and brought our lips together, tasting herself. I was so turned on it physically hurt.

When her hand traveled down to feel just how she affected me, I couldn't contain the groan. "Blair," I breathed.

She chuckled softly as she licked the side of my neck and continued her soft caress of my clit. "Hmm?" she hummed.

"I'm not going to last much longer if you keep doing that," I panted.

Clearly she didn't care, because her hand didn't stop, and I could feel the orgasm building. It had been building for months, but a few touches from her, and it was going to come crashing down.

I should've stopped this in the car. I should not have followed her inside, but I couldn't find it in me to regret it.

Right before that blissful peak, she slowed down and inserted one finger a few times before inserting two.

"Oh my God!" I moaned when she simultaneously pumped in and out of me and rubbed my clit with her thumb. She increased her speed and pressure until my tits were bouncing and she was fucking me senseless. I guess she was working out some frustration. With the intensity at which she fucked me, I was going to explode.

"Blair!" Her name came out in a euphoric cry as my orgasm came crashing out, and she didn't stop until I was a limp mess.

She gave me one last kiss before she fell onto the bed next to me. "Well, that's one way to say goodnight," she whispered in between breaths.

"I'd say so. Shit, Kenzie is going to kill me if she ever finds out about this." I groaned, remembering I had just broken my promise.

She laughed. "Why? Isn't she getting married?" She sat up suddenly. "Oh my God! Do you have some sort of poly relationship with them? Did I break some rule?"

I laughed. "No. Fallon is like my sister. I would never go there. No, it's ... it's stupid. Forget it."

She turned to me. "What is it?"

I sat up and sighed. "I'm not supposed to be having sex." I rolled my eyes, not believing I was about to share this with her. "This is so stupid... Two years ago, my ex of three years and I broke up. I had been taking it kind of hard and sleeping around. A lot. And drinking. A lot. We had our closure and she's with someone else now and living in New York, and I'm happy for her. It's just been hard. She was all I knew for so long. I guess I should've seen the signs that we weren't meant to be, you know? I mean, we were on and off our whole relationship. We always fought about the dumbest things. Anyway, Mackenzie had this great idea that I needed to ban myself from sex in order to find myself or whatever." I shrugged. "Look how well that turned out."

She blushed. "I'm sorry I broke your ban. It was one time, though. She doesn't have to know you fell off the wagon, as long as you get back on it again... if that's what you want."

"Do you want me to get back on the wagon?" I asked, caressing her leg. I hoped she would say no, because after this night, with her, I had no intention of looking at another wagon again.

"Well—" She stopped when the doorbell rang. "Shit."

Chapter Twenty

BLAIR

"Shit, shit! That's probably Cara." I started frantically looking for our clothes.

I had to get rid of her before she saw Drea. This was so not good.

"Uhh... okay. You stay in here and do not make a sound! I'm going to get rid of her." I threw on a robe and fled out of the room, not waiting for a response.

I almost stumbled when I saw the trail of clothes we left in our lust-filled haze. A blush crept up my neck at the images of how they got there in the first place, but another ring of my doorbell quickly dismissed any lingering throbbing I felt.

"Shit," I whispered, rubbing my face. What was I thinking?!

I fixed my hair and cleared my throat, taking a deep breath before opening the door.

Cara was standing there with a smile, completely oblivious to the chaos that her arrival had ensued within me. I had to play it cool and pray that Drea listened to me and stayed in the bedroom. Cara needed to go, or else she would receive a deliciously naked surprise.

"Cara! Hey, what's up?" I sounded as if I was hiding something from her, which I was, but I didn't want my voice to betray that.

She narrowed her brows. "Hey, are you okay?" She leaned around me and took in the hot mess of my house and grinned. "Am I interrupting something?"

I blushed a few shades of red, following her gaze behind me and praying Drea wasn't standing there. Relief washed over me when I only saw my empty living room. "Actually yes. Can I help you?"

"I was just coming by to check on you. After the storm the other night, I wanted to make sure you were okay, but clearly I wasn't the only one. Who's in there?"

She tried to peek further into the house, but I blocked her view and scowled. "Excuse me, a woman never kisses and tells."

She laughed. "Right, of course. Apologies, madame." She pretended to tip an invisible hat, and I rolled my eyes but failed to hide a smile.

"Well, since it's obvious that you're alive and entertaining company... I'll be on my way. Goodnight, doll. Have fun and call me later. I want to know all the juicy details." She winked.

"Good night." And I shut the door, double-checking it was locked.

I was such an idiot! I should have known she'd come to check on me. If I didn't answer my phone after a storm, she always dropped by.

That was way too close for comfort. I felt like a horrible friend for not remembering, but when I was with Drea, all rational thoughts flew out the window.

I picked up the clothes while heading back to my room, where Drea was lying, covers off, naked in all of her caramel gloriousness...

"I was right, it was Cara." I let out a relieved breath. "She was just checking in after the storm."

"How sweet of her," she said softly as she pulled me into the bed with her.

I giggled when she began kissing my neck. "Drea, it's time for you to go now." I didn't sound very convincing as I moaned out my demand.

The last thing I wanted was for her to leave. I had zero regrets, just as I told her I wouldn't, but I knew it wouldn't be a good idea for her to stay.

"You never answered my question earlier. I could get back on the wagon, or I could stay here, far away from the wagon."

I moaned when she sucked at my collarbone. "Drea, I..." I let out a shaky breath, trying not to get distracted by what her mouth was currently doing. "I think it's best if both you and your wagon go home. As spectacular as this was, it can't happen again."

I shouldn't have groaned in protest at the loss of contact between us. It was my words that caused it to end.

She stopped and sat up again. "I know," she begrudgingly said as she took one last look at my body.

She kissed me softly, and I wanted to kick myself as I watched her perfect naked body leave my bed. I threw on a night shirt and walked her to the door after she got dressed.

"So, this is me," Drea teased with a grin, pointing to the front door.

I laughed. "I guess it is. Thank you again for today." I smiled.

She took a step closer and pulled me by my shirt. "You're very welcome, and thank you for the orgasms, love." She kissed me passionately, and I held on a little too tightly, refusing to let it end so quickly.

She broke the kiss, and I was out of breath as she turned around and left. I brought my hand to my mouth, still feeling her lips, demanding myself not to call after her.

After a very cold shower, I slid into bed when my phone went off with a text notification:

> Cara: Is your mysterious date still there?

> Me: She just left.

> Cara: Wow, I didn't expect you to be the casual type.

I groaned.

> Me: I'm not.

> Cara: So you have someone special in your life and didn't tell me?! I am hurt! 🙁

Me: It was one time, Cara. I don't know what's going to happen.

Cara: What do you want to happen? Do you have feelings for this woman?

I froze. I didn't know what to say to her. I couldn't lie to her—she was my best friend—but I also couldn't be totally honest with her. If she ever found out about Drea... It was one time. She wouldn't find out.

Me: I don't know. Thanks for checking in on me ♥ Goodnight.

She replied with a moon emoji, and I turned off my phone.

Did I have feelings for Drea? The thought terrified me...

Chapter Twenty-One

DREA

After my night with Blair, anytime I needed a release, the image of her riding my face came to mind. It was so incredible, but I knew it wouldn't happen again. Nobody needed to know, and I could just move on with my life.

We didn't have to see each other for another few weeks, but I was still nervous to see how it would go. I wondered if I should call her, maybe see if she wanted to hang out, but I admit, I was scared. I was scared I wouldn't be able to handle being around her, knowing that one perfect night was all I would ever get. I was scared to admit that I might have wanted a lot more than just one night with Blair.

Today I was meeting Cara for lunch at the Luna Rosa before our weekly pickleball game. There were a few things about the signing she wanted to discuss.

As I walked into the restaurant, my stomach was in knots. The last person I wanted to discuss with Cara was Blair.

I didn't know how to be honest while also not telling the whole truth. It was only one time, but I didn't know what I would do if Cara ever found out about it. I wasn't sure how she would handle it, considering how difficult we had been for her over the years.

"Hey, doll, you look great!" Cara greeted me with a hug and a double-cheeked kiss. I showed up to lunch in a silver silk button-up blouse and black trousers, and Cara was wearing a white sundress.

I gave her a wide grin. "Hey, love. Thanks, so do you. Did you order already? I'm starving."

She laughed. "Not yet, I was waiting for you."

We both ordered the chicken and fettuccine pasta with asparagus along with a caesar salad. Luna Rosa had the best chicken.

"So, what did you want to talk about?" I asked as the waitress left the table.

"Oh, right! I wanted to talk about the signing. I know you approved the capacity and a few other things, but I wanted to talk about the fees, just the two of us. I know we've done this before a handful of times, but I wanted to clarify and make sure we are on the same page, especially since I know things might be a little tight, hence the reason for the signing in the first place."

I laughed. "I almost wish I couldn't afford it."

She rolled her eyes. "Drea, honestly, you two are ridiculous! This sounds absolutely insane, but you two bicker like an old married couple. The way you both argue almost makes me think you could have feelings for each other or something."

My water went down the wrong way as I began to violently choke.

"Oh my God, Drea! Are you okay?"

Barely breathing, I responded in between coughs, "Yeah... I'm fine... water went down the wrong way."

If only she knew the feelings I had for Blair... Wait, what feelings did I have for her? I was sure the attraction was just my deprived libido talking. I was convinced that after we had sex, my feelings would go back to normal, back to the way they had been before I started to get to know her.

We slept together once, and until then, we hated each other. But the more time I spent talking to her and just being around her, the more I realized I could be content if I never did anything else. *Get it together, Dre!*

Thankfully, our waitress came back with our food before she could press the issue anymore.

"Where were we? Oh, right, you and Blair."

"What?!" I yelled out, unsure as to why I raised my voice so much. I cleared my throat and tried again. "What about me and Blair?" As far as I knew, there wasn't a "me and Blair." It was just one night, and I was not going to tell Cara.

"How are things going with you two, anyway? Are you even getting along at all?"

My fork stopped mid-air and my face heated. There was hope in her tone, and I knew I couldn't tell her the truth, but I could throw her a little bone.

I cleared my throat. "You could say that, yeah."

"Good. See, I told you things would work out! She's great once you give her a chance and get to know her." She smiled and took a drink.

Didn't I know it...

"I went to see her the other night. She doesn't handle storms very well, so I wanted to make sure she was okay." She got this look in her eyes as she talked about her best friend. The love she had for Blair was evident on her face.

"Oh really, and was she?"

She laughed. "Actually, she was. She had company over, so I would say she was well taken care of."

My face scorched at the memory of exactly how Blair was cared for...

"I tried to pry, but she won't tell me who it was. She seemed to be happy, though." She shrugged.

I didn't let myself ask for more details. "Well, that's good."

"She usually tells me if she's seeing someone, and it's been a while since I've heard about anything."

I scolded myself for the slight smile that tugged on my lips at the thought of Blair not being with anyone else. We slept together once, and it wouldn't happen again, so I had no right to feel any sort of claim on her.

I needed this subject to change. I couldn't talk about her anymore. "So, have you talked to Fallon or Mackenzie? You know they're getting married, right?"

She laughed. "Yeah, I know. I ran into Mackenzie the other day. She apologized for the hundredth time and told me. I'm happy for them. That situation was weird, but it's laughable now, and I'm glad we can all be friends. It must be nice to find your other half. Not all of us can be that lucky. To find someone who envelops all your thoughts during all hours of the day. Someone you just want to be around, even if it's just to look at them. I would give anything to have a feeling like that, you know?"

Yeah, Cara, it's really something...

I cleared my throat. "Uhh... yeah, totally."

She laughed. "Oh, ignore me. I'm just in my feelings right now. I know relationships aren't really your thing. Let's change the subject."

They didn't used to be my thing, but... sometimes people's opinions on life could change.

"You know me so well." I laughed nervously. I had to get it together.

We finished our lunch before heading to the club for our weekly game.

Chapter Twenty-Two

DREA

"So, have you and Blair tried to kill each other yet? I'm surprised Cara doesn't attend every meeting between you two." Penelope laughed.

It had been a few weeks since our "meeting," and I would be lying if I wasn't tempted to call her at least a few times a week for a repeat. As much as I liked Cara, I wasn't interested in having Mother Goose around asking questions or even worse, finding out about what happened.

I rolled my eyes. "We are adults. We can be civil... sometimes. No one has been threatened, yet. It's actually been going pretty decent, to be honest. We have a mutual understanding."

Fallon looked at me skeptically. "What, are you two best friends now? A month ago you wanted to strangle her."

I tried to hide my smile at the memory of her strangling my face with her thighs as she was coming apart from my touch. "We are not best friends, love. That spot is taken already. But I guess you could call us casual acquaintances?"

She snorted. "Okay, if you say so. Anyway, are you bringing anyone to the wedding?"

"I still can't believe you're getting married!" Penelope grinned widely at our friend.

It was still weird to hear Fallon talking about marriage. How did time pass by so fast? Pen was trying to get pregnant and Fallon had found her other half. Was I the only one refusing to grow up?

A softer smile replaced the playful look on her face. "Every day I wake up, thinking it's all a dream, but then I turn to see Mackenzie next to me and I realize it's not. I'm really getting married, you guys."

Tears started forming behind her eyes, and I playfully swatted at her. "All right, that's enough. You better not cry or you're going to make us cry!"

"Exactly! We are insanely happy for you, babe," Penelope added. "We love you, and we can't even put into words how it feels to see you with your person."

My face lit up with joy at Penelope's words, but I couldn't ignore what my heart had desired for sometime now. I was so happy for my best friend. She had been through a lot, even with Mackenzie, and she deserved her happy ending.

I couldn't deny, though, that I felt a tinge of jealousy. Getting married had never been on my bucket list; hell, even being in a committed relationship never made it onto that list.

But as I sat there with my two best friends, one happily married for over a decade and one soon to be married, I had no choice but to think about what my future would look like.

Who would be in it, if anyone? Would they have warm hazel eyes and soft skin? Or was I destined to spend the rest of my life alone and going from bed to bed because I was afraid any relationship I had would end the same way as the ones I grew up surrounded by?

The thought came out of nowhere, and I blinked it away, clearing my throat. "So, actually, I was thinking of asking Blair to the wedding. I really don't want to go alone, and going with an employee doesn't sound too appealing, as much as I like Kaia."

Fallon and Penelope stared at me. "Wow, Drea. You want to bring Blair, as your date, to my wedding?" Fallon asked.

I rolled my eyes. "As a date, no. As my... casual acquaintance, yes. I don't want to go alone. Is that a problem?"

She raised her hands in surrender and shook her head. "No, no problem at all. It's just a little surprising, that's all. But I'm glad you made a new friend."

"I guess. Listen, I love you, babe, but I need to take care of a few things at the store. Call you later?"

"Of course, boss lady. Love you, too." Fallon looked at me warily, like she didn't totally believe me. I didn't totally believe me either, to be honest.

I hugged my friends before heading to work. It wasn't a total lie; I did have some things to take care of, but none of them needed to be finished today. I just didn't want to stay for more questioning about my... Blair.

We went from fighting to kissing to having sex, which neither of us have brought up since then. She said it couldn't happen again, and I agreed. It would make things too messy.

That didn't mean I was happy about it, though. I wanted nothing more than to feel her coming apart for me. To taste her orgasm above me. To see what she looked like from behind, shaking and desperate.

Several hours later, I was sitting in my office, going over last month's receipts, when I heard a knock on my door.

"Come in," I said without looking up.

"When are you going to get some paintings for this office? It looks so boring." My eyes darted up to see a smirking Blair looking drop-dead gorgeous in a tight little black dress that hugged every curve and made me want to smother myself in her tits. *Good fucking God!*

"What..." I cleared my throat. What had I done in a past life to deserve this sight? "What are you doing here, and why are you dressed like that?"

Now was not a good time for Kaia to be on break. Being alone with Blair while she looked like that was very dangerous. My mind was running wild with all the dirty things I wanted to do to her. On top of my desk, specifically.

She pouted and looked down at her dress. "What's wrong with my dress? I thought it looked good."

That was an understatement. Saying she looked good would have been an insult. She looked like the definition of pure perfection, and I swallowed hard.

"That is definitely not what I said. There is no denying how good you look in that dress." I didn't add that she would look better with the dress on the floor... "Back to my original question, what are you doing here?" I asked.

She smiled and walked closer. I met her on the other side of my desk as I leaned against it. "I wanted to talk about the other night, when I said it couldn't happen again."

I frowned at the mention of how that night ended. "I remember vividly."

She played with the top button of my shirt. I had gone for a professional look today with a burnt-orange button-down shirt and black pants.

"Well, I've been thinking a lot about it, and maybe I made that decision a little too hastily."

"Is that so? I'm inclined to agree with you there, darling. What are you saying, then?"

She undid another button and didn't take her eyes off me. "I don't think one night is nearly enough for all the things I want us to do, and I'm pretty sure you don't either."

"Again, I'm inclined to agree." I smirked. "You have to know, I'm not one to put a label on things, but I enjoy spending time with you, and I'd really like to keep doing that."

"That's fine with me. I'm not asking for a commitment or anything. I'm usually the opposite and need to label what I'm doing with someone. Casual dating is not really my thing, but at the same time, wanting you was never my thing either, but here we are." She grinned.

"Yes, here we are."

"So, we're going to keep seeing each other?" she asked.

She was looking so nervous that I couldn't help but chuckle. Did she honestly think, after our night together, I wouldn't want to experience her again?

"I guess we are." I smiled and lifted her dress, but she stopped me.

"Not here, at my place. I don't want to have to be quiet."

I groaned. Fuck, this woman! "I'm off now." I winked.

She frowned. "I can't tonight. I really need to get some writing done. I have a deadline, but I'll call you?"

I lowered her dress and tugged it closer to me. "I don't want to interfere with your work. That sounds like a plan."

I propped myself onto my desk and spread my legs, pulling her closer. She settled in between them and placed her hands on my thighs. "So, how do you feel about straps, darling?" I asked as I caressed her arms.

She moaned, pulling my shirt so we were inches apart. "I really like the sound of that."

"Good," I whispered. "I look forward to being able to fuck you properly." I grabbed her chin and kissed her.

Kissing her was like floating on a cloud that had been warmed by the sun. I wanted to melt into it every time and let the kiss consume me.

She grinned into the kiss when I lifted her dress up to her hips and rested my hands on her ass, just underneath her underwear. Her ass felt so soft that I had to give it a light squeeze. I reveled in the little sound she made when I did.

"I'm sorry, I didn't know you had company. I... I should've knocked." A familiar voice brought us back to reality, and a flushed Kaia was standing at the door with her eyes covered.

Blair took a step back, cheeks fire red, and fixed her dress, smoothing out the wrinkles and ensuring no glorious body parts were in view.

"I should go." Blair cleared her throat and ran out the door without another word.

"Blair!" I yelled after her but she didn't stop. I sighed and covered my face.

"Drea, I... I'm so sorry. I didn't..." Kaia stammered but I put a hand up, stopping her.

"Kaia, stop."

"I'm sorry," she whispered. She was trembling, and I could see her watery eyes from my desk. She was scared, as if she was in trouble. Normally, she might've been, but I was still high from Blair, so I let it slide. Nothing was going to happen, anyway. But once I was home and alone? That was a different story.

I sent her a look and motioned her to my desk. "Kaia, sit down." I sat in the chair next to her.

"So, you and... I'm confused. I thought you hated each other?"

I groaned. "We did... It's complicated. Listen, can you pretend you didn't see anything?"

She frowned. "Of course, Drea. But I thought you weren't supposed to be having sex?"

I rolled my eyes. Fucking Fallon! "Who said anything about sex?"

She smirked. "I mean, that didn't look like a business meeting. Aren't you?"

I groaned. "Like I said, it's complicated."

"Right. Well, again, I'm really sorry, and I will keep this to myself. I just came in to tell you I was leaving."

She stood up and headed to the door. "Oh, and Drea? Whatever is going on, I'm happy for you." She smiled sweetly, and I couldn't help but do the same.

"Goodnight, Kaia."

Chapter Twenty-Three

BLAIR

Walking into Drea's office was the best and worst thing I had done. After she left my house, I couldn't stop thinking about her. I tried everything I could think of to get her out of my head, but it was pointless. She had burrowed into my brain with no way of getting out.

I finally couldn't take it anymore, and I decided, why not do something for me? I wanted sex, and I wanted it with Drea, anywhere and everywhere I could. So why not ask for it?

Even though I'd told her we couldn't do it in her office, once she started to kiss me and her hands found my ass, I was willing to forgo that thought.

I was beyond mortified when Kaia had walked in. Although the idea of having sex in Drea's office turned me on more than it should've, getting caught didn't. Poor innocent Kaia, if she ever saw that...

Drea and I had had sex a solid four times since we agreed to keep sleeping together, and every time had been better than the last. My body had been doing things I didn't know it could do.

If I would've known how good it felt to be with Drea, I would've tried it years ago.

I wanted nothing more than to spend every waking hour in bed with her, but unfortunately, today was a workday and I was meeting with Cara at the bookstore.

Kaia was at the counter, talking to some woman, when I walked in. I smiled when I noticed she was speaking sign language with the other woman. I couldn't tell who she was from the back of her head, but Kaia looked very happy, so I assumed everything was all right.

"Hi, Blair. Drea's in her office." She turned back to the woman and began talking again. I had no clue what she was saying, but I waved anyway.

"Thanks, Kaia."

I walked into her office and was confused when Cara was nowhere to be found. Maybe she was arriving late.

"Well, hello there, beautiful." Drea grinned from her desk and stood up when I walked in.

"Where's Cara? I thought she was supposed to be here, too."

"She was, but something came up and she had to cancel, so it's just the two of us, I'm afraid. Sorry to disappoint you."

I walked over to her, wrapping my arms around her neck. "So I have you all to myself? Whatever will we do to pass the time?"

"I can think of a few things, but they will have to wait until later. We have to get going." She smirked and kissed me, causing all thoughts to disappear.

When she broke the kiss, I whined in protest. "What do you mean? Where are we going?"

"You'll see. It's a surprise." She gave me one last kiss before heading for the door. As soon as I turned around, she smacked my ass and my core heated. Later couldn't come soon enough.

Ten minutes later, my eyes darted to Drea, and I furrowed my brows when she stopped the car in front of Bud and Bloom, a small flower shop.

"Why are we here?" I asked.

"I know you haven't been happy with my decisions for the previous signings, so I wanted to bring you along to pick out your own floral arrangements. We're going to Sugarleaf after this, too. I want you to be happy with this signing."

She smiled, caressing my thigh. I looked down at the contact and something in my chest warmed.

It was in that moment, whether it was the sheer thoughtfulness of the gesture, or the warm feeling spreading through me while she was touching me—whatever it was, it caused something to shift between us. I didn't know if she felt it, too, but the way she was looking at me only confirmed my notions. I was past heading into dangerous territory. I was already there.

"Oh, these are gorgeous!" When we walked into the flower shop, I stopped to smell a beautiful blue dahlia on the way to the counter. I had always thought they were gorgeous, like soft little puff balls. "And they smell amazing! We should definitely have a few of these." I turned to Drea with a grin. She smiled and nodded at the florist, who jotted something down on a notepad.

"Those are actually Fallon's favorite flowers. They have been for as long as I've known her."

"Really?" I asked. "We should buy some for her as a wedding present."

She brought me in for a sweet kiss and my legs could have turned into jelly at the warmth of her. "I think that's a wonderful idea."

"Which dahlias are her favorite?" I didn't know Fallon that well, and I wanted to make sure she loved them. If anyone asked if I had ulterior motives for buying her favorite flowers, like trying to win over her best friend, I would deny it.

"Well, she loves the pink, purple, and white ones, and she always has at least one black one when she buys them for herself," she said.

I was practically floating as we headed to the counter with our goodies.

Leaving the flower shop had me in a bright, cheery mood. Feeling the warm sun mixed with the cool fall breeze, while holding a gorgeous bouquet of flowers and walking with Drea to one of the best bakeries in the city, I was in blissful heaven.

The only thing that would have made the moment even more perfect would be to feel her hand in mine, but I knew we couldn't risk the chance of seeing Cara.

When we got to the bakery, the aroma of baked pastries and bread swarmed my nose and made my lips form into a smile. It smelled heavenly.

"Okay, what's our first choice?"

I placed my finger on my chin, contemplating this tough decision.

"Well, it goes without saying, cookies are a must. Chocolate chip, and maybe macadamia nut. Oh, and these red velvets look incredible!"

"Got it. What else? Do you want any bread? The banana bread looks amazing. Fallon would love you for that too, by the way." She winked.

I smirked with no ulterior motives in mind. "Banana bread it is, and maybe a few of those almond croissants. I think that should be good. We don't want too much."

We walked up to the counter and after Drea paid, I looked questioningly at the small box the woman had given her. "What did you get?"

She held the door open for me and stopped once we were outside of the bakery, handing me the box. "Red velvet cookies." She shrugged.

"You didn't have to do that, Drea."

She took my hand and forced the box into it. "You liked them, so yes I did. They're just cookies. It's not that big of a deal." She laughed.

I grinned, desperately wanting to wrap my arms around her and never let go. "Thank you. For everything today, seriously."

It was a big deal, at least to me. All I did was mention that they looked good, and she thought of me enough to get them for me. It had been a long time since someone had thought of me enough to do something like that.

"You're welcome. I think we had a successful day."

"I think so. I am very happy with how this day has turned out."

"So, while we are on the happy train, I was wondering how you feel about weddings?"

I paused, almost dropping my delicious-looking cookies. "Drea... I mean, I like you, sure, but... marriage? Isn't that a little—"

Her dying laughter cut off my ramblings. "Oh, for fuck's sake, love. I'm not proposing. I was trying to ask if you would go to Fallon and Mackenzie's wedding with me."

I picked up my heart from the floor and exhaled sharply. "Oh. Sure, that sounds fun, but ... won't Cara be there? It might look weird if we show up together."

She shook her head. "No, Cara will not be attending. Considering she technically dated both brides, that would be weird. And we don't have to make it a big thing." She paused for a moment before she added, "Unless you want to."

I frowned. "I don't know what you've told your friends about us, whatever we are, but I'm okay with going as just your friend or as your date."

"Date. I like the sound of that. I told them I was asking you as my friend. I didn't want anything getting back to Cara, but I like the idea of calling you my date." She nudged my side.

"Then it's a date." I grinned in return as we left the bakery.

Chapter Twenty-Four

DREA

> Mother Dearest: Our flight just landed, darling. Are you on your way?

I groaned and tried not to roll my eyes as I looked down at my phone. I'd told my mother a dozen times what time I'd be at the airport. My mother and my sisters just flew in from Portland, and I was literally getting out of my car to pick them up when she texted me.

> Me: I'm walking in from the car park as we speak.

> Mother Dearest: Okay, dear. See you soon!

I didn't bother with a reply. I told them I'd meet them at baggage claim to help with their luggage.

They were only staying for a few days, but I was anxious to see them. I loved my family and honestly had missed them, but they could also be a lot sometimes.

Between my mother complaining about my father and asking me a million questions about my love life, and my sisters gloating about their accomplishments, I always looked forward to racing them back to the airport by the end of their visit.

While my sisters and I all went to college, I majored in business. Not as prestigious as psychology or creative as art. But I knew I wanted to own my own business. I wanted to be my own boss.

Owning a bookstore definitely wasn't in my top list of career choices. I thought I wanted to work at some big corporate Fortune 500 company and go to fancy parties and catch red-eye flights to close business deals. But when I stumbled into the bookstore for sale and talked with the owner, I knew it was where I was meant to end up. It just had a little charm about it that I knew I needed in my life. I bought the bookstore right then and never looked back.

It took a lot of arguments and conversations with my parents, who seemed to think owning a small bookstore was beneath the Voss family name, but eventually they gave up, and I don't regret my decision for even a second, even if it did strain my relationship with my parents a little.

On my way to baggage claim, as I took in all the people walking to and from their gates holding hands or walking with their children, I couldn't help but think about Blair and wonder if we would ever take a trip together.

Would we be like the thousands of people who littered an airport every day, racing to check our bags and get through security? Would we grab a drink at the bar and share our thoughts on what we were looking forward to the most on our trip? I wondered where we would go. Would we go to Paris or Italy? Texas or Florida? Would we take a cruise to the Bahamas or Turks and Caicos? Would we sunbathe on the beaches of Hawaii and talk about the future? I smiled as my thoughts ran wild with all the possibilities.

The fact that I was thinking about any of this at all was enough to glue my feet to the floor of the SEA-Tac Airport. We weren't even dating, not officially, and I'd *never* had thoughts of taking a vacation with someone before, so why now? Why *her*?

What was it about Blair freaking Sterling that had me making imaginary plans for a future vacation? More importantly, why was it making me smile so brightly? The whole airport had to have thought I was very drunk with the way I was walking around the place, smiling to myself.

I tried to think of something else besides a future with Blair, because that was the last thing I needed to be thinking about, but for some reason, now that she was there, my brain wouldn't conjure up any thoughts besides those of her.

I laughed to myself when I remembered the look on Blair's face when she thought I was proposing. She looked so adorable and terrified. I should've been grateful for that kind of reaction. It wasn't like I wanted to get married or anything, but it almost had me wondering, if only for a second, if I—

"Drea!" The sound of my three sisters and their banshee screams shook me out of my thoughts of marriage and Blair.

I almost considered pretending I didn't know them. They were so loud that every single person in the building glanced their way.

A security guard ran over to see where the screams were coming from, and when he noticed my obnoxious sisters, he rolled his eyes and shook his head in disapproval.

"Ladies, there is no screaming allowed in this airport. If I have to come back here, you will be asked to leave and not come back!"

The color drained from my sisters' faces, and I had to stifle my laugh. "Apologies, Officer. My sisters are still learning their manners. We'll just be on our way, sir." I replied politely.

The officer grumbled and walked away, and embarrassment was written all over my face. *Someone please save me...*

"You lot aren't even in town for two minutes, and you're already giving me a migraine," I grumbled as I tried desperately to hide my smile. For as annoying as my sisters were, I had missed them. Seeing them get into trouble was also a delight.

They suffocated me in a group hug until my mother came up and joined in. "Look at all my babies together! Makes a mother so happy."

"Okay, okay, I can't breathe!" We all let go, and my mother immediately started checking me for injuries.

"Oh, honey, I've missed you! Are you eating enough? You look paper thin."

Rolling my eyes, I tried to contain my grin. "Yes, Mother, I'm eating plenty. Why don't we get your bags and head out, yeah? Are you guys hungry?"

After lugging everyone's bags in the car, because for some reason their arms were broken, I fell into the driver's seat and headed out of the airport.

We rode to the restaurant in a comfortable silence. My sisters were busy on their phones, and I kept glancing over at my mother in the passenger seat, where she was beaming at me.

"Yes, mother? Why are you looking at me like that?"

"I'm just happy to have all my girls together. It's been too long and we miss you, Drea." My mother's voice was quiet when she spoke.

I reached over and placed my hand on hers. "I've missed you, too, Mother."

"Where are we going, Dre? I'm starving." Eliza, the youngest, popped her head in between Mother and me.

I turned to look at her and elbowed her head to get her to scoot back. "We are going to lunch. Relax, runt."

My mother scowled at me and I grinned with a shrug. Sighing when she didn't find me hilarious, I added, "We are going to Social Kitchen. Is that okay?"

Eliza flicked my arm where Mother couldn't see, and I wanted to backhand the bitch. "Sounds perfect, Sister Dearest." When I scowled at her, she smirked and returned to her seat.

"Honey, are you sure you don't want us to stay in a hotel? I'm sure you and Skylar wouldn't want us imposing. Alone time is very important in a relationship, you know."

My eyes widened with surprise at the mention of Skylar. I had told my father about our breakup, but I never got around to telling my mother. It was easier to talk about things like that with him. He didn't care about personal details, so I never had to explain anything further.

I only told him things so he would know what's going on in my life, and I wouldn't have to worry about him bringing up something that I didn't want to talk about, because he didn't know about it. He was very cut and dry, and I admired that about him. My mother, on the other hand... very different.

"You aren't imposing, Mother. I want you there. I have plenty of space." I put on a genuine smile. Thankfully, we arrived at the restaurant before she could press the issue any further.

We settled into a table, and I desperately needed a drink, but that would have to wait until later.

"Vosses do not drink in public, dear. It is positively ghastly," my mother would say. I didn't think it was "ghastly" at all, but what did I know?

"What's new with you three? How's school going?"

"School is..." Eliza began.

"Ugh! We haven't seen each other in so long and you want to talk about school?" Poppy groaned, rudely interrupting Eliza. "Did I tell you about the red Mustang Dad bought for me? It was an early graduation present."

"No one wants to hear about your stupid car! Seriously! You brag about it to every person you meet!" Sophie interrupted. "I, for one, will be moving to Italy after graduation to pursue a career in art restoration. Did I tell you about the salary? I could never see myself working in something as ridiculous as psychology—"

"Well, at least I will actually help people, instead of fixing someone else's work!" Poppy said as she stuck out her tongue toward Sophie.

"Girls! Stop fighting. If you have nothing nice to say, don't say anything at all!" my mother intervened.

Eliza shyly spoke up. "As I was saying, school is going great. I am planning on going to Costa Rica after graduation to explore the effects of the environment on wildlife. I may even go to Antarctica to research the polar ice caps after."

"That all sounds amazing. I'm really proud of all of you." There, their one compliment for the year.

"What's new with you, Dre?" I could hear the sincerity in Eliza's tone, and I couldn't hide my smile. Even though the triplets were the same age, Eliza seemed to have a maturity about her that I got along with better than the others.

"Well, the bookstore is still doing well. I have an author coming in for a signing in a few months. It's been going pretty well, actually. Oh, and Fallon is getting married."

"Oh, isn't that nice, dear? Soon, both of your friends will be married ladies. I do hope you'll follow in their footsteps, hmm?"

Groaning, I took a long sip of my tea, choosing my words carefully. "The store keeps me rather busy at the moment, Mother."

When would she learn to stop meddling in my love life? She should've known by now that I didn't want to get married, not when I knew how it could break apart a family.

"Well, Skylar isn't going to wait around forever, darling. Speaking of, where is that lovely woman, tonight? Is she meeting us later?" My mother smiled sweetly while drinking her tea, and I tried not to choke on mine.

I sighed, taking a long drink, wishing the tea was from Long Island. "No, she will not be meeting us later. We are no longer together. She moved to New York." Four forks crashed to the table as my mother and three sisters stared at me.

"What?! When?" Poppy asked.

"Why? What did you do?!" Sophie so lovingly chastised. She was always the bitchier one of us.

I rolled my eyes. "I didn't do anything. We broke up two years ago. She got a promotion in New York, and I didn't go. End of story." That wasn't the end of the story apparently, as my mother spoke next.

"Two years?! Why didn't you tell us sooner? Didn't you love her? You were together for a long time. Why didn't you go with her? She was such a lovely girl. You could have made it work if you wanted to."

I groaned. I really didn't want to talk about it anymore. "I'm sorry, Mother. I've been busy with work, and it was complicated, okay? I cared for her, yes, but... I have a store to run, and I couldn't just drop everything and leave. She understood that. She's doing great and she met someone else."

My mother frowned like I'd told her Michael Kors went out of business. "Oh, Drea, I'm sorry. You'll find someone, too, don't worry. You have a lot to offer a woman."

Eliza snorted. "Like what, Mother?"

I scratched my nose with my middle finger at Eliza. "Eliza Jane, that's enough!" my mother scolded.

I laughed when she bowed her head sheepishly. *That's what you get, bitch!*

"I'm fine, really. I've moved on and I'm happy for her."

I realized my first mistake of the day when my mother's eyes shimmered with excitement. No, scratch that, mistake number two. My first mistake was picking them up from the airport in the first place.

"Oh, really? Do tell! Who is she? Where did you meet? How long have you been dating? When can we meet her? Is she coming to lunch?"

I groaned. "Please stop. I've moved on from our breakup, but I haven't physically moved on. Well, I mean—"

"Do not finish that sentence!" Sophie scrunched up her nose. "We know exactly how physical you can be. You forget we used to share a room with you."

I rolled my eyes. "You know what, I'm not talking about my sex life with you. Let's just finish our lunch, please."

"You're lying!" Sophie called out when she must've noticed my red cheeks and how I wouldn't look them in the eyes. "You've met someone, haven't you?"

Mistake number three...

"Drea Elise, are you lying to your mother?"

I laughed nervously, still not looking directly at her. "What? No. You know me."

"Then look me in the eyes, dear."

I hesitated before slowly looking at my mother, who raised a perfectly polished eyebrow, and I sighed. She could get me to confess to something I had only thought about doing. "Okay, fine. I may have met someone, but it's... complicated."

Complicated was the only word to describe my life these days. Between the issues at the bookstore, my relationship with my friends and how little I let them in, and now adding Blair to it all... It was enough to make my head spin. Life would have been so much easier if I wasn't so fucked up.

Sophie scowled at me. "Which is Drea's way of saying she's sleeping around with half of Seattle."

"Piss off, Soph!" I wanted to be anywhere else but at this table, having this conversation.

"Drea! Sophie, must you be so crass?"

Sophie put up her hands in surrender. "I'm not the one doing it, Mother. I was just saying."

"I know what you were saying. Drea, is this true? Are you sleeping around? You know I don't want to judge you, but—"

"No, I'm not sleeping around, okay? I..."

I hadn't slept with anyone else for months. Since I started sleeping with Blair, I hadn't even thought about anyone else. Why would I need to? Oh, shit... What was happening to me?

"Drea? What's going on?" my mother asked softly.

I think I'm falling in love and I'm scared!

Who was I kidding? I was so insanely in love with Blair it was sick. When I was with her, nothing else mattered, and when I wasn't with her, I wanted to give anything to be with her. Now I knew how Mackenzie felt. I would have to remember to apologize later for giving her shit for being wrapped around Fallon's finger.

I was kicking myself for agreeing to pick up my family from the airport, but I didn't really have a choice. That morning, I was trying to convince Blair to stay in bed all day, and even though she was screaming yes, I knew she wasn't talking about staying in bed.

"Fuck, baby. Yes!" she screamed as I sucked her clit into my mouth when she shattered underneath me.

"As much as I would love to do that all day, you already promised to go to the airport, and I really need to find a dress for the wedding."

I groaned, bringing myself back to the present. Besides my failed attempt to convince her, she had a point. Poppy had called and practically guilt tripped me into picking them up, so I was having an interrogating lunch while Blair was trying on dresses, probably looking sexy as fuck without me.

I sighed when I realized my mother had asked me a question. I was so caught up in my thoughts that I forgot to answer her, and they were all staring at me as if I had completely lost my mind, which in a way, I supposed I had.

"Talk to me, honey. What's going on?" There was no judgment in her tone.

"I have been kind of seeing someone. It's still new and very complicated. I don't know what we are, okay? So don't ask. We haven't really talked about it. I don't want to talk about it anymore. Can we please just move on?" I was desperate to talk about literally anything else.

"That sounds like a splendid idea, dear." My mother smiled. "But just know, I want you to be happy, however that looks for you. Just please make sure you are being safe."

"Okay, Mother! Jesus." I wanted to gag at the thought of my mother knowing anything about sex. I liked to think she'd had sex twice in her life, and the results were sitting at the same table, and she would never do it again.

Aside from the nauseating conversation about my sex life, I was happy to have this family time. It wasn't often that I got to talk to my mother or sisters, and it was nice. Except for Sophie—she could've stayed in Portland.

Chapter Twenty-Five

BLAIR

It took two hours and eight dresses to find the one I wanted for Fallon's wedding. It was powder blue and simple, but I absolutely loved it. I just hoped Drea would too.

I went into the dress shop with the intention of getting something I would love, not thinking of anyone else.

But as I started trying on dresses, I couldn't help but think of her. Would she like this one? How would it feel to have her take it off? Was this one easy to put on and slip off? Would she think I looked beautiful or would she tell me if she didn't?

After that, every dress I tried on, I asked myself if she would like it. The employee who was working was very helpful and asked me what I liked and didn't like about the dress. Eventually, I broke down and admitted that I was going with someone and I wanted her to like it too.

"Oh, sweetie, I wouldn't worry. You are gorgeous, and I'm sure she will like you in anything you pick. Choose something for you," she told me after the sixth dress I tried on.

I knew she was right, so I tried on a few more until I found the one I loved. I felt confident in it, so I knew it was the one.

After I left the store, I walked around the mall for a little while longer, stopping to grab a pretzel since I hadn't eaten all day.

As I was heading out toward my car, I noticed a store I would've normally walked by without another glance, but being with Drea, I'd been doing things I'd never even thought about doing before, so why not?

I walked into the lingerie store and smiled shyly at the cashier who greeted me. I told her I didn't need help, that I was just browsing, and I was thankful she didn't try to insist. Perhaps she noticed my red cheeks and shy demeanor and decided to leave me alone.

I had never worn anything like these before—lacy and barely there. But I was still thinking about Drea. I wanted to do something she wouldn't expect, and I wanted to get her reaction.

The thought of her getting so turned on just by how I looked, and fucking me senseless while wearing one of those, turned me on so much I had to clench my thighs together. I was definitely leaving this mall with two bags.

I walked around the store, taking in all the different options. The lace, the leather, the strings. It was all too much and I felt out of my element, but I had made it this far, so I was determined to at least circle the rest of the store.

I made it to the back of the store where they had things that were more up my alley. Lacey corsets and babydoll dresses. They had school-girl outfits and other kinds of costumes as well.

There were so many options that I didn't know what to go with. I knew I wanted something I could be confident in, but also something comfortable.

I started looking at the babydoll styles. They looked cute and very comfortable, and I could wear them without underwear, so that could work.

They had different colors, but I felt like a forest green would be the best. Partly because I loved the color, and partly because Drea's first compliment to me was when I was wearing a forest-green dress.

This babydoll dress was short, as I suspected it was supposed to be, and left the boobs exposed. I knew my boobs were her favorite part of me, seeing how she could never keep her hands or mouth off them anytime she was around them, so I knew this dress was the perfect choice.

I took it off the rack and headed for the counter to pay, when I stopped. A display right before the counter had a variety of toys and other pleasurable items. A hot-pink one caught my eye. I'd been wanting to try something like it for a while, but the idea of trying it with Drea sent a spark of pleasure through me.

I grabbed it a little too eagerly and made it to the counter. The cashier greeted me with a bright smile. "Hi, did you find everything you needed today?"

I tried to hide my blush. I wasn't used to buying anything from a sex store. "Um, yes, thank you."

She started scanning the items, and I couldn't help but fidget and look anywhere else. "Oh, this is a very good choice. My partner and I have used it on more than one occasion. You're really going to enjoy it."

I blushed at the thought of using it with Drea. I had an idea as to what we could do with it, and now I was even more excited, in more ways than one. "Oh. Thank you," I said nervously.

I was grateful she seemed to have picked up on my shy expression and didn't continue to try to have a conversation as she finished checking me out.

I left the mall in a good mood and desperate to try out my new purchases.

When I got home, I immediately headed for my room and started unpacking my bags from the mall. I hung the dress I was planning on wearing to Fallon's wedding in the closet and paused when I pulled out the lingerie I had purchased.

I stripped off my clothes and replaced them with the dress. When I looked in the mirror, it lit my whole body on fire. I looked good; more than that, I *felt* good. I felt sexy and could not wait to wear it for Drea. I just hoped she thought I looked as good as I did.

Thinking of wearing this for Drea, I could almost feel her fingers on my skin as she slowly slipped it off my shoulders, watching it fall to the floor. I closed my eyes and let my hands roam over my body, wishing they were her hands instead. I snaked them up my chest and to the back of my neck slowly, taking my time and exploring myself.

I had masturbated a handful of times since meeting Drea, but this somehow felt different. It felt tender and loving, like I was cherishing every moment.

After my hands found my breasts and I began to squeeze and tug them with more pressure the more turned on I got, I slowly trailed one hand down past my stomach and in between my legs.

I didn't want to use any toys this time. I wanted the feeling of skin on skin, even if it wasn't the skin of the person I craved more than anything.

After feeling my own wetness coating my fingers from just a few gentle strokes, I decided to make myself comfortable on the bed. I didn't lie down right away. Being at the mall and trying new things, I wanted to try a different position, so I put my forehead on my pillow and got on my hands and knees.

I'd never tried this position alone, but if I've learned anything from exploring my sex life with Drea, I really loved the filthy way I felt from getting fucked with anything from behind. Maybe that was just with her, but I was about to find out.

I put one hand above my head, gripping the pillow, and the other sliding down my neck and back to my breasts. I flicked and tugged on my nipple until a burst of pleasure shot straight to my core. I loved touching myself and feeling my reactions. I knew my body well, and I knew the right buttons to push, but I wasn't the only one.

From our very first time together, Drea seemed to know all the right things to get me to combust almost instantly. She knew the right things to say and the right outfits to wear. She knew how to hit the right spots with her tongue or fingers to have me whimpering and begging for more.

As I started to insert two fingers deep inside, I cried out from the sensation. I was so wet, and they went in with little to no friction. Thinking about Drea always got me so hot, but it also warmed something in my chest.

I wasn't just falling in love with her; I was already there. It was crazy to think about where we were in our lives just a few months ago. I hated her, God, did I hate her! Anytime Cara mentioned her name, I would tense up and force myself not to go on a rant on how much I truly despised that woman!

Seeing her at our first meeting after not seeing her for a long time triggered some of the old anger, but it also brought out some new feelings. On the outside, she didn't look any different, not really. But something about her energy drew me to her. It was like I was blinded by my anger for so long I didn't give myself a chance to really see her.

Something about her looked different. Maybe it was the way she looked at me, like it was the first time she truly saw me. Whatever was going on in our lives that caused us to see things differently I was beyond thankful for because it brought us to this point in our lives, together.

I moved my body up and down on my fingers as I thrusted harder and harder inside. "Fuck! Oh, yes!"

I was so close to coming I could feel it in my teeth. My muscles were tensing, and that familiar spark of pleasure was building in my lower stomach.

I slowly took my fingers out and coated my clit in my arousal. A few strokes had me screaming Drea's name and coming all over my sheets.

"Shit!" I breathed out as I collapsed on the bed with a smile on my face.

Chapter Twenty-Six

DREA

"Okay, what is going on?" Cara looked back and forth between me and Blair with a concerned expression on her face.

We were sitting at Brewed Awakening, having our weekly book signing meeting. Since it was getting closer, we met more often.

This morning, I'd left Blair's before Cara was supposed to pick her up, but not without a struggle. I was not ready to say goodbye, and I had to show her exactly what she was going to be missing.

"What are you talking about?" I asked Cara. We were trying not to give anything away, but I guess we weren't trying very hard, because she was looking back and forth between the two of us, trying desperately to pick up on something she shouldn't have been, and it was making me force myself not to fidget.

It was a struggle to sit there with Blair and not think about what we had been doing hours before this meeting with Cara. I wanted to slide my foot up and down her bare leg. I was starting to regret our decision not to sit next to each other, but there would've been no way I could've kept my hands to myself if she was centimeters away from me.

She gestured between the two of us. "I mean this. You two, right here. You're being nice to each other and no one is yelling. What is happening?"

I laughed. "You wanted us to be professional and get along, so that's what we're doing."

"Well, stop it. I don't like it. It's freaking me out."

Blair laughed, and my chest warmed at the sound. I would never tire of hearing any sound she made. "Relax, Cara. We're putting our personal differences aside to get this project done, just like you asked us to."

She looked skeptically between us before sighing in defeat. If she saw through our lie, she didn't show it. "I'm glad you two can finally get along. Honestly, I never thought it would happen. It's just weird. Anyway, I'd love to stay and chat but I have another client meeting to get to. I'll call you guys later?" She stood up and hugged us both good-bye. "Blair, do you need a ride home? It's on my way."

Blair snuck a quick glance at me, to which I smiled, and she shook her head. "No, babe, I'm good. I'll get a car."

"Nonsense. Since you guys are such good friends now, Drea, why don't you take her home?"

I snapped my head up. "What? Cara, I don't think that's a good idea. We aren't exactly friends." I looked at Blair, who gave me a look that told me I would pay for that comment later.

"Yeah. I'll get a car. It's not a big deal," Blair replied.

"Oh, come on, it'll be good for you two to spend more time together, and at least I'll know you made it home safely." Little did she know, it had been very good spending more time with Blair.

Blair sighed like it pained her to agree. "Fine, Drea can take me. Happy?"

"Not really, but I'll do it anyway," I replied sarcastically.

"Ahh, there's the two women I know and love. Okay, bye, ladies."

Blair turned to me and scowled when Cara was out of earshot. "Don't sound too heartbroken about taking me home. I can find another way, you know."

I stood up and walked around the table to where she sat. She followed me the whole way but looked straight ahead when I bent down and lowered my mouth to her ear and whispered, "Baby, I'm taking you home so I can slowly take that dress off and worship every part of your delicious body." She shivered when I nibbled her ear a little.

She cleared her throat and stood up. "Yes. Let's go... now."

. . .

Blair had barely closed the door to her house before I was on her, keeping to my word and taking her dress off one strap at a time. She moaned when I kissed her neck while my hands worked at her bra. Her tits were like magnets and my hands found them every time.

"God, you're so beautiful," I whispered as I kissed her against the door.

I groaned in protest when she broke the kiss. "As much as I am enjoying this," she said in short breaths, "I think maybe we should slow down, just a little, you know. I mean, we have the whole night ahead of us. Why don't we go for a swim, maybe cool down for a bit and talk?" She seemed to have lost her confidence and quietly added, "Unless this is just sex for you?"

I froze, one hand on her hip, one hand on her neck. I wasn't prepared for that conversation, especially right before I had other plans for my mouth.

I took a small step back. "Is that what you want? Just sex?" I asked. I didn't know what to say.

"That's never been my thing, but if that's what you want this to be, just sex, then we can talk about it. I just want to know what we're doing."

"I can tell you what we were about to do." I grinned, but she rolled her eyes.

"I'm serious. We need to be on the same page, or this can't happen anymore."

Damn she was good. She knew threatening to take sex away would sober me up.

I didn't like the serious turn the night had taken, but she was right, and I would be damned if this didn't happen anymore. "Okay, honesty time. I don't know what is happening between us. Clearly there is a physical connection here that I can't deny. We went from hating each other to this rather quickly, and it's all been a lot. Don't get me wrong, it's been good... so damn good, but it's also been a lot to process. I'm not good at putting a label on things and commitment and I are estranged acquaintances."

She looked as if I had just run over a dog, so I quickly added, "But I can't sit here and pretend I don't feel something strong for you, Blair. What that is, I don't know, but what I do know is I enjoy every second with you, no matter what we are doing. If you want this to be just sex, I'm okay with that. If you want to have sex and cuddle afterward, that's cool, too. I'll take any part of you that you're willing to give me. I can't promise any sort of commitment right now, but I can promise to be honest with you and to try."

She smiled and brought our bodies closer together. "That's all I ask, Drea. I'm not asking for a ring or for you to change your lifestyle for me. I just want to know if I matter in some way to you."

But I wanted to change. For her, I wanted to try, and the thought scared me more than I cared to admit. I felt so strongly for her, and it scared me how comfortable I was. If she didn't like something, I'd fix it. "Darling, you matter more to me than I can understand." I smiled and kissed her softly.

"So, how about that swim? I've got this bikini I've been dying to try out." She smirked.

"Or... I can finish undressing you, and we can forget the bathing suit altogether."

"Mmm, I think I like that idea even better."

Ten minutes later we were naked and making out in her pool. I should've won a damn medal for the patience I showed. Her naked body straddling my naked body while we were floating in the heated pool and I didn't fuck her? Damn heroine over here!

She groaned in protest when I broke the kiss. "Why did you stop? I was enjoying myself."

"I know, sweetheart. I can feel just how much you were enjoying it."

Eventually I gave in and started massaging her clit under the water. It wasn't enough pressure for her to have an orgasm or anything, just a little teasing. But I forced myself to stop for only a moment. "Because we need to talk about us."

"I thought we already did?" She tried to navigate my hand to its original spot, but I grabbed it and intertwined our fingers together, kissing each of her knuckles. I was obsessed with touching any part of her I could.

We had been making out in her pool for a good twenty minutes by that point and had only just come up for air. She was still straddling me, and I didn't know how much longer I was going to last out there, so I wanted to get this conversation over with while my mouth wasn't otherwise in use.

"We need to talk about Cara."

She frowned and got off me. "If you don't want to have sex, just say so, Drea."

I pulled her back to me and rolled my eyes, gripping her hips and sitting her on me once more. She wrapped her legs back around me and I was rewarded with a sweet wet kiss.

"First of all, I will never not want to have sex with you, Blair Sterling. But I'm serious, what are we going to tell her? That we're dating? That we are just sleeping together? That I take you from beh—"

She shut me up with a splash of water to my face. "Definitely not telling her that last part, thank you. I don't know how she's going to take it. We've been pretending for so long that we hate each other. I don't know how it'll go, going from one extreme to the next."

I shrugged. "I don't think we've been pretending to hate each other. We did hate each other at one point, but we haven't exactly been honest with her either. Mixing business with pleasure might cause some issues with her. As you know, her career is very important to her and she is very big on professionalism."

She snorted. "That's an understatement. And yes, I agree. So maybe we just don't tell her, at least until after the signing when we technically aren't working together anymore."

The idea of hiding her from anyone made me sick to my stomach, but she had a point. It would just make things messy if we said anything right now.

"You're right. So maybe it's best if we don't tell *anyone*? Mackenzie and Fallon are friendly with her. Kaia already knows from the last time you were in my office, but I will have another conversation with her to make it very clear it stays between us."

She started kissing me, and when her hand traveled down to my wet clit, my legs wanted to give out. "So, I'm like your dirty little secret? Kinky."

I laughed at her use of the word kinky and shamelessly pushed myself into her touch. "As long as you're mine, you can be whatever you want to be."

I carried her out of the pool and walked toward her house, closing the door behind us.

I didn't want the neighbors to see what I was going to do to her next.

Chapter Twenty-Seven

BLAIR

After our late-night swim, I hadn't seen Drea in a few days and I was having withdrawals, but not just from the sex.

It was weird to say, but I missed her. I missed her laugh, her witty personality, and the warmth of her touch, even as we sat on the couch watching trashy television shows.

I had been working on my new book a lot these past few days, and she had maid of honor duties to handle, but she was supposed to be coming over for dinner tonight, not that we would even make it to dinner. We rarely did. I didn't make anything for that exact reason. I planned to order something after we said hello.

When I heard a knock, I was too eager as I ran to open the door, dragging Drea inside. She wore a black crop top and I could see her nipples through the fabric. Her boobs were making my mouth water and her stomach was begging to be touched. She'd paired the top with a pair of gray sweatpants that looked so comfortable I wanted to slip inside them with her.

"You look so freaking sexy today." I groaned as I kissed her against the door. "Ahh!" I screamed. I felt something hard between us and it scared the shit out of me.

"I see you two have met." She smirked.

I went back to her and felt the outside of the spot that had hit me. "What?"

For a second I was confused until I felt around a little and instantly became drenched. I was so aroused I couldn't see straight. "Are you packing, Drea Voss?"

Her wink told me all I needed to know. I reached my hand down her pants to confirm she, in fact, was packing. A thick dildo was attached to a pair of boxer briefs. Holy shit, I was about to get wrecked.

I started kissing her as I slowly massaged the toy. I must have been doing something right, because she started to moan and I swore I could've fallen apart at the sound.

The sounds of her pleasure only fueled my desire, and I wrapped my hand around the cock and pumped it a few times, twisting and applying a little bit more pressure as my boldness grew.

"Baby," she panted, "if you keep doing that... I'm going to make a mess on your pretty hand. It's double-sided, and I can feel... every time you... shit, Blair."

"Then why don't you do something about it?"

I pulled my hand out, pulling the sweatpants down in the process. She stepped out of them, and I squealed when she picked me up, causing me to wrap my arms and legs around her, before she placed the cock inside of me, the sudden fullness causing me to gasp for air.

This wasn't the first time we'd used a strap, but having her inside me while the other end was inside her was on a whole other planet of pleasure. It fused us together and somehow made us connect even more.

A piece of her had permanently tattooed itself on my soul in that moment. Our moans echoed against the walls as she walked us to my bedroom, the movements causing the sweetest kind of friction.

We barely made it a step into the room before my back was against the wall and she was kissing me harder than she had ever kissed me before.

This wasn't just rough sex. It was intense and passionate, like we wanted to drill into each other until we were cemented to one another with no way of getting undone.

The harder she thrusted into me, the harder I fell for her. All hope was lost in that moment, and nothing else existed in the universe.

Jesus, I sounded pathetic! I *was* pathetic, but I was being filled and fucked so good I didn't have room to care.

"You... are so... fucking... perfect." The words came out one thrust at a time as she slowed her pace.

I was so close, but she stopped and walked us over to the bed, laying me down slowly before pulling out.

I shivered at the loss of contact. "What are you doing?" I breathed out.

She smiled. "Don't worry, sweetheart. I'm not done with you yet."

And she wasn't. Seconds later, a buzzing noise filled the room, and my whole body heated. *Of course it vibrates, as if I wasn't already on the brink of death!*

"Tell me if it's too much, and I'll stop—"

I silenced her with a kiss and whispered, "Don't you dare fucking stop."

I felt a pang in my chest at her reassuring words. Even before she was about to ruin me, she always made sure I was comfortable and felt safe.

She grinned and was back inside me shortly after. "Oh, fuck!" I screamed so loud I knew the neighbors heard me.

I wanted to pass out from the sheer pleasure. Not only from watching her fuck me, but using a double-sided vibrating dildo? I had to have been dreaming. There was no way this was really happening to me.

My orgasm was getting closer and closer with each thrust, and I knew she was following right behind me. Her movements became erratic, her eyes were closed, and her head was tilted back. I caught a glimpse, and that was all it took for me to come crashing down.

The messes we'd made in the past didn't hold a candle to the one we made now. Both of our orgasms hit at the same time and a mixture of my pleasure and hers coated the dildo and dripped onto the bed. In that moment, I couldn't have cared any less. She was the only thing I cared about.

Once we both came down and were spent, she slowly pulled out of me and turned off the vibrating purple-colored toy. She collapsed on the bed next to me, and I snuggled up to her, caressing her chest while she played with my hair.

"Holy shit, that was incredible," I whispered, smiling at her.

She leaned down and kissed my forehead sweetly. "Yes you are."

I rolled my eyes and lay down on her chest again, making sure to hide my blush. She never seemed to run out of ways to make my heart swell. Just a smile from her and I would collapse at her feet if she asked me to. There were very few things I wouldn't do for her.

She lay there stroking my hair as I just listened to the soothing sounds of her breathing. I drew circles on her chest, wishing we could have stayed like that forever.

Of course, the sex was phenomenal, but nothing was better than snuggling up with her, our naked bodies connecting intimately, and just being in the moment together.

"I can't believe you're going to be gone for the whole weekend. You better leave that thing so I can get through it."

She lightly tugged on my hair, a pleasurable pain, and I looked at her grinning. "You are not using that without me! You'll just have to manage. If I can do it, so can you. I did go months without sex, you know."

"Yeah, but have you ever had sex with you? It's pretty spectacular. I'm not sure I can hold out."

She laughed. "Yes, I have, and I agree, but it's only for two days, darling. I think you can manage."

I sighed as I relented, like I had a say at all in the first place. "Fine, but you better not fuck anyone else when you're there! I'm the only one you can defile, got that?" I tried to come across very intimidating, but I wasn't sure I succeeded.

We hadn't talked about not sleeping with other people, so I was worried how she would respond. I knew casual was more her thing, but I just couldn't stand the thought of anyone else getting to share these special moments with her. I also hated the idea of anyone looking at her naked body. It was all mine. Or at least, I wanted it to be all mine.

If it bothered her, she didn't show it. She only furrowed her brows in a mock serious expression. "Yes, ma'am. Only you can take my dick."

Her words had me ready for round two. "Well, if I have to wait a whole week for it again, we better make it count. You need to make sure you fill every hole by the time you leave here."

I laughed when she sat up and ripped the covers off the bed, but my laugh fell away at her next words. "Turn around and get on your hands and knees."

My blood boiled at her filthy words, and without hesitation, I obeyed.

Chapter Twenty-Eight

BLAIR

Other than a text this morning saying they made it to the hotel, I hadn't talked to Drea all day, and I missed her. We had been dating for only a few months, if that was even what we were doing, but I did. I missed her and I felt pathetic.

I had no idea what I was to her, and I was afraid to ask. I wanted to stay in my blissful bubble for as long as possible, and I hoped we were on the same page. What page that was, I had no clue, but what I did know was that whatever we had, I was getting used to it and I wasn't ready for it to go away.

It was a little after ten at night, and I finally couldn't take it anymore, so I texted her, telling myself I just wanted to check in:

> Me: How's it going? Has anyone gotten arrested? Are you missing me yet? ☺

As soon as I saw the "sent" label under my message, I wanted to throw my phone into a river. Why would I ask that? Of course she doesn't miss me. *Stupid, Blair!*

. . .

Drea: It's going! No one got arrested, yet. And of course I miss you! Since the second I left. We are all pretty toasted right now, and Mackenzie just brought out more wine! 😊 🍷

I laughed and rolled my eyes. It was just the sex she missed, but something inside of me still smiled. At least there was something about me she liked, even if it was just the physical aspects.

It must have been that little ego boost, along with the fact that she wasn't with me in person, that caused me to be a little brave.

Me: What would you do if you were here right now?

I anxiously waited for a response. A few minutes later, one came through:

Drea: Anything you would let me do... 🍆

I gulped, the images of the night she had me against the door flooding my thoughts. It still blew my mind that I could need her as badly as I did, and it wasn't even just the sex. I needed her voice, her laugh, her encouraging words, I needed all of her.

> Me: Such a shame you aren't here then. The ideas I just came up with would have you begging to fuck me again.

Where did my cockiness come from? You would've thought I was the one getting drunk and not Drea.

> Drea: It doesn't take much for me to want to fuck you, Blair. Surely you've gathered that information by now. I can't seem to stay away from you.

I didn't want to seem like I was solely dependent on her, but I wanted to agree. I just couldn't bring myself to stay away, not that I had tried very hard.

Every internal alarm was going off on why we were such a bad idea, and yet... she always found a way to silence them.

Whether it was feeling her body close to mine or during the little moments when she would text me just to share a funny meme she found or tell me to have a good day, I craved every aspect of her.

> Me: Do you wish you could right now?

> Drea: Yes, I really do. I want to bury my face in your pussy until you beg me to stop.

Holy shit! This was turning me on. The images my brain was coming up with were enough to ruin me. I probably could have come just from hearing her voice tell me everything she wanted to do to me.

> **Me:** God, I'm getting so turned on, Drea.

> **Drea:** Fuck! I wish I were there to take care of you.

> **Drea:** Call me in five minutes? I'm going to sneak away.

I grinned and waited. When the five minutes passed, she answered on the first ring.

"Blair, fuck, I need you."

I laughed. "Well, hello to you, too. What did you tell your friends?"

"I told them I had to go have phone sex and I'd be right back."

I gasped. "Drea! No you didn't!" I sighed in relief when I heard a sexy chuckle on the other end.

"Of course not, love. I told them I had to call my father."

I smiled. "You're not funny!"

"I thought I was rather funny. Are you actually wet, or was that just to get me turned on?"

I hummed. "Did it work?"

"Yes, Blair, I'm so fucking turned on! Just thinking of you over there, touching yourself, I could come."

I laughed. "Well, I wasn't lying, Drea. I'm so wet." My voice sounded sultry, and I had never heard it before. This wasn't something I did. I didn't talk dirty on the phone, and rarely did I do it during sex.

Drea was opening up a different side of me. She was making me more confident in myself, and it made me want to try new things. I found out early on there were things I *really* liked during sex, or at least with Drea.

"Jesus Christ! Are you touching yourself right now?"

My breathing became heavy at her voice uttering those words, and I had no choice but to slip my hand between my legs. "Yes," I breathed out. "What would you do to me if you were here?"

I heard an unzipping, and my clit pulsed at the thought of her touching herself.

"First, I would slowly pull down your underwear, kissing my way down softly as they rested at your feet."

I moaned as I slowly started circling my clit.

"Then I would lay you down and start kissing your neck as my fingers found themselves around your swollen clit."

"Fuck!" I breathed out. "Are you touching yourself?"

"Listening to you fuck yourself on the phone, how could I not? I'm so fucking wet, Blair."

I hummed my appreciation. "What else would you do?"

"Before you were about to come, I would stop circling your clit and replace my fingers with my mouth, licking slowly while inserting two fingers inside of you, feeling that perfect pussy clench around them."

Holy shit. The images she was painting were driving me wild. I was so tempted to beg her to take the next flight back here, but there was no way I could stop now.

"Drea, I'm so close," I moaned.

"Fuck, I want to taste you when you come."

"Wait!" I stopped my movements and sat up, thinking of something to make this moment even better. "There's a toy I want to use."

"Blair!" she whined, and I let out a little moan at hearing it.

I rolled over and reached into my drawer for my favorite toy. When I came back, I saw that I had a facetime call. "Drea?" I asked.

"I want to see you come, baby. Please," she begged.

"Since you asked so nicely," I teased, and answered the call.

"Hi." She looked like she was in a hotel room, and she was sitting in a chair in only her bra and underwear. The sight alone almost made me want to forget the toy altogether.

"Goddamn you are amazing. Hi, sweetheart," she muttered, staring at my bare chest. I was completely naked and lying in bed.

"You flatter me. Are you still touching yourself?" I asked. She nodded and lowered her phone to show her hand inside her underwear. *God!*

"I bet you're so wet right now. I want to taste you!" I whined.

I angled the phone so she could see all of me and tried to hide my blush when I heard a pained, "Fuck!"

I circled my clit a few times before turning on the toy. It was a vibrating clit sucker that cost almost a hundred dollars, but it had more than paid for itself over the years.

I turned it on my favorite setting and positioned it on my already pulsating clit. The setting had made me squirt within thirty seconds more times than I could count. It gave a few pulses that were fast and intense, then a few that were a little gentler.

Seeing as how I was already wet from touching myself and seeing Drea, I was about to hit a personal best with that thing.

"Oh fuck!" I screamed so loud I hoped no one could hear me.

"Blair, you are so fucking sexy!" she moaned as she inserted a vibrator into herself.

Yeah... I wasn't lasting thirty seconds.

"Drea, I need you," I panted. My pulse was erratic and I could feel my orgasm coming. My moans became more frequent as I watched Drea fuck herself.

"I bet that vibrator feels so good sucking on your clit. I know you're seconds away from coming all over it, aren't you, baby?"

I nodded, mouth parted as I was reaching my peak. "Yes, it feels so good. It's going to keep going until I squirt."

"Mmm, I want to see you squirt so badly. Can you do that for me? Can I see you?"

"Yes, baby." I moaned. "I want to squirt for you. I'm almost—"

I lowered the phone as my orgasm came rushing out with so much force. I had never come that hard in my life, and it wasn't over. I didn't stop even as I heard Drea's own orgasm shortly after mine, and I came again at the sound.

I fell onto the bed, spent and almost deeply satisfied.

"I miss you," I said softly, in a moment of vulnerability. "If it's too soon to say that, I get it. Or if we don't have that kind of relationship, I—"

"Blair? I miss you too... a lot, actually." I looked at my phone and grinned.

"You better get back to your friends, I don't want to be the reason you miss out on Fallon's bachelorette party," I added quietly, feeling guilty.

"They are hammered. They won't miss me too much. Besides, I'm happy right where I am." She smiled.

"Me too. But seriously, you better go. It's getting late, anyway. I'll see you when you get back."

She sighed in defeat. "Yeah, you're probably right. Fallon may seem like an angel, but if she's pissed off enough, you're going to know about it." She chuckled. "I'll call you tomorrow, okay? Sweet dreams, darling."

I blushed at her sweet tone. "Goodnight, Drea."

I hung up the phone and fell asleep with a warmth filling my chest.

Chapter Twenty-Nine

DREA

"Oh my God! I'm never drinking that much again!" I whined to Kaia as we were closing up the store. I had been repeating the same sentence all day, and I was sure she was getting sick of hearing it.

"I know. I don't think I've ever drunk that much in my life, nor will I plan to in the future. I think I can still smell wine in my hair." She winced.

The store had been pretty consistent for most of the day, which I was not happy about. I was still massively hungover, and I wanted to sit in a dark room all day instead of pretending I hadn't been obliterated this past weekend.

It was safe to say it had been a very successful trip. We were a walking Katy Perry song, literally driving to California and getting drunk on the beach. It was good spending some quality time with Fallon and Penelope.

Mackenzie and her bridal party went, too, but they separated after a few hours to do their own thing.

As much as I loved my best friends, the highlight of my weekend was video calling with Blair. That was by far the best solo orgasm I'd ever experienced, and if I wasn't hooked on her before, I definitely was now. It wasn't even just about the sex. I wouldn't care if it never happened again. She was just spectacular in every way, and I was literally and mentally fucked.

"Are you good to close up, Dre? I have plans with a friend." Kaia's words shook me from my euphoric thoughts about Blair. She blushed, and I knew which friend she was going to see.

I chuckled, putting a hand on her arm. "Of course, Kai. Go, have fun, and tell Daisy I said hello."

She grabbed her bag, pushing a stray hair behind her ear and looking down as she walked past me and headed out of the store with the pinkest blush and the biggest smile on her face.

I had just locked the door when my phone buzzed in my pocket:

> Blair: Where are you?

> Me: At the store, just closed. I still have a few things to finish up before I leave. Why?

> Blair: Don't leave... I want to see you.

I sent a smiley face emoji, one that matched the one on my stupidly giddy face, and put my phone away.

I was just finishing up at the counter when a knock caused me to jump. I opened the door and smiled at an adorable Blair. "Hello, welcome to Open Book. Please, come in." I grinned and kissed her before turning to lock the door.

"Hi." She greeted me with a playful smile.

"I'm almost done, and then we can go," I said as I headed to the counter. "I just need to file these receipts away and finish up a few things."

She didn't speak until we were in my office. "That sounds good, but..." I turned around, and she had already taken off her coat. I swallowed.

She was wearing a bright smile and the thinnest green babydoll dress I had ever seen. It left her tits out perfectly for my perusal, and I groaned when my gaze traveled down and I could see she wasn't wearing any underwear.

"I had another idea," she teased and I dropped the papers on the floor. This was going to be the perfect ending for my day, but the thought of her outside this room dressed like that had me feeling a possessiveness over her I didn't have a right to feel. I wanted to be the only one who could see her in, and out, of an outfit like that.

"I..." I was speechless. I was convinced if this was how she would've shown up to our first meeting, our rivalry would've never started.

She smirked. "If you're busy, I can go—"

I cut the distance between us in two long strides and grabbed her by the waist. Tilting her chin up, I kissed her before I whispered, "You're not going anywhere."

I was starving for her. After we'd been apart for so long, my need for her had only grown. I needed to feel her skin on mine. I needed to hear her voice, her laugh, in my ears. I needed to see her, all of her. I just needed to be in her orbit... always.

The kiss sent shivers down my whole body, and I tangled my hands in her hair, slightly pulling back to gain access to her neck. She moaned when I licked and started sucking her collarbone.

I didn't protest when she lifted my shirt, and she gaped at me when she saw I wasn't wearing a bra.

"God, you're perfect." She groaned.

I hissed when she took an already hard nipple into her mouth. "Fuck, your tongue is incredible."

She brought her mouth back to meet mine, and I gently caressed the side of her face, making the moment more intimate.

Anytime we were together, whether it was rough and fast or gentle and slow, I always wanted her to feel safe and cared for. It wasn't just about sex for me, and I wanted her to know that, even if I couldn't find the words to express it.

She moaned when I felt her reaction to me, rubbing her clit in between my fingers.

"Oh, wow, baby, you're so wet."

Her moans became more frequent as she got closer to release, but I wasn't relenting. I wouldn't stop until she had my hand drenched from her pleasure.

She stopped my hand and panted, "Drea, I need you inside me, please."

I groaned at her words. Licking my fingers, she stopped me before I could enter her.

"No," she breathed. "Not your fingers. I need... fuck! Drea, please."

"Damn, you're needy tonight. Well, lucky for you, I'm always prepared."

I walked around my desk and unlocked the drawer where I kept my spare straps and other essentials. Hey, you never knew when the mood would strike you.

Lowering my underwear, I put on the strap, and Blair didn't take her heated eyes off me the entire time. This one wasn't double-sided, but it still did the job.

I applied the lube, and her eyes shot to the movement, her lips parting. Knowing it turned her on, I continued my motions a little slower.

I walked back over to her and kissed her, the cock creating more distance between us.

I broke the kiss and whispered in her ear, my voice growing feral. "Turn around, Blair. I want you bent over my desk, that perfect ass bared to me while I fuck you." I rubbed her clit a few more times, feeling her reaction to my words before she kissed me again and spun around.

The sight of her from behind was something ungodly. Her ass inches away from me while she was bent over the desk, legs spread, waiting for me, was one I never wanted to forget.

I lowered myself behind her, spreading her legs a little more so I could stroke her pussy with my tongue, just once.

She shuddered, and my clit instantly pulsed. "Drea..." she moaned.

In that moment, I was thankful Kaia had gone home early. I hadn't expected the night to take this kind of turn, but there was no way I could've stopped now.

I stood up and positioned the cock behind her. "Are you ready for it?" I asked. This wasn't our first time, but I still wanted to make sure she was ready. Lord knew I was...

"Yes. Please!" she begged.

God, hearing her moans was my own personal aphrodisiac. "Spread your legs, sweetheart," I commanded.

She did as I asked, and I couldn't help but reach out and touch her. "Good girl." I caressed her ass before I gave it a decently hard smack. She moved forward slightly and gasped, causing me to release a moan.

After a few more caresses and squeezes, I finally fisted the cock and moved it to her entrance before very slowly inserting it.

"Is this okay?" I asked. Before I fucked her senseless, I wanted to make sure she was comfortable. I was a lady after all.

"Oh my God. Yes," she breathed.

I grabbed her hips before starting my movements, pumping in and out of her a little faster.

I couldn't begin to describe how it felt as Blair's perfect ass made contact with my center as she took the cock deeper. I wanted to taste her when she came, but I couldn't leave this position. It was too perfect. *She* was too perfect.

"Faster... fuck."

I grinned and did as I was told, holding on to her hips tighter as I pounded into her. I wanted to come just at the sounds of our bodies slamming together. It was so filthy, yet it felt so right.

"Blair... fuck, you feel incredible," I groaned.

I wanted to keep fucking her until the end of time. I only wished I had my double-sided dildo to make this all the more intimate.

"Baby, I'm so close. I need to come... please," she begged.

Dear God! This scene, with her words, I was so close, too.

I quickened my thrusts as both of our orgasms hit at the same time. "Shit! Come all over my cock, sweetheart."

After we came back down to earth, I slowly pulled out of her and she turned around, pulling me in for a sweet kiss. I didn't bother getting dressed as I walked her over to the couch, dropped the strap to the floor, and covered us with a blanket as she laid her head on my chest.

"That was... wow," she breathed out.

She wasn't the only one out of breath, as my reply came out the same way. "Yeah, it really was."

"You are really good with that thing, you know that?"

I laughed. "What can I say, I've had a lot of practice... That's not what I meant. I mean—"

"Drea, relax. I'm not an idiot. I know I'm not your first, and I probably won't be your last." She smiled, but it didn't look like the genuine one I had become addicted to.

I didn't dignify that with a response, so I kissed her softly instead.

She laid her head back on my chest, drawing idle circles. I was so content at that moment, but I couldn't get her words out of my head. *I know I'm not your first, and I probably won't be your last.*

She wasn't the first, but I thought maybe I could've wanted her to be the last, and that scared me. I was afraid to admit it to myself, and I didn't know how to make the words come out.

The what-if's played in the back of my head on a loop. What if she didn't feel the same way? What if she *did*? What if we fell in love for a few years, but it ended badly? What if we got married and started a family, but resented each other and were stuck together because of the kids?

Blair was worth more than those thoughts. She deserved more than me. Someone who wasn't broken. Someone who could give her what she wanted.

But as we lay there together, I realized I wanted to be that person for her. I wanted to be good enough for her. I wanted to be someone she could be proud to be with. I wanted to be the person she loved.

She looked so beautiful and peaceful lying on me. Like she was at home in my arms, and I didn't dare think to move us as her breathing evened out and I noticed that she had fallen asleep. She felt like home.

Chapter Thirty

BLAIR

I woke up in an unfamiliar room, a warm body beside me. I snuggled into the warmth, remembering who I was with. She must've carried me all the way to the back room in the middle of the night.

I felt tender arms wrap around me, and I melted into the embrace. I wanted to continue waking up in Drea's arms. She made me feel safe and secure. She made me feel like she would always be there to protect me from anything.

"Mmm, good morning, beautiful." A sleepy Drea smiled at me and kissed my forehead softly.

"Good morning, sleepy head. Did you carry me back here last night?"

She shrugged. "You fell asleep on the couch, and I didn't want to wake you to take you home, but I also didn't want you sleeping on that hard couch. So I brought you back here to the bed. I'm sorry. I should have slept in my office."

I frowned. "What? Are you crazy? No, this was—" My phone interrupted me, and I cursed when I saw it was Cara calling.

"Shit, I better take this. I'm sorry."

She kissed me gently. "Don't be sorry, love. I'll be right here when you get back."

I groaned, not wanting to get out of our warm bubble.

"Hey, Cara." I cleared my throat, trying not to sound guilty of anything. "What's up?"

"Hey, doll. What are you doing? You sound like you just woke up or had sex."

I let out an embarrassing sound somewhere between a choked laugh and a squeal. "Sex?! What? No, don't be ridiculous. I wasn't having sex... I just woke up." It wasn't a lie, so why did I have to make it sound like one? *Play it cool, B!*

"Are you okay? You sound off? I just wanted to see if you were free next weekend for lunch. I know Drea has a wedding to go to, so I thought we could have a meeting to finalize a few things for the book signing and talk about your next book. I also want to catch up with my best friend. I feel like it's been forever, and I miss you."

I looked over at Drea, who was looking so peaceful as she snuggled in the bed. "I miss you, too, Cara. Next weekend?" Drea looked up at me and tilted her head. "I can't, I'm sorry. I'm going out of town... family thing. How about the following week?"

"Sure, that sounds good. I'll call you with the details later. Get some more rest. You sound tired. Love you, doll."

I smiled nervously. "Love you, too."

I sat down on the bed and groaned, covering my face. The bed shifted, and I felt a soothing hand drawing sweet circles on my back. "What's wrong, darling?"

I turned to her. "I hate this, Drea. I hate lying to her. She's my best friend, and I'm hiding one of the most..."

I hesitated for a second. I almost admitted to Drea that she was the most important thing in my life. Last night, I'd told her I knew I wouldn't be the last woman she had in her bed. It broke my heart in half, and part of me wanted her to disagree, but it was silly to expect her to.

Drea was not someone to be tied down to one person. I tried very hard not to think about what would happen when she left. Who her lips had been on. Who had been touching her or getting sweet moments like these. It wasn't any of my business, and I shouldn't be caring about those things.

"I mean... hiding the most fun I have had in a very long time. I can't wait to be done with the signing."

She wrapped me in a tight hug, and all my worries drifted away and were replaced with the feeling of being with her. "I know, I can't wait either. It hasn't been easy hiding you from her or my friends."

I forced myself to get up and gather my things. I couldn't stay in this moment forever, no matter how much I wanted to.

"I better go before Kaia gets here. Call you later?"

She kissed me so softly. I wanted to forget everything and fall back into bed with her. "You better."

As I left the bookstore, I realized something that caused me to stop in the middle of the sidewalk. I was falling for Drea Voss, and I was falling hard...

~

"Come on, brain!"

When I got home, I locked myself in my office and started writing. Well, I *tried* to start writing, but nothing came out. For three hours, I sat at my desk and... nothing.

I was ready to pull my hair out. I texted Drea to vent about my writer's block, but her only suggestion was to offer a way to... massage the block out of my hand. Which in turn made me lose even more focus because I started thinking about what that would look like... and I almost said yes.

Writer's block was a normal part of writing, and I knew that. I had been struggling for years, but I thought it would get better. The more I wrote, I thought the less it would happen, but boy was I wrong. It made imposter syndrome a bitch to deal with, and being on the best-seller list hadn't made it any easier. If anything, there was even more pressure to produce amazing quality books.

After another forty-five minutes of just staring at my computer screen, willing the words to appear, I finally shut it down and walked away. I needed a break. I needed something else to occupy the space in my brain, and hopefully in the process, make space for new ideas to form.

Sighing in defeat, I turned off my office light and left the room. I knew the perfect thing that would put me in a better mood.

The first time I showed Drea my... rather unconventional hobby, I expected her to laugh at me as Cara had. Instead, she simply kissed my temple and smiled brightly. "The most old lady hobby to exist, but still very you."

I headed out to the backyard, where I had a gnome garden set up. My grandmother used to be obsessed with gnomes, and the hobby kind of stuck with me.

A Japanese maple tree guarded the garden. I had carefully pruned it so the canopy fanned out to create a shaded area. The leaves constantly changed colors throughout the seasons, beginning with a deep purple color, then green at the height of summer, and bright orange and yellow in the fall before being bare in the long winter.

Looking closer at the ground, I could see small stone paths, about two inches wide, carefully laid out, leading in several directions. Following the path to the right, I noticed the small mushroom-shaped house surrounded by a white picket fence. Moss and dark beach pebbles surrounded the tiny house.

On the miniature garden bench sat a gnome and a honeybee, each holding teacups. Looking left, I noticed two more gnomes that needed to be moved further out from the bleeding hearts so they could survey their little world. I carefully moved the two girl gnomes underneath the little white gazebo that had once been a small birdcage.

One of the gnomes was particularly special to me. She had a light-pink hat with white hearts all around, and her dress was the same shade of pink with white frills at the bottom. I had inherited her from my grandmother and rightfully named her Mellie. She was her favorite, and growing up, I saw her take extra special care of her. I never learned why she was so special to her, but it didn't matter anymore. She was now my favorite. Whenever I needed to talk to someone, I'd pick up Mellie and go sit somewhere and talk.

I settled down with Mellie under the maple tree like I had countless times over the years. "Hey, Gran. I know, it's been a while. I'm sorry about that. Work has been hectic, but that's no excuse." I could already feel the tears coming, but I pushed them back.

I always got like this whenever I talked to my grandmother. She had been such an important part of my life, and I would come out here to talk to her about anything and everything. Whenever something was going on in my life, Gran was the first person to know about it.

I settled further against the tree and took a deep breath. "Things are going pretty great right now. I've been writing almost nonstop and spending a lot of time getting ready for this book signing. Cara is still amazing, and..." I trailed off, my thoughts instantly going to Drea.

My grandmother was *very* familiar with Drea and our history. I had come out to this tree to complain about her so many times, but afterward, I always felt better. It was as if the shade of the tree was her way of comforting me from beyond. Like the shadows were her hands caressing my shoulders, letting me know it would all be okay. I knew it sounded silly, but it calmed me to think about it.

"There's a new development in my life, Gran. You won't believe it. You remember Drea, the bookstore owner? So, our... rivalry, I guess you could call it, it's kind of over. We've been..." What should I even say? We'd been dating? I definitely wouldn't be using the words *fucking* or *having sex.*

"I think I'm falling in love with her, Gran. I know, it sounds... crazy. Believe me, I feel crazy just thinking about it. It hasn't even been that long. I don't know how it happened, to be honest. We had a horrible first meeting, as always, but after that? I started to see beneath her icy layers, and eventually, I wanted to see more. I won't give you all the glorious details, but I'm happy. For the first time since... they died, I'm truly happy."

At that point, the tears found their way out, and I just let them fall. It had been so long since I lost both my parents and my grandmother, but the wound was still fresh. I knew I had my brother, but he wasn't as close as I would've liked him to be, and I still felt alone. Except when I was with Drea. With Drea, I felt safe, secure, seen.

"You would like her. She's quite the looker, as you'd say, and she has the biggest heart. The way she took care of me when we had a bad storm would've made you happy. And did I mention she's British? You know that's my weakness. Oh, and I'll be flying out to see Chris and the twins soon. It'll be their birthday. Ten years old, can you believe it? I can't either." I laughed. "I wish you could be here to see them grow up. I love you, Gran, and I miss you like crazy. I wish you were here with me." I kissed Mellie and placed her back safely, wiping the tears from my face. I went back inside, feeling a little sad but a little more motivated to write.

Chapter Thirty-One

DREA

"So, let me get this straight. You want me to go out for a movie night. To the same place Skylar and I broke up three years ago? Not only that, you want me to sit through an entire movie with Cara *and* Blair?"

I could hear Fallon's eyes rolling from the other end of my phone. Surely I'd heard her wrong. Of course I had no issues with spending the night with Blair, although it would be torture not to touch her. I would make up for it once we got home. But I had no interest in going back to Pinstripes. Not after the last time I was there.

"First of all, that was a long time ago. You need to get over her—"

"I *am* over her, Fallon. I just don't understand why you want to go out with both of them."

"Kenzie and I thought it would be good for all of us to get together, and it's where we reconnected. It has sentimental value, and we want you guys to be there. It's only for a few hours. Surely you can manage. Cara already agreed. She said she would talk to Blair, and Kaia even said she would go. Roxxy has to work, Greyson is sick, and so is Pen. Dre, you're being so difficult right now. It's just a movie. Come on, babe, don't make me pull the maid of honor card."

I rolled my eyes and let out a sigh, knowing I would cave. "You can really be a pain in my ass, you know that?"

"You know you love me, and you'll have a good time. You and Blair are friends now, right? Since you're bringing her to the wedding, this should be a piece of cake."

I groaned. "Yeah, I guess so."

"I still don't understand why you're bringing her as your date. Is there something going on I should know about?"

Yes... no... I don't know!

"I already told you I don't want to go alone, and Kaia is an employee. Yes, she is also my friend, but it would be weird. Blair and I... tolerate each other and she likes you. Nothing is going on."

"Okay, babe. I don't understand, but I believe you. You know you can talk to me, right? I'm always here."

Of course I knew, and that made this situation even harder. I wanted nothing more than to sit with my best friend and share all the details about what had been going on in my life and how happy I was with Blair. But I couldn't, and I could feel the guilt slowly starting to eat away at me.

"I know, love. I appreciate you. If there is something to talk about, you'll be the first person I call. Listen, I gotta go, okay?"

She sighed in defeat, and I wanted to spill everything. "Okay, Dre. Don't forget tomorrow night. Bye."

I hung up the phone with a loud sigh and lay back down on the bed. I guess I was spending a night with all my friends who were oblivious to what was going on in my love life.

"Is everything all right?" Blair had just gotten out of the shower and hadn't bothered putting on pajamas... lucky me. She strode toward me, looking sexy and glistening from her shower. I had planned on joining her, but of course Fallon had decided that would be a perfect time to give me a ring.

I smiled as she crawled into bed beside me, resting her head on my chest. Those were my favorite moments with Blair. Aside from the mind-altering sex, nothing compared to having her with me and hearing her steady breathing as she rested on top of me.

It was in those moments, though, when I was the most scared, too, because the comfort and safety I felt with her should have terrified me, yet it never did. I kept waiting and waiting for the feeling of needing to run to come, but instead, I pulled Blair closer, tethering me to the spot so the feeling couldn't drag me away from her.

"Yeah, that was Fallon. Apparently we are all going to a rooftop movie night tomorrow. Expect to hear from Cara very soon. Fallon said she was going to ask you about it. She cheated and tried to play the wedding card, so I'm going too."

As if she were spying on us, Blair's phone chimed with a text notification. Blair checked her phone and laughed. "Word travels fast, doesn't it? She said Fallon invited us to the movies tomorrow night and said Mackenzie is going... and Kaia? She said it will be good for us to all spend more time together outside of work."

"She is always trying to get us to spend more time together. Maybe she'll be happy when we tell her about us?" I hadn't meant for it to come out as a question, but I wasn't so sure how Cara would react.

"Maybe if we would've told her from the beginning, but since we have been hiding it from her and basically lying to her, she might be upset at first. But I'm sure once she sees us together, she'll understand. At least, I hope so."

She shrugged and typed out a quick message and put her phone back on its charger. "I told her it sounded fun and sent a thumbs-up emoji. At least I didn't have to lie to her. I've done that enough already."

I heard the sadness and regret in her voice, and I wished I could take it away. I was counting down the days until the book signing was over.

"It should be quite an interesting night, to say the least, but in the meantime, maybe we should make up for the time I won't be able to touch you tomorrow?" I smiled when I felt her shiver as I ran my fingers along her sides.

"You're impossible." There was no bite to her words, and I only smirked in response.

I grabbed her chin and kissed her sweetly before I pulled her on top of me and began making up for the time we would lose tomorrow.

∼

Me: ETA ten minutes

Blair and I had made the smart decision not to ride together. For one thing, I was worried we would be late and we wouldn't be able to hide the reason why. For another, it would have looked too suspicious.

I was looking forward to a night out with everyone even though I was sure it was going to be a little awkward.

I had picked up Kaia since her place was on the way. When we got to Pinstripes, Fallon and Mackenzie were just walking in. "I don't know if this is a good idea."

I stopped walking and turned to her. "Why wouldn't it be? It's just a movie, Kaia."

She sent me a glare. "I don't know if you've noticed, but you two don't exactly hide the way you look at each other. You just better hope you don't get stuck sitting next to her, or everyone is going to pick up on what's going on between the two of you. I honestly don't know how they haven't already." She shrugged before continuing to walk away, as if she didn't just try to out me.

There was no way we were that noticeable, right? Surely Cara would've said something by now if so.

We waited up for Cara and Blair, who weren't too far behind. When they walked up to us, I had to clench my fists to my sides so I didn't reach out and touch Blair. I was now hyper aware of everything I said, of every movement of my eyes as they landed on Blair, every lick of my lips as I thought of relieving her of her sexy-as-hell dress. How had I gotten so lucky to find a woman who always wore dresses?

She was wearing a brown babydoll summer dress that exposed her sexy legs and matching wedge shoes that made her long legs seem infinite. Her hair was down in curls, and I wanted to run my hands through the strands. Jesus! How did she always manage to take my breath away?

We all said our greetings, everyone hugging except for Blair and me, who just smiled politely at one another. Cara rolled her eyes in annoyance but didn't bother commenting as we all headed inside.

After Fallon gave her name, the hostess led us to a table in the back. It was a perfect spot away from loud conversations. We ordered our drinks, and Fallon and Mackenzie put an order in for appetizers.

When the waitress brought our drinks over, I raised my whiskey glass to toast. "To Fallon and Mackenzie, who we all love and adore. I'm so grateful you found each other, and I can't wait to see where the future takes you both!"

Mackenzie put her arm around Fallon's shoulder and kissed the top of her head, which caused Fallon to blush slightly. I would never get bored of seeing my best friend so happy.

We chatted more about the wedding, and I was silently thanking Fallon and Mackenzie for not bringing up the fact I was bringing Blair to the wedding. Once our food came, all conversations stopped as we ate and drank.

Any chance I got, I snuck a glance at Blair, who was doing the same, and I couldn't hide my smile. I was glad we weren't sitting next to each other, because I wouldn't have been able to keep my greedy hands to myself. When she'd smile at me and lick her lips, I wondered if she did it on purpose to mess with me. I had to shift in my seat every time.

"Are you okay over there, Drea?"

I stopped and turned to see Kaia looking at me with a concerned expression. To anyone else, that was what it would have looked like, but I barely caught the subtle raise of her eyebrow and the faintest lifting of her lip.

I cleared my throat and took a drink. "Of course. Why do you ask?"

"You're just moving a lot in your seat, that's all."

"I'm fine," I bit out, silently threatening her with my eyes.

What was her deal today? Suddenly she wasn't so shy and was trying to test me? I knew she wouldn't actually say anything to anyone, but it was still making me on edge.

Mackenzie was literally seconds away from catching on, I was convinced. If she knew, then Fallon would know, and eventually it would get back to Cara and—

"So, Blair, what's new with you?" Mackenzie took a sip of her drink, but I didn't miss the smirk she was trying to hide as she eyed me over the rim. I gave her a confused look, because what the hell? Why was she looking at me like that? Did she suspect something? I hoped not. I had a feeling she wouldn't keep her mouth shut about it if she did.

"Oh, you know, I've been writing a lot and getting ready for the book signing. I live a pretty boring life most of the time."

"That is so not true!" Cara laughed, and all eyes at the table turned to her. What did she mean by that?

"Are you joking? I write and hang out with you or Milo. That's literally all I do!" Blair smiled, and it felt good to see her interacting with her friend.

"That's not all you do, but you still won't tell me about it." Cara smirked, but I could see the hurt laced in between her words.

I really wished Blair would slip up and say something. Holding all of this in was driving me crazy.

The whole table showed a wide variety of emotions. Fallon furrowed her brows in confusion, Mackenzie quirked an eyebrow, I tried to show no emotion, and Blair looked as if she would cry at any second. I hated that look Cara forced Blair to paint on; I hated not being able to wash it away.

"What does that mean?" Mackenzie pressed. I was sure I didn't want to know.

"I went to check on her the other day, you know, after the bad storm? But it seems I wasn't the only one. When I got there, she looked like she had just finished... entertaining company. She still refuses to tell me who was in there."

"Really? How very interesting." Mackenzie looked at me, and all I could do was look away. I wasn't going to give her the satisfaction of giving a reaction.

"Why are you talking about me like I'm not sitting right here?" Blair scowled at Cara, and I hoped things weren't going to escalate.

"Why are you still hiding it from me?" Cara smirked, and I sagged in relief.

"Do we really have to do this right now? I already told you it wasn't a big deal. If it was important enough, I would have told you about it, Cara." She took a sip of her drink and gave me an apologetic look. I knew she didn't mean anything by it, but her words still hurt.

"Maybe we should get the check? The movie will be starting pretty soon." I finally took over the conversation. I had to get some fresh air, and I knew Blair did too.

Once I paid our tab, with only little resistance from everyone, we headed to the rooftop. On the way out, I sent Blair a text:

> Me: You look absolutely gorgeous tonight. How are you doing? I'm sorry about Cara's comment.

Blair turned back to me after she pulled her phone out of her purse. I sent her an innocent smile.

> Blair: Thank you! You don't look so bad yourself. I'm sorry about what I said. I wanted her to let it go. I hope you know I didn't mean it.

> Me: It's all right. I know you didn't, and it seemed to have worked.

"It feels so crazy being back here." I was just about to send another text to Blair when Fallon's voice stopped me.

We had made it to our seats and were settling in. Fallon and Mackenzie sat next to each other, obviously, with Cara following next to them, leaving Kaia, Blair, and me on the edge. Luck must have not been on my side, because Kaia scooted in next to Cara, leaving the last two seats for Blair and me. This was going to be a long night.

Mackenzie looked down at us and smirked. I swore she was onto us. I had to be very careful around her. "It's wild to think the last time we were here, I was desperately trying to get Fallon to forgive me, and Skylar was trying to get you to move to New York with her. Crazy, isn't it?"

I glared at her but softened at the look Fallon was giving her fiancée. I bit out a quick, "Yes," and hoped she would drop it.

Luckily my phone chimed with a text, and I was grateful for the distraction. I silenced it before checking it:

> Blair: They are so cute! Also, I'm sorry she brought up your ex. For what it's worth, I'm glad you didn't go to New York.

I risked a casual glance at Blair and chuckled softly at her flushed cheeks.

> Me: They make me sick! But I love them, anyway. And I am too.

As soon as the movie started playing and it got darker, I took a chance. I glanced at Fallon and Mackenzie, who were wrapped in each other's arms. Cara and Kaia were watching the movie, and the coast seemed to be clear. I slowly moved to interlace my fingers with Blair's, and my heart calmed when she accepted the contact. I kept glancing at everyone to make sure they weren't looking at us. Thankfully they never looked over.

I was so nervous about getting caught, but I needed her touch to calm me. I kept rubbing her hand with my thumb and I loved the way it felt. I loved feeling any part of her, and I wanted her to feel comforted by the motion.

After several minutes of holding her hand, I gently squeezed it three times, hoping she would pick up on the three words I didn't have the courage to say. I wanted to convey my feelings in that one small gesture.

About halfway through the movie, Blair tapped my shoulder. "I'm going to the restroom. Will you let them know?"

"Of course. Do you want me to go with you?" I smiled hopefully.

She grinned and glanced at our friends who were paying no attention. Of course, Fallon and Mackenzie weren't even watching the movie at this point, and I was so jealous.

"Give me five minutes? I do actually need to go."

She got up, and I had to pinch my thigh so I didn't smack her ass.

"Where's she going?" Kaia asked.

"The bathroom." I returned to the movie and kept glancing at my phone, counting down the seconds.

It was risky; I knew it was. I couldn't help it, though. I would've risked my life for just a moment of her time. I was so addicted to her, and I was in no rush to find a cure.

After what seemed like an eternity, I turned to Kaia. "I'm going to the bathroom. I'll be back."

"Okay... have fun." She looked at me quizzically, and I suppressed an eyeroll.

"Oh yeah, I'm going to have a blast," I mused. At that moment, I was glad she knew better than to question me.

I made my way to the restroom, which was thankfully empty aside from Blair. She was washing her hands when I came in. I locked the door behind me, and as soon as I turned around, she was on me.

I grabbed her waist and kissed her like I was starving for her. Like I hadn't explored her body hours prior to this moment. It didn't matter; it never mattered.

"Hi," I finally said when she broke the kiss. Her hair was out of place, and I had never been more turned on than I was at seeing her looking perfectly a mess.

"Hi," she replied with a smirk. "I've been wanting to do that all night. You think they would let us sneak out early?" She was playing with the buttons on my shirt, and I had to remember to breathe.

"I highly doubt it. Fallon would murder me if I left, and they would ask a million questions."

She gave me the sexiest little pout, and I had no choice but to capture her mouth in an intense kiss. She was the most beautiful creature on the planet, and I sincerely hoped she understood just how perfect she was. I would spend as much time as I had to prove it to her if not.

I lifted her dress slightly, and my hands found their happy place resting on her hips, my thumbs tucked into the band of her underwear. God, I wanted to rip them off her!

I groaned when her hands found their way under my shirt and around my bra-covered nipple. I'd decided to wear a matching lace set tonight, so I could feel every caress she made and it drove me wild.

I had to break the kiss. If I didn't, I was going to fuck Blair in this small bathroom. We were both panting heavily, trying to catch our breaths. I finally managed to let go of her and help fix her dress.

"We better get back," I said, trying to cool down the heat building inside of me. "If we keep going, I won't be able to stop, and then we'll really be in trouble."

"Maybe I like getting into trouble with you," she whispered before she nibbled on my ear.

My knees began to feel like jelly, and I really thought they were going to give out. "Jesus Christ, woman," I breathed. I grabbed her chin and kissed her one last time before I let her take a step back.

I gave Blair a head start before following after her. When we finally made it back to our seats, Kaia was giving me a look I couldn't name. One of her eyebrows was quirked up, and she had the faintest smirk on her lips. Seriously, what was her deal tonight?

"Was there a long line? You guys were gone a while," Fallon whispered across our seats.

"Uh... yeah," I answered unconvincingly.

"Damn, did you guys get into a fight or something?"

I frowned at a smirking Mackenzie. "What? No, why?"

She laughed. "Well, did you fall or something? Blair, your hair looks a little..." She pointed to the top of Blair's head, which was disheveled and looked like she had been making out in the bathroom. "And, Dre, you have something on the corner of your mouth. Is that... blood?"

I wiped at my mouth and wanted to crawl into a hole. Sure enough, Blair's lipstick had found a home at the corner of my mouth. I didn't have to look at Blair to see the embarrassment all over her face. Everyone was looking at us, waiting for an answer I couldn't give them. *We are so fucked. This is it. This is where Cara kills us both!*

"I... well—"

"It's okay, Drea, you don't have to cover for me." Blair interrupted my stuttering, and I gaped at her, unsure of what would come next.

"I tripped, and Drea tried to catch me before I hit the ground. Thanks again."

She gave me a genuine smile, and my returning one wasn't forced.

"It... was nothing." I shrugged and turned back to Mackenzie who was shaking her head with a knowing smirk. We were so screwed.

I was relieved no one else bothered to ask more questions, and we returned our attention to the movie.

Not even ten minutes later, my phone buzzed with a text. I was expecting it to be Blair, but the disappointment was evident on my face when I opened the message:

> Kenzie: You saved her from falling? Why do I find that hard to believe?

> Me: I don't know, Kenz. Watch the movie.

> Kenzie: You still have "blood" on your face, savior Dre. 😂

Oh my God, she knew! Also, I was mortified! I could only hope Cara was oblivious and Mackenzie kept her mouth shut.

> Me: Shut up!

> Kenzie: Did I strike a nerve? 😌

> Me: No. Watch the damn movie, or I'll tell Fallon all about the time you drunk sexted me thinking it was her. I still have the messages, you know. You really are whipped!

I chuckled as I looked over at a wide-eyed Mackenzie, who quickly put her phone away and snuggled back into her fiancée.

We managed to get through the rest of the movie without incident. However, the car ride was a different story. Kaia seemed to have gained some confidence, because she chose to speak up when I had nowhere to escape.

"So, she fell, huh?"

I took a deep breath and glanced over at her. She was looking straight ahead, but a smirk danced across her face. "Is there something you would like to say, Kaia? Just say it."

She laughed and shook her head, seemingly fed up with me. "I can't believe you, Dre."

I shrugged. "What? I can't help it. Have you seen her?"

"I love my job, so I'm going to say no. But seriously, in the bathroom? You two are ridiculous."

"It was only harmless making out. And why are you attacking me right now?"

I didn't know what had gotten into her these days. She was usually so much more reserved. She would have never thought to call me out like she was doing.

I wasn't sure if I should have been proud of her for starting to find her footing in this world, or upset that she had the nerve to question me. It was probably a little bit of both, but only because I was on the other end of it and I wasn't happy about that.

"I'm not attacking you. I'm happy for you, I really am. I'm just worried. You guys are lucky Cara is so oblivious."

My grip tightened on the steering wheel, knuckles turning bleach white. She was right, but I couldn't find the words to say so. "I appreciate your concern, but it's not necessary."

"When are you going to tell her? She'd probably be happy for you. She's been trying to get you guys to get along for years, you know."

I groaned in frustration. "We will tell her when the time is right, okay? Can you just drop it, Kaia?" My tone was anything but friendly. I was still on edge from almost getting caught and I didn't want to talk about it anymore. It wasn't any of her business, anyway.

She sighed and turned toward the window, lowering her voice. "Fine."

Internally, I kicked myself. I knew I shouldn't be getting short with her, but holding this secret was causing my brain to short circuit. I wanted to tell Cara so badly.

I wanted to hold Blair in public, announce to the world that she was mine, in whichever way that was. I wanted to breathe easier and not be constantly looking over my shoulder every time I looked at her, worried Cara would show up out of nowhere.

"I'm sorry." My voice was so low I didn't think she heard me.

"It's okay. I know it's not easy keeping something from the people you care about. I mean... I imagine it's not."

I wanted to ask what she meant by that, but looking at her next to me, head down and fidgeting with her bracelet, I didn't think it was the right time.

"Yes, well..." I let the rest of my thoughts hang in the air as I drove Kaia home.

Chapter Thirty-Two

BLAIR

"Mm, yes, baby. Shit!" I had never paid much attention to how big a shower was or needed to be until now. I was grateful I had a decent-sized one. One that two people could fit into perfectly.

I was lying on the floor while Drea was going to town on my clit and stroking my G-spot at the same time. The water was raining down on us, and it was so erotic.

She moaned into my pussy, and I could feel the orgasm building. We had started standing up, but my legs quickly turned into jelly, and she lowered us down to the shower floor. It was cold at first, but after the first few licks and sucks, I couldn't feel the floor beneath me.

"Please don't stop, baby," I whined as my eyes rolled back into my head and she forced every drop of pleasure out of me, causing my back to arch as if she were sucking my soul out of my body. It sure felt that way, anyway. She devoured me until I entered another universe entirely.

"Delicious every time." She grinned as she brought her fingers to her mouth and sucked them one by one.

"Good fucking God," I panted. She chuckled and helped me up, applying another lather of shampoo to my hair before the conditioner.

"Darling, do you know how truly exquisite you are?" She rinsed her hands and started washing my body, reveling in the little jolts it produced when she touched a particularly sensitive area.

I groaned and pulled her to me for a perfectly wet kiss. "This is not what I had in mind when I told you I wanted to take a shower before the beach," I said as I broke the kiss and tried to catch my breath.

She laughed while rinsing the conditioner from my hair. Having her play with my hair was one of the most relaxing things for me. "I'm sorry, love, are you complaining right now? Because kiss me if I'm right, but I heard nothing but positivity in those screams a second ago."

I turned around and pulled her in from the waist, our wet bodies connecting again, and I had to muster all the strength I could manage not to go for another round. Shower sex was one of my favorite pastimes. "No, baby, I am not complaining at all." I rubbed my thumb across her cheek before connecting her lips with mine.

I broke the kiss, and she turned off the water, stepping out to get the towels. She wrapped me up first, pressing a kiss to my forehead, before getting her own towel.

It was always the little things like that that sent a flutter through my stomach. The forehead kisses. Washing my hair in the shower or wrapping me up before getting her own towel.

"I just meant I don't always expect sex when we're together. It's definitely a big plus, but... it's not the reason I stay. I just wanted you to know." I was fidgeting with a piece of the towel, trying to contain my nerves.

I hadn't brought up our arrangement since our late-night swim, and I was nervous to. I knew of Drea's dating history and how commitment was not her friend. I mean, she was with Skylar for three years and never once called her "her girlfriend." I was afraid of what I felt for her, and I was scared it wouldn't be returned. I just wanted to enjoy being with her, in whatever way I could have her, for a little longer.

She smiled at me and placed two fingers under my chin to tilt my head so we were eye to eye. "Darling, I'm so glad you stay, whatever the reason. And just so we are perfectly clear." She leaned in to place the softest kiss on my lips. "I don't expect anything either. I am here for *you*."

God, I wanted to melt into the earth for her.

I cleared my throat, trying to gather myself and not drag her back to the bed. "Glad we cleared that up. Now, should we get ready? I can make us breakfast before we go."

She dropped her towel, and all thoughts of the beach were forgotten. "On second thought, the beach isn't going anywhere. We have plenty of time to get there."

"I couldn't agree more, darling. Why don't I help you... dry off, hmm?" She removed my own towel, and I knew we were going to have to use them again pretty soon, but did I care? Absolutely not.

After *another* shower and eventually stumbling our way to make breakfast, we finally made it to the beach only two hours after our original plan.

I wanted to forget the beach altogether, but Drea thought we needed some fresh air and Vitamin D. I tried to make a sex joke as an excuse to stay home, but she didn't buy it.

"Are you sure this is a good idea? What if someone sees us?"

"Darling, please relax." We had just parked the car, and her hand was still lightly caressing my thigh. Anytime we were in the car together, that was where her hand landed and where it would stay until we got out of the car.

I laid my head back, eyes fluttering closed as she inched higher and higher up my thigh. The parking lot was surprisingly empty, so I would've been more than okay if she wanted to help me relax in the car.

I let out a moan when she started kissing my neck, but it was over before it began. "Tease," I pouted.

She chuckled and rubbed my cheek with her thumb. "I'm trying to help you relax. Everyone is out of town for the Fourth of July weekend. Let's just enjoy a nice day together, okay?"

I gave her a sweet smile, knowing she was right. "You're right. Let's go." I stole one final kiss before we gathered all our things and headed to find the perfect spot on the beach.

We ended up finding a decent spot before more people started to fill the beach, and nobody really sat near us.

I was still on edge, wondering if we were going to get caught by someone, but literally everyone we knew was out of town for the holiday.

I just hoped no one caught on that we were both the only ones deciding to stay in town. Luckily we were able to use our jobs as an excuse.

"Babe, would you mind putting sunscreen on my back, please?"

I turned around with the sunscreen in my hand. "Great minds think —" Words seemed to have floated out into the ocean when I turned to see Drea taking off her cover-up.

She'd gone with a coral bikini set. The halter top fit her boobs perfectly, and it was so transparent I could see her delicious nipples peeking through. I trailed my gaze down to her stomach that was already glistening with sweat from the heat, down lower to the bottoms that I assumed barely covered the ass I so desperately craved to bite.

She cleared her throat, and I jumped. I must've been drooling because... goddamn! "Like what you see, Ms. Sterling?" She quirked her eyebrow, and I could feel my cheeks burning.

Yes, I most certainly do. "I... Turn around?" It came out as a high pitched question, which caused her to chuckle.

"Yes, ma'am." She winked, and I stood up on shaky legs as she turned around.

When I was done, she took the bottle from me and motioned for me to turn around so she could apply it to my back. I turned around and took a deep breath.

Of course she took her sweet time applying the lotion, and I had to suppress a moan when I felt her warm breath on my ear as she whispered, "All done."

"Great!" I spun around and wretched the bottle from her hands and applied it to the rest of my body. "Thank you," I said at a normal volume. She smirked and waited for her turn.

After we set up our towels and chairs, I got out the book I'd brought with me. It was a vampire book that Mackenzie had recommended to me. The vampire's love interest was a hunter, and the two had a very interesting past. It was very dramatic and very spicy. The perfect combination.

I must've dozed off, because I felt a wet hand on my leg and jumped, forgetting where I was briefly. "Sorry, darling. I just went for a little swim. How's your book?" Drea was now crouching in front of me, applying more sunscreen to my body and I closed my eyes, enjoying the contact.

"Nothing exciting was going on. I must've fallen asleep. How's the water?" I asked.

She leaned in and placed her arms on my sides, caressing them as she had at the book festival. The memory of her body so close to mine as she pressed me against the wall had a heat filling my body that had nothing to do with the sun.

"It was refreshing," she said in a sultry voice that had me squeezing my thighs together. She knew what she was doing, and I didn't want her to stop.

She smiled and brought her lips to mine, and I hesitated for a beat before she grabbed my chin in the way she knew made my knees weak. I grabbed the back of her neck and kissed her back with everything I had. It was over in a second but the aftereffects lingered for several minutes.

"I was thinking, we should build sandcastles. Thoughts?"

I shook away the tingling feeling her kiss had left. "I think that is an excellent use of our time, Ms. Voss."

After hours of building sandcastles, laughing, and stealing kisses, my skin was starting to get a little toasty, so we decided to call it a day and pack up. We had just gotten in the car when my phone went off.

"Are you going to answer that, love?" Drea asked as she was packing up the car.

My eyes widened when I saw it was Cara trying to video call with me. "Um... I'm not sure if I should. It's Cara. She wants to video chat."

She shrugged. "I can make myself scarce. It's okay, Blair, answer it."

I huffed out a breath and swiped to answer the call. "H... hey, Cara. What's up?"

She grinned brightly when I answered. "Hey, B! How's your weekend going? I miss you! Are you going to watch the fireworks later?"

"It's good, just taking a little break from writing. I was starting to get blocked. Yeah, I think we're going to watch them later. How about you guys?" My smile wasn't forced.

Cara looked like she was having a great time with her family, and I was happy she was taking a break. She worked way too hard sometimes. But who was I to talk about working harder than was necessary sometimes?

"We? Are you with your mystery guest right now? Is that her car? Let me see!" She gasped and I turned bright red.

I fucked up. We? We?! How could I have let that slip? I needed to think of something to say, but I didn't want to lie to her.

Thankfully, someone in her family saved me from having to come up with an excuse. "Maybe next time, doll. The family is beckoning me." She groaned with a sweet smile. "I want to meet this woman, Blair... soon!"

You already have, Cara... "Go. Tell your parents I said hello." We said our goodbyes just as Dre was getting into the car.

"Well? How did it go?" Drea was rubbing sweet circles on my thigh, and my anxiety from the call was slowly diminishing. She always had a magical way of doing that.

"I almost ratted us out, and now she's demanding to meet my 'mystery guest' soon, but luckily we're both going to be pretty busy, at least until the signing, so I should be okay. This is killing me, Drea. I'm tempted to just tell her, but now I'm too scared it'll blow up in my face."

"I'm sorry, sweetie. I know it's not easy to keep it from her. I'm having the same issue with Fallon. She is my family, and I don't like lying to her. Soon enough, this will all be over, and I can brag about you until the end of time." She smiled softly and kissed me with a passion that had me forgetting whatever I was upset about to begin with.

"Let's go wash off this sand," I said. She winked and I blushed, remembering how our day had gotten started.

Chapter Thirty-Three

DREA

I had been a mess all day. It was finally time to see my best friend get married, and I didn't know how to handle it. She was more like a sister than a friend.

I usually didn't gravitate toward dresses, but unfortunately I had to wear one today per the bride's selfish demands. The only time I would wear one was for very special occasions, usually involving Fallon. It was a simple white dress that hugged my body and stopped just above the knees.

While Fallon got ready, we all sat around laughing and crying until it was time for the show to start.

When we asked her, she said she wasn't nervous. "I'm so in love with her, you guys. I don't see my life going anywhere that she isn't. I'm beyond ready to marry her. I've been ready for so long," she said while her mother touched up her tear-stained makeup.

Penelope and I said our goodbyes, as it was time for us to head to the altar. That thought gave me pause.

This was the first time I'd be walking down a wedding aisle, but would it be the last? Did I see myself taking these steps later down the road? Finding my own person to call home? I never used to want those things, but lately, I wasn't so sure anymore.

When I walked down the aisle, Mackenzie was there looking gorgeous in her long white V-neck wedding gown.

"Damn, you clean up rather nice there, Wildcat," I teased.

She rolled her eyes at the nickname, but there was no real irritation behind it. "You don't look half bad yourself. I have to say, I'm shocked you're in a dress. It's been what, a few years?"

"Since Fallon's birthday at Pinstripes. The things we do for that woman, right? Don't get used to it, though." I turned to face the crowded venue and instantly lost my breath when my eyes found Blair's perfect hazel ones.

My friends were polite and welcoming to Blair when we got there, and none of them asked any questions, although I didn't miss the sideways glances and smirks they sent my way when she wasn't looking. I made it a point to prove she wasn't there as my date; she was there as a friend I sort of tolerated. But Jesus was it hard!

Sitting in the crowd, grinning at me, she looked like an angel in her lace two-piece maxi dress. It had been nearly impossible to keep my hands off her all day.

Kaia was standing on the other side of Penelope, but she seemed to be in her own world, staring off into the clouds, and didn't catch me drooling over Blair. I couldn't help it; she was stunning.

"She looks gorgeous, don't you think?" Mackenzie whispered.

I replied without taking my eyes off Blair. "Yes, she really does." A warm smile played on Blair's lips, mirroring the feeling in my chest. I had never seen anything more awe-inspiring than Blair Sterling and her damn smile.

"You know, I've never looked at any of my friends like that, Dre. You can't even take your eyes off her. It's almost as if you don't want to look away. How interesting. How is your sex ban going, by the way? Is there something you would like to tell me?"

I whipped my head to see her raised eyebrow. I opened my mouth to say... Well, I didn't really have anything to say to that, but I was saved when the music started playing as Fallon came into view, her stepdad, Brandon, walking by her side.

She was absolutely glowing in her dress, and I couldn't stop the tears from coming out. It was a long strapless ball-gown style dress with pockets, freaking pockets! Those were her exact words when she found out, and needless to say, that was the one.

She looked absolutely perfect walking down the aisle. I still couldn't believe my best friend was getting married.

Of course, I wasn't surprised when she told me. Besides the fact that I helped pick out the ring, those two were the most perfect pair I had ever seen. But now that the day had finally arrived, it was bittersweet. I was gaining a sister, but I also felt like I was losing one in a way.

I wouldn't be able to call her at all hours of the day to come over if I needed her. I supposed I could if I really needed to, but I'd feel guilty for making her take time away from her wife. I had to share her now, and it wasn't going to be easy.

Apparently, I wasn't the only one who thought she looked beautiful. I turned to Mackenzie, who was now looking so brightly at Fallon without a dry eye.

"She looks beautiful," I whispered.

She shook her head. "No. She's perfect."

After the sweetest exchange of vows and a loving kiss, I officially had two married best friends. How fucking surreal!

The wedding was absolutely perfect, and Fallon's little brother, Caleb, was the cutest little ring bearer, and instead of a flower girl, they had Rylee's son, Greyson, as the flower boy.

I was even surprised to see Mackenzie's dad sitting in the crowd next to a sweet old couple I knew as their neighbor's. The man, Robbie, I believe, gave Mackenzie's dad a skeptical glare here and there, but her father's smile never wavered as he watched his daughter marry the love of her life.

After the ceremony, I found Blair and forced myself not to reach out for her. "That was a beautiful wedding." She smiled sweetly as we walked to the reception, which was inside the venue space.

"Yes, it really was. I'm glad you came with me." Kaia was several paces ahead of us, and I took a chance during the rare private moment to graze my fingers against hers, just barely.

My heart warmed when she smiled softly at the contact. "I'm glad I could be a part of it."

When we sat down at our table, I took the opportunity to rub her leg underneath where no one could see. Her skin was so soft, and I wanted to move my hand further along her thigh.

"You look incredible," I whispered. Everyone else was in their own deep conversations, and Mackenzie and Fallon were making heart eyes at each other and in their own little world.

I was grateful everyone was distracted enough not to notice how close I was to Blair. We were sitting too close for "just friends," but I wouldn't have wanted it any other way. Okay, maybe if she was in my lap, but I figured that might've given us away.

Kaia was the only one at the table who knew part of the truth, and I suspected Mackenzie wasn't too far behind. She was annoyingly perceptive sometimes.

Blair blushed as if she had no idea how perfect she was. "Thank you. I must say I could get used to seeing you in a dress. You look very sexy." She caressed my thigh, and I begged for her to move her hand up a few more inches.

"I much prefer for you to see me out of my dress, darling," I whispered, causing her to choke on her drink.

The whole table turned to look at us as I started lightly patting her back.

"Are you all right, Blair?" Kaia asked.

Blair nodded. "Yeah, sorry. It went down the wrong pipe, I think. All good here."

Luckily, that seemed to assuage the group, and they all returned to their conversations while Blair turned back to me and glared. I was barely able to contain a chuckle, so I shrugged. "What?"

"That was not funny!" She tried to sound angry, but the small smirk and the tint of red coloring her cheeks gave her away.

I placed my hand on her thigh and drew dainty circles and leaned in closer, seeing the slight fluttering of her lashes as she tried to keep her composure. "I wasn't joking, love. You will see this dress on the floor later," I whispered with a wink. She shivered under my touch, and I decided to stop teasing her. For now.

It was so easy to get her going, but I wasn't immune to my own words. Just picturing how the night would unravel later had me desperate to get her alone.

We sat and watched the couple's first dance before everyone else joined in. While we were sitting in a comfortable silence, I couldn't help but graze my fingers against hers. I wanted to hold her as I watched my best friend dance with her wife.

I snuck a glance at Blair and noticed she was doing the same as she returned the favor and linked our fingers together. She was smiling brightly at me, and I couldn't handle it anymore. Seeing how perfect she looked in her dress and the way she was looking at me forced me onto my feet.

"What—"

"Dance with me, darling." I held out my hand and she hesitated for a moment.

"Are... are you sure?" Her gaze bounced from all the couples dancing, to the brides, and back to my outstretched hand.

"Baby, my best friend just got married. and all I want is to celebrate with you. Dance with me... please?"

She continued to hesitate, pulling her bottom lip in between her teeth.

"Sweetheart," I started, pulling her to her feet. "Mackenzie and Fallon are not even on this planet right now. Kaia already knows about us, and Cara is not here. Even if all eyes were on us, who cares? It's just dancing." We both knew damn well it wasn't, but neither of us had the good sense to admit it.

Finally she nodded, and I led her to the dance floor, trying my best to keep a respectful distance between us.

As soon as she laced her hands around my neck, and mine found their home around her waist, I knew I had simultaneously made the right choice and the wrong one. On one hand, I knew there was absolutely no way we looked like friends, and a small part of me was nervous about Cara somehow finding out. But on the other hand... we were like two final pieces of a puzzle, fitting perfectly. Her body was made for mine, and I felt completely at home. *Okay, Dre, maybe ease up on the champagne!*

"Are you okay, love? You seem distracted." When her eyes connected to mine, she would smile, but they barely latched on because they kept darting around the room.

I trailed lazy circles on the skin just above the waistband of her skirt, causing a sexy shiver. "I am when you do that," she whispered, eyes fluttering closed for a brief moment. "I'm sorry, I'm just nervous. I know friends dance together all the time, but Kaia knows. What if she tells Fallon and what if she tells Cara, and what if—"

I silenced her with a chaste kiss. I pulled back to see her lips glistening from our kiss and her eyes looking into mine with a softness that wasn't there before.

"Blair, sweetie, take a breath. Cara is not here, and no one is paying any attention to us. Even if they were, I wouldn't care. All I care about is dancing with you. As far as I'm concerned, we are the only people in this room."

That was how it was anytime Blair was in the same breathing space as I was, no one else mattered. I might have been a little fucked here, and I might not have even been mad about it.

"How do you do that?" Her question came out a little breathless and with pink-tinted cheeks.

"Do what?" She was caressing the back of my neck and looking at me with those dark hazel eyes, and I couldn't form a coherent thought.

"Make all my worries disappear with a kiss? Even just a smile from you, and I forget how to breathe. How do you do that?"

I shrugged. "Everything is easy with you."

It was the honest truth. Everything had been easy with Blair. Perhaps not from the start, but as I had gotten to know her, she'd slid into my life seamlessly. Talking to her, caring for her... falling for her. It had all happened right in front of my eyes without me even knowing it.

She smiled and tried to hide a blush as we continued to dance to the music. I could have held Blair like this all night, but right now there was something else I wanted to do.

Leaning in a little closer, I whispered in her ear, "Want to go somewhere a little less... crowded?"

She pulled us apart slightly. "I thought you'd never ask."

We made our way out of the reception hall, the noise of the crowd growing distant. It had been a chore to keep my hands to myself all night, and I was about to rectify that problem.

I had been to this venue only about a dozen times, so I knew where we could be alone. There was a little room in the back corner of the space that was used mainly for extra storage.

As soon as the door closed, she was on me, pressing me up against the door.

"I thought I would never get you alone," she breathed as she grabbed me and kissed me.

I grinned and gripped her waist, pulling us closer together. "We're a little needy tonight, aren't we? I'm glad I'm not the only one. I was beginning to think this was one-sided."

She stopped and frowned. "Really, so all of my screaming orgasms didn't give me away?" I laughed and kissed her. I pushed her up against the wall, and she hooked one leg on my hip.

"God, Blair! The things you do to me..." I trailed off, replacing words with actions as I kissed her again.

Feeling her tongue had me drenched. I lowered the straps of her dress until her tits were bare for me, and I cupped one.

"Fuck," she moaned as I lightly pinched her nipple.

I was a boob woman if there ever was one. Hers were so perfect I had to touch them anytime I could.

I groaned before I scooped one into my mouth, and she moaned when I flicked her hard nipple with my tongue. I was addicted to every part of her—mind, body, and soul.

"Everything I thought I wanted before you has changed."

Before Blair, I was content with being a one-and-done kind of woman. I was perfectly okay with not having someone to go to bed with or wake up to in the morning. I was okay with my empty house and empty life.

Even when I had relationships, it didn't feel like one. We wouldn't talk every single day. We never lived together. And that was fine; I never wanted any of that. But now?

"What... Drea," she moaned when my greedy hand found her swollen clit.

"You feel so good," I said.

Everything about her felt good. The way she shivered underneath my touch. The way she screamed my name and writhed in those moments of ecstasy. The way she looked at me as we cuddled on the couch together and watched terrible movies. Seeing the way she did a cute little dance when she ate some good food or took a sip of her chai latte. All of it made me feel like I was constantly floating on a cloud.

I kissed her as I inserted two fingers inside her. I didn't think I could ever grow tired of seeing her like this, of feeling her.

"Drea," she breathed as I thrusted into her harder, pressing her more against the wall.

Seeing her in that moment, with her perfect tits bouncing as I fucked her against the wall, and feeling her coming apart for me, cemented my feelings for her.

"You are so perfect, Blair. Everything about you... God! How did I get so lucky?"

"Shit, Drea," she breathed in between thrusts.

"Yes. You are so gorgeous like this," I groaned.

I was seconds away from my own undoing, and she hadn't even touched me. But that was the thing about Blair—she could look at me and smile, and with that smile, I would crumble into the earth if that was what she wanted. I would do anything, go anywhere, be anyone she wanted me to be, as long as I got to be hers.

"Well, this is certainly not the restroom, is it?" A familiar voice caused us to freeze, and I rolled my eyes before I turned to see Mackenzie grinning at us like a damn fool.

Chapter Thirty-Four
DREA

"What are you doing here?" I asked, not bothering to hide my irritation.

I was trying to act calm, but inside, I wanted to vomit. I was so embarrassed. Blair, on the other hand, acted like she had just been electrocuted, pushing off me and adjusting her dress.

Mackenzie laughed. "I could ask you two the same thing. Fallon told me to come find you, something about wanting a few pictures together."

"We... we were just..." Blair was getting flustered, and I tried not to giggle, not that it was a laughing matter. There was nothing funny about the situation I had found myself in. She just looked so adorable with crimson-red cheeks.

"I know what you two were doing. I got the visual. I've had my suspicions for some time now, but when I saw you two walking off the dance floor holding hands, I knew I was right. So this is why you have been so nice lately, Dre. I guess I have you to thank for that, Blair. Her attitude was getting to be a bit much." She smirked.

I groaned. "Mackenzie, you are insufferable. Can you please keep this between us?" The last thing I needed was for this to get out to anyone. Not for my sake—I didn't care if anyone knew what I was doing in there, or who—but for Blair's.

Her personality outside of the bedroom, or closet, for that matter, was very different from inside, and I knew how embarrassed she would be if anyone found out.

"It doesn't feel good to be on the other side of the sex door, does it?" She laughed.

"What is she talking about?" Blair turned to me, face still flushed.

I sighed. "I caught her and Fallon in the back room at a book signing a few years ago. That's why there are cameras everywhere now."

Blair's face created a new shade of red as she gaped at me. "Even in your office?!" she whisper-shouted.

I chuckled. "Of course not, but that can be arranged if you're interested." I winked and laughed when she swatted my arm. At least Mackenzie didn't totally ruin the mood.

"Like that would've stopped me, anyway." Mackenzie winked. I turned my attention back to her, forgetting for a moment she was there.

"Mackenzie! Promise me you will keep this between us!" I demanded. My heart was still racing, but after seeing the look on Blair's face, I needed to make sure this stayed between us. Her face was flushed, and she looked like she could have cried at any moment. I hated seeing her like that, and I hated that I was the reason.

Keeping this from Cara had been hard on both of us. I was sure once we told her she would understand, and maybe even be happy for us, but it was the other side of what her reaction could be that stopped us every time. I didn't want her reaction, or anyone else's, to ruin what we had. I wanted to stay in our little bubble just a little longer.

She must've seen the same thing I did, because she turned from Blair and sighed. "Fine, this stays between us and Fallon." I glared at her. "Hey, she's my wife now. I can't start my marriage off with a secret, especially one as good as this one. My marriage would be over before it began."

I sighed in defeat. I should have known that was coming. "Fine, but she can't tell anyone! Kaia already knows, but if this gets back to Cara, we can't—"

"Don't worry, Dre. After everything you've done for me, I owe you at least this. So I guess this means your ban is over. What have we learned?"

I glared at her but looked at Blair, who was still blushing. "We've learned a lot of things."

Mackenzie didn't shame me like I thought she would. Instead, she smiled, perhaps knowing what it was I learned. "Well, I'll let you two get back to it. I have a bride to get back to, but don't keep her waiting too long, Drea. Have fun!" she yelled over her shoulder as she left.

My shoulders sagged and I knew there was nothing to get back to anymore. "I'm sorry about her. She can be a real ass sometimes."

"No... uhh... it's okay. That was the first time I've gotten caught in public. You've corrupted me." She grinned.

"Welcome to the dark side, love." I winked.

"Yeah, well, we should get back out there." She walked back over to me, and I wrapped my arms around her. "But first, we need to fix this. I can't have everyone looking at your boobs." I looked down to see my dress almost around my waist, and my tits were, in fact, almost out in the open.

"No, we can't have that, now can we?" After she fixed my shirt, I kissed her softly, and took her hand in mine. "Shall we? I better go find Fallon." She smiled as I led her back to the party.

"They seem really happy... The Bennetts, I mean."

I smiled at the mention of my best friend. "They do, don't they? I'm glad they figured things out."

She stopped and turned to me. "What do you mean?"

"For a long time they kept trying to tell us they were 'just friends,' but we all knew from the beginning. The way they both looked at each other. I've never looked at any of my friends that way."

None of them except for Blair. She was the exception to every rule I had ever put in place for myself.

"Fallon has been through a lot over the years, and I am thankful she found Mackenzie. They have been through their fair share of bullshit together, and Mackenzie has come a long way to earn back her trust, but I honestly don't know what would have happened to Fallon if she never found her. After she went through a really bad breakup and moved here, I didn't think I would ever get my best friend back. In my eyes, Mackenzie saved Fallon's soul just by loving her without fail. No matter where they were in their lives, together or apart, she never stopped loving Fallon. She never stopped showing it either." My eyes watered at the memory, but Blair squeezed my hand in comfort.

She didn't speak as we started walking in a comfortable silence. Walking with her, our hands interlaced together, was a feeling I could have gotten used to. Having Blair in my life was something I could have gotten used to.

When I locked eyes with Fallon, I knew there was going to be no way out of this conversation. "Good luck, baby." Blair squeezed our joined hands before letting go and kissed my cheek.

Hearing those words made something in my chest tighten. I squared my shoulders and headed to Fallon as Blair headed back to our table.

"There you are. I've been looking for you, babe!" When I reached her, there was nothing short of amusement in her eyes. Mackenzie was standing next to her, mirroring the same expression as her wife. They really were perfect together, despite the current mischief brewing in their expressions.

"Here I am." I smiled. "Kenz said you wanted some pictures?"

She gasped. "Oh yes, right! Rylee is waiting for us over in the garden."

"Sounds good, love. Lead the way." Good was the last thing it sounded like. I knew there was no way for me to avoid talking about what I was doing with Blair, and I couldn't deny what Mackenzie saw. I wanted to relive the moments before she walked in, but I couldn't deny it.

"I'll be right back, Mrs. Bennett." Fallon kissed her wife sweetly, and I wanted to gag.

"I'll be waiting for you, Mrs. Bennett."

"You two make me sick. Let's go, Fal."

Despite my sarcastic comment, I was beyond happy for them. Fallon was my family, and I wanted nothing but the best for her. She was truly happy for the first time in a long time, and I would never tell her, but I was forever indebted to Mackenzie for that.

"All right, boss lady, let's go. I thought getting laid was supposed to make you more relaxed?" she said as we walked away from Mackenzie.

I groaned. "Word travels fast, doesn't it? It does when your wife doesn't interrupt before I have an orgasm!"

198

She laughed. "Well, I guess we're even now. At the book signing, I was literally seconds away from com—"

"We are even!" I interrupted. I didn't need to relive that horrible day. It still haunted me whenever I saw that godawful chair... I really needed to get rid of it.

"Anyway," she continued, waving me off, "when you said you were bringing her, you told me you guys were barely even friends. Why did you lie to me?"

She sounded a little hurt, and I felt awful. Her wedding was not the place I wanted to discuss this with her, but I owed it to her. She was my best friend, and this was sort of something pretty big happening in my life.

I sighed. "I didn't lie, not technically, anyway. We *are* friends, I mean, we were. It's just..." I stopped when we approached Rylee.

"Hey, Rylee! How are you, love?" I was all too eager to change the conversation and Fallon knew it too. She scowled at me, but I ignored her as I ran up to Rylee and gave her a hug that was probably a little too long, trying to draw out the moment.

She laughed into the hug. "I'm good, sweets. You look amazing, Dre. And Fallon, my God, if you were straight, you would definitely be getting pregnant tonight!"

Fallon couldn't hide her laugh. "I can almost guarantee Roxxy said the exact same thing to Mackenzie, but thanks. Where do you want us?"

"Could you guys turn away from the camera? I would love for you both to be holding the bouquet between you."

We did as Rylee asked, and I knew the pictures were going to turn out beautifully.

"Don't think I forgot about our conversation earlier. What is it you two are doing? You clearly aren't just friends, babe. Are you just existing together?" She raised her eyebrows, emphasizing the words I always spoke when asked about what Skylar and I were doing. She was quiet for a few poses, and I honestly thought she was going to drop it. I guess I was wrong.

"We were friends. We *are* friends, but..." I just couldn't find the words to label what we were doing. I knew what it looked like and what it felt like, but something stopped me every time I tried to say the words out loud.

"Dre, you know you can talk to me." Her voice was so calm and devoid of any judgment. I couldn't hide it from her. We were family, and family didn't keep things from each other.

I sighed. "You know me, I'm not one to put a label on things. I like her... I *really* like her, Fal."

"I do know you, and I can see how you two are together when you think no one is watching. I saw the way you looked at her when we were all dancing. I know you thought no one was paying attention, but of course we were. She's the first woman you've brought around since Skylar, and we can see why. She was the only person in the room in your eyes, wasn't she?"

I remained quiet. I couldn't admit it out loud, least of all to myself. She wasn't wrong. Blair was something to me I was scared to define. I was scared it would go away, and I didn't want it to. Like saying how I felt out loud would somehow jinx everything and it would disappear.

"I just want you to be happy, babe."

Fallon's eyes started to get damp, and I wanted to push her down into the grass. "Don't cry, you bitch, or I'll start to cry."

"I'm sorry," she said, sniffling while she wiped away her tears. "I've just never seen you like this over someone before, not even Skylar. I know you loved her, but you weren't in love with her. If you were, you would've left with her and gone to New York without giving it a second thought. I'm not pressuring you to label anything with Blair, but I can see things are different. I can see she really means something to you."

I didn't respond. I didn't have the guts to say what I should have known from the beginning. Instead, I smiled as Rylee continued our pictures.

"Okay, guys. That should be enough."

We thanked her and linked arms as we headed back to the party.

"Do you love her?" Her question caused me to stop fidgeting with my dress and look up at her.

That was the million-dollar question, wasn't it? I cared for her deeply. I would have done anything for her. My life was better because she was in it. When she wasn't around, I didn't feel like I was truly living life; I was just existing in it. Like I was an NPC in a video game, waiting for the player to interact with me.

I took a deep breath and sighed, too tired to come up with a lie. "I'm scared," I whispered. "You know I didn't have the best role models for love growing up. If my parents, who had four children together, couldn't love each other enough to work it out, then I can't see why I deserve anything different. What if I fuck it up and lose everything?"

I'd never spoken the words out loud before, and if anyone knew the dynamic of shitty parents, it was Fallon. Still, I was relieved when she didn't press for more details and just pulled me in for a hug.

"Babe, I love you, and I understand where you're coming from. It's scary, giving up a part of yourself when you can't guarantee it will be treasured, but you are not your parents. Just please promise me, whatever is going on with you two, you will embrace it and be honest. You deserve to be happy, and that's all I want for you." Fallon laid her head on my shoulder.

"I never said 'I love you.'" The admission came out in a whisper. So low, in fact, I couldn't be sure she heard me.

"What? What are you talking about, Dre? There's still time. I mean, if that's how—"

"To Skylar. I never said 'I love you' to Skylar. I wanted to. I cared about her so much, and I wanted to love her. I wanted those feelings for her. The way I feel about Blair, God, I really wanted to feel them for Skylar, Fal, I really did."

The look on her face was pure shock, and all I could do was shrug. I hated being so vulnerable. Even with my best friend, it was still difficult sometimes. "Wow. I... I had no idea. I saw the two of you together, and how long you were together, and just assumed you loved her."

I shrugged. "I know. I wish it would've been that simple, but then I wouldn't have gotten to know Blair, and..."

"And fallen in love with her?" she asked.

I stayed quiet, knowing the truth but still afraid to say the words out loud. I didn't have to, though. Fallon knew me as well as I knew myself.

She gave me a sweet smile and pulled me close for a hug. It was a struggle to keep my eyes dry. "I bet Cara is thrilled about all this. She's been trying to get you two to stop arguing for years!"

Her comment was met with silence as my eyes roamed around the garden.

"Drea... she *does* know, doesn't she?" Her glare was terrifying.

"Not... exactly."

"What do you mean, not exactly? She doesn't know you two are... together?"

I shook my head slowly. I hated all of this. I was seconds away from just calling Cara and telling her everything. The guilt was tearing me up inside, not to mention I wanted the whole world to know who had a part of me—all of me.

She groaned. "Drea! You need to tell her. She deserves to know, and I don't like the idea of hiding something from her, especially about her best friend. I won't bring it up, but if she asks, I'm not sure I can lie to her. We're just getting to a good place in our friendship, and I don't want to jeopardize that."

I sighed. "I know, love, I know. We're going to tell her; we *want* to tell her. We just... we just want to get the signing out of the way first. We don't want our working relationship to complicate things with her."

"Fine. I won't say anything. I haven't seen you this happy in a long time, and I don't want you to lose that feeling. I just hope you know what you're doing, babe."

So did I...

Chapter Thirty-Five

BLAIR

Dancing the night away with Drea at the wedding was an incredible experience. I had never felt more at peace than I was when I was in her arms.

A small part of me felt lighter knowing that people knew about us and seemed to be happy. It felt freeing, in a way, to be able to spend the night with her, not worrying about what someone would say. To enjoy being with each other without looking over our shoulders and wondering if Cara was going to see us and start asking questions.

A huge part of me was still weighed down by the thought of my best friend being the only one who didn't know I was with Drea. Anytime we were together, she kept trying to get information out of me.

Ever since she came over that night Drea was still there, she couldn't seem to let it go. I kept telling her it was no one, or I would change the subject. I hated lying to her, but I told myself it was only for a little bit longer.

I wanted to share this part of my life with her, and I just hoped she'd be happy for me when the time finally came for me to tell her. How could she not be? She had been trying to get Drea and me to see eye-to-eye for years, and now we had. Granted, we had seen a lot more than each other's eyes, but that didn't matter.

The whole ride home I couldn't hide my smile, and I was so at peace

I even fell asleep in the car, which I never did, not since after the accident.

I woke up the next morning wrapped in a warm Drea blanket, and we snuggled for at least an hour until snuggling turned into the best morning sex of my life.

She had left for work shortly after, against my protest, and I spent the day missing her and catching up on some writing.

After the wedding, she asked me out on a real date. I was nervous, of course, not for the date, but for the chance we might be seen by Cara, but she told me she had it all taken care of and all I needed to do was to be ready at 9:15 and to dress comfortably. I thought it was a little late for a date, but I didn't question it. I loved surprises.

I went with a plaid mini skirt and black tights, a black cropped sweater, and some red ankle boots with a chunky heel. I had no idea where we were going or how cold it was going to be. It was early fall, so I didn't expect to be that cool, unless we were going to be indoors. She gave me zero details other than to be comfortable, which was easy enough. With her? It was impossible not to be.

The doorbell rang promptly at 9:15, and I raced to the door. "You're very punctual," I said, swinging the door open and wrapping my arms around a very sexy-looking Drea. She was wearing a pair of black skinny jeans and a maroon crop top, matching my outfit and shoe color.

"And *you're* very beautiful. Are you ready? Your chariot awaits." She grinned, gesturing to her car. I couldn't help but laugh and shake my head.

"And what, my dear, is so funny?" As we walked to her car, her scowl made me laugh even more. She was so freaking cute.

"I'll never get used to seeing you drive a purple Beetle," I finally said.

If someone would have asked me what kind of car I thought Drea Voss drove, the last answer I would have come up with was a Volkswagen Beetle.

She grabbed my ass and squeezed, causing a small moan out of my throat. "Hey! There is nothing wrong with my car!"

"You're right, baby, I'm sorry for making fun. I especially like the daisies on the rims." I grabbed her wrist to stop her from walking away.

She turned around and I wrapped my hands around her neck, playing with the back in the way I knew she loved.

"You look so sexy tonight, but where are we going?"

Instead of an answer, I got her lips pressed against mine, and I suddenly didn't care where we were going. All I cared about was her.

She pressed me against the car, and I deepened the kiss, ready to drag her back inside and forget whatever she had planned for our night together.

I pouted when she pulled away. "Come on, love." She opened the passenger door for me, and I got in with a small ache between my legs.

As she drove, her hand never left my thigh, and I had to take deep breaths. The smell of her cologne mixed with the feeling of her soft hand rubbing delicate circles on my thigh had me feeling very heady, and I wasn't sure how long I was going to last.

It still felt crazy to me how much I could crave another person—at least, not until I met Drea. Even when I hated her, I craved the banter. It made life not so boring, and I didn't feel so alone, even if I'd been fuming most of the time. Now it was all of her I needed. Her smile, her laugh, her body, her touch, *her*.

The drive to our mystery date was torture. I wasn't sure if it was the anticipation of what it was or how Drea's hand would occasionally find its way into my lap. After an eternity, we finally arrived at our destination, and I was left with so many questions.

We arrived at the Coral Cove Aquarium, which seemed to be closed. Drea must have sensed my confusion as she grinned and made her way to open my door.

"Drea, I'm so confused... I thought we were going on a date, not breaking and entering into the aquarium."

"Blair, honey, have some faith in me," she said as she walked us to the employee entrance of the building. She then knocked three times, and a familiar face smiled at me as the door opened.

"Well, hello there love birds. Here are the keys. Please make sure to clean up after yourself. I don't want to burn any furniture," Mackenzie said with a wink toward Drea.

"Thanks, Kenzie, I'll be sure to tell your future children about the time you and Fallon—"

"No need! Have fun and watch out for Houdini the penguin. He's a bit of an escape artist," Mackenzie said, as her cheeks turned beet red and she rushed off.

"What was that about? I would love to hear *that* story!" I said as soon as Mackenzie was out of earshot.

"Trust me, you don't want to know. Fallon and Kenzie can't seem to keep their pants on these days, even at Mackenzie's place of business, apparently." Drea chuckled.

"Well, you can't seem to keep your pants on these days, either," I joked.

"Says the one who is *always* wearing a dress."

I scoffed. "You've never had any issues with them before."

She took a step closer, and my pulse quickened when she brushed my bottom lip with the pad of her thumb. "I definitely don't have any issues with your dresses, darling," she said in a low voice as she started to play with the hem of my skirt. "Especially when they're on the floor."

"We... better go." It took everything I had in me to force us apart.

As we made our way in, Drea delicately grabbed my hand and led me through the dimmed hallways. Part of me wanted to stop and look at every display. There was something different about visiting at night, but my curiosity wanted to know what Drea had planned for us.

We arrived at a room that had one of the largest fish tanks I had ever seen, with fish of all colors. In the dark, it felt like we were actually underwater.

In the center of the room, Drea had placed a small picnic area down on the floor with candles and a few pillows. As we got closer, I noticed she also decorated a small table with violet peonies. Next to that was a box of pastries from my favorite bakery, Sweets.

"Drea, this is gorgeous..." I said, as I forced the tears back into my eyes. "How did you....? When did you...?" I was speechless. No one had ever done something like that for me.

Drea placed a soft kiss onto my lips as she led me to the pillows. "Kenzie helped me set this up tonight. I wanted our first real date to be special," she said, as she kissed a trail down my neck.

We sat, talked, and laughed for what felt like hours. Part of me regretted not getting to know her sooner. It had been a while since someone had made me feel *loved*.

Maybe it was the way her eyes glittered in the light or the way her lips curved into a smile, but I couldn't stop the words that came out of my mouth.

"Thank you for tonight... for everything, really. I... care about you, and I hope we can continue what we've been doing. I haven't been this happy in a long time."

A few moments of silence passed. And for a second I wished that I hadn't said anything. What if it was just a fling for her?

"Drea, you don't have to say—" My words were interrupted as her lips came crashing into mine.

She wrapped her arms around my body and started to push me toward the pillows. A second later, I threw my cropped sweater across the room and Drea continued to move her lips lower and lower down my chest.

She teased and pulled on the lacy material of my bra. The things she could do with her mouth were unimaginable.

Then, from the corner of my eye, I saw a shadow in the hallway. I shot up, holding my chest, and screamed.

The color drained from Drea's face. "Blair, what's wrong? Are you okay?"

"No! There is someone over there watching us!"

Drea turned around and ran toward the direction of the shadow. I quickly pulled on my sweater and ran after her. When I got to her, I couldn't stop laughing.

"Houdini! Go home, you little peeping Tom," Drea said as she ushered the terrified bird back into his exhibit.

We made our way back to our ruined picnic. "Well, that was a bit of a buzzkill." I giggled as I tried to pick up the flowers and ruined pastries.

"Sorry, love. Kenzie did mention that Houdini could be a bit of a cockblock. Want to head out and go back to your place?"

I couldn't stifle a laugh. "Sure."

The drive back home was quiet, and the silence made me uneasy. "Can I ask you something?" I finally said, unable to handle the silence any longer, curiosity getting the better of me.

She smiled, caressing my fingers with hers. "Of course, darling. You know you can ask me anything."

I looked down at our joined hands and took a deep breath. "Why do we always go back to my place? Not that I mind, of course. I love having you there. I just... You've never invited me over to yours, and I was curious, I guess. I'm sorry if that's stupid." It had been nagging at me for a few weeks, but I never found the time to ask.

My cheeks were turning red, and I wished I could have jumped out of the car. I never should've said anything. What if she thought I was ungrateful or something? *Don't be ridiculous, B!*

Her hand froze and she looked at me with an expression I couldn't quite name. "I... uhh..."

After what felt like several minutes of contemplating, she cleared her throat and put a soft smile on her perfect lips. "Any excuse I was about to give wouldn't have been a good one. I can explain more once we get there."

I looked at her, not missing the meaning behind her words. "Drea—"

"Blair." She squeezed my hand. "I *want* you there, okay? I'm sorry I haven't asked you sooner. It's a habit, but it wasn't my intention to... I would love for you to come over. Should I prepare the guest room?"

"Only if you're sleeping in there with me." I answered hesitantly. Of course I wanted to, but why was she being so weird about it? I wanted to know the real reason she hadn't had me over yet. Was she ashamed of where she lived? Was she a slob? Did she have—

The questions swirling in my head died off as we turned onto a driveway that seemed to go on forever. It was surrounded by lines of trees, and that made it seem like you were driving down a back road, not a driveway to someone's house.

Finally, after what seemed like another mile of driving down the driveway, the largest house I had ever seen came into view. I didn't think my brows could raise any more as I turned to look at Drea, who was slightly shaking. *What is going on?*

I tried to speak, but I could only sputter out a few words. "What... You live... Huh?!"

She chuckled, but I didn't miss the redness coating her cheeks. Why was she embarrassed? Because she was rich? No—not rich... *filthy fucking* rich?

"Okay, I'm sorry if this seems rude, but what the actual fuck?!"

She groaned. I was still confused as to why she seemed so weird. "Can we talk inside, please? I'll explain everything."

I nodded as she walked around the car to open my door for me. She took my hand as I stepped out and pulled me closer to her, nearly taking all the air out of my lungs. She always had a way of doing that.

"I had a really great time tonight, and I hope my weirdness hasn't ruined the mood. Tonight was... special to me, and I don't want it to end."

A rock lodged itself in my throat. I wasn't used to seeing Drea so vulnerable, and I didn't know what to make of it. All I could do was smile and accept the kiss she offered me. I found out early on that as much as I tried to, I couldn't deny her anything. If she wanted it, it was hers.

"Tonight was perfect," I said when she broke the kiss. "Thank you. I can't believe you planned all of that for me. But this house..." I took in a breath and shook my head. It just didn't make sense. She owned a small bookstore and drove a tiny purple car. None of it was adding up. "I just don't understand."

"I know. I should have brought you sooner... I should have explained things sooner, but I just..." I turned to see if she would say something else, but she didn't. She shook her head and led us inside where any further words I had in my vocabulary swiftly died off.

As soon as I walked in, the largest space greeted me. It was lit by a giant crystal chandelier hanging from the ceiling, and straight ahead of me was a double staircase. I was almost convinced that I'd open a door and find a library straight out of a Disney movie.

I was truly speechless. I wasn't sure if I should've been upset that she had hidden this from me, and I was more confused as to... how?! Math wasn't my strong suit, but I was pretty sure bookstore owners didn't make millions. Apparently, I didn't know jack shit, because there I was in basically a mini version of the White House.

She led me to a living room that looked bigger than the bookstore. She sat on a tan couch and motioned for me to sit next to her, which I obliged.

"The house was a gift," she started, and my eyes nearly fell out of my head.

"I'm sorry... a gift?!" Who the hell gave someone a mansion the size of the White House as a gift?!

She nodded. "When I moved here, my parents didn't want me staying with friends or in some strange hotel. They wanted me to be comfortable and have my own space."

"Naturally." I nodded, as if I had a fucking clue how to relate.

She sighed. "My father was a cybersecurity expert in the military. And my mother is the CEO of my grandparents' jewelry company.

"So you're like super rich? Richy Rich! No, wait! Regina Rich!"

She chuckled and kissed my cheek. "I inherited the money when I turned twenty-three. I purchased the bookstore with the money, but I have worked my ass off to get it where it is now. I don't flaunt my money. No one knows I live here besides my close friends, Skylar, and now you."

"Wait... Kaia doesn't know? She works for you. And what about Cara?"

She shook her head. "No, neither of them know. It took me almost two years of being with Skylar to bring her around and let her see all of me. I don't want to be treated differently because of my family's money, and it takes me a lot to trust someone enough to let them in. Fallon and Penelope are my family, and now Mackenzie is, of course, and while Kaia works for me, and I would consider us *friends*, as well as Cara, I don't know, I just..." She shook her head again, seemingly trying to shake whatever emotions were building up away.

It takes me a lot to trust someone enough to let them in... Her words kept replaying while she spoke. Her ex hadn't known about this big part of her life until they were together for years, and here I was, someone she hadn't even known that long, not really known, sitting on her couch while she opened up about an important part of herself she kept hidden from the world.

So many emotions were running through me. I had to fight hard to tamp down the tears that were so desperate to spill out.

"But why?" I asked softly. "Why keep this big part of your life hidden?"

She shrugged. "I don't know. I... I don't want someone to try and take advantage of me because they think I just have money to throw away. If I did, I wouldn't need to do a signing to get people in the door. I try not to use my family's money unless I absolutely need to. I don't want to depend on them for anything. They've already given me so much, most of which I didn't ask for and certainly don't want. I want to make my own way in the world."

"What did they give you that you don't want?" I asked, unable to help myself. She was opening up to me, and I would get every drop of information I could. Any scrap of what made Drea tick I would collect and hoard forever.

Chapter Thirty-Six

DREA

Tonight was a night of firsts, not only for Blair and me together, but for me personally. I'd roped Mackenzie into helping me plan my first official date with Blair at the aquarium, which was a success.

It had been absolutely perfect, even with Houdini clit-blocking me. He was so adorable, and Blair fell in love with him, so he was forgiven.

And now I was sitting on my couch with her. Skylar was the only woman I had brought back to my house, and it took me over a year of being with her to do that.

Yet, I was sitting at home with Blair, completely comfortable and at peace. I couldn't quite place it, but there was just something different about her. How I felt when I was with her, it wasn't even worth comparing her to my previous... situations with women. None of them held a candle to her.

"What did they give you that you didn't want?" Her question left a sharp pain in my chest. I hated talking about myself. I didn't want anyone else to see how fucked up I was, especially since I was almost thirty.

I sighed, not wanting to talk about my family, but not wanting to ignore her question either. She had already buried herself this deep into my skin, and I would've given her anything she asked for.

"My parents are far from perfect, no matter how much they pretend to be. They were married for almost fifteen years before they divorced, proving to me and my three sisters that nothing is forever. I learned that lesson pretty early on, so I've kind of kept everyone at arm's length."

"But why? I mean, you have an amazing group of friends, and you're doing well for yourself, so why hide so much of yourself from new people?"

She was so cute, and her genuine care for me made something in my chest soften. I had never felt this way about another person, platonic or otherwise. I never wanted to open my eyes and not see Blair smiling at me.

"I've found it to be a better solution than letting someone in only to inevitably be hurt in the end. My father taught me to never show weakness. Opening yourself up to vulnerability and the potential to be hurt is weak." I shrugged, as if it were a normal fact that was spilling from my lips and not a fucked-up thing to tell a child.

She took my hands in hers and caressed them sweetly, calming the storm brewing inside me. "That's dark, Dre. I'm sorry." I didn't hide my smile at hearing her call me Dre. It was the first time, and it sounded heavenly.

I shrugged as if it weren't a big deal. "Enough about me." I put my hand on her leg and relished the grin she gave from the contact. "I've been a terrible host. Can I get you something to drink?"

"I would love some water."

I led her to the kitchen, and she took a seat at the island. We'd definitely be utilizing it later. I handed her a bottle of water, and we both sat there, silently hydrating ourselves.

"Are you hungry? I think Charlotte put some leftovers in the fridge."

She blinked at me. I wasn't sure what I had said—

"Oh... Charlotte is my chef. Not my... I'm not... Blair, I'm not with anyone else."

I blushed, so embarrassed at my rambling, but I needed her to know. She was the only woman I wanted.

She nodded slowly before letting out a breath. "That's good, and no, I'm fine, thank you. I... for the record, I'm not either. And of course you have a chef. Do you have a butler too?" She chuckled and shook her head, and I was glad for the mood shift. This night had been perfect, and I wanted to keep it that way.

I laughed. "No, but I have a housekeeper, Stella. She only comes twice a week. None of the staff live here if that's what you're worried about. It's just us."

She blushed, and I loved the sight. "I wasn't worried, but that's good to know. I just can't believe I didn't know any of this about you. You live in a mansion, and you have 'staff.' I feel like we're so different. I... I feel like I don't know where I fit into your world here." She gestured around the large space, and I frowned at the worry on her face.

I set the glasses down and walked over to where she sat so perfectly perched on my barstool. I took her face in my hands and looked into her stunning hazel eyes.

"Blair Sterling," I started before I leaned in and captured her mouth in a sweet and gentle kiss. Like so many of our kisses before tonight, I treasured every swipe of our tongues as if they were the last. Every second we were connected was a second I wanted to last forever. I was reverently hers with every passing moment in time.

Reluctantly, I broke the kiss and smiled at her rapid breathing and flushed face. "You fit in everywhere. Please know that. If there was a part of my life you felt like you didn't fit into, I would simply change it."

She pulled me in for another kiss, and I instinctively placed my hands on her thighs, desperate to get those tights off. She pulled back and chuckled at my pouting expression. I wasn't ready to let her go.

Still, she hopped off the stool and handed me a glass of water while holding on to the other as she led us back to the living room.

I watched her make herself comfortable on my couch once again, and I couldn't help but smile at seeing her in my home. "So, what's your story? I mean... I know about your parents, but what about after that? Where did you go?"

The smile quickly fell from her face and she shifted, sitting up a little straighter on the couch. "Well, my grandmother, Amelia, took me and my brother in. He was fourteen at the time. He was with her at the time of the accident, so thankfully he wasn't hurt. She raised us until we left for college. She was amazing. We spent every Sunday baking in the kitchen. Christopher and I always put on little plays for her, and she never once rolled her eyes or seemed annoyed."

Her eyes started to fill with unshed tears, and I wanted to reach out and wipe them away, but she kept going.

"She was so supportive when I told her I wanted to be a writer. I was nineteen, and she had all the faith in the world in me. She bought at least three copies of every book I released for the first three years of my career before... before she passed."

Her eyes had released the pools of water they held, and I leaned over to wipe some of them away. I hated seeing her like this. I would've given anything if it meant she was never sad again. God, I had it so bad for her.

"I'm sorry, darling. She sounded wonderful. I'm sure she knows what an amazing job she did raising a perfect woman."

She huffed out a sobbed laugh. "I don't know about perfect, but she was pretty wonderful."

I reached for her, grabbing her chin and tilting her gaze up to meet my soft eyes. I needed her to hear every word I was about to say and really believe them.

"I need you to listen very carefully to me, Ms. Sterling," I said, using my other hand to caress her side. "You are as close to perfect as a person can get, do you understand?"

She blushed and looked away, but I knew she didn't believe me. I would just have to take matters into my own hands and show her just how I felt about her.

Without another word, I grabbed her chin again and turned her head toward me. I needed her to look into my eyes and believe my truth. I stared into her eyes for a few seconds, hoping to convey everything I was too afraid to say.

Finally, I had enough of torturing myself, and I leaned in to kiss her. Feeling her lips on mine, her hands on my thighs, felt otherworldly. I needed so much more in that moment. I needed everything.

My hands left her face as I grew more desperate to explore the rest of her. Both of us were wearing too many clothes, and I was going to fix that very soon.

Blair broke the kiss as my hands started roaming underneath her shirt. "Dre," she whispered while licking her lips.

"Yes, darling?" I loved calling her that, and I loved the response it got. My voice was a similar decibel as hers, as I was still trying to catch my breath. I tried to show that nothing affected me and I had a tough outer shell, but for Blair Sterling, I was a total mess.

"Take me upstairs." I didn't have to be told twice. I would've taken her anywhere she wanted to go.

"You know I love how needy you get." She chuckled and kissed me again, making me forget everything we had been talking about.

I broke the kiss, but not before taking her tongue and sucking on it like I knew drove her wild. She let out a little moan and gripped my arms tighter. I grinned, knowing that little move would be rewarded later.

We stood up and made our way up the stairs. It was times like these that I regretted not living in a studio apartment. We got halfway up the stairs, and I had to stop us. "Stop, Blair."

She turned around and frowned at me. "Is everything okay?"

I shook my head. "No, it's not. Take off your tights. Now."

She took her bottom lip into her mouth and grinned, doing as I commanded and removing her bottoms and showing me all of her.

I groaned and kissed her. She melted into the kiss, and I sat her down, knowing her legs were about to become very unstable.

We were only feet away from my bedroom, as it was the one at the very top of the stairs, but I didn't care. I needed her, and I was going to have her right there on the stairs.

"Drea." She gasped when my impatient fingers found their way to her already drenched pussy. I was rubbing slow circles around her clit, making her grip me tighter.

"I love when you say my name, sweetheart, but I'd rather hear you scream it instead," I teased before I entered two fingers inside her. She was so ready for it they went in with ease, and I could feel myself growing wetter by the second at the feeling. I wanted to put my whole hand inside her. I wanted to go as deep as possible. I wanted to be as connected to her as a person could be.

As she clenched around me, I started sucking at her collarbone, determined to leave a mark. I wanted the whole world to know Blair was mine.

"Don't stop, baby. That feels so good." Her words came out in breaths and in between moans. Blair was vocal, and I reveled in it. I didn't think I could ever get enough of her. Of any part of her.

"You are so fucking perfect. Don't ever forget that. God, I love seeing you like this. Such a mess, and only for me."

I started fucking her harder in the way I knew she liked. And when I curled my fingers to hit the right spot, her moans told me I was on the right track to seeing her come apart.

"Shit. I'm about to come. Fuck!" As soon as the words were out, so were my fingers.

She gasped at the sudden loss of contact, and her whine was the sweetest sound. "I was so close."

I grinned and stood her up. "I know, baby. I know." I said nothing else as I grabbed the side of her face and kissed her, walking us the rest of the way up the stairs.

I didn't break the kiss until I felt the bed hit the back of my legs, and I sat down, pulling her down on top of me.

She looked around the room, taking it all in. I knew I would think about what it meant having her in my room, but right now, I didn't want to think about anything else but her and me making a mess on my sheets.

"Blair? You can see the rest of the house later. Right now, I want to see the rest of you."

She gave me one of her heart-stopping smiles, and seconds later, she was completely naked in front of me. The sight never failed to take my breath away.

She didn't know it yet, but this wasn't just sex for me. I wanted to take my time with her tonight and show her what she meant to me, even when I didn't have the words.

She helped relieve me of my own restricting clothing, and soon she was the one who couldn't pull her eyes away.

"Like what you see, darling?" I asked, knowing damn well she did. The way she looked at me in that moment made me feel like the most beautiful woman in the world. Which wasn't true when she was in the room. Everyone paled in comparison while standing next to her.

"Oh, you know I do." She grinned and made her way onto the bed.

"Come up here," I demanded. I wanted her in my favorite spot—on my face.

She hesitated for a second and pulled her bottom lip between her teeth. "Is everything all right, Blair?" I asked. I was starting to get concerned. Usually, she loved that position.

She shook her head, and I sat up a little more. "Yeah, yeah. Everything's fine. I just... I was wondering if we could try something new? I mean, I *really* love that position, but I was wanting to do the same to you... at the same time."

My eyes lit up at her suggestion. I loved feeling any part of her on me, but feeling her at the same time I'd be devouring her? "Hell yes we can absolutely do that!"

She let out a small laugh. "Are you sure? I know we've never done it before, and I—"

"Blair?" I cut off her hesitation with a crook of my finger. "Get up here."

She still hesitated, but I let her gather herself before she eventually made her way up to me.

When she turned around and settled herself in between my legs, her ass bare to me, I wanted to cry. I loved every part of her, and I was going to enjoy every second of this.

"Are you ready, baby?" I asked, wanting to make sure she was comfortable.

She nodded, and when I felt the first swipe of her tongue on me, my eyes rolled back. Fucking shit! I hadn't been touched like that in so long I didn't think I'd be able to take my time with her like I wanted. I wanted to fucking devour her. To show her just how much I needed her. How much I craved her.

I opened my legs further for her and grabbed her hips, preparing to have my way with her.

"Fuck," she moaned when I licked her clit before gently sucking it.

"Shit, baby. That feels incredible." I couldn't describe how it felt. Devouring her perfect pussy while a similar sensation was happening to me? I didn't know why we hadn't done this before, but I wanted to only be doing it for the rest of my life.

She moaned when I inserted my tongue inside her. I want to drink up every drop she could give me. She tasted sweet and so fucking mine.

No matter what I told myself, she *was* mine, and every part of me belonged to her. She could do whatever she wanted to me as long as she didn't break my heart. I had no intention of breaking hers, but I'd seen what could happen when someone claimed to love you and wanted to guard your heart forever. It never worked out.

I was scared. Hell, I was terrified, but you couldn't choose who your heart wanted, and all I could do now was just go along for the ride and hope we wouldn't crash. That would all be a problem for future Drea, because present Drea was getting her shit rocked by the most perfect woman to exist.

When she pushed two fingers inside me, I moaned into her, ready to come apart.

This scene would've played in my memory for years to come. She was breaking down every defense I'd ever had until I was completely surrounded by her and her alone.

I was seconds away from coming, and I didn't know if it was from the feeling of her tongue and fingers on me, or from the taste of her and the feel of her from behind. It was probably a mixture of the two, but it didn't matter. As long as I could taste her when she came.

She came first, but I wasn't too far behind. I held on to her, desperate not to miss a single second of her orgasm.

"Fuck, Blair," I groaned as my orgasm hit just as hard. "Don't stop, baby. Please don't fucking stop." I loved the reaction she always gave when I squirted for her. It didn't happen all the time, but when it did, she loved it.

Eventually, and against my protests, she came up for air and tumbled off me and onto the bed, trying to catch her breath. She was so beautiful in that moment. Freshly fucked and thoroughly satiated had never looked so good on another person.

It still blew my mind that she chose me. That even knowing every-thing about me and my past, about my fucked-up family and my views on relationships, she still chose to give me a chance, to give whatever this was a chance. I didn't know how I could've ever repaid her for that gift. It was a gift I didn't know I needed, and one I would cherish.

"Holy shit. I can't... I just... shit!"

I chuckled and kissed her forehead. "My thoughts exactly, love."

She looked up at me and held my face, giving me a soft smile. "Thank you," she whispered.

I frowned at her. "You're thanking me? I should be thanking you.

You're definitely getting a gift basket tomorrow. That was fucking incredible." In a quieter voice, I added, "*You* are incredible."

I wanted to say so much more, but I couldn't. I wasn't strong enough to admit out loud how much of me she had. How much more I wanted to give her. I wanted to give her everything.

She blushed, and I had no choice but to kiss her again. When she bit my lip and her hands traveled to trace circles around my nipples, I knew our time for conversation was over.

Chapter Thirty-Seven

BLAIR

Screwed. I was completely screwed. There was no other way to put it. I was so in love with Drea. There was nothing else to call it, and I couldn't tell her.

I was too scared she wouldn't feel the same way. That was not how Drea lived her life. She didn't settle down with one person. Even in her last relationship, she couldn't commit. She loved, but she couldn't be in love. I knew she cared for me, but how deep did that run?

I didn't want to think about it anymore, so I slipped out of bed before I got too comfortable and let the words slip out.

She was still sleeping soundly when I left, and she looked so perfect I didn't want to wake her. Instead, I grabbed my notebook and a pen and headed to the patio.

I always carried a notebook if I didn't have my laptop in case inspiration struck. Her patio was enclosed, so I could feel like I was outside without actually being outside.

I had wasted about two sheets of paper by the time Drea came out. I was trying out ideas for a title, and they were all terrible.

I warmed when I felt soft lips on the side of my neck and smelled the delicious scent of coffee. "Mmm, good morning." I turned into her waiting lips.

She kissed me softly, and I wanted to melt into her touch. "Good morning, sweetheart. What are you working on?" She sat the coffee down, and I scooted over on the couch so she could sit.

"I'm working on a title, but so far I have nothing." I groaned and snuggled into her warm body. She had put on some plaid pajama pants and a tank top before she'd come out.

"I know you'll find one you love. Do you want me to leave you to it?" She got up to leave, but I stopped her.

"No!" I squeezed her tighter so she couldn't leave. "I need a break, anyway." I looked up at her, and she smiled.

"Okay, then." She kissed my forehead.

My smile fell as I whispered, "Please don't leave me." I hoped she picked up on the meaning behind my words.

Don't leave me out here. Don't leave me for someone else...

"Blair, I'm not going anywhere, okay?" I snuggled deeper into her embrace, wanting to believe her words.

I sat there for another hour, trying and still failing to think of a good title, before my alarm went off, reminding me of my meeting with Cara.

After Drea insisted on helping me take a shower, I called a car to take me to Cara's. I was thankful she wanted to stay in today and not go to some fancy restaurant.

The past few days with Drea had expended more than enough energy, and I was exhausted, but in the best way. I'd never complain about being too tired from spending time with her or having way too much sex.

Cara was already out on her porch when I pulled up, and I was grateful we didn't track each other's locations.

"Hey, doll!" She waved to me as I paid the driver and headed up the driveway.

My steps quickened until I was basically sprinting to give her a hug. I had missed her. "Hey, I'm sorry I'm late."

I would've gotten there sooner if Drea hadn't "helped" me in the shower. I had to learn to control myself around her. One look at her naked body, one lick of her lips, and I was against the wall, coming and screaming her name.

"God, I've missed you, doll! I feel like it's been way too long since we've had a chance to spend some time together without work!" Cara's voice broke me from my horny thoughts, and I shook my head, bringing myself back to the moment.

I had to agree. The past few months had been crazy busy for both of us, and while I loved my job, I missed my best friend.

"I know! What's been going on with you outside of work? Today is a no-work day!"

She laughed, leading us to her couch. "Well, I've been going on a few dates, but nothing too exciting. I don't know what's wrong with me. Am I trying too hard? Am I looking in the wrong places? I feel like all I do is go on dates, but I don't *date*, you know?" Her smile fell, and I reached over to place a comforting hand on her arm.

"I'm sorry, Car. I don't think you're trying too hard or looking in the wrong places at all. You're doing what everyone else does. You'll find your person, I'm sure of it. If you're feeling lost or frustrated about it, then maybe it's time for a break? They say once you stop looking, that's when you find what you need." I shrugged, but it was true. At least for me.

Once I stopped trying to find someone in bars or on dating apps, that was when I found Drea, although she was right there all along and I just didn't see her.

She exhaled sharply. "Maybe you're right. It's getting to be exhausting, and I've been feeling deflated about it all. Maybe I should focus more on my career for a while. Anyway, enough about me, I want to talk about you. Your life is more exciting than mine. How was your trip? How's Chris?"

I snorted. "You think my life is exciting? That's sad. And what trip? Chris is fine." I gave her a confused look.

"Your trip out of town? You said there was a family thing and that's why you couldn't hang out."

Shit. I had completely forgotten about that. I should've known she would bring it up. "Oh. Yeah, Chris is good. He just needed help with the boys," I lied. I hated lying to her more, but I couldn't tell her where I really was.

"Right. Is everything okay with you? You've been acting kind of weird for a while."

"I'm fine. I've just been, you know, writing and preparing for the book signing. You know how I get when I work with Drea."

I really hoped she would drop it. I honestly didn't think I was acting any different, and I didn't think she would've called me out on it if I was. She was always so busy with work and trying to find her person that I honestly hadn't thought she was paying much attention to me at all these days.

"You guys seem to be getting along better these days, huh? Especially at our movie night. She saved you from falling? Months ago she probably would've been the one to push you down herself."

I laughed nervously. "Uh, yeah, probably."

"So, how are things going with your mystery date? Are you going to tell me who it is yet? When do I get to meet her? Or him? I feel like I don't know you these days, Blair."

She looked sad, and I was so tempted to tell her everything, but I was scared. I didn't want to do it without Drea with me, and I didn't know how she would react. I decided to give her a little something.

"Things are still fresh, but you'll meet her soon, I promise. I don't want to jinx anything with us right now. I'm sorry I've been acting so weird. The signing will be over soon, and then it'll be time for our recharge vacations." I smiled, hoping she would believe me.

I sighed in relief when she seemed to. "Good. I want to meet her, Blair, and I'm serious! I understand things are new for you, and I don't want to ruin your happiness. That's all I want for you. You're my best friend and I love you. I'm looking forward to a much-needed break."

I stood up and gave her a hug. "I love you too, Cara. I'm sorry if I haven't been a good friend lately."

"Oh, honey. You've been a great friend, as always. I just want to meet the woman who makes your eyes sparkle when I bring it up. I haven't seen you this happy since Gwen, and I want to know who is responsible."

My chest tightened at the mention of my ex. I hadn't heard that name in over six years. After we'd broken up, she'd moved to Montana, and I hadn't seen or spoken to her since, and I had no plans to. Even before I met Drea, that chapter of my life closed and I wanted to move on.

We were together for three years, and I kept waiting for her to propose, but she never did. We never had screaming matches or anything, but we would always argue about little things.

I had overheard her talking to someone on the phone, and she'd referred to me as her "friend." We had a long conversation about it, and I found out she wasn't out to her family and wasn't sure she ever would be. I understood that, and I was patient with her.

Coming out was never easy, and I wanted to be there for her and give her whatever she needed. A year later she told me she was going home for the holidays and was taking some guy who was pretending to be her boyfriend.

We had a long fight after that, and I finally stood my ground. I loved her, but I just couldn't do it anymore. I couldn't hide our relationship, especially if she was making no moves to change things.

I shook my head, letting that memory go. I wanted to tell Cara so badly about what had been going on in my life. I was happy with Drea, and I wanted her to know. But we'd agreed to wait until after the signing to tell her.

I only had to wait a few more weeks. Things were going to be even more crazy the closer we got, so I was sure it'd be easier to hide it from her until then.

"Thank you for this today. I needed a break, but I need to get back to work."

"You work too hard, Cara. You need to take a vacation."

She laughed. "In a few weeks, I will. Do you need a ride home?"

I nodded. Usually I'd take a car home, but I wanted just a little more time with my best friend. "That would be great. Thanks."

It wasn't a long drive back to my house, but I was anxious she would try to bring up Drea again. If she did, I wasn't sure I'd have any more lies to give.

Chapter Thirty-Eight

DREA

When Cara called me last week to invite me to a wine tasting, I was all for it. She had come up with the idea to get Blair a bottle of wine to celebrate the book signing.

She didn't need to know that I had already planned on having Blair open something else on that night. She could enjoy the wine while I enjoyed her.

Between getting ready for the signing, running the store, and adding Blair to my to-do list, I was looking forward to a relaxing night.

When I walked into Queer Quarters, I headed for the bar and ordered a whiskey while I waited.

"Do you want a refill?" Rylee asked. Rylee, who was Mackenzie's best friend, was also the barista at Brewed Awakening.

I laughed. "God, no. I'm here for the wine tasting. If I mix my drinks too much, I'll be crawling out of here! I'm just waiting for Cara. She wants to get a bottle for Blair to congratulate her on the book signing, so I'm helping out."

"Oh, *Cara* wants to get her a bottle?"

I rolled my eyes. "Oh, shut up!"

"What?" She shrugged innocently. "I think it's cute you want to do something nice for your girlfriend."

"Aren't there other patrons you could be bothering?" I adored Rylee, but I didn't want to talk about Blair with the chance Cara could walk in at any second.

She smirked. "Funny how you didn't deny she's your girlfriend. But actually, I do need to check on my other customers, so you got lucky this time. Let me know if you need anything else."

"Of course, love. Thanks." I let out a massive sigh of relief when she walked away. I wasn't ready to label what we had yet, especially not without talking to Blair about it first.

It was crazy to think about how much things had changed since two years ago. I celebrated my best friend's birthday. I went through a breakup while she had gotten back into a relationship. She got engaged while I stayed single and worked in the store. Blair came into my life and completely turned things around for me. My best friend was married, and my other best friend was thinking about children.

Marriage and kids were never on any list I had, except for one of the things I would never do, but being with Blair has made me reevaluate some of my previous opinions on things.

And now here we were, a few months after we'd started working together again, happy and getting ready for a big accomplishment for Blair. I was finally in a good place in life and I was happy, really happy.

I had been waiting only five minutes when a familiar voice interrupted my thoughts. "Hey, doll!" Cara slid into the barstool next to me with a hug.

"Hey, love. You're right on time. I just got done with my drink."

She sat down and ordered a gin and tonic and we spent a few minutes catching up on life.

"I really needed this tonight. It's been non-stop work between my other clients, and you and Blair... speaking of Blair, you know she still hasn't told me who she's been seeing? I'm starting to wonder why she won't tell me. It's not like I would judge her. Has she said anything to you?"

I choked on my drink, the contents coming out of my mouth and nose and spraying onto the bar top. That was the last thing I was expecting her to bring up, and something inside my chest cracked at the hurt in her voice.

"No, she hasn't said anything, but we aren't that close. I wouldn't worry about it. Maybe it's just not that serious? I don't know."

I hoped she would buy the lie. She had no reason to believe I was remotely involved with Blair.

She shrugged. "I guess. I just want her to be happy, you know? Hopefully she'll tell me some day."

She looked down at her drink, and I wondered if she could feel the guilt radiating off me. I hated hiding this from her, especially seeing how hurt she was by Blair not telling her something so important about her life. If Fallon did the same thing, I couldn't imagine how broken I would have felt.

I nodded and took another long sip of my drink. "Speaking of, how's your dating life going?" I needed to shift the topic of conversation anywhere besides Blair, and I genuinely wanted to know what was going on in Cara's life.

"You know how it is, going on dates but never dating. I still have hope, though. Someday I'm sure my person will show up and sweep me off my feet."

"Don't worry, they will. You're amazing and anyone would be lucky to have you!"

The host of the wine tasting came around and brought us all a tray with half a dozen tiny cups. Each cup was accompanied by a label, indicating the name of the wine.

They introduced themselves and told us a little about their winery and what they did there. It was really interesting to hear about, and I made a mental note to take Blair sometime. She wasn't really a big drinker, but it still sounded like something romantic for us to do together.

Cara and I started swirling and smelling the wine as if we had the slightest clue what to look for. We really just wanted to have an excuse to drink and catch up, as well as find something to give to Blair as a celebration for the book signing.

"What about you? I haven't heard any of your crazy forgotten dildo stories in a while. Are you seeing anyone?" Cara asked. If I had been drinking anything, I would have choked again.

I hated lying to her just as much as Blair did, but I'd made a promise, so I laughed and put a blanket over the truth. "Oh, you know me. Work keeps me busy."

She gasped. "Good! I have someone I think you will like!"

I groaned. I should've seen this coming. This was my payback for setting her up with Fallon, I was sure of it. "I don't know, Cara. I'm really busy with the store, and I'm supposed to be celibate, remember?"

It didn't matter that that orgasmic boat had sailed a long time ago, and if I had my way, after experiencing sex with Blair, I would never be celibate again.

She scoffed, taking another drink. "You don't have to have sex to go on dates, Drea. You've been so busy with the store that you need to take time for yourself, and I have a few friends I think would be good for you. My friend Kelsie is—"

"Cara, please stop. I'm not interested, okay? Can we talk about something else?"

What I really wanted to say was, *I'm sorry, Cara, I can't go out with any of your friends. I am with Blair and she is the only one I want.*

But of course, I couldn't say that, so I had to hope she would take my word and just leave well enough alone.

"But why not? You're the queen of dating. It's so weird for you to be single. Just go on one date. What could it hurt?"

Clearly that wasn't happening. At this point the wine was mixing with the whiskey from earlier, and it was starting to affect my nerves and I was getting frustrated, so my voice raised a little. "Because, Cara, I don't want to go out with anyone, okay? Just drop it!"

"Why? Give me one good reason why you won't even consider—"

"Because I'm sleeping with Blair!"

Cara's drunken smile fell, and she became dangerously quiet.

Shit, shit, fuck, shit!

She slowly sat her drink down and cleared her throat. I was in so much trouble. Fuck!

"I'm sorry, what was that?" she asked. She folded her hands and placed them on the table. I wasn't sure why the move terrified me. Maybe because she looked like a very pissed mob boss.

"I mean... I..." I stammered, trying to find the words.

I sighed in defeat. Having said the words I wasn't supposed to say, there was no point in trying to take them back. "I can't go out with anyone because I've been seeing Blair."

"You and Blair?" She shook her head and let out an incredulous laugh. "Not *my* Blair. You hate her. You have made that perfectly clear to me time and time again. You've made my job so insanely fucking difficult for years because of this fact. I just don't understand. You're seeing *that* Blair?"

I sighed. "I don't know another Blair, do you? Yes, Cara."

She scoffed. "You have no right to get an attitude about this, Drea. If anyone is going to be upset, it's going to be me! I literally just asked you if you knew anything about who she was seeing, and you sat there and blatantly lied to me?! How long has this been going on?"

I bit my lip, not wanting to be honest. I was not in a clear headspace to be having this conversation. "That doesn't matter. Let's just take the wine and go—"

"You lying directly to my face doesn't matter? Are you serious right now? Do you just not care about anyone else's feelings anymore or what?"

"Cara, I—"

"How long have you been sleeping with my client, Drea?!"

"I'm sorry, I don't really see how that is any of your business. We are both adults, and she is more than your client, Cara. She is your best friend."

"You may be adults, but you and my 'best friend' are hiding things from me and fucking with my business. How long?!"

"For months! Is that what you want to hear? I have been making your precious client come anywhere I get the chance. In my office, on her couch, against her door, even in her pool. I was the one naked in her bed the night you showed up. Those clothes all over her living room floor? Yeah, those were mine. She was probably making me come as you were pulling up, actually. Is there anything else you would like to know? Do you want to know what kind of strap I used when I fucked her against my desk? Do you want to know the sounds she makes as she begs for me to make her come?"

Okay, so maybe I didn't need to go that far. I knew I should've stayed home. I should have made some excuse as to why I couldn't come out tonight, but it wouldn't have mattered anyway. This altercation was bound to happen one way or another. Perhaps not in a drunken admission and not that vulgar, but it was too late to take it back now.

"Wow, really classy! That's exactly why you two being together is a terrible idea!"

"And what is that supposed to mean?!"

"You know what it means, Drea. Blair isn't Skylar. She isn't going to wait around until you decide she's good enough to keep. She isn't someone you can just fuck when you feel like it and then move on to the next. She's better than that, or at least I thought she was."

"Excuse me? How dare you! You don't know anything about—"

"That is enough!"

I froze at the angry voice and turned around, wanting this to all be a dream.

"Blair... what are you doing here?"

Blair looked between us confused, which told me she hadn't heard what I'd said, thank fuck.

"Rylee said you two were wasted and screaming, and asked me to come get you," Kaia answered.

Blair scowled, looking between us. "What is wrong with you two, fighting in the middle of a bar?! What is going on?"

"Don't come in here acting all high and mighty. When were you going to tell me you were fucking her?!" Cara stammered out, pointing at me.

Blair blinked. "What... What are you talking about?"

I turned to Kaia. "Why the hell would you bring her here?!"

Kaia frowned and opened her mouth, but Cara interrupted. "Don't change the subject. When were you going to tell me you two had been fucking for months? Everywhere, according to Drea. I cannot believe she was there the night I stopped by, and you hid it from me!"

"Cara, I'm so—"

"I'm supposed to ask what strap she uses, but I really don't need to know that. And I *definitely* don't need to know the sounds you make."

Blair gaped at me, darkness in those once soft hazel eyes. "Are you serious?!"

Cara shook her head. "I can't believe you, Blair! I expected this from Drea, but not from you. I really thought you had more self-respect than this."

"Excuse me? What is that supposed to mean?" I glared at Cara, trying to ignore the anger in Blair's eyes while my own was boiling to the surface.

"It means that fucking around and disrespecting the people who care about you is kind of your thing. Look what happened to Skylar. She—"

"That was a long time ago, and this is different."

"Different?" She scoffed. "Please, you're still the same person you were when Skylar dumped you. Crawling into anyone's open bed. I just didn't think Blair would be stupid enough to fall for it, but I guess desperation can get the best of us some—"

"That is enough! You can say what you want about me, but you will not disrespect Blair!" I stood up and took a step closer. I was seconds away from putting my hands on someone I had respected for so long.

"Like you didn't just do the same thing, Drea! Honestly, you are such a—"

"Drea, you know I love you, but you guys need to go," Rylee said in a polite but authoritative voice.

"We were just leaving," Kaia spoke out, grabbing me by the hand while Blair tried to get Cara.

"Don't fucking touch me. I don't know where that hand has been. I'm going! Goodnight, Rylee!"

"Sorry, Rylee," Kaia said apologetically.

Once we got outside, Blair refused to even look in my direction. "Blair, please look at me," I pleaded. This whole night had just taken a twisted turn.

"Kaia, can you please take me home?" she said, completely ignoring me.

"Of course. We can get your bag from the store on the way. Cara, do you need a ride?"

She scoffed. "With those two? Not a chance. I'll find my own ride."

"Cara, can we—"

"No, Blair, we can't! I don't even have the words for how angry I am. You've been going behind my back and lying to me for months?! Do you have any idea how that makes me look, how that makes *you* look? Were you really out of town when I wanted to get together, or were you two having a fuck fest?!"

Blair blushed and sighed. "I *was* out of town... at Fallon and Mackenzie's wedding." She winced.

"They know too?! This is insane!"

When I saw the look in Cara's eyes, I wanted to take a step closer to Blair, but I knew it would make the situation worse.

"Cara, I'm really sorry. We didn't mean for any of this to happen." I was desperately trying to diffuse the situation, but all I could think about was getting Blair to look at me. Even just a glance would calm the fire spreading through my veins.

Cara shook her head and scoffed. "I can't fucking believe this! I really hope the sex was worth it, because it may have just cost you your publishing deal and our friendship. Fuck you both!"

"Cara, you can't be serious? This is what you wanted. You wanted us to get along—"

"You think I wanted this?! You think I wanted my best friend to lie to me? You think I wanted to find out that my best friend was sleeping her way for a check? You think I wanted everyone in my fucking life to be sneaking around behind my back and lying to me? Get real!"

"Cara!"

Cara stormed off before Blair could get a reply, and she turned to me, eyes turning dark. "Real fucking nice, Drea."

We all got into Kaia's car without another word.

The car ride was dead silent until we arrived at the bookstore. "I'll be just a second, Kaia," Blair said as she got out of the car, not even glancing my way.

I got out of the car, following behind her. I was going to find a way to fix this somehow.

When I opened the front door, I spoke. "Blair, I'm—"

She walked right past me into the store, ignoring me completely.

"Blair!" I called after her, but she didn't turn around. "Blair, just stop and talk to me, please."

This time, she stopped in the center of the store and turned around slowly. "Talk to you? You want me to talk to you? I barely want to look at you, let alone speak to you, Drea, so why don't you start? Where did you get the fucking nerve to speak about me like I am just some whore you can play around with? Is that really all I am to you? Just someone to screw when you're bored?"

I frowned. "Blair, of course not. I wasn't thinking. We had a lot to drink, and things got way out of hand." I took a few steps closer to her. When I got closer, I saw tears starting to form behind her eyes. "I'm so sorry."

She scoffed. "You're sorry? So am I, Drea. I hope you're happy, because my career is probably over now! What were you thinking?"

"It just came out! She was trying to get me to go out with her friends. I kept telling her no, but she wouldn't stop pressing, and finally I couldn't take it anymore! I just blurted it out in the heat of the moment."

"Well, maybe you should go out with them."

"I don't want to go out with any of them, Blair. Just... let me fix this, please."

"There is nothing to fix. I knew you had commitment issues, but damn, that was taking it to another level. If you aren't happy with someone, just end it, Drea. You don't need to get drunk and make a fool out of yourself in order to do so."

She started to walk away, but I grabbed her wrist, stopping her abruptly. She yanked her arm away and looked at me, tears streaming down her face.

"Blair—"

"Don't you dare touch me! I am not yours to touch. Apparently I never was."

"I'm sorry, please," I begged. I couldn't hide it as my voice mirrored the cracking in my chest.

"I... I can't." Her voice broke, and I hated myself a little bit more with every passing second. How had I fucked up this badly?

I watched her walk away without another word. I waited until I saw Kaia's car drive off before I slumped against the counter, and let the darkness take over until I felt something wet and warm slide down my face and onto the floor.

I was sitting in my office when the door opened. It had been over an hour since Blair left, and I was embarrassed that a small part of me hoped she had come back.

"Blair's home safely. Do you want to talk about it?" Kaia's sweet voice used to cheer me up, but now, mixed with the whiskey and the wine, all it did was fuel my internal fire.

"So you can go run and tell everyone everything? I don't think so."

"Drea, no, of course not. I—"

"Why on earth would you bring her with you knowing Cara didn't know anything about us?!" I yelled. "You know what, it doesn't matter now. It's done. Just leave so I can be alone."

"Drea, please talk—"

"I said leave, Kaia! I don't want to talk, especially not to someone who couldn't keep a secret if you paid them!"

I must have been really drunk, because I could have sworn I heard Kaia curse at me.

"What?" I asked.

"You heard me. I said fuck you!" Nope, I definitely heard it that time.

In the five years I'd known Kaia, I had never, and I did literally mean never, heard that woman say a bad word about anyone, and certainly not those words.

"First of all, I don't know if you forgot that I have been keeping your secret about whatever you two were doing even long before you asked me not to tell anyone. Do you not realize these walls are thin?" A slight blush appeared on my face. No, no, I had not realized...

"I heard everything, but I kept quiet because I respected you and it wasn't my business to tell. But that doesn't matter anymore. You aired your own dirty laundry."

"We may be friends, Kaia, but I am still your boss, and you will—"

"Oh, don't play the boss card... God, I am so sick of this, Drea! I cover for you when you are hungover after your random hookups. I hear you bitch and bitch and bitch about Blair for months, yet you still work with her and make all of us deal with the tension between you two. I had plans with a friend, but I canceled them to help Blair while you were out getting drunk and insulting her! Rylee called me to come get you and said you two were yelling in the bar, and Blair insisted on coming. She told me what you were saying about Blair, but I didn't tell her because I was loyal to you and I would never do that, even if she deserved to know what you really think of her."

"Excuse me? You don't get to—"

"I have canceled plans to be here for you when you needed me the most, and you don't appreciate it! You have never once shown you give a shit about me, Drea."

I had never seen this side of Kaia, and any other night I would have been taken aback. But tonight was just a never-ending shit storm, and I was not in the mood to be disrespected in my own store.

I stood up. "Then leave! Just like everyone I care about in my life, fucking leave! I don't need to take this, and I don't need you!"

"They leave because you push them away! You pushed Skylar away because of your selfishness, and now you've pushed Blair away. Are you that blinded by your own self-importance that you can't see the hold you had on that woman? She is devastated over you, and you don't care. Did you even care about her at all, or were you just using her to get over Skylar because she was convenient and—"

"That is enough, Kaia! I will not stand here while you question me about my relationship with Blair, which is none of your concern, by the way!" I wouldn't stand for her talking to me that way. She had no right.

"What relationship? You don't have one anymore, and your friendship with Cara is certainly not doing any better. You did this to yourself, Drea, and now you have to live with the consequences, alone, because I'm done."

"With what, this conversation? Good, shut the door on your way out."

"No, with all of it. I am done being your punching bag. I'm done being your servant you think you can call at all hours, and I am done being a witness to your self-destruction." She dropped her keys on my desk and walked out, slamming the door behind her.

She was right, and I had no right to be angry with her. She'd just happened to get caught in the line of fire. I wasn't blind to Blair's feelings for me. I should have told her how I felt. I should have done a lot of things, and now I wouldn't get the chance. I really fucked up, but I did this to myself—

Something I said earlier gave me pause. My relationship with Blair...

Relationship. In my twenty-nine years of existence, I had never once so casually referred to a situation I was in as a relationship. But I had said it to Kaia without batting an eye. Without even so much as a thought. Blair had integrated herself into a part of my life, my heart, and I had so willingly accepted it.

But that was what we had... what we used to have. I had been in a relationship, and I'd ruined it. I was so undenyably in love with Blair, and I'd driven her away.

Not three seconds after the door closed, the sound of glass breaking filled the room as I picked up the wine bottle we had bought for Blair and threw it against the door.

Chapter Thirty-Nine

BLAIR

Walking into Cara's office at ten on a Monday morning was not my idea of a good time. After everything happened, we still hadn't spoken. All my calls and texts had gone unanswered. Drea's messages had been the same.

I refused to talk to her. I didn't even want to think about her, but I didn't have control over that. From the second I woke up to a text from Drea—

> Drea: Good morning, beautiful. Please call me. I'm so sorry.

—until I went to bed with a text from Drea:

> Drea: Goodnight. I'm so sorry.

I ignored her for a week straight before the messages and calls stopped coming in. Part of me was relieved when she stopped reaching out, but the other part missed them. I wanted to forget everything that had happened between us, all the feelings that weren't there before.

Cara emailed me prior to this weekend, requiring my presence for a "mandatory meeting," which was where I was about to walk in.

I knocked on her office door and stood there with shaky legs. My palms were clammy, and my heart was pounding out of my chest. I had a strong feeling I knew what this meeting was going to be about, and I didn't want to attend it.

"Come in." A dry voice on the other side answered after the second knock. I really wanted to turn around and run off. Confrontations and I were not best friends, and I knew this wasn't going to be a lovely little chat between us. I wasn't even sure Cara and I were still friends at this point, and I was too afraid to find out.

"Hey, Cara... you wanted to see me?" I asked nervously.

"Sit down." Another quick reply. No sign of her usually chipper demeanor.

I didn't want to. I wanted to go back to when I first started having feelings for Drea and tell Cara. I wanted to go back to before I caught feelings for her to begin with. Maybe I wouldn't be hurting so much if none of this ever happened. But then I wouldn't have lived through all the amazing moments with her, either. I didn't know which was worse.

I sat down and rubbed my hands together, trying to get my legs to stop shaking. "Cara, please let me start by saying that I am *so* sorry you had to find out like that. It—"

"Save your breath." She stopped my apology with a hand. "Do you have any idea of the situation you have put me in? I have been your publisher for seven years, and your friend for almost as long. The fact that you felt the need to hide this from me hurts the most. Not to mention, you two have put me through *hell* these last few years! Bickering and creating hostile working environments, even just a few months ago! And now all the sudden you're dating, fucking, what?"

"I am really sorry. It all happened so fast, and I know I should have told you sooner, but it's over now, so none of that even matters."

"See, that's where you're wrong. It does matter, Blair. It's unprofes-

239

sional, it's disrespectful, and I cannot, in good conscience, keep that kind of person in my life, business or otherwise."

"Seriously? You can't just drop me over a little disagreement. What about the book signing? It's next month."

"A little disagreement? Blair, you were sleeping around with a business partner, and you lied to me. So yes, I can, and I am!"

"We didn't lie. We just didn't tell you, and this is why. We knew you would react like this!"

"Excuse me? So you two made it a point to discuss hiding a big part of your life from me? Isn't that perfect?!"

"And I wasn't sleeping with her for a check, Cara. I'm in love with her!" This was not the time or place I wanted to tell my best friend that I was in love, but she wasn't giving me much of a choice in the matter.

She continued, not caring at all that this whole situation was killing me. "As far as the book signing is concerned, it's too close for us to be able to cancel, so we are still going through with it. But effective two weeks after it's over, your publishing contract is terminated, and our friendship is done... starting now."

I looked at her, desperation in my eyes. "Cara, please don't do this. I'm sorry," I whispered.

During the whole meeting, Cara was professional and didn't show an ounce of emotion. Until now.

A single tear was falling down her face, and I could feel my own building up. "Please don't make this more difficult than it already is. I need you to leave, Blair. I don't want to see you again. Eloise will handle all further communication with you until the signing is over."

"Can I just—"

"Now!" she yelled, throwing a finger to the door. She tried to hide the crack in her voice, but she couldn't.

I sighed and stood up. As I got to the door, I stopped when she spoke. "I hope she was worth losing everything."

I didn't turn around as the tears fell down my face, and I shut the door behind me.

Chapter Forty

DREA

Blair had walked out of the bookstore over two weeks ago, and I hadn't left since. I rarely went home, except to shower and sleep, which I didn't get much of these days.

Most nights I slept at the store so I didn't have to be in my big house alone. It didn't matter, though. Everywhere I went I was alone.

I was handling this breakup in a different way from my last one. Fucking and drinking my way out of it wasn't an option this time.

For one, I didn't think I could just get over someone like Blair, and for two, I could not even fathom looking at someone else, let alone sleeping with them. She was the only one I wanted and the only thing on my mind.

That was why I kept busy at the bookstore. I knew if I stopped long enough, I would think about her and break down, and I couldn't do that.

Luckily, on top of running the store, I had the book signing to get ready for, so staying busy wasn't a problem. Cara sent her assistant, Eloise, over a few times to make sure everything was finalized and ready for next week. One more week until I saw Blair again.

I tried to ask about Cara, but she refused to give me any details. It was strictly business anytime she came into the store or sent an email.

I'd also tried to reach out to Kaia, but all communication methods went unanswered; even the Instagram DM I sent was never seen.

I noticed a shift in Daisy as well. I knew they were friends, so I assumed she'd told her what happened. Daisy didn't come in as often, and when she did, she hardly smiled at me anymore. I still tried, though, but I hadn't tried to talk to her until today.

I waved at her when she came in. She gave me a small nod and went to sit down. I rounded the counter and followed after her.

Hey, Daisy, I signed when she looked up at me.

After her and Kaia started talking a lot more, I thought it would be a good idea to start learning sign language. Before I drove her away, Kaia was even helping me. I was still learning, but I knew a few phrases.

She sighed before giving me the most uninterested wave back.

Did I do something to upset you?

No, I just... Kaia told me what happened and it was a pretty crappy thing to do, but it's not my business.

She was right, but I wasn't going to tell her that. She was too sweet and I had already ruined things with Kaia, but add being rude to Daisy on top of that...

I know I messed up. I'm trying to make things right. I don't want to put you in the middle of it.

Thank you for that. I just want to enjoy my book, if that's okay?

I nodded. **Of course, sorry to bother you.**

Every time the bell above the door rang, my eyes shot up with hope it was either Cara or Kaia. I wasn't stupid enough to think it could have been... anyone else. My chest ached at even the thought of her. It hurt too much to say her name out loud.

I wanted to call her every day, but after she ignored my calls for a week straight, I took the hint and decided to give her some space. I wanted to go to her house and talk to her directly, but I knew that would make things worse.

I wanted more than anything to make things right between us, but I respected the hell out of her, and she deserved her space. Hopefully we could talk at the book signing and I could make things right.

This time, my smile didn't fall when I saw who came in.

"Hey, love, what are you doing here?" Penelope walked in holding a bag of takeout by the looks of it. I frowned when she locked the door and turned over the closed sign.

When she came up to the counter she looked warily at me. "I brought lunch. Let's sit, babe."

The store had emptied by this point, and I was nervous. "Why did you lock the door?" I said cautiously.

"You look like you haven't eaten or slept in about a week. Sit down and eat!"

"You're really taking this parenting thing seriously, and you're not even pregnant... unless—"

"No. I'm not pregnant. I'm just worried about you. You've been working nonstop since Blair—"

"Don't. Talk about her. I'm fine, Pen. I have a store to run. I can't put that on hold because... because she..." I couldn't say the words.

"Because she left? You say you're fine, but you can't even say her name. Drea, I know it hurts, but working yourself to death won't bring her back. You need to rest and take time for yourself." Her tone was soft and not judgmental, but that didn't stop the pain in my chest.

"I fucked up, Pen. I don't deserve time for myself."

"Drea, yes you do. If you love her—"

"Love? Who said anything about love?"

She glared at me. "Really? You're wallowing and working yourself sick, not eating and barely sleeping, because you *aren't* in love with her? Stop lying to yourself, Drea. Not every relationship is going to be like your parents. You are not them, and neither is she. You can deny your feelings all you want. I don't care. But if you want her back, then get up, close the store, get some sleep, maybe take a shower, and come up with a game plan to do so. But step one, get some damn rest!"

"Jesus, Pen, did Fallon plan that speech?" I laughed when she swatted my arm.

"You can afford to close the store for a few hours. Go home and get some sleep."

I groaned, knowing she was right. "If it gets you to leave and stop talking about her, then fine, I'll go."

I reluctantly closed early and headed home. I walked into my empty house, checked my empty phone before I put it on the nightstand, and climbed into my empty bed.

As soon as my head hit the pillow, all the feelings I'd kept in for the past several weeks came rushing out. One tear for every fucked-up word I said, until I ran out of words and tears and fell asleep.

"Blair!" I woke up from a nightmare screaming Blair's name and panting. It was the night we broke up, but instead of being in the bookstore, we were outside in a storm. I was yelling for her as she walked away, and she was about to walk off a cliff when I woke up.

I instinctively reached over to her side of the bed to reassure myself she was safe, only to realize my sleeping nightmare was similar to my waking one... She was gone.

Penelope was right, though. After thirteen hours of sleep, I felt a little better and ready for what I had planned that day. I wanted to make things right, and my first stop was Cara.

I knew if I went to her office, her assistant would most likely not let me in the door, so I did the next best thing and went to her house. I might regret it, but I needed to try.

"You have got to be kidding me!" Cara groaned as she opened the door to my timid smiling face.

"Hi," I said nervously.

"What on earth do you want? Haven't you done enough?"

I expected her to slam the door in my face, and there was still time for that, but so far, all she did was cross her arms over her chest and lean against the doorframe with an angry expression.

"Can we talk? Please?"

"I don't think we have anything else to talk about. You fucked my client, lied to me, and ruined our friendship in the process. Did I leave anything out?"

I groaned. "No, just, please let me in so we can talk, Cara."

She sighed but reluctantly opened the door for me to step inside. "Five minutes, Drea!"

She walked me to the kitchen, and I sat down at the table. "Water?" she asked. She might hate me, but she was still a good host.

I shook my head. "No, thank you. Look—"

"Don't waste your breath. I already know what you're going to say. You're sorry for keeping it from me, you're sorry for lying about it, and you wish you could take it back, right?"

"I really am sorry, Cara. It was not my intention to fall—"

She scoffed. "What? Fall in love? Don't tell me you actually love her. You aren't capable of that emotion. Just ask Skylar. Oh, wait, you can't because she left you."

I sighed. "That was a low blow, Cara, but I deserved it, I know."

I didn't want to tell anyone before telling Blair how I felt, but I needed Cara to know I was serious.

"She wasn't just another lay to me, Cara. I did; I fell in love with her. I know I can't take any of it back, but I am sorry for everything I said. I was drunk, and you wouldn't stop pressuring me to go out with someone, and I was tired of hiding it from you. I never got the chance to tell her how I felt because I was scared, but I'm sorry. I know none of that is an excuse for hiding it from you. You deserved a lot better, and I wish I could change things."

"You really think you can come here with a sob story about love and I'll forgive you? You lied to me, Drea. You were dating my best friend, or whatever the fuck it was you two were doing, and you both felt the need to pretend nothing was going on, and you even had a discussion about hiding it from me. That is the part that hurts the most. If you would have told me from the start, I wouldn't have been so upset. Shocked, hell yes, but I would have understood."

"I know. We wanted to tell you. She was heartbroken that she couldn't share it with you, but we both thought it would be for the best. Maybe that wasn't for us to decide, I don't know. Maybe we shouldn't have asked Kaia to—"

"Wait, Kaia knew beforehand?!"

Shit! "She kind of caught us kissing at the store, but I made her promise not to say anything."

"Wow, you guys are so fucking classy! Who else knows?"

"Cara, Please don't ask me—"

"Who else knows, Drea?! Can you spare me the truth for once? Don't I at least deserve that?"

"Of course you do, Cara. That's why I am here. I'm so sorry we—"

"Who else knows about you two, Drea?!"

I winced. "Everyone else."

She was quiet for a moment, and I wondered what she was going to say next.

"This is un-fucking-believable! You all must think so little of me to have hidden this. The fact that literally everyone knew—"

"Cara, we don't think little of you at all. It was my fault. I asked them not to say anything. If I'm being honest, at the beginning, I didn't know what we were doing or if it would last, and I didn't want to complicate things for something that might have been short term, but I quickly realized that what I felt for her, what I still feel for her, wasn't going anywhere. At that point, it was too late and it would have made things too messy, which I guess it still did in the end. I don't expect you to forgive me, but please don't cut Blair out of your life. She really cares about your friendship, and no part of this was her fault."

"I honestly don't care what your excuses are. The point is, everyone thought it was okay to hide something from me like we were never really friends to begin with. You are wasting your breath and my time. I think it's time for you to go and take your half-assed apology with you. We are done here."

She left no room for discussion as she opened her door, waiting for me to pass by. I hated everything about this situation, and I sighed in defeat. I didn't think I could have said anything else to change her mind.

As I walked out the door, I turned around and gave her one last pleading look. I hadn't noticed how red her eyes were until now. She was trying to look away so I couldn't see them. "Cara, I am so sorry."

She looked at me, and all I could see was hurt and sadness in her gaze. "Me too, Dre." And with that, she shut the door and I was left on her front porch, alone.

Chapter Forty-One

BLAIR

I hadn't left the house since I left Cara's office two weeks ago. I had tried every way possible to reach out. Phone calls, video calls, texts, emails—hell, I even tried to send her a Facebook message. None of them were even opened.

I wasn't stupid enough to show up at her office, and it would have been embarrassing for me to take a car to her house just so they could see the door getting slammed in my face.

I'd been trying to forget about everything and everyone, so I spent my days sleeping in and writing as much as I could.

I reached for my phone more often than I cared to admit, tapping on Drea's contact information, only to start crying again as I threw my phone on the bed.

I was getting cabin fever, though, and I needed to get out of the house. I called a car and put my stuff in a bag while I waited.

I didn't have many places to go, but I had an idea in mind. My first stop was to the shelter where I took Milo for a walk and got him a cup of whipped cream from Brewed Awakening.

My heart stopped when I went in, worried I would see Drea, but I was able to go in and out without a sighting.

After a few hours of spending time with Marcus and Milo, I called for another car, which arrived in three minutes. I took the car twenty minutes away until it stopped in front of an apartment building.

I had only been there once, and I really hoped she was home. I hadn't thought to call before I showed up, but it was Sunday, so I knew she wasn't at the bookstore.

I knocked on the door and was thankful when I heard footsteps a minute later.

"Blair? What are you doing here? What's wrong?"

"Hey, Kaia. Nothing's wrong. I'm sorry to bother you. Are you busy?"

She shook her head. "No, of course not. You aren't bothering me at all. Please come in."

"I'm sorry to just drop in without calling. I was out walking Milo and wanted to come see how things were going, you know, after everything." I hadn't talked to Kaia since that night she took me home. "You know, how's Daisy? How's... work?"

She smiled. "Daisy's good. She's becoming a really good friend." After the mention of Daisy, her smile fell, and it had me worried. "Work on the other hand, I... uh... quit the night you left."

My eyes shot up to hers. "Wait, what? Kaia, you can't quit. You love working there."

She sighed. "I did, but I couldn't take it anymore. She didn't appreciate everything I did for her. After I took you home, I tried to be nice and be there for her, like I always do, and we got into a big fight, and I finally snapped. I've never yelled at anyone before, Blair. I still feel guilty about it, but she needed to hear it. She ruined her relationship with Skylar because of her commitment issues, and now she ruined her relationship with you—"

"Woah, Kaia. I don't think we had a relationship. I mean, yeah, I was in love with her, but I don't know how she felt. We never talked about it aside from our initial conversation and our conversations about not telling Cara."

She scoffed. "It's not my place to say—you two need to have that conversation if that's what you want to do—but your feelings were not one-sided. Everyone could see it."

I didn't respond to that. I didn't have it in me to ask more. "I'm sorry things got this messy, Kaia, and I'm sorry we brought you into it."

She frowned. "It's not your fault. I should have stood up for myself a long time ago. She's not a bad person, though. She just needed some tough love, and she needed to know I was serious."

I knew she wasn't a bad person. The total opposite, actually. Things would have been a lot easier if she were a piece of shit.

"Oh, before I forget, I brought you something."

She looked at me, puzzled, and I smiled. "I wanted to thank you for everything you've done. Taking me home that night and helping with all the signings in the past. I know working with the two of us hasn't been the most pleasant experience. I made you some snickerdoodle cookies. Drea told me once that you liked them." I shrugged.

"*All signs point to love*," she said, reading the cover of a sapphic romance novel I picked out at the store.

"Well, I always see you signing with Daisy, so I picked this book up a while ago. It's a romance novel, and the main character is deaf. I'm sorry if you don't like it. I can take it back."

She shook her head, a slight glossiness in her eyes. "No, no, it's amazing, all of this. I... thank you, Blair." She came over and gave me a hug and I leaned into the warmth.

"I'm sorry things got shitty," I whispered. My eyes burned as she squeezed me tighter.

"Me too." She pulled away and wiped at her own tears. "I'm sorry things turned out the way they did. I hope everything with Cara works out. She should come around eventually."

I really hoped so...

I was heading for the door when she stopped me. "Oh, Blair?"

"Yeah?" I turned back around.

"She really cares about you. I've never seen her like that with anyone else. I just wanted you to know."

My smile disappeared at the mention of Drea. I cleared my throat. "Goodbye, Kaia." I turned and walked out the door.

As I was stepping into the elevator, a familiar young woman was getting off and startled when she saw me. I had only seen her a few times, and I smiled before waving to her as she passed me. She returned the gesture and headed down the hall.

. . .

I didn't have a specific direction in mind once I left, so I just mindlessly strolled down the street. I had missed seeing Kaia so often, and it was good to see her again, even if the circumstances weren't ideal.

My thoughts, of course, took me back to Drea, as they always did. I hated to admit that I missed her. I had to wipe away the tears that were threatening to wash me away right there on the sidewalk. I had to stop giving her the power to break me with just a memory.

I finally pulled myself together long enough to take a look at my surroundings, and I had to chuckle at myself. Even in my mindless wandering, I still ended up in front of Cara's office.

I wasn't foolish enough to go in, but I stood there for a few seconds, letting the memories of our friendship and partnership wash over me.

I would have reacted the same way had the roles been reversed. I held our friendship so close to my heart, but all I did was prove the opposite. I showed her that all those years meant nothing to me, which couldn't have been further from the truth.

I didn't know how I was going to make it up to her, but I knew I had to try. I had to get her to talk to me one way or another, but I would wait until after the signing. I would give her some time and space to think. Maybe when I got back from spending time with my brother, then we could talk.

I had done everything I could think of to forget about the signing. It would have been a lot easier if it wasn't part of my job and livelihood.

Eloise and I had been in constant communication, making sure everything was finalized. Anytime I asked about Cara, she would immediately change the subject, and I stopped asking after a while.

We were days out now, and I was dreading it but also looking forward to it. I loved my job, and although the current state of it was still hanging in the balance, this was one of my favorite parts and I had worked so hard on this book. I loved connecting with readers and hearing their thoughts. I always loved when someone felt the same obsession with the characters as I did.

I hoped things were cooled down enough by now that Cara would show up. I wasn't keeping my fingers crossed or anything, but I desperately wanted her to be there.

I doubted I would see Kaia. She had made it pretty clear she was moving on and had no intention of going. Although she did wish me luck, I hoped Daisy talked some sense into her and convinced her not to leave things the way they had.

Every time I thought of seeing Drea, I wanted to curl into a ball and cry. I had missed her so much since I'd left, but I was still so fucking angry. I knew I shouldn't be. I was stupid. So unbelievably stupid.

Going in, I knew how things were. I had heard the stories of her ex and their rocky relationship. I had also heard how she handled that breakup before me. I was so stupid to believe I could be the one to change things. I should have known that people like Drea weren't the settling-down type.

I had been so blinded by the sudden and fiercely strong attraction to her that I hadn't cared. I'd wanted any part of her I could have, and I'd forgotten all about my feelings and what my brain had been telling me I knew all along.

I finally pulled myself away and continued on my walk until I ended up inside the warm and inviting doors of Brewed Awakening. I had to stop and take a deep, calming breath. I almost wished I had brought my laptop to get some writing done.

"Hey, Blair! It's so good to see you." Rylee, the barista, was always so sweet anytime I came in.

I walked up to the counter to greet her, cautiously looking around for any sign of smooth skin and devastating brown eyes.

Her bright smile instantly turned sad as I turned back to her. "She's not here. She actually hasn't been in here for a while." She let the meaning of her words hang between us like a dark cloud.

I sagged in relief and planted on the most genuine smile I could manage. "How are you, Rylee? How did the wedding pictures turn out? I cannot wait to see them!"

Her warm smile returned and I was thankful to see someone not looking at me like a sad sick puppy. "Oh my God! They are stunning, if I do say so myself. I am dying to see everyone's reactions, but..."

"But?" I supplied, hoping she would continue.

She let out a sigh and went on. "But there are some... Well, I don't know exactly what is going on with all of you, but what I've heard is..." She shook her head and started again. "Sorry, I just hate bringing up past issues, but I took some pictures of you and Drea."

My eyes grew wide. "Oh."

"Not that it matters anymore, but I was going to make sure you guys saw them first before I sent them to Fallon and Mackenzie. I just... You guys looked truly captivating. I couldn't help myself."

I could feel my eyes burning, and I had to clench my jaw to prevent the tears from falling. "No, it's all right. Thank you for telling me. Has she...?" It hurt way too much to say her name out loud but I knew Rylee picked up on what I was asking. *Has she seen them?*

"I offered to show her the last time I talked to her. She refused." She paused before her voice grew softer. "She wanted you to see them first and decide what you wanted to do with them. Please feel free to tell me to delete them if you wish. I had to... The two of you looked so happy and in love that it would have been a shame to miss out on the opportunity to capture it, but I understand whatever your decision."

This time, clenching my jaw wasn't nearly enough, and a few tears escaped anyway. I quickly wiped them away, but it didn't matter. No matter how hard I tried, I couldn't hide all the pain and anger I felt.

I cleared my throat and tried to gain control of myself again. "Thank you, Rylee. Looks can be deceiving, I suppose, but I appreciate the gesture, nonetheless. I would love to take a look, but I'm not sure I can right now. I'm sorry. Would you mind emailing them to me?"

She nodded. "Of course, Blair. Whatever you need. I'm sorry I brought it up. I just thought you would want to know. Can I get you anything while you're here? A chai, maybe?"

I smiled and agreed. "That would be lovely, thank you."

After I got my drink, I settled myself in a chair in the back corner. Luckily the coffee shop was just about dead this time of day, but it felt nice to sit somewhere that wasn't in my office and have a change of scenery.

I watched the hundreds of people walking outside, living their own lives. I made up stories about men on their phones having important business calls on the other end, or their mothers asking when they were going to settle down.

Eventually Rylee went on break, and I invited her to sit with me. We chatted until a customer came in and she had to get back. It was nice to socialize and not think about what a mess my life had become, if only for a little while.

Chapter Forty-Two

DREA

The day of the book signing had finally arrived, and I was on edge, per usual. Usually when it came to book signings with Blair, I was stressed because I wanted to get them over with so I wouldn't have to see her again. This time was different.

I was anxious to see her, I was nervous, and I was dreading the end. I didn't know what was going to happen. Would she want to talk to me? Would she leave without a word? If I was being honest with myself, I was terrified she would walk out the door for the last time.

Normally I had Fallon and Kaia with me to help calm the nerves. Fallon was coming later, and Kaia...

I wasn't naïve to think she would show up. She didn't owe me anything. I hadn't given too much detail when I'd texted Fallon weeks ago asking if she would help like she normally did. She'd been on her honeymoon, and I hadn't wanted to upset her.

She'd spent three weeks in Bali, and I'd wanted her to enjoy every minute of it. I planned to tell her about Blair and me when she got to the bookstore, or after the event. Maybe I didn't have to tell her at all. That seemed like a way better option.

I still had another hour before the store even opened, and I was setting up the table when the door opened.

"Hey, babe. Thanks for—"

"Andrea Elise Voss! What the fuck is going on? I leave to go be bliss-fully married and in love, and I come back to complete chaos?!"

"Whoa, Fallon! No need for government names. Relax, will you?"

She scoffed. "Relax?! How am I supposed to relax when my whole life got turned upside down without me even being here?!"

"Okay, Fresh Prince. Let me guess, Kaia told you?" I asked. "I should have known."

"Actually, no, you ass hat! She wouldn't tell me anything other than that she quit. Rylee just told me all about your fight at the bar when I got my coffee. What possessed you to insult Blair like that? I thought you liked her? It sure seemed that way at my wedding, but maybe I read it wrong. Maybe she really was just another name in your book."

I glared at her, giving her a pass for just coming back from her honeymoon, and also not in the mood to piss off someone else I loved. "Don't do that, Fallon. You know damn well she wasn't."

"Well, then what the fuck happened?!" I had never seen Fallon so angry at me before. Mackenzie was right, though, it wasn't a pretty sight.

"I was drunk! And Cara kept pressuring me to go out on dates, but I couldn't tell her why I wouldn't, and I just couldn't take it anymore!" I yelled.

"Seriously, Drea, what is wrong with you? You could have gone about it so differently without tarnishing her name and essentially ruining everything between you two."

"I know, Fallon. I fucked everything up. I was really drunk and upset. It just slipped out. I wish I could take it back."

"I get that, but you can't. And what about Kaia quitting? She is the sweetest, most loyal person I know, and you made her quit?!" She rubbed her fingers between the bridge of her nose, and I felt like I was a disappointing child being scolded.

"I am gone for three fucking weeks and come back to a shitshow. God, I really need my wife right now," she muttered under her breath. "Oh, and thank you oh so very much for ratting us out to Cara! We were finally at a good place, and you had to throw me under the bus? Now she refuses to talk to any of us, even Rylee!"

"I'm sorry. I didn't want to lie to her anymore. And you agreed not to say anything, remember?" I wasn't trying to place blame, but I was tired of everyone yelling at me, even though I knew I deserved it.

"We agreed because you promised to tell her yourself. I told you from day one that you were putting Cara in a shitty situation. And I convinced myself that it was okay to lie for you because I was tired of seeing you miserable after Skylar, but now you put us all in a fucked-up position, Dre!"

"I know! I did tell her... just not in the way I wanted to. I fucked up, okay? Kaia was right." I couldn't help but yell. I wasn't yelling at her; I was yelling at myself for being so fucking stupid and making a huge mess of things.

"Yeah, you did! And back to Kaia, what the hell?!"

I groaned. "She said she'd had enough. I was still drunk and dealing with the breakup and I was upset and yelled at her. She shouldn't have brought Blair with her, but I know it's not really her fault. She told me that I deserved everything that happened, and she was right. I drove Blair away, and now I have to live with it. I should have told her how I felt and figured out a way to tell Cara, before things got ugly, but I didn't." I rubbed my face in my hands.

"And how do you feel, Dre?"

I sighed. "I can't explain it, but she was different. I didn't even have to try with her. I know it hadn't been that long, and we didn't start off on the greatest terms, but I think something has always been there between us, at least for me. Maybe that's why I kept agreeing to work with her. I think a part of me wanted her in my life, no matter the circumstances."

She sighed. "It sounds to me like you have feelings for her, strong ones, if I had to guess. Do you love her, Dre?"

She spoke so softly and sweetly I wanted to cry. My best friend knew me too well, and there wasn't a trace of anger or judgment in her tone.

I glared at her. "Fallon, seriously? You're asking if I love her? Of course I love her! I wouldn't be feeling this way if I didn't. My world doesn't exist without her in it. It feels like a piece of my heart disintegrates bit by bit with every day she's not here."

I hadn't realized I was crying until Fallon came up to me and wiped a tear with the pad of her thumb. "Babe?" she whispered softly, and I leaned into her touch.

"I know, I'm a mess. What am I supposed to do? I need her, Fal. She's like a telescope, and without her, I can't see the stars shining in the night sky."

"First of all, wow, that is some poetic sappy shit that I did not expect from you, like at all."

I nudged her arm. "I'm serious, babe."

I hated feeling like this, and I needed my best friend to cut the bull-shit and tell me the truth like I had done with her so many times before. I couldn't imagine a life where I didn't have Blair, so I needed to come up with a plan, and fast.

She let out a loud, dramatic sigh. "Okay, well, first things first, clean your face off. She'll be here soon, and you have a business to run. You need to clean up and get your shit together. Handle the signing like you do every other one and be professional."

I nodded, words failing me as I tried to calm my nerves. I knew she was right. I couldn't let Blair see me like this. I couldn't let her see how miserable I was without her, but I wasn't going to lie to her and make her think I'd already moved on without her.

"Get through the signing. Then when it's all over and everyone is gone, try to talk to her, but don't make her think she has no choice but to listen, but also make her listen. Does that make sense?"

"Yeah... kind of?" It didn't make sense to me at all, but maybe that was because my brain had no space for anything that wasn't daily basic functions, and Blair.

She rolled her eyes. "Honestly, Dre, do I have to spell out everything for you? Just finish the signing and then talk to her. Don't put pressure on anything but be honest and say what needs to be said. Then let her decide what happens next and go from there."

That sounded doable, I supposed. My nerves were running rampant, but I would have to put them aside for now because the door opened and every organ in my body stopped altogether.

Blair walked through the doors, the picture of perfection. She wore a long and flowy army-green short-sleeved summer dress. It crisscrossed in the front, over her abdomen, showing just a little bit of skin, and she looked radiant in it. She wore brown gladiator sandals with it, and it made my chest ache. She was so fucking beautiful, and she used to be mine.

Seeing her again for the first time since our breakup was like time stood still. Like I was looking at a photograph of her and not the real thing. I wanted to wrap the moment in bubble wrap and keep it safe and out of harm's way. I never wanted anything to taint the moment.

Unfortunately I wasn't looking at a photograph, and time resumed when Fallon started heading over to Blair. She turned her head when she noticed Fallon, and our eyes met. She took in a breath as her lips parted. Neither of us said a word as we silently stared at each other. I had to grip the counter so I didn't get tempted to get too close.

Thankfully I could hear their conversation from where I stood. "Hey, Blair, you look amazing!" Fallon went in for a hug, and Blair looked happy for the first time since she'd walked in.

"Thank you, Fallon. Marriage looks good on you. How's Mackenzie? How was Bali?"

Her eyes never left Fallon the entire time she gushed about her honeymoon and her life as a newlywed.

"Drea's over there if you want to..." She trailed off as she hitched her thumb and saw me staring at them.

I hated the distance between us. I hated that I couldn't just go over there and say something or hold her and kiss her. To tell her how proud I was of her and how amazing I thought she was.

Blair cleared her throat and still didn't make eye contact with me. "Oh... uh, actually, I was just going to get set up at my table, if that's okay? It's probably best if I just stay over here and do my job."

I turned away to grab some things from the back, giving them privacy and giving myself a chance to pull it together. I only had to get through a few hours of looking at Blair, and I could move on. I didn't even have to interact with her. She had already been paid, and so had I. There was nothing left to say or do.

That was a fucking lie. There was a lot to say, but now wasn't the time. I was going to give her space, and as Fallon said, I was going to get through the signing before I could even *think* about talking to her.

I should have known better. I was never going to make it through the signing!

Why did I ever think this was a good idea?

I should have just broken the contract and paid the crazy fees or done whatever I had to do. Anything would have been better than staring at Blair in her element without being able to be there for her like I wanted.

I couldn't help but stare at her and watch as she sat at the table with a genuine smile on her face that never wavered, even after talking with fans one after another. Not being able to receive that same expression made my heart ache.

She barely looked at me all day, and when she did, I was desperate to run up and hug her. To comfort her and let her know I loved her. She never smiled when she looked at me, and it broke my heart all over again every single time.

Fallon was working her ass off today, and I made a mental note to pay her accordingly. She always refused anytime I tried to pay her for helping, but somehow, I would force her to take it this time. She was running interference between me and Blair and helping with any issues that came up. Mackenzie showed up for two hours to help before she had to get to work, but luckily they actually worked the entire time and never looked freshly fucked.

The book signing was *finally* finishing up, and I told Fallon I was heading to my office to finish up a few things. I didn't have the courage to say goodbye or to stick around to watch Blair leave.

Fallon gave me a look that screamed, *You're pathetic*, but I didn't have it in me to care. It hurt too much. Of course, she didn't say anything about it and promised to give my thanks to Blair and finish up out front.

I was replying to some emails when there was a knock on my office door. "Babe, I'm not sure why you're knocking when you can just—"

"Hi."

Chapter Forty-Three

DREA

"Kaia... hi."

I honestly didn't know what else to say. There was so much I wanted to say, but I needed to play it smart. This might be my last chance, and I didn't want to fuck it up again.

"What..." I cleared my throat and tried again. "Please, have a seat. Would you like anything to drink?" I was a mess. My emotions and words were all over the place.

She shook her head. "No... I'm not here to stay."

My heart sank. Of course, I knew that. I knew we couldn't pick up like nothing had happened, but it still hurt to hear it.

"Right, of course. How... how are you?"

She blew out a breath and slowly walked over to my desk. "We aren't doing this, Drea. I just came for my last check. Maybe I should have waited until you mailed it—"

"No!" I stood up, stopping her from turning around. "No," I said in a more inside-voice type of way.

"Right... So if I can just get it, I'll be on my way."

I nodded. "Of course, please have a seat. It'll just take a minute." I motioned for her to sit down, but she didn't move.

"Drea..." She sighed and relented when my stare didn't waver. "Fine."

She sat down and refused to make eye contact with me. I knew this was hard for her as much as it was for me.

I didn't waste time and got out my checkbook. After pulling up her file and seeing her hours, I wrote the appropriate numbers on the check and handed it to her without a word.

She took the check and stood up, heading to the door. "Thank you... What is this?"

I was sitting in my chair with my legs crossed, exuding professionalism and acting as if everything was totally normal, when she stopped and turned around sharply to glare at me. "It's your check. Is something wrong? I paid you for your hours of work. I thought it was an adequate amount."

She scoffed. "Adequate? You think this is adequate? Drea, you overpaid me... by a lot!"

I smiled and sat up in my chair. "I paid you based on what I feel you are owed."

She shook her head coming back to my desk and throwing the check on top. "Is this some sort of joke or a bribe? To forgive you? I don't want your money, Drea. I just want to get paid for what I worked and move on. Please don't make this any harder for me."

Her eyes were filled with tears, and I didn't want to play games anymore. I stood up and took the check, handing it back to her. "Read it, Kai."

She furrowed her brows. "What?"

"Read it, Kaia."

She sighed and took the check, clearing her throat. "Pay to the order of Kaia Rhodes for the amount of... Drea, I already read how much it's for. Why do I—"

"The bottom, Kaia. Read the bottom."

She looked skeptically at me and rolled her eyes, clearly getting more annoyed with every second.

She cleared her throat and continued reading. "An advance for the new... co-owner of Open Book Bookstore if she chooses to forgive her idiot boss? Drea, what... co-owner?"

She slumped in the chair opposite mine and stared at me, complete shock on her face.

I sat down and took a deep breath, preparing the courage I needed to say what I had to.

"You were right, about all of it. I didn't appreciate everything you did for me. I knew you would do anything I asked, so I took it for granted, and I'm sorry. I was so wrapped up in my own life and dealing with things, or trying to deal with them, that I lost sight of what was really important—making sure *all* aspects of my life were taken care of. That includes this business, and you. This is just the start of my apology. I want you to come back, Kaia. I want you to be your own boss and have fifty-fifty ownership of the bookstore, with contracts and everything. Legit businesswoman-type shit." We both laughed, and I was grateful for the lightness that filled the air.

"You were right about Blair. I drove her away, just like I did with Skylar. But you were wrong about one thing. I do care about her, quite a lot, actually. I love her, Kaia. I am a mess without her. I was addicted to her, and I don't know what I'm going to do without her. I'm still trying to work through my issues, but I can admit that I fell head over fucking heels in love with her, and I'd move to Antarctica with nothing but a towel if she asked me to."

The entire time I was talking, Kaia stayed in the chair, fidgeting with her jeans. Her eyes never left mine, and I hated the redness that formed around them. I was determined to get the words out, though. If this was the last time she would be in this office, I had to lay everything out on the table.

"I know I'm rambling. What I'm trying to say is that I'm so incredibly sorry for not acknowledging how amazing you are and not appreciating everything you do for me. Honestly, if it weren't for you working for me, I would have closed down a long time ago, especially with the way I had been acting for the past two years."

"Isn't that the truth." Kaia laughed, and I let out a tear of happiness at the sound. "But you really think I can be part owner of the bookstore? You really want *me* to be your partner?"

I smiled and nodded. "Yes, Kai, I really do. I'm so sorry for everything. I want you to be co-owner of the bookstore, but more than that, I want our friendship back."

Kaia grinned and stood up. "Thank you... for everything. This is all too much. I—"

I stood up and pushed the check back to her. "No, Kaia, it's not. I don't think it's enough, to be honest. You are truly amazing at what you do, and I should have seen how lucky I was to have you in my corner. I see how you interact with the customers, even the bitchy ones, and *especially* how you are with Daisy. You didn't see her as a loiterer, someone who just comes in to lounge around and not buy anything. You saw her as a young woman who may have just needed someone to talk to, and you have been there for her, just like you were always there for me. She is very lucky to have you in her life."

She blushed and looked away at the mention of her friend, but I kept going, afraid if I stopped, she would vanish out of my life again. "Of course this is just an advance, but when... *if* you agree and sign the contract, you will get another check to cover your salary for the next five years, which—"

"FIVE YEARS?!" Kaia's eyes blew wide open and I tried to hide my chuckle. "How is that possible?"

I laughed. "Kaia, love, I'm what you kids would call fucking loaded."

"What? How?" She looked at me with wide eyes.

I sighed. "Well, technically, my family is the one with money. My grandmother left me a good amount of money, some of which I used to open the store, but I haven't touched it since. My parents bought my house for me when I moved here, but I pay them monthly for it. Granted, it's not nearly as much as it would've been had I purchased the house myself, and I won't bore you with all my family drama and money technicalities."

Her eyes seemed to have gone back to their normal size, but she still sat there without a word.

"Anyway, that's not the point here. The point is, you deserve this and I would really like you to say yes. I mean, if that's something you even want. I understand I have thrown a lot at you, and if you don't even want to continue to work with me, I totally understand."

I waited with bated breath for a reply. I hadn't expected her to sit there for so long already. I expected her to just take the check and leave. If I was being totally honest, I expected her not to show up at all. Even if this was the last time I saw her, I was relieved knowing everything was out in the open.

"I have one condition."

"Is that a yes?"

She smiled. "*If* I can hire a manager and *two* people to work the front, especially on the weekends. *And* someone to teach a sign language class once a month."

I laughed. "Why am I not surprised? This wouldn't have anything to do with a certain beautiful deaf woman that frequents my store would it?"

"*Our* store... and maybe... okay, yes. I really like her, okay? As a friend."

I raised an eyebrow. "Just a friend, huh? Are you sure about that? I've seen the way you look at her, Kaia. The same way Kenzie and Fallon look at each other."

The way her cheeks flushed, I knew I was right. No matter what a person said, you could always tell what they were really feeling with their eyes.

I also didn't miss the way she corrected me by saying "our store." That made my heart soar, and I wanted to crush her into a hug. It was still a fragile situation, so I refrained until I knew we were in smooth waters.

"And how you look at Blair?" she asked.

Something large in my heart broke at the mention of that glorious woman, and my smile fell into one of sadness and loss. I lost the best thing that came into my life, and I had no one to blame but myself.

"Yeah." My voice cracked at the only word I could manage.

Her face turned a few shades of red. "I guess it's something like that. But we are just friends, seriously. I don't want to lose her, and besides, I'm pretty sure she's straight. Just my luck, right?" She huffed out a laugh, but it sounded painful.

I smiled softly at her. "Kaia, she would be lucky to have you. Just enjoy spending time together and see what happens, yeah?"

She nodded, standing up. "Thanks, Dre. So do we have a deal?" She held out her hand and I laughed, rounding my desk and pulling her in for a hug.

"Of course, Kai. Anything you want."

"Well, I better get out of your hair. Thanks again, Drea. I can't tell you how much this means to me."

"I'm so sorry again for everything, Kaia. I promise to show you every day how much you mean to me." I went back to my desk and sat down as Kaia headed out of my office. I couldn't contain my smile as I thought about how the day seemed to have turned around.

"Thank you, Drea... Oh, hey, Blair, congratulations on the signing." I looked up to see Blair standing in the doorway.

"Hey, Kaia. Thanks." She gave her a soft expression as Kaia walked past and closed the door behind her.

I tried to keep my composure as I looked at her, but it was almost impossible.

I had been catching glimpses of her all day and tried not to torture myself by staring for too long. But seeing her in my office was the worst kind of torture. She was so close I could smell her vanilla perfume, and there was no one else around. I could have easily captured her lips in a kiss, but I couldn't. Not anymore.

"Hi," I finally said, unable to control the shake in my voice and my legs as I stood up.

She hesitated before slowly walking over to my desk without sitting down. She had no intention of staying, and I couldn't say I blamed her.

"I just came to see if I left my bracelet here. The last time I was here when we... I think I dropped it. It was from my mother," she said with no emotion. Maybe Kaia was wrong and she wasn't in love with me...

Without a word, I opened my desk drawer and retrieved the gold bracelet. It was a dainty little thing with a few small gold balls spaced around the band. I remembered it wrapped around her wrist, fitting so perfectly, just as she had fit into my life, into my heart. I'd found it a while ago when I was cleaning and kept meaning to give it back, but I never got around to it.

If I was being totally honest, I never mustered up the courage to seek her out to give it back, and I selfishly wanted to hold on to any piece of her I could. If I had known the special place it held in her heart, I would have forgotten all about my feelings and found a way to make sure it got back to her safely.

I walked over to her and held it out without letting go. Feeling her skin on mine for the first time in so long felt too good, and I didn't want to lose it again.

"Drea," she whispered. I could tell by the trembling in her voice and the shaking of her hand in mine that she was trying to hold it together. I wondered if she could tell how much that was breaking me even more.

"I... was hoping we could talk." I didn't want to push her, but I was desperate for any chance to talk to her. To fix this. It took all I had to hide the tremor in my voice. To force a strength I didn't possess into my words.

She sighed heavily and closed her eyes for a beat before opening them again. "There is nothing to talk about. Please... just let me go."

My grip held tight as I shook my head. "I can't do that. You made the mistake of letting me have you, and now?" I pulled her closer. "I don't want to let you go," I whispered as I softly and slowly pressed a kiss to her lips.

If she'd wanted it to stop it would have in a heartbeat, but she made no move to pull away and her hand found its way to my arm, causing the bracelet to crash to the ground.

I wasn't dumb enough to think this meant we weren't going to talk about things, but I wasn't questioning anything as we walked to the couch and she straddled me, her hand finding that sweet spot between my thighs. That was a problem for me to handle tomorrow. I didn't know how much time we had, and I didn't want to waste another second.

She broke the kiss, both of us panting and not taking our eyes off one another. "This doesn't mean—" I stopped her with a kiss, not wanting to break the spell over whatever this was.

I brought my hands up to roam her body. I needed to feel her everywhere I could. She stopped my hands and took them off her, and I immediately missed the contact.

"Blair—" She cut me off with a firm shake of her head.

I was left confused as I watched her get off me without saying a word. Realization dawned on me when she opened the drawer next to my desk and pulled out a small bullet, and I was instantly turned on again.

She walked back over to me and I had to fight the urge to drag her down with me again. I could see she wanted to be in charge, so I let her. If it was going to get her to forgive me, she could do whatever she wanted with me.

"Take off your shorts," she commanded. My shorts and underwear hit the floor within seconds, and I tried to reach out for her, but she put her hand out to stop me.

"Lay back." She straddled me as I lay back, and my hands traveled to her ass, but she stopped them again with only a shake of her head as a response.

"Blair, please—"

"Hands above your head." I didn't understand why she wouldn't let me touch her, but I could tell in her tone she was angry. I did as I was told and placed my hands above my head. She turned on the toy, and it buzzed to life, causing a jolt of pleasure to shoot through me.

I instinctively closed my eyes as soon as she swirled it around my clit. "Fuck," I breathed.

I kept trying to move my hands, hoping she would let me touch her, but her grip only tightened and it was killing me. I wanted to touch her. I wanted to feel her and kiss her. Fuck, I wanted everything!

"Blair, can I, Oh God!" My words melted into a moan as she inserted the vibrator inside of me and circled my clit with her thumb. I was a mess, and I was completely at her mercy.

She was not taking her eyes off me, and she was fucking me without saying a word. I wanted her to yell at me. I wanted her to tell me off, to insult me. I wanted... anything but this. Her silence caused more pain than any words could have.

"I'm so close. I need to touch you, Blair, please," I begged. I was desperate to be close to her again.

Her only response was to thrust the toy harder and deeper, somehow knowing I needed it that way. She was angry and hurt, and I wanted her to take it all out on me.

Tears started falling down her face, and I would have given anything to be the one to wipe them away. I felt like I was losing her all over again and it fucking sucked.

"I'm so sorry," I whispered before the vibrator moved one last time and my orgasm hit me at the same moment tears started burning my eyes.

She didn't stop thrusting the toy into me, and her tears didn't stop their descent on her perfectly devastated face. It was breaking me all over again.

"Shit, Blair." Her name came out in a moan, and my eyes never left hers.

After she rang out every ounce of pleasure from my body, she slowly removed the vibrator and turned it off. I lay there unmoving, waiting for her to say something... anything.

"Can I..." I stopped myself when she got off me, and I sat up as I watched her place the vibrator on my desk.

She turned and headed for the door without another word, and I immediately stood up. "Blair, wait."

She stopped with her hand on the doorknob and turned around to face me. Tears were still running down her face, but she made no move to wipe them away as she cleared her throat. "Feel free to tell Cara what color the vibrator was... Oh, and make sure to tell her you were the one who came in your office this time." She turned and walked out of my life again, closing the door behind her.

I put my shorts back on and slumped on the couch. "Fuck!" I groaned out. I knew I deserved that, but it still hurt.

Chapter Forty-Four
DREA

Two weeks later

I hadn't been able to stop thinking about the signing and everything that had happened afterward. The signing itself was a success, and I was thankful to have Kaia back.

It also felt really fucking good to be honest with her and open up a little bit about my past. I could tell she appreciated it and knew I was serious about how much she meant to me. Things hadn't been the same since she'd left, and I was proud of her for standing up and telling me how stupid I had been.

I promised to work hard and show her more than tell her how much I appreciated her, starting with letting her run the store alone for two weeks. But the events after the signing...

I couldn't believe Blair had left, again. I mean, I could, but not in the way she did. I was blinded by my love for her, and I hadn't thought to question any part of what was going on.

I'd hoped it meant we were going to work things out, but clearly I was wrong. I couldn't blame her for walking out on me again, though. I deserved it. I had made her feel the same way when I'd spoken to Cara, and it was only fair that I got a taste of my own medicine.

I was packing up my office to head out to catch my flight. I wasn't taking anything related to work this time. I desperately needed a break, and I knew Kaia could handle the store. I made sure to take the key to my drawer. Poor Kaia didn't need to know what was in there.

I was heading home to Portland to visit my family. One week with my mother and sisters, one week with my father.

When I left my office, Kaia was talking with Daisy at the counter. It looked like they were making plans to go to the movies, or something involving ducks? My sign language was still a little rusty, and the person Kaia had hired to teach the class wasn't starting for another month.

"Do you have everything you need? You have my number, you have access to the cameras, and you have the emergency numbers, right?" I asked Kaia as she rolled her eyes at me.

"Drea, yes, I will be fine! If you didn't think I could do it, why did you hire me back?"

I sighed. "Of course I know you can do it. I'm just nervous. I've never been away from the store for this long. Two weeks is a long time, but I trust you."

"Good! Go, enjoy your trip."

I planned to. I needed to get out of Seattle for a little while. Everywhere I went reminded me of Blair, and I needed to clear my head. I hadn't given up on us yet, but I thought some space would be good for both of us.

I'd respected her wishes and hadn't tried to contact her. According to Kaia, she'd left town shortly after the book signing, and she wouldn't tell me where she went. As long as someone knew where she was, I was happy.

It wasn't unusual for her to skip town after a signing, or so I was told. From what Cara had told me, she used that time to get inspiration and regroup. I never asked where she would go, because at the time, I didn't care. Now I wished I would have asked. I just needed to know she was okay.

I hadn't heard from Cara, so I didn't know if she was speaking with Blair again or not. I decided it was best to give everyone space. Maybe after my trip I would try to reach out, when the wounds weren't as fresh.

"I will try. Let me know if you need anything, and tell Daisy to keep an eye on you."

She blushed, turning to tell Daisy what I'd said, and I left the store nervously. I had to put more faith in Kaia and show her that I trusted her. At least I knew I could trust her not to have sex in my store. That was exactly why Fallon was never allowed to be in charge while I was away.

Since the book signing, I had been away from the store a little more, but I still managed to stay nearby if Kaia needed anything.

The store had been picking up a little in recent weeks, and Kaia said she needed help. It was nice to see that even as part owner of the store, she still wanted to be present and work on the floor, but I needed to remember to give her an office.

I stopped at Brewed Awakening before the drive for liquid encouragement, and Rylee was shocked when I didn't get my regular order.

I had been ordering the same chai latte with cinnamon since I moved to Seattle, but now it just reminded me too much of Blair.

I'd made the mistake of asking about her and if she ever came in there. The look Rylee had given me was filled with sympathy and irritation.

I apologized again for that night. She had heard every horrible thing I'd said about Blair, and I could tell she still remembered.

She told me that yes, Blair sometimes went in, and no, she didn't ask about me. Of course not. Why would she?

The drive to the airport was forty-five minutes, but it was going by pretty quickly. It was raining a little, but as I got closer, it started to pick up, and visibility became a little more difficult.

I was in my own world, thinking about my parents, my sisters, Blair, and the store, and I hadn't noticed I was going twenty miles over the limit. A flash of lightning pulled me from my thoughts, but not quick enough, because when my eyes focused, it was too late as I got closer and closer to the back of a semi-truck. Then everything went dark...

Chapter Forty-Five

BLAIR

"Auntie Blair, Auntie Blair! Are you coming to our party? It's coming up, and Dad said we had to share... again! Tell him we want our own parties. We're too old to share. We aren't babies anymore!"

The twins had been running me ragged all day talking about their party decorations and fighting over who got to pick out the piñata and who got to cut the cake first. I loved them, but I had only been at my brother's for three days, and I was already exhausted.

"I think Brenden is right, Chris. They're little men now, and they have different styles. Maybe they should have their own parties."

My brother huffed. He could rarely say no to his boys. "Perhaps you're right, little sister. I'll talk to your mother, and *if* she agrees, we will start planning separate parties. But I don't like it!"

I rolled my eyes and laughed when Brenden and Cole rushed to tackle me in a hug.

"I'm ashamed to admit I haven't been back here since the last time you were here," Chris said as we were getting out of the car.

Chelsea kept the boys home so we could see our parents. We waited until after dinner and left while they were getting ready for bed.

"You have a family and a busy life, Chris. They understand." I smiled and squeezed his arm.

It had been way too long since I had seen them, too. I talked to them almost every day, just as I talked to Gran, but it wasn't the same as coming to see them.

We took our usual spot on the grass and took turns telling them how much we loved and missed them. Chris told them about the boys and their birthday parties they were now having. I was surprised to see his eyes water at the mention of them growing up.

I told them about being a best-seller and how I hoped they were proud of me. I also told them about Drea, and I started crying when I told them that we'd broken up. Chris was there to comfort me, and it was nice.

"I'm sorry," I whispered to no one in particular.

Chris helped me stand as I wiped the tears away. "Let's say our goodbyes and get back to the boys, okay?"

I nodded, and we took our turns saying goodbye before heading back to the house.

I said goodnight to everyone early, but I couldn't sleep. I was still thinking about Drea, and whenever I closed my eyes, they would fill with tears, picturing all our memories together. Mostly the hurt I felt hearing all the things she had said to Cara. Making it sound like I meant absolutely nothing to her, while she meant everything to me.

It was nearly two in the morning and I still couldn't sleep, so I gave up and headed to the kitchen for a late-night snack.

When we were younger, my brother and I used to sneak into the pantry after our parents had gone to sleep, and we'd eat chocolate chips right out of the bag. They never caught us, or if they did, they never said anything.

"I should've known I'd find you in here."

I was sitting with my laptop in the kitchen when Chris came in. I'd gotten my computer before I'd come down, knowing I shouldn't have.

Sometimes when I was upset and crying, I thought it was helpful to have something to make me cry harder. It was a weird coping mechanism of mine, and I still didn't know if it was healthy, but it made me feel better... eventually.

I was already thinking about her, so I'd decided to bite the bullet and open the email from Rylee. She had sent me the pictures from the wedding, and they were gorgeous... until I got to the ones she'd taken of me and Drea. Dancing together. Kissing. Looking perfectly happy and in love... at least one of us wasn't faking it.

"Blair?" I was so lost in thought I had forgotten Chris was standing in the doorway.

"Hey," I said quietly, quickly trying to wipe the tears away. "Why are you up?"

He walked over to me, and his face softened when he saw me. He took some chocolate from the bag. "I couldn't sleep. You?"

"Same." I shrugged, turning my attention back to the pictures.

"Is that the wedding you went to? They look happy."

I nodded. "Yeah. They really do, don't they?"

"They aren't the only ones. You two look quite smitten with each other, you know?"

I huffed out a sad laugh. "Yeah, well, looks can be deceiving. I was, but I guess I was delusional."

I slammed the laptop closed and covered my face with my hands. I didn't like anyone seeing me cry. Least of all over some woman.

Chris enveloped me in a hug, and I leaned into it, unable to hide the pathetic sob that escaped me.

"Do you want to talk about it?" he asked.

"I loved her, Chris. Like fucking seriously loved her. I thought I could see us settling down together. How pathetic is that? Months ago, I despised her!"

"Hey, hey. It's not pathetic at all. Love doesn't have a time require-ment. It happens when it happens, and you can't change that."

"Yeah, well. I can make sure it never happens again. This feeling fucking sucks, and I'm not going through it again."

"Oh, don't say that. It only sucks because it was real. You can't give up on love, Sis. Just take some time for yourself. But don't give up! I know how much it hurts right now, but it will get better."

I snorted. "I know you're right, but right now, it sucks."

It did suck. I was still so angry with her, but the love I had for her was still just as strong. I was determined to get over her and move on.

∿

We were sitting in the living room two days later still talking about the boys' parties. Now that they were getting separate parties, there was a lot more to manage.

"Hold on, Chris, someone's calling me." I reached for my phone and froze when I saw Cara's name light up on the screen. I hadn't talked to her since I'd left her office. She never even messaged me after the signing, but I didn't know why I expected her to.

I furrowed my brows and answered hesitantly. "Hello?"

"Oh my God, Blair, I'm so glad you picked up!" She was frantic and sounded like she had been running.

"Why, what's wrong?" She was starting to freak me out a bit.

"Blair, it's Drea... There's been an accident."

Everything in my body felt as if it had stopped working. My eyes couldn't see, my ears couldn't hear, and my lungs couldn't absorb oxygen.

"What?" I whispered, almost dropping my phone. I had to sit down.

I was in the middle of the living room, and I didn't even make it to the couch before my legs gave out and I sat in the middle of the floor.

"It's all over the news. There was a storm a few days ago—"

"Days?! What happened? Is she okay?" *Is she dead?* I couldn't bring the words out of my throat. I was too afraid to hear the answer.

"I don't know. There was an accident on the highway, near the airport. There were five cars involved. One of them was her car. She was being carried out on a stretcher. They said there were a few fatalities and some in critical condition, but they aren't giving any details."

I couldn't breathe. "Does Fallon know? Kaia, Penelope, her parents?"

"Yes, her parents are flying in from Portland, and Fallon called me. She's a mess, so I told her I'd call you. I'm sorry this is how we have to speak for the first time, but—"

"Where is she?" I was already packing my bags before the words had left my mouth.

"Blair, you're in—"

"Where is she, Cara? I'm coming home."

"She's at Northwest Medical. I tried to call, but they wouldn't tell me anything because I'm not family. Fallon called her parents, though."

"I'll be there as soon as I can. Call me if anything else happens. This is all my fault. If I hadn't left—"

"Blair Ameilia, don't! This is not your fault. Just get here when you can."

I didn't bother saying goodbye when I hung up.

"Chris, can you drive me to the airport, please? I have to go home." I could barely get the words out through the tears. I didn't know what was going on, and I didn't know if she was alive or...

"Blair, calm down, please. What happened?"

"I'm sorry. It's an emergency. I... Drea was in an accident, and I don't know what's going to happen. Can you please take me to the airport or get me a car so I can finish packing?"

He grabbed my arms and stopped my frantic movements. "Breathe. It's only a few hours away, and it's cheaper if I drive you. I'll leave the boys with Chelsea. Let me grab my keys and let her know."

He hugged me, and I cried into his shoulder. "What if she's gone, Chris? What if she's gone and I wasn't there? I should have been there. I should have—"

"No. Don't say that. She's going to be fine, I promise."

He couldn't possibly promise something like that, but I didn't have the energy to argue, so I nodded in agreement and finished packing.

Chapter Forty-Six

BLAIR

The car ride back to Seattle was the longest ride of my life. I stared out the window the whole time, not saying a word. My brother tried to get me to talk, but I couldn't find the energy.

When we got to the hospital, I practically jumped out of the car while it was still moving and booked it down the hall.

I called Kaia, and she got the room number from Fallon. When I got outside her room, Fallon had just come out, tears filling her eyes. Mackenzie was next to her, holding her up, and I knew that wasn't a good sign.

They both looked up at me, and I froze in place. The second I moved, I was admitting it was all real, and I didn't want any of it to be real.

"What... is she..." I couldn't say the words. I didn't want to put them out in the universe.

Fallon took a step toward me and wrapped her arms around me. "She's alive, yes. But..."

I pulled back and frowned at her, trying to hide my own tears. This was exactly why I was an author and not an actress. "But, what? What happened?"

"She... she's not..." She turned to Mackenzie and fell into her without a word.

Mackenzie soothed her wife and spoke for her. "She is breathing, but she is unconscious. We don't know how, but she ran into the car in front of her, going pretty fast according to witnesses. The storm was bad and the cars behind her couldn't stop in time without slipping, and they caused a five-car pileup. Her airbags didn't deploy, and... she hit her head." She squeezed Fallon tighter and tried to force her own tears down to be strong for her wife. "She... Uh... she's been unconscious since the impact. They don't know when she will wake up, if at all."

My legs became weak as the ground became closer. Fallon and Mackenzie rushed over to me, but I couldn't hear them over the pounding of my heart in my ears.

She might not wake up, and it was all my fault.

After a few minutes, I finally gained enough energy to speak. "I want to see her."

"Blair, I don't think—"

"Fallon, please. I need to see her, okay? I just... I need to."

She nodded, and I stood up, brushing myself off before walking to her door. I was shaking, but I forced myself to go in. I had to see her for myself.

My legs almost gave out again when I saw her hooked up to all those machines in her hospital bed. She looked so peaceful, yet fragile and alone. I hated this. She was one of the strongest people I knew, and I couldn't handle seeing her broken and weak.

I wondered where she was, if she could hear us. If she knew I was there for her. Did she blame me like I blamed myself?

I walked closer to her and took her hand. It had been weeks since we'd last touched, but this touch was different. It wasn't filled with sadness and revenge; it was filled with love and regret. Regret for everything we didn't say. Love, because despite everything that was said between us, I still loved her, and that would never go away.

I sat down in the chair by her bed and caressed her hand softly. "Drea?" I whispered. I didn't know if she could hear me or if she would want to, but I had to believe she could. The machines told me her heart hadn't given up yet, so I tried to have hope.

I squeezed her hand three times, letting her know I was there, hoping she could feel the love I still had for her. "Drea, if you can hear me, baby, please come back to me. I'm so sorry for everything I said, and for the night I left. If I wouldn't have left, then maybe you would still be here. I need... I just... Please come home." I started crying again, and I felt a warm hand on my shoulder.

"Blair, maybe we should get you home. You can come back tomorrow, if you'd like. It's been a long day, and you should get some sleep."

I wiped my tears and stood up. "I appreciate that, Fallon, but I can't... I'm not leaving her, not until she wakes up and I know she's okay. I can't leave her again. I just can't."

"Are you sure? The doctors will call if anything changes," Mackenzie added.

I nodded my head. "Yes, I'm sure. I know no one believes me, but it's my fault she's here. She wouldn't have been leaving if I hadn't left the way I did after the signing. I have to be here."

"It's not your fault, but if you want to stay, then fine. Just please eat something and try to get some sleep, okay?" Fallon gave me a hug and squeezed tight.

It sucked that it took a shitty situation for me to feel like I had friends, but I though that was what they were. Fallon, Kaia, even Mackenzie, they were my friends.

Fallon and Mackenzie left, leaving me in an empty sterile hospital room, while the love of my life was possibly gone from this world.

A few hours later, I was dozing off when I felt a warm hand on my shoulder. "Mackenzie, I already told you—" I looked up to see a woman I'd only seen in pictures, and the same man from the pictures standing several feet away from her.

"Sorry to scare you, dear. I'm Joy, Drea's mother. That's Vincent, her father." If I hadn't already known about their divorce, their body language would've given them away.

"It's okay. I must've fallen asleep. I'm Blair—"

"Drea's beautiful girlfriend. We know. It's so nice to finally meet you. We have heard nothing but wonderful things about you. I'm just sorry we have to meet under these conditions. How is she?"

Joy walked closer, and I gave up my seat on the bed, figuring she had earned it more than I had. "Oh, my baby," she whispered softly, tears filling her eyes.

"She's unconscious but stable. They haven't given me any more information than that."

She nodded and wiped the tears away. "Thank you for being here for her. I can see why she loves you."

I chuckled softly. "We haven't... It's complicated." I didn't know what else to say.

"I don't know much about your relationship with Drea, but from what she's told me and the way she talks about you, it's so obvious to see she's crazy about you, dear. I'm sorry to cut this short, but I would like to speak with the doctors. Please don't leave on our account. You can stay as long as you would like." She gave me a warm hug and a double-cheek kiss like I was royalty, and then she was gone.

Vincent kind of just sat in the corner and didn't really say much, but as soon as Joy left, he seemed to have cheered up. We talked until she came back with the same news I had gotten, and he made an excuse to leave. They stayed for another few hours, and Joy asked me if I needed anything when I told her I was staying the night. I assured her I was fine and sent them on their way to their hotel.

It was nice to talk with her parents. They were both so warm and reminded me so much of Drea. I finally broke down when her mother asked about going to visit for the holidays, and I told her we weren't together anymore. I didn't go into the details as to why, but she didn't press for any more information.

She told me it said a lot about me as a person, and how I felt about Drea, to come see her after things had ended. I admitted that while, yes, we were no longer together, I was still in love with her, and I needed to make sure she was okay.

I tried to keep it together, but the tears wouldn't stay in. I was grateful Joy let me have my moment and cry it out. If Drea ever woke up, I would have to remember to tell her how lovely her parents were to me.

Chapter Forty-Seven

BLAIR

I spent the next two days in the same chair, eating the hospital food they brought up for her. I never understood why they kept bringing it for her, knowing she couldn't eat it.

I held onto her for most of the day, just rubbing her hand and repeating the same phrase. *Please come home. Please come home. Please come home.*

I washed her face and watched as the doctors came in and checked her every so often. Every time, they gave me pitiful looks before leaving.

Kaia came by yesterday and sat with me for a while. She had closed down the store for the day, which she didn't think Drea would be happy about, but I told her she would get over it.

Fallon came back to check in. She sat with her while I took a shower and got some real food.

Mackenzie had offered to run me home to pack a bag and made sure to keep Fallon on the phone the entire time in case something changed. It didn't.

For four days, her status never changed. She never got worse, but she never got better, and every second longer, I was filled with guilt. I knew accidents happened, but she wouldn't have been a part of it if I had stayed in Seattle. If we had worked things out sooner, maybe things would be different.

Cara hadn't come by while I was there, which I was thankful for. I wasn't ready to see her, not like this. I had Fallon send her text updates. Apparently she saw her before I arrived.

I had just gotten out of the shower when I could have sworn I saw movement. Fallon and Mackenzie were sitting on the couch on their phones, so I couldn't ask one of them.

I sat next to Drea and took her hand, waiting to see if it happened again. Sure enough, a minute later, I felt a twitch in my hand and jumped.

"What?!" Fallon yelled.

"I think..." I stopped when I felt her finger twitching. "Call a nurse!"

Mackenzie got up and yelled for the nurse, who came in quickly after.

"What's going on?" one of the nurses asked as the other checked the machine.

"I was coming out of the bathroom when I thought I saw her hand move. I sat down and felt her fingers twitch in my hand." It sounded crazy to my own ears, but I knew what I saw.

The nurse walked over and checked all the monitors and then checked Drea. When her hand twitched in mine again, I jumped. "There!" I yelled, pointing to her hands. "They twitched again!"

The movements became more frequent, enough that the nurse took notice and paged the doctor. I couldn't have stopped the tears if I'd wanted to. I was sure she wasn't going to wake up, and there she was, alive. Drea was alive, and she was coming back to me—to her family and friends. Not to me.

With everything going on, I had forgotten what I was to her, or what I wasn't. I was happy she would be okay, but that didn't change that I meant nothing to her.

A few other nurses had come in just in time for Drea to start waking up. She was blinking slowly a few times, and trying to give her eyes time to adjust to the bright hospital lights.

When she finally opened her eyes, mine were filled with tears as I held her hand.

"Blair?" she groaned." She winced at a pain she must have been feeling, and I squeezed her hand.

"Hi." I smiled through the tears. I couldn't believe she was awake.

She looked around the room and saw Fallon and Mackenzie, who were both crying and holding each other. "What's going on?"

We sat and listened while the nurses told her everything that had happened, and her face went pale. "Did I kill anyone? Oh my God, how could I have been so stupid? I should have—"

"Drea, relax," Mackenzie soothed. "There was a bad storm, and it was an accident. It's not your fault. These things happen."

She turned to me, and I grinned, forgetting the past hurt, forgetting the things we'd said, at least in that moment. I was just thankful she was alive. We could resume the real world later.

"Blair, I am so sorry. I was so stupid. Everything I said, I was scared. I should have told you sooner. I lo—"

"Don't." I stopped her. "Just work on getting better. We can talk later."

The doctor came in before she could say anything else, and I was grateful for that. I didn't want to fight with her when she had just woken up.

He checked her vitals and asked her dozens of questions. I didn't take my eyes off her the entire time he was talking. The part of the conversation I did catch had me turning my attention toward him.

"Also, you'll need someone with you for a few days, just to make sure there isn't anything that arises. Do you have someone who can look after you?"

Drea looked to Fallon, who nodded. "Of course, babe, we can—"

"I'll do it." The words left my mouth before I could think them through, but I didn't need to.

All eyes were on me as Fallon spoke. "Blair, that's sweet of you, but we can handle it. You guys aren't exactly—"

"Can you guys give us a minute, please?" I asked. They looked at Drea, who nodded.

Drea looked at the nurses and the doctor. "I'll go put in an order for some pain meds and let you get some rest." I thanked them as they all left, leaving me and Drea alone for the first time in weeks.

When everyone was gone, Drea released our hands that were still joined together, and I looked down at the loss of contact. I had forgotten I was still holding her hands. I hated to admit it felt good. It felt really good to be connected with a piece of her again.

"Blair, I appreciate you wanting to help, but you don't owe me anything. You were right to leave the way you did. Fallon can look after me. You should go home and get some rest."

"You really want me to go?" I asked. I couldn't stand the thought of leaving, but I wouldn't stay where I wasn't welcome.

"Of course not, I never want you to go. I just—"

"Then please let me help. I wasn't able to take care of my parents, and now they are gone. The thought of losing you too... I can't handle that." I couldn't say the words I wanted to say: *I love you and it would destroy me if you left.*

"Okay, okay. I can't argue with that logic. If you're sure. Will you let me tell you how I feel now?" She grinned.

I shook my head. "No. You almost died, and you wouldn't mean it. Just get some rest and feel better so you can go home tomorrow. We will talk when you're better."

"Fine, but my feelings won't change whether I'm dying or not."

That word didn't sit right with me. I couldn't imagine a world without her—my world without her. Even though she wasn't technically in my world anymore, I still hated the thought of losing her forever. A part of me still belonged to her... loved her.

"You're not dying! I'm not letting you off the hook that easily."

"I didn't think you would." She smirked.

"Drea, I... I owe you an apology for how I left things between us."

She furrowed her brow and tried to sit up, but winced at the pain. "Apologize? Blair, you have nothing to apologize for. I understand why you left the way you did. I treasure any time spent with you, even if it was out of anger on your side. I hurt you, and you had every right to leave."

I sighed. I was angry. I was so angry, but seeing her like this? The thought of losing her, like this? "Just work on getting better."

I wanted her to get better so I wouldn't feel guilty about leaving. I didn't know how things were going to work out. Did I forgive her for everything? Was there a future for us? Only time would tell...

Chapter Forty-Eight

DREA

I thought I would never make it out of that hospital! I had one hell of a headache and a few broken ribs, but overall, I was lucky.

The one thing that made everything a little less painful was having Blair by my side for a few days. I was shocked when she insisted on helping.

She still thought it was her fault, but I tried to tell her it wasn't. We all did. If it was anyone's fault it was mine. I knew I didn't intentionally space out, but it was still my car that hit the truck, causing the pileup. I hoped everyone else was all right.

I was still lying in bed two days later. Blair refused to let me get up unless I had to go to the bathroom. She even slept next to me, and I had to fight the urge not to touch her. I didn't get to do that anymore.

Every few hours I was awoken by her jumping from her sleep and trying to find me, probably making sure I was still there. I hated that I made her feel that way. I was so happy to have her back, but I knew she wasn't back in the way I wanted her to be.

I still planned on trying to make things right, but I didn't want to use the accident as an excuse for her to stay. I was going to wait until I didn't need supervision anymore. That way she could walk away guilt-free if she wanted to, which I imagined she would.

"Blair, I can't thank you enough for being here for me, but don't you want to see the outside world, maybe go visit Milo, or the Taj Mahal?"

She was sitting in a chair she'd made my housekeeper help her bring up from the living room. She'd tipped her a pretty penny for it, but still.

"I'm sorry for wanting to make sure you're okay. Next time, say no to my help and come home on your own!" She pouted.

I smiled. She looked so cute like that. "When have I ever said no to you? Wait—" I paused at something she'd said.

"What?" she asked, confused.

"Okay, this is going to sound totally crazy, but did you talk to me when I was unconscious?"

She snorted. "What? Don't be ridiculous, I..." She groaned. "Fine, yes I did. It's stupid I know, but why do you ask?"

I shook my head, adjusting myself and wincing at the pain.

"Stop moving!" She jumped up and positioned me again.

I grabbed her hand and she froze. "Blair, stop. I'm fine, okay? None of this is your fault, so please relax. I promise." I caressed her hand, but she slowly pulled away. I'd pushed too far.

"Why are you asking if I talked to you? Why does that matter?"

I ignored the way she shook off my touch, and continued. "Because you said 'come home on my own.' I kept hearing a voice inside my head telling me to come home, but I thought I was dreaming. Maybe I was, I don't know."

She looked at me and smiled softly as tears started to pool in her eyes. "You heard me talking to you? What else did you hear?" She seemed embarrassed, like maybe she'd said something she didn't want me to know.

"That's all I remember," I answered honestly.

She nodded and hummed, leaving it alone for now. "How's your dinner?" she asked, nodding to my almost empty plate of steak and potatoes.

Blair had cooked for me every night since I'd come home from the hospital. I'd tried to insist it wasn't necessary, but she wouldn't hear it, and I learned it was best not to argue with her. When it came to her, she would always get her way, whether we were together or not.

I grinned. "Just like the chef, it's amazing."

She gave a faint smile. It was odd how I enjoyed the domesticity of the situation. Eating dinner together, watching TV, talking. Although we didn't do too much talking, and never about us. I hadn't wanted to bring it up if she didn't.

"Thank you again for everything you've done, Blair. I mean it. You didn't have to do any of this. I'm sure I've more than earned my punishment to heal alone."

"I know," was all she said.

I didn't press anymore as I stood up and headed for the bathroom, but she stopped me before I could even get out of the bed. "Where do you think you're going?"

I groaned. I was an adult, dammit, and I was perfectly capable of moving on my own, sort of. I still had a nasty headache, and it was a little painful to move, but I could do it.

I'd cleaned up with help from the nurses before I left the hospital, but I desperately needed a shower, and I wasn't stupid enough to ask for help this time. I had a bench in there I could sit on, and I would manage just fine.

"Blair, I'm fine. I'm going to take a shower. I'll leave the door open so you can see me, okay?"

"You're joking, right? You may be able to walk fine, but there is no way I'm letting you take a shower on your own. The chances of slipping for a normal person are already high, add your disabled state to those numbers, no thanks."

She tried to help me up, but I stopped her. "I know you want to help, but this is something I can't ask you to do. I feel like this crosses a line I know you don't want—"

"Drea, stop. It's just a shower. I've seen you naked plenty of times, and I'll be... I have to know you are safe before I leave." She said it as if it were that simple. As if it were that simple for us to be vulnerable together and not feel what we had before. As if it were simple to walk away from us, and maybe for her it was.

We had been in every state of undress together, but never when I couldn't just reach out and hold her. Her words were saying the opposite of her body as she shakily reached for my hand.

I was in no position to argue, so I had to trust her words, even though I knew they were a lie. At the end of the day, she was right, and I didn't want to risk another accident. I simply nodded and let her help me up.

The shower was big enough for at least six or seven people, with a rain showerhead above and a bench against the wall underneath it. She walked us over to the bench, never taking her hand off my arm, and sat me down.

"Are you okay?" she asked.

I was partly okay. I was okay in the sense that I wasn't hurt. I was okay in the sense that a naked Blair stood only a few feet away from me.

But I wasn't okay in the sense that we weren't together and I couldn't take advantage of this moment. That there was an emptiness in her eyes I had put there.

"Fine." I had to force the word out past all the thoughts running through my mind.

Before I'd sat down, she had washed off my back, and I could feel her trembling, but I stayed silent. The whole time neither of us spoke, the water raining down on us being the only sound in the room.

I stiffened when she walked back over with a freshly soaped loofa and started washing my body, starting with my neck and shoulders.

If she washed only my back, I could have survived without a problem, but the second I came face-to-face with her, staring into those sad hazel eyes, it became more of a challenge.

When she started to make her way to my breasts, she paused and looked at me, waiting for permission. "You never need permission to touch me, Blair," I said with a nod.

She didn't respond as she continued to clean me, and my muscles spasmed when she got to my stomach and worked her way down to my thighs and legs. I was thankful the water and soap were able to cover up just how she was affecting me.

The moment was anything but sexual, but she always had a way of getting my body to react to her, no matter what.

When she came back up to my arms and shoulders, I couldn't resist. The tension was mixing with the steam from the shower, and it permeated the air. She was being so gentle, looking so beautiful, and I needed to touch her, even if it wasn't sexual and even if it would be for the last time.

I reached up to push a stray hair behind her ear before I cautiously wrapped my arms around her waist, slowly bringing her closer to me.

She hesitated before allowing the contact and placed her hands on my shoulders. "Drea."

I hugged her, breathing her in, committing every part of her to memory. I wanted to stay like this forever, but I knew we couldn't.

"God, I've missed you," I whispered. She didn't respond, but as soon as I began to lightly dust her hips with soft kisses, she tensed and slowly pulled away. I grabbed her wrist, making sure there wasn't too much space between us, as I slowly stood up.

I pulled her closer and brushed my thumb across her lip. "Blair, I—"

"I think we're done." She shook her head and rinsed me off before she turned off the water, handing me a towel. I didn't think she was only talking about the shower.

"Blair, please—"

"Just dry off. I'll be right outside." She turned and left me alone in the steamy bathroom.

I walked out and saw Blair on her phone, sitting on the edge of the bed. She had already gotten dressed, and her bag was at her feet, ready to leave with her.

She looked up when she heard my throat clear. "I'm going to go downstairs and call a car."

I frowned. "You're leaving." It wasn't a question. We both knew what she was doing.

She stood up and sighed. "I think it's best if someone else takes over. Now that I know you are okay, there is no reason for me to stay." Her words sounded confident, but her wandering eyes that refused to land on me told me a different story.

"I don't think that's true." She turned to leave without another word, but she didn't get more than two steps before I grabbed her wrist again. "Wait."

She stopped but didn't turn around. "Drea, please don't." I could already hear the crack in her voice, but I had to push the words out.

"Please just let me say this, Blair. I'm so sorry."

She turned around, and I let go of her wrist. "You think an apology is enough to make up for everything you said? You made it sound like I was your whore to use around whenever you liked, like my feelings meant nothing."

"I don't think that at all, Blair. Your feelings mean everything to me. I was upset and drunk and it just came out. I know it's not an excuse and I can't take it back, but you have to know that's not how I feel about you at all. I..." I stopped myself.

"You what, Drea?"

I sighed. I would not let her leave again without getting the words out. "You weren't just something I added to my to-do list because I was bored. I've never been good at expressing my feelings or putting a label on anything. But for you, I wanted to try. If you were to ask me to do just that and label what we were, I would say we were in a relationship. We were in a committed exclusive relationship, at least for me. I can't imagine sleeping with anyone else when you are all I want. I am still committed to you, and I will do whatever it takes to keep that relationship, because I am in love with you, and I cannot even fathom the thought of losing you."

She stood there, unmoving. This was not how I wanted to tell her I loved her, but if she was really walking away, she had to know the truth.

"You love me? How could you possibly know that? You had a funny way of showing it to Cara."

I chuckled, taking both of her hands in mine. "Are you kidding? How could I not be in love with you? You're beautiful, inside and out. You're compassionate, brave, hardworking, and you see the beauty in even the ugliest parts of life. You encourage me, you don't put up with my bullshit, and you challenge me. When I'm with you, I feel like I can accomplish anything as long as I have your eyes to look into. Loving you feels effortless. It's something I do subconsciously, and when I'm not with you... my heart doesn't beat. I love you, and that isn't up for discussion, Blair. I loved you before you left, and I love you now. It's the only thing I am meant to do in life, and I think you might love me too or you wouldn't still be here. When you asked me to come home, you didn't mean just to Seattle, did you? You wanted me to come home to you."

"Don't you fucking dare use your accident to get me back. That is not fair!" Her eyes were filled with tears, and she took a step back.

I shook my head. "No, that's not what I am doing. If you genuinely want to be done, I'll let you walk away without another word. But look me in the eyes and tell me we are done. Tell me you don't love me."

She didn't say anything for a long minute, and I honestly thought I got it all wrong. I was convinced she was going to walk away again.

At this point she couldn't hide her tears, and I was ready to accept defeat. She shook her head. "You know I can't do that, Drea."

"Why not?" I asked. I wanted to hear her say the words.

"Because I haven't thought about anything else except for you since I left. Because my world came crashing down when I thought you died. Because I didn't want to think about going a single day without you on this planet. Because... goddammit, because I love you, Drea! You're my safe space, my home, and I need you here, okay?!"

I brought her closer to me and brushed my thumb under her tearful eye. "Baby, I'm not going anywhere unless you're going with me. I'm so irrevocably and undeniably in love with you, and I will never forgive myself for letting you go a single second thinking otherwise." And I kissed her.

Chapter Forty-Nine

BLAIR

"Relax, babe. I'll get it." We were sitting on the couch watching *Stuart Little*. I had never seen it, and she said it was Fallon's favorite movie, so I decided to see what the hype was all about.

I had made the mistake of texting Fallon to let her know we were watching it, and I got about eight voice messages that were three decibels too high telling me how much I was going to love it and praising Drea for "leading me down the right path in life."

I kissed Drea's cheek and stood up to get the door, barely missing the smack on my ass. I would never get tired of these small moments with her. I still had to remind myself every day that she was alive and she was mine.

I was laughing as I opened the door, but it quickly died off as I stood in front of the last person I'd expected to see.

"Cara." I was stunned, and a little confused. I hadn't seen or talked to Cara since she'd called me a few weeks ago. She had gone through Fallon or Kaia to check in on Drea, but she hadn't personally contacted us until now.

What was she doing here? Did she come here to yell at us some more?

"Blair, hey. I don't know why I'm surprised to see you here. I guess I was expecting Drea to answer the door. I just wanted to check in, but I can see you've got it covered... Tell her I stopped by."

She went to turn around but I stopped her. "Wait! Come in. She's in the living room."

She hesitated before turning around. "Blair, I don't know if that's a good idea. I don't think—"

"Please, Cara. I know she wants to see you, and we should talk. We have too much history for things to end like this."

She didn't say anything for a minute until she sighed. "Fine... Just for a minute."

I beamed and opened the door further.

"Who was it, darling?" Drea called from the living room. I stopped in the doorway and let Cara come into view. Drea's playful smile fell as shock washed over her.

"Hey, Drea." Cara gave a faint smile.

Drea stood up suddenly, and I worried she would fall over. She was walking a lot better, but I was still scared when she did anything strenuous. I almost lost her, and I would be damned if I let it happen again.

I ran to her side and made her sit back down. She did, but not without an eye roll. "Cara. I'm glad you're here. Please, sit down and make yourself comfortable."

Cara hesitantly took the couch in front of us looking around like she had never seen the place before, which I guess was true. Only a select few people knew where Drea lived. How did Cara know now?

"If you weren't sick, I would be upset that I had to force Fallon to give me your address. But now I can see why. Why didn't you tell me you were loaded? After all those lunches I paid for, I should send you a bill!"

Drea laughed, and it felt so good to hear it again. "I'm not sick. And I don't like anyone knowing where I live. I try not to use my family's money if I can help it. This house was a gift when I moved to the city. I was afraid people would get the wrong impression or try to use me for what my family has. That's an issue I have to work through, which I am, but I'm sorry I kept it from you."

"Well, you look good. You gave us a damn heart attack!" Cara laughed softly.

Drea grinned, and I was just glad nobody was yelling. "I'm doing a lot better. I had a really good nurse." Drea turned to me and rubbed my thigh. I smiled at the familiar warmth and placed my hand on hers.

"I can see that. Listen, I'm sorry about—"

I shook my head, cutting her off. "No, Cara, you have nothing to apologize for. We should be the ones apologizing. Well, I can't speak for Drea, only myself, but... I hid an important part of my life from you and risked your business. That was fucked up, and I know I can't take it back. I need you to know that I had no intention of any of this happening. Falling for Drea was never part of the plan, nor was hiding it. You're my best friend, and I wanted to tell you from the moment I started feeling something for her. At the festival, I—"

"The festival? You told me nothing happened, Blair. Was that another lie?"

I shook my head, determined to get her to believe me. "No! Of course not. Technically nothing happened. You called before something might have, though, but I should have told you everything anyway. We don't keep secrets, and I kept a very big and important one. I knew it would complicate our working relationship, and that it was selfish of me to hide it from you. I know words can't fix things, but I really hope you will forgive me someday and give me the chance to earn back your friendship. You are my best friend, Cara, and you mean the world to me."

I sat there while Drea caressed my thigh, waiting for a response. I wasn't sure what she would say, or if she would walk out on seven years of friendship. I'd said all I could say. Now it was just time to wait.

After several agonizing seconds, she finally spoke. "It did hurt, but thank you for owning up to everything and apologizing. I do have to apologize too. I was angry and hurt, and it wasn't fair to take away your livelihood because of petty feelings. It wasn't even the fact that you were together. I've been trying to get you to get along for years. Sitting here seeing you two together, I can see it's real. It was more that I considered you both friends, and I was hurt that you hid a part of your life from me and lied while everyone else knew about it. I promise that in our new contract, I'll be sure to add a 'no pettiness' clause," she said with a smile.

"Again, Cara, I am so incredibly sorry for lying to you. You mean the world to me, and I—Wait, so does that mean—"

"Yes. If you would have me, I would really like to continue representing my best friend... on one condition."

I nodded. "Anything!" I said eagerly.

"You have to promise to always be honest with me."

"Of course. You got it!"

She smiled and stood up to hug me. "And promise to take care of this one," she said, pointing to Drea. "She has proven she literally can't live without you."

I sobbed out a laugh. "I promise. She's not going anywhere if I have anything to say about it."

"If this reunion is over, can I have my chance at begging?" Drea stood up and rubbed my back.

I looked at Cara, who nodded. I returned to my spot on the couch to give her the floor. I wanted her to have her own moment with Cara.

"Cara," Drea started. She looked like she might fall down, so I rushed to her and tried to make her sit on the couch, but she stopped me. "Honey, I'm fine. Please sit down and relax. I swear if she has her way, I'll never pee alone again." She laughed when I swatted her arm gently.

"I appreciate you more than you'll ever know, my love." My chest warmed as she turned to Cara. I would never tire of that nickname. I knew she called almost everyone in her life "love," but I was the only one who got the "my" in front of it. I was her love just as much as she was mine.

"Drea, you don't need to—"

"Yes, I do. I directly lied to you about Blair and that was fucked up. We have been friends for years, and you didn't deserve that. Part of it was because I made a promise to Blair not to say anything. We didn't want to complicate things or make you upset. But the other part was because I was scared. I don't typically get too close to anyone, and I felt like I was getting too close too fast, and if I acknowledged it out loud, then it would have made it real and it would have gone away, just like it did for my parents. But I couldn't deny it. I was falling for Blair the longer I spent time with her, and it was as real as it got. To be honest, I think I started to see her differently at the festival. Seeing how she was with everyone and how she handled herself on that stage—you should have seen her, Cara. It was the most real thing I have ever witnessed, and it was beautiful."

I didn't have words. I mean, I'd known she was going to kiss me, but I'd figured it was just to see how I would react. I didn't think...

Drea was sounding like she was on the verge of tears, and I had to force myself not to reach out to comfort her. She needed to get through this on her own.

"I also need to apologize for keeping you at arm's length. Not only with Blair, but with myself. No one outside of my family and close friends, and now you two, knows where I live or why I keep this part of my life hidden, not even Kaia, but she will soon enough. Skylar knew, but only after a year of being together. I honestly don't have a reason for not telling you. Maybe if you'd asked, I would have told you, but maybe not. I consider you a dear friend, and I am sorry that I was blinded by my own issues to tell you how much I appreciate you and let you into that part of my life. I will do anything to show you that."

"I appreciate your honesty, but I'm going to need a lot more groveling than that. You two have put me through hell for the past three and a half years! For starters, you owe me a wine bottle from the wine tasting, and several expensive-ass lunches!" Cara laughed, and I sighed in relief. I wasn't stupid enough to think we could all become best friends right away, but I hoped with more time and more groveling, it would all be okay.

"That sounds fair enough. You can pick any bottle from my wine cellar downstairs, and how about I take you to lunch next week?"

"You have a wine cellar?!" Both Cara and I yelled simultaneously before taking off down the hall.

We laughed as we ran, but I stopped, forgetting something in the living room. "Hold on, Cara, I'll be right back."

The feeling of this moment was indescribable. Having Cara back in my life was amazing. I had missed my best friend, and I wouldn't waste another second I had with her in my life. But having Drea back...

Having Drea not only back in my life, but alive and happy, was a true blessing. I was never the religious type, even growing up, but I would make sure to thank anyone I could that Drea came back to me that day in the hospital. I would never take another second of life for granted again, that much I was sure of.

I ran back to the living room where she had just gotten up from the couch. She looked happy. She looked content. She looked like home.

I grabbed her face and kissed her hard, causing her to take a small step back, but making sure not to hurt her.

"Whoah, what's this for?" she asked. "You don't even drink wine."

I wrapped my arms around her and squeezed her tightly. She was here, she was real, she was mine, and I was never letting her go. "Thank you for coming into my life and being the reason I know I can weather any storm."

Epilogue

Two years later

"Good morning, baby." Blair's sleepy voice awoke me from my dreams, and I couldn't have been more okay with it. My reality was better than any dream could be. The way she called me baby always made my heart skip a beat, but when it was in that sexy, early-morning sweet tone, I might as well have still been dreaming.

She peppered my neck with soft kisses as she caressed my shoulders and back, sending shivers through me. I couldn't help but smile when I turned over and saw her naked body so close to mine.

"Morning." I grabbed her chin and brought her in for a soft kiss.

"How did you sleep?" She asked me that every morning, as if the answer could ever change.

"With you in my arms? Perfectly."

It had been six months since Blair had moved in, and she still hadn't explored every part of the house. We had been rather... preoccupied with getting her acquainted with our room, all three showers, the pool, and even the patio.

She was insatiable, and I wasn't any better. After a long day apart, we would barely make it to the room most nights. My housekeeper learned to knock on any door before she entered. Voyeurism wasn't our thing, and it made both of us uncomfortable and embarrassed at the thought of being caught, but we couldn't help it sometimes. The need was too intense, even after two years of being together.

"You know you say that every morning. I'm starting to think you are just trying to get on my good side." She smirked.

"Is it working?" I hissed when she pinched a nipple. I wasn't sure why she thought that of all things would be a punishment. It made me want to act out even more.

"Maybe." She was lying on me, drawing idle circles across my chest while I squeezed her tightly and kissed the top of her head. I never wanted to leave this bed.

A throbbing sensation began between my thighs as I felt something wet and cold on one nipple and a flicking motion on the other. Her tongue had a way of getting my body to react in a severe way. Even if it wasn't touching a sexual place, it always felt like it was.

"Baby... you know what that does to me." I moaned as she continued her sucking and flicking motions on my now even harder nipples.

She didn't respond. Instead, she moved her hand down, feeling exactly what it did to me. I took in a breath when her fingers made contact with my clit. Even after all this time of being with her, I could still get turned on just from looking at her, especially in moments like these when we were at our most vulnerable.

I moaned softly as she inserted two fingers into me while rubbing my clit with the pad of her thumb. She knew we couldn't lay lazily in bed all morning. She knew we had somewhere to be, and she wasn't wasting any precious time.

I was on the edge of coming undone, and I groaned in protest when she slowly pulled out of me, but it quickly died off when she brought her hand to her mouth and took in those fingers, sucking and licking them erotically.

"I love you," I whispered as I kissed her so fiercely, tasing myself on her lips. The action was filthy yet so sweet and intimate.

"I love you too, but I'm going to fuck you like I don't. Get on your hands and knees, baby," she whispered. Music to my fucking ears. If I was wet from her touch before, I was soaked from her promise. It wasn't a threat.

Blair did anything she set her mind to and if she said she was going to fuck me, then by God, I was getting fucked. But you would never hear me complain. It wasn't often that Blair became the dominant one, but when she did, I never took it for granted.

I expected her hands to find their original position, or her mouth. Hell, I would have even expected her own pussy to find mine, but out of all the possibilities, I wouldn't have ever expected my favorite strap to find its way into me.

It was my favorite because it was the first one I had ever used on Blair. The memory of her naked and bent over my desk still played in my mind when she wasn't around, and sometimes when she was. But this was a first.

"Do you know... how fucking perfect... you are?" I said in between desperate breaths. Desperate to come, but desperate for it to never end. This vision of her wearing a strap, gripping my hips as she pounded into me—I was moments away from crumbling into the earth. I now understood why she loved this position so much.

"God, you look so good like this, Dre." Hearing those words was all it took for me to tumble over the edge.

"Don't stop, Blair. Shit!" I screamed as my orgasm tore through me, but she never faltered, even when her own orgasm followed mine and her thrusts became irregular as she moaned out in pleasure.

After the hardest orgasm of my life, I dropped onto the bed, limp and breathless.

"Goddamn, baby. You never cease to amaze me," I breathed as she crawled back into bed, snuggling up to me and kissing my neck gently.

She smiled, and I wanted to capture it forever. "I'm not sure what I love more, getting fucked from behind by you, or seeing the cock move in and out of you."

I kissed her hard, whining when she broke us apart. We were going to be late if we kept at it, and I had every intention to keep going if she didn't stop me.

. . .

After we took the longest shower—partly my fault because I loved eating her out in there—we finally made it to the bookstore.

We had been closed for months while the renovations finished up. Business had been doing better after my accident. Maybe people felt sorry for a business owner who almost died, but I wasn't looking a gift horse in the mouth.

When we got there, Kaia was already opening up, of course. Since becoming co-owner, she had really grown into the role. She took her job seriously, and sometimes I had to be the one to tell her to relax. Not that she listened. If your name wasn't Daisy, you might as well be talking to a wall.

Their friendship had really grown over the past year. Daisy was at the store every day, and once a month she got paid for it. When Kaia had demanded I hire someone to teach sign language, I didn't have to ask why, but I had given her the go-ahead to hire whoever she saw fit. I shouldn't have been surprised when Daisy showed up on the day of the first class.

"There you are! We thought you two weren't going to show!" Fallon smirked from the counter where Rylee was stocking up beside her.

Rylee still bartended on the weekends, but she had quit Brewed Awakening without a second thought when I asked her to come work at the store. I didn't hesitate when Blair had the idea to offer her the opportunity to run her own café. It probably helped that I offered her double what she was making, which let her work more on her photography business, but I liked to think she did it out of the kindness of her heart, not her wallet.

"Of course we made it. We just got a late start this morning." I winked at Blair and smirked at the reddening of her perfectly soft cheeks.

"Oh, I'm sure you did." Mackenzie came out from the back, holding a box of receipt paper, a furry friend by her side.

"Is she causing you trouble, Milo?"

"Hardly. She treats him like our child." Fallon shook her head.

Two months after Blair had moved in, I had Marcus help with the arrangements to adopt Milo. I knew Blair adored him, and I adored her, so it was a no-brainer.

"He is! Our godchild, anyway. Besides, it's good practice for the future." She smiled and kissed her wife's forehead.

It was still surreal to say that I had two married best friends, one thinking about children and the other one...

"Isn't that the truth? I've been getting my steps in, taking him for walks all the time. At this point, this baby is going to be walking out of me," a very pregnant Penelope added from the couch.

Milo walked over and positioned himself at her feet, settling there. Penelope and her husband, Greg, were expecting a baby girl in four months, which was insane!

The past two years had been a whirlwind. A lot of good moments and a lot of bad ones. Losing Blair being one of the worst, alongside my accident. I learned how short life can really be, and I promised myself to make the most of it.

I didn't even think about it when I asked Blair to move in. After not being with her, I never wanted to have that feeling again. I needed her, and I needed her close. She still worried sometimes when I got sick or hurt, but I couldn't fault her for being protective. If the roles were reversed, I would never let her out of my sight.

Since Kaia had taken over half the company, it gave me more time to experience life, and the love in it. I had even traveled out of state for a few days to go to signings or other literary events with Blair, something I would have never done before, but I never had to try with Blair.

"So who drove here?" Cara sat up from the couch next to Penelope and grinned.

Our friendship was finally back to the way it had been. I still owed her about three hundred dollars worth of meals, but a few bottles of wine had certainly helped. She came over about once a month for dinner before helping herself to our hot tub. Blair insisted on cooking every time, even though I kept telling her that we had a chef for a reason.

"Drea did today. I was too..." She looked at me and the redness of her cheeks deepened to a crimson, and I tried to suppress a chuckle. She was so unbelievably adorable when she got flustered. "Tired."

After we'd reconciled, Blair told me she had started seeing a thera-pist. She was embarrassed to tell me because she thought it made her seem weak that she couldn't overcome the obstacles in her life on her own. I did my best to reassure her that it was perfectly normal to feel that way, and it was also perfectly normal to ask for help. We were only human, and we couldn't do everything on our own.

I thought it had really been helping. If there was a storm, she would come and find me, wanting me to hold her until it was over. If I was not there, she'd call me and we'd talk about whatever she wanted to talk about. Sometimes I had her count to one hundred or describe some-thing she saw, smelled, heard, and tasted, if anything. I'd heard about the five-senses method on a podcast about PTSD, and it seemed to work.

Six months ago, she'd started taking driving lessons and had been doing really well. Sometimes we went on the back roads, which I knew were typically quiet. Sometimes we went in residential areas, or to parks where the speed limit was low, and sometimes we stayed in large parking lots.

She experienced her first storm while driving, and I was terrified. Not only did her parents die in a car accident during a storm, but I almost died in one. I expected her to never want to learn to drive, so I was shocked when she mentioned it after one of the hottest shower sex nights of my life. It was the first, and most definitely not the last, time I used the strap in the shower. Whoever invented rain showerheads deserved a raise.

I was prepared for her to stop the car abruptly, maybe to even crash into something, but I wasn't prepared for what actually happened.

At the first boom of thunder, she jumped slightly, and I could see her breathing start to quicken. Instead of doing any of those things, she calmly pulled over to the side of the road and started describing her surroundings using her senses as I rubbed her leg.

"I can smell the vanilla from the air freshener. I can see the little pellets of rain starting to form on the windows. I can hear the faint lyrics of the song playing in the car. I can touch the leather of the seats." She turned to me and pulled me in for a passionate kiss.

In that moment, nothing else mattered. Not her PTSD. Not the storm. Not the fact that we were already late for our dinner reservation. None of it mattered as I held Blair in my arms and could feel her panic slipping away as her breathing regulated.

"And I can taste the love of my life on my lips." She grinned as she wiped her lipstick off the side of my mouth with her thumb.

She took a deep breath and squared her shoulders, putting the car in drive, and signaling she was merging back onto the road. The storm continued but she remained calm. She flinched at every thunder boom or lightning strike, but she never lost control. She took calming breaths and reached for my hand, which was never far away.

Saying I was proud of Blair didn't even begin to describe the feeling I had. She had come a long way from our first meeting; we both had. Snide comments, backhanded compliments, and heated tension were a thing of the past. Replaced with flirtatious comments, genuine compliments, and still heated but now sexual tension, but only temporarily.

If I wasn't driving, working, or sleeping, some part of my body was on her. I had to touch her at all times to remind myself she was real. She was here, and she loved me just as much as I loved her.

Blair and I walked over to the couch opposite Cara and Penelope. Penelope frowned as Milo's loyalty shifted when his mother sat down, curling herself into my arms.

"Are you comfortable there, sweetheart?" I asked jokingly. She knew I didn't want her to be anywhere else.

She looked up at me and smiled, pulling my shirt so I brought my face to hers, placing a soft kiss on her delicate lips. "When I'm with you? Always."

"Okay, you two, we know you're a fan of public exposure, but how about we focus on the store for today?" Mackenzie's grin turned evil, and I flipped her off as Blair buried her head in my chest, embarrassed.

"Oh, for fuck's sake. Fallon, you couldn't have married someone with a little more class?"

Fallon was sitting on Mackenzie's lap on the couch next to Penelope. "Why marry someone with class when you can marry someone with ass?"

"Exactly, my baby gets it." Mackenzie smacked Fallon's ass, causing a groan to slip out of my mouth.

"You two make me sick." The insult died off as soon as my smile broke free.

"Talk about class. Did you forget our wedding? Your closeted—"

"Alright, alright. Thank you, Mackenzie. I get your point." I rolled my eyes even as my chest warmed when all my friends were gathered together. I loved my chosen family.

But as I sat with all the people closest to me, at the re-opening of my store that I'd worked so hard for, I couldn't believe I had waited so long to let people in. The feeling of loving wholeheartedly and being loved just as intensely was a feeling that didn't compare to anything else in the universe.

I had been blinded by the comfortability of Skylar and keeping my guard up with everyone around me that I couldn't see what, or rather *who* was right there all along... *Blair freaking Sterling.*

Acknowledgments

Thank you to my wife for inspiring quite a few things in this book and for being my hype woman through it all. I love you 3,000.

Thank you to all my amazing readers for helping me along this journey.

Thank you to Melissa for talking me out of my spirals and not letting me become a dumpster fire! And thank you for your invaluable contributions.

Thank you to Kris for bringing this book to life with the cover. I am so in love with it, and I will never be able to thank you enough!

And finally, a huge thank you to everyone who has read TMNTKY and has shown it some love. Your support means everything to me!

About the Author

Elee Rose is a lover of all things smutty and sappy, which inspired her to start writing her own stories.

A hopeless romantic at heart, she writes the kind of books that make her swoon, sweat, and maybe even sob.

Happily married, Elee often draws inspiration from her own life, and you'll rarely find her without her wife. When she's not writing about love, she's reading about it or living it.

Stay Connected!

Follow Elee Rose for updates, sneak peeks, and more behind-the-scenes content.

Instagram: @authoreleerose

Facebook: Author Elee Rose

Join our smutty Facebook group: Sapphic Sap and Smut

Join my Patreon: patreon.com/eleerose

E-mail: eleeroseauthor@gmail.com

www.ingramcontent.com/pod-product-compliance
Lightning Source LLC
Chambersburg PA
CBHW050021120726
47903CB00006B/1866